Hell West of the Pecos

Hell West of the Pecos

V. J. Rose

WHEELER PUBLISHING
A part of Gale, a Cengage Company

Wheeler Publishing Large Print Softcover Western.
The text of this Large Print edition is unabridged.
Other aspects of the book may vary from the original edition.
Set in 16 pt. Plantin.

**LIBRARY OF CONGRESS CIP DATA ON FILE.
CATALOGUING IN PUBLICATION FOR THIS BOOK
IS AVAILABLE FROM THE LIBRARY OF CONGRESS.**

ISBN-13: 979-8-88578-739-0 (softcover alk. paper)

Published in 2023 by arrangement with Wolfpack Publishing LLC.

*Dedicated to my father, uncles,
and the rest of the Mundine boys who
"always had blood on their hats."*

Chapter One

Dudford Washburn rolled over, hoping to blot out the snoring of his cell mate. The blanket underneath him smelled of stale sweat and vomit. Dud closed one eye tighter — the other eye was already swollen shut. Aching all over, he tried to recall the events of the night before. Running his thickened tongue over his teeth, it relieved him to find them all there. Twenty-five years old and he felt like fifty.

"Get up, Washburn!"

Dud opened his good eye and rolled over. The sheriff stood on the other side of the bars, looking none too happy with him. He got up on one elbow, but had to pause before rising because all the blood seemed to whirl in his head instead of his legs.

"Hurry it up. I ain't got all day."

Dud stood up while the sheriff unlocked the door and motioned him to get out. With a pounding head and shaky legs, Dud did as he was told.

"Your uncle paid your fine."

Dud nodded and followed the sheriff into his office. The sheriff went around to his desk, taking out Dud's holster and gun from a drawer. The door opened, and the sheriff's daughter entered carrying a basket. Dud removed his hat and nodded his head.

"Ma'am."

A look of horror came over her face. "Oh, Mr. Washburn, you've been hurt!" she cried.

"Daughter! Leave my supper on the desk and get on home. You leave Mr. Washburn alone. He's a married man."

"Not any more I'm not," Dud said under his breath.

Dud put on his gun belt and checked to make sure his Colt revolver was loaded before putting it back in its holster. The sheriff's daughter left with obvious reluctance. Her father watched her go out the door before turning to glare at Dud.

"You ain't much to look at Washburn, especially since you come back from the war. I don't know what it is women see in you. Skinny bag of bones with mousy brown hair is all I see."

"Oh, yeah. They are all in love with me," Dud replied. Except his wife. Or rather, his ex-wife. "Where's Ponder?"

"Outside waiting for you. Git."

Dud walked out, shutting the door behind him as softly as he could. If he slammed it, his head might blow off. Ponder stood leaning his tall, lanky frame against a post, looking out over the street, his big hat pushed back and to one side, showing his thinning dark hair. He turned, running his eyes up and down over Dud, his great dark mustache silent and still in disapproval.

"Thanks for paying my fine," Dud said, rubbing the right side of his face and eye. "I'm surprised you left the poker table long enough to find out I was in jail."

"Poker is what paid your fine," Ponder said, standing upright and pulling his hat down. "What is the matter with you, Dud? Tearing up the best saloon in San Antonio. Couldn't you have picked a less expensive dump to start throwing punches?"

Dud sighed. "Come on, I'm going back to the ranch with you. And don't talk so loud."

They began to walk down the Main Plaza, dodging pigs roaming the streets, stepping over lazy dogs. Poor-looking mules with destitute ex-Confederates rode by, while Union officers escorted their ladies in fine carriages and buggies, staring with disdain and curiosity at Dud and the Mexicans and Germans mingling around them. They had only walked a short distance when Ponder spoke.

"I've got to get some bait first. What about your job?"

"Forget that. And I can't eat nothing. I'd probably throw up on the table looking at food."

"I don't care. You can sit and watch me eat, and if you think you are going to throw up, you can go outside."

Dud stopped. "Uncle Ponder, can't you get it through your thick head I want to leave this town right now?"

"Well, get it through your dunderhead I'm going to eat first."

Dud shook his head. "Why did Pa have to die at Palmito?"

He had gotten along so well with his pappy, but he and his uncle crossed swords at every turn. He didn't wait for Ponder to answer, but began walking again. Ponder kept in step with him and spoke his mind fast enough.

"Why did Rayford have to die at Gettysburg? Why did Milford and Bradford have to die at Shiloh? I don't know the answer. I just know I'm stuck with you, and you're stuck with me 'cause we are the only two Washburns left."

Dud said nothing, knowing they were

headed for Ponder's favorite dive that sold beans and heaven only knew what else wrapped in tortillas. Mad that Ponder insisted on eating first, Dud nevertheless didn't object as strenuously as he might have, knowing it would be unlikely they would meet anybody they knew except a few Mexicans who would not ask questions.

The little café was crowded, but they found a table in the center, next to a wall. They were the only white men in the place, but in due time, a pretty little señorita came to take Ponder's order. She looked knowingly at Dud and smiled at Ponder before walking away to yell to the cook in Spanish what was wanted of him.

"What about Beatrice? She ain't going back to the ranch with us?" Ponder asked.

"She doesn't want to be known as Bee-at-trice anymore; she wants to be Bee-ah-trice. She says it's more refined. And no, she's not going back." She hardly ever did, but Dud understood Ponder was just hoping this would not be one of the rare occasions she decided to leave the city.

"My things are waiting for me at the stage office. She was getting ready to ship them to me. I returned faster than she thought I would."

The waitress brought Ponder his food.

Dud looked at it and decided he might could eat a little something after all. "Bring me some of that, please, ma'am."

She nodded and walked away, shrugging her shoulders at the *caprichos* of white men.

"What brought this on?" Ponder said, digging into his food.

Dud shrugged. "She doesn't want to be married to a rancher or a mule skinner. I don't make enough money for her."

He had to admit it had been hard on her, being the daughter of a pastor to a wealthy church, where all the patrons wore fancy clothes and lived in fine homes. She was drinking coffee adulterated with ground okra seeds and eating pork belly while everyone around her was feasting on champagne and oysters. Since the war, ninety-five percent of the people in Texas were too poor to pay attention, but there was always that five percent who managed to live high on the hog.

"I told you and told you not to marry that woman, that she was too high-toned for you. But you had to do it anyway."

Dud rubbed his forehead. How many times had Ponder said that? He was not being entirely truthful. "Aw, she was tired of me being jumpy all the time since I came back. I'd wake in the middle of the night, thrashing around in the bed, thinking somebody was after me."

The war had affected them in different ways. He had nightmares. His brother-in-law hardly spoke and spent hours alone. When Ponder was not working cattle or around the ranch, he would be in a saloon or the back room of a store, compulsively playing one card game after another until he dropped with exhaustion or ran out of money.

"What does her pa think about this, him being a man of the cloth?"

"It doesn't matter what he thinks; you know that, Uncle Ponder. It's whatever Beatrice and her mother tell him to do. And they told him to get her the quickest and quietest divorce he could."

The waitress brought Dud's food. As he nodded his thanks, she gave him a sly wink before leaving. Conversation swirled at the tables around them, all of it in Spanish. He was a fair hand at Spanish, and Ponder spoke it better than some Mexicans did, but he wasn't interested in what they were saying. He sat for a minute before blurting, "She told me not to be coming back to San Antonio, and if I did, to pretend I didn't know who she was. They are going to tell people her husband died. She said it was better for her reputation."

"You gonna take that lying down?"

"Yeah, Uncle Ponder, I am," Dud said, his voice getting loud. He strove to lower it. "What difference does it make? It's not likely I will to be moving in her circle of friends no how."

Ponder stared at him while chewing on his food. He swallowed and spoke. "There's more to it than what you're telling me."

Dud did not know if he should keep it to himself or not. He decided to admit part of it.

"She wants to have children, and she thinks she ain't gonna get any out of me."

Her exact words were, "Let's face it, Dud, you're shooting blanks just like Ponder." Ponder had been married two or three times, and none of those women had missed so much as one monthly cycle. But they had not left him because of it. Fever and disease killed them, not childbirth or lack of it.

That painful confession stopped all conversation, and the two men ate in silence. Dud ruminated in his own world. Maybe if he had made plenty of money, she would have overlooked not having children and stayed with him.

The men behind him were loud and boisterous, and it irritated him that he could not eat in peace when his world was crumbling. He could feel his heart pounding and his blood getting hotter and hotter as they kept on talking and boasting.

He looked up to see Ponder staring at him.

"I ain't got no more money to get you out of jail."

Dud nodded and felt his anger draining away. It was not anybody else's fault his wife did not want him. He bent his head down and took another bite.

He had just started to chew when a fat man one table over jumped up and began screaming, running the words together so fast, Dud could not at first catch what he was saying.

The irate man was hollering toward the kitchen, and picking up something from his plate, he threw it at the cook. He spouted a lot of Mexican cuss words, and something about the cattle roaming the outskirts of town being as thick as fleas, so why did they have to serve him a cat's jaw?

As soon as Dud heard *mandíbula de gato,* he spit his food out, he and Ponder leaping from the table at the same time. Throwing money down, they escaped in a hurry, before chairs started being thrown and knives were drawn.

Dud took one last look through the doorway at the commotion beginning inside before striding away, keeping up with Ponder and his long legs.

"That's the last time you are taking me into that place."

"Quit bellyaching, Dud. You know you've had to eat worse. Come on, let's go to the station and pick up your things."

Dusk began to fall on their way to the stagecoach station, and they argued back and forth. Dud wanted to go leave San Antonio immediately and lick his wounds in the privacy of darkness. Ponder wanted to sleep in the stables and head out just before daylight.

Approaching an itinerant preacher standing on a chair and exhorting a crowd in the fading light, they stopped cussing one another long enough to get past the preacher.

"For God has tested us; He has tried us as silver is tried. He has laid a crushing burden on our backs," the preacher cried in a loud voice. "We have gone through fire and through water, yet God has brought us to a place of abundance, brothers and sisters."

Someone picked up a rock and threw it at the preacher, narrowly missing his head. "You lie, preacher! There ain't no abundance here!"

He stooped to pick up another rock, but before he could, Ponder lifted one of his boots and kicked him in the back. The man fell face down and rolled over on his side. Ponder kicked him again in the stomach.

"Show some manners. That ain't no way to speak to a man of God."

All he did was groan and vomit. Dud pulled on Ponder's arm.

"I ain't got no money to get you out of jail either, old man."

They walked in silence along the darkening street, Dud again inwardly lamenting his lack of funds. If he just had a big enough wad of money to buy her a fine house, maybe she would come back to him.

The stagecoach station operated out of one of the finer hotels. Always a busy spot, the sidewalks hummed with activity despite the fading light. The stagecoach had been late coming in, and people jockeyed around it, reaching for their baggage or greeting the folks waiting for them. Dud and Ponder pushed their way through toward the hotel doors. The flickering street lanterns above their heads lit the face of a severe looking woman with a harsh New England accent who had just alighted. She upbraided her husband with little care that anyone around them could hear every word spoken. Dud forced himself to shove down the anger that always rose when he saw people of the North flocking to Texas to take advantage of a broken and defeated people. They had asked for the trouble they had, but that did not make it any easier to swallow.

". . . bring me to this godforsaken place," the woman was saying. "Those cattle with those beastly long horns, blocking the road, making travel impossible . . ."

Dud looked at the husband — nodding, trying to calm his wife while he felt completely out of place and unsure of what to do — and he suddenly felt better. Men in the North had just as many marital troubles as men in the South. He felt like patting him on the back and saying, "I understand, brother."

He and Ponder went inside, making their way through the bustling crowd to the ticket counter. Polished wood and shining brass were everywhere, gleaming in the glow from overhead lamps that managed to hold on to the illusion of genteel prosperity in a state now raw with upheaval. Just as Dud was about to introduce himself to the clerk, a tall man in a well-cut suit cut in front of him.

"I need two tickets for Corpus Christi and

get with it. I'm in a hurry."

Dud glared at him — he was one of those men who had stayed home from war "to take care of business" and somehow managed to amass a personal fortune while everyone around him went hungry. His nose looked like it had a peach pit on the end of it, and Dud was getting ready to rear back and hit it when Ponder strode on his boot.

Dud scowled at Ponder but let go of his anger. All he wanted to do was get out of San Antonio as soon as possible.

"That will be twenty-five dollars, Mr. Karling," the ticket clerk said.

He threw money on the counter, grabbed the tickets and left. Dud and Ponder in their cowboy attire were invisible to him. Dud stepped forward and gave the clerk his name.

"I'm here to pick up some crates that were addressed to me in Goliad."

The clerk in his visor and gartered sleeves gave him a keen look. "There's only one package here with your name on it, Mr. Washburn."

He reached under the counter and brought out a lump wrapped in brown paper, throwing it on the counter in front of Dud.

Dud took it, like a man in a dream. It was

soft and pliable, and he knew inside would be the few clothes he owned. All the tools he had collected, his books, the rifle that had belonged to his father — all of them gone.

He turned around, looking at Ponder with unbelieving eyes. He swallowed hard and made his way out of the hotel with Ponder at his heels. At the stable, they saddled their horses in the dark and left San Antonio with barely three or four sentences spoken between them.

"At least she left me the ranch."

"You better check at the courthouse when we get home and make sure."

After that, conversation bit the dust, and all that could be heard was the sound of horses' hooves pounding on the parallel dirt trails that served as a road. Keeping a steady pace, it would take them four days to get to the Washburn ranch. Despite the blackness of the night, they knew the way well, and late into that first evening, they stopped at the home of a longtime friend.

"I got nothing, Dud," he said as they sat outside with only an occasional star peeking through the clouds for light. "The Confederate Army swept through here and took every animal on the place. It took me a year to raise enough money for a horse and one old mule that I got to guard ever night like they was gold."

With a shotgun across his lap, he talked about a mutual acquaintance who was making a little cash rounding up wild mustangs on the prairie and selling them.

"He rides with them for miles, never letting them stop for food or water, until he can work them to getting into a pen he made around an old watering hole."

They talked far into the night, discussing horses, cattle, politics, and naturally, women. Dud gave their host a brief account of his divorce. While sympathetic to Dud's troubles, he and Ponder mercifully did not press him for more details. Not that there were that many to tell.

They left the next morning, refreshed and feeling better, with their friend standing on the veranda waving goodbye and calling, "Y'all come see me now and then."

They intended on spending the following night in the next town. Because they had stayed later at their friend's ranch than they had planned, it was dusk when they finally rode into town, stopping to stable their horses before heading for a saloon where they hoped to meet an old acquaintance or two who might invite them home for the night. Otherwise, they would go back to the stable and sleep with the horses.

As they made their way to the saloon, Dud looked up and down the empty streets. “Where is everybody? This looks like a ghost town.”

“Danged if I know,” Ponder answered.

The saloon, however, was crowded. Ponder immediately found a poker game to join while Dud stood at the bar. He was not much of a drinker and could nurse a beer for half the night if he had someone to talk to, and thankfully, several men he knew came in and joined him. They answered his question readily enough.

“The Union Army has taken up residence. You know we’re under martial law. Don’t go anywhere at night by yourself, Dud. It ain’t safe.”

Dud looked around. “Then why aren’t they in here? I never knew a career army soldier that couldn’t drink his weight in whiskey in one night.”

“They will be. Their money is welcome, but they ain’t. If they settle in for too long, the place will slowly empty until they ain’t nobody left but them, so old Joe there,” he said, motioning his head to the bartender, “makes sure they don’t overstay their welcome.”

Dud glanced at the bartender with his

striped shirt, bowtie, and dark hair parted and slicked down with bear grease. “How does he do that?” he asked, turning back to his companion.

The man took a long drink and turned, placing his elbows on the bar as he surveyed the room.

“Varnish solvent,” he said, not looking at Dud. “It gets stronger as the night goes on, until their bellies begin to feel afire.”

Dud grimaced into his glass and took another sip. Outside, a lamplighter was going up and down the street, lighting coal oil lanterns that gave the night a soft glow. The lanterns in the saloon had already been lit in readiness for nightfall.

Shadows were flickering on the wall when the soldiers came in about an hour later, six of them. As soon as they entered, men stopped talking, and the saloon became as quiet as a church house on a Friday night. Knowing better than to stare openly and invite trouble, Dud gave discreet looks into the mirror behind the bar. He counted five enlisted men led by a big, burly sergeant who looked like he chewed glass for supper.

They sat at a table behind him, boisterous and noisy at first, pretending they were not the cause of the unnatural silence in the room.

Dud glanced in the mirror at the table where Ponder sat playing poker. It was as if they were playing in some kind of sign language, because no lips moved.

After a while, when the soldiers had started in on their second and third bottles of whiskey, they began to complain and speak disparaging remarks about Texas in general, hoping to get a rise.

"If New Mexico Territory was the devil's playground, then this place is hell's kitchen."

"Fort Sumner with its starving Indians was a picnic compared to this."

"The only thing that smells worse than an Indian is a Texan."

When no one responded, they started in on Confederate soldiers. Still, the room remained silent.

"And you know who were the worst cowards of them all?" the sergeant blared. "The Eighth Texas Cavalry, that's who."

Dud did not think he let his back stiffen, but they must have picked up on some vibration from him. He had been one of Terry's Rangers.

They continued their verbal assault on the Eighth Texas, mocking their reputation, calling them yellow cur dogs and the like. Men who had been standing by Dud at the bar silently drifted away, until he was left standing alone. Two nights before, he had been looking for a bar fight, now that one was offered to him, he did not necessarily want it.

He looked in the mirror at Ponder. When Ponder was ready for a brawl, he would spit out his wad of chewing tobacco so he did not accidentally swallow it. But Ponder's lower lip still had a telltale bulge, and he concentrated heavily on his cards. Ponder, who never backed down from a fight, for some reason did not want Dud to start one in this barroom.

As Dud looked into his beer glass, and the soldiers behind him continued a rant against his fallen comrades that ordinarily would have had his fists flying, he realized why. All of Texas was under martial law. The newspapers reported Major General Phillip Sheridan, the military commander of Texas and Louisiana as saying, "Texas has not yet suffered from the war and will require some intimidation." And he intended to see that they got it.

If the army wanted to, they could arrest every man in the saloon and keep them in jail so long, they would not be able to feed their family and could possibly lose everything they owned. Instead of fighting, they had to sit in silent hatred, and they were asking Dud not to make them join him in a public fight that could cost them their livelihood.

So, he said nothing, believing the soldiers would approach him any minute and start one on their own. To his surprise, they did not, and glancing in the mirror, he saw the sergeant put his hand out to stop someone in midsentence. He looked at Dud and motioned to his men to leave.

They rose from the table and departed, the sergeant the last one out the door.

The noise level did not rise immediately. It took some time before the saloon returned to normal. In the meantime, Dud remained at the bar, starting his second beer as his companions drifted back to him. All of them, himself included, began to talk about horses, cattle, and women again as if they had never been interrupted.

After a while, Dud grew restless. He walked over to Ponder's game to stand and watch for a while. But Ponder's pile of money stayed more or less the same, and Dud knew he would continue to play as long as he had money and someone to keep dealing the cards to him.

Dud left him and went to the door, looking over the batwings at the dimly lit street.

A young woman appeared, walking timidly, looking over her shoulder as if she was afraid. Dud glanced back at the poker players. Ponder's pile had grown larger, not smaller. He turned to look outside again at the woman who seemed so all alone and scared.

Without hesitation, he pushed open the swinging doors and walked across the street.

Chapter Two

The wind blew in little gusts, picking up bits of trash, lifting them up to swirl and depositing them farther down the street. Dud looked right and left, but the streets remained deserted. He removed his hat as he approached the woman.

When she saw him, she put a hand to her breast. "Oh, you frightened me!"

"I'm sorry, ma'am. You look a little scared out here. May I escort you somewhere?"

In the light of the lantern, she looked older than he had first thought and a lot harder. But he did not retract his offer. She gave him an unsure glance, and said, "I guess so. I stayed at my friend's house longer than I intended."

Dud held out his arm, and she put her hand on it. They began walking together on the wooden sidewalk.

"My name's Dud Washburn, from down Goliad way," Dud stated.

"Oh, yes, I know exactly where that's at," she said, her eyes glancing anxiously up the street.

As they walked by an alley, she paused, moving her hand up his sleeve. She raised her lips, and before he knew what was happening, she was kissing his lips and groping him all over. At the heels of the first shock came a tremendous rush of pleasure, and just as the warning bells were beginning to make themselves heard, she removed her hands and melted into the darkness.

His hand went to his holster, but the pistol was gone. Before he could chase after her, the six soldiers from the saloon stepped out of the alley, casting long shadows and blocking his way. One of them held an ax handle in one hand that he used to pound rhythmically in the palm of the other. The big burly sergeant was rolling up his sleeves with a look of glee on his face.

Dud knew he was in for it; nevertheless, he took the offensive and charged in. He managed to knock two of them down before the others grabbed his arms and held him. The sergeant took a sadistic swing at his abdomen, and Dud bent over, his mouth filling with vomit. While they laughed, Dud shot out a foot, kicking one of them in the groin. Dud used their surprise to escape, but they rallied, catching him in one vicious pounce.

They dragged him into the alley where the blackness was like dark ink painting every surface. Making himself dead weight, Dud managed to slip their grasp long enough to fall into a ball on the ground. As they kicked him and swung at him with the ax handle, he did what he could to keep the blows away from his head and kidneys.

Wave after wave of pain came over him, and he tried to block it out while at the same time protecting his body the best he could. With blood spurting from his wounds, the voices of people in San Antonio and the saloon played over and over in his mind. "I'm tired of being married to a freight hauler." "A place of abundance." "Cattle as thick as fleas." "Starving Indians on the reservation."

A roar of gunfire blotted out everything. The alley lit up with fire belching from pistols, and the smell of gun smoke burned in his nostrils. The soldiers no longer beat him. Instead, they fell beside him in pools of blood.

Dud could barely open his eyes. He saw Ponder with a smoking pistol in his hand, and the men from the saloon behind him, holding guns that reeked of gunpowder.

"Get him on a horse if you can, Ponder," one of them was saying. "Ride out of here and don't say nothing about tonight. We'll handle it from here."

Ponder walked to him and looked him over. "Can you ride, Dud?"

Dud felt his head nod.

Later on, he could barely remember what he did. Somehow Ponder got him on his horse, and somehow, he managed to stay on until Ponder found an abandoned shack far from town. Dud remembered Ponder making a pallet on a dirt floor and helping him to lie down. How many hours or days he slept; he was not sure. He only remembered awakening and seeing Ponder bending over him.

"You gonna be all right, boy?"

Dud struggled to raise up on one elbow. All he could think about was getting to his brother-in-law.

"We got to go to Fitz's, Uncle Ponder. I've got to talk to him."

Ponder nodded, placing his hand on Dud's shoulder and gently pushing it down. "We'll go. Just rest for a while first."

The next day, Dud kept assuring Ponder he was well enough to travel. That evening, Ponder helped him on his horse and handed him a new army-issue Colt revolver stolen from one of the dead soldiers to replace the one the kiss had cost him. The kiss had been delightful, and the pistol was of a much better make than the one it replaced, so perhaps it was worth all the hide that had been extracted for it.

To avoid any militia that might be looking for them, they traveled by night, taking it easy and stopping at daylight to visit at the ranches of people they knew. News traveled slow, but it did travel, and no one said a word about any army soldiers being murdered. Neither did they ask Dud where or how he received his bruises. Instead, they welcomed them, eager for company, and shared what little food they had. Dud felt guilty for taking their grub, but since he was a poor cook and Ponder an even worse one, he couldn't help but feel grateful. He and Ponder brought in squirrels or rabbits, even a possum if nothing else, to every house they stopped at.

Nevertheless, Dud rode on, every bounce of the horse causing shocks of pain. He could not complain, because now that Ponder knew he was not going to die, he would just say he was paying for his sins. All he could think about was getting to his sister and brother-in-law's ranch.

"How come you so all fired in a rush to

see Fitz?" Ponder asked.

"I'll tell you when we get to Fitz's." He didn't want to argue with Ponder while on the road.

There were no signs of anyone following them, but still they traveled by night. The weather had turned sharp, and they clutched at thin jackets, trying to stay warm while the horses seemed to enjoy the cold air and walking through darkness.

"I'll bet you they stripped them soldiers of anything that could identify them and buried them miles out of town," Ponder said. "I know just where, too. There's a swampy spot near the creek, and I bet you anything that's where they buried those bodies so deep, won't nobody find them excepting maybe somebody a hundred years from now, and they still won't figure out it was them army fellers."

"What's the army going to do when they finally figure out them soldiers are missing?"

"I bet nothing. Everything is in such an uproar right now; it will take them forever to realize they is missing. And when they do, they'll think they deserted, and that will be that."

Dud hoped so. He had fought against the Union Army for four years, and he did not want to fight them anymore. The war was over; the South lost, and that was it. But there were always people on both sides who kept hanging on to hatred. That part of Dud's life had finished. He would meet with Fitz and explain the plan that had come to him as he was being beaten.

When they did arrive at his sister and brother-in-law's cabin, it was late afternoon. Callie ran out to greet them, blonde hair shining and cheeks pink with happiness. Dud thought she had gained a little weight, but always a slender girl, it became her.

When Fitzhenry Callahan came courting a few years previous, people laughed at his audacity. Callie Washburn was an effervescent, goodhearted girl who always looked like she had some special piece of fun just waiting to happen tucked up her sleeve. Her list of beaus was legendary. Fitz Callahan was older, big and slow moving with a quiet, dry wit that caught people off guard when it became devastatingly sharp. He had a shaggy head of black, curly hair and was brawny on top, slender on the bottom, reminding Dud of a buffalo. But he won Callie's heart, the hearts of her parents, her uncle, and lastly, the hearts of her brothers.

"Dud!" she cried when she saw him. "Uncle Ponder, help me get him off his horse and into the house. Oh, my, Dud!"

They helped him into the log cabin and set him in Fitz's favorite big chair. When Ponder had seen him situated, he left to tend to their horses.

"Dud, were you in a bar fight?" Callie fussed.

"This eye was," he said, pointing to his right eye. "But this here other eye wasn't."

She shook her head and made clucking noises. "I'm going to get you some coffee, and then I'm putting on water to boil for a bath. You are a mess, Dud."

His sister's answer to every illness was to first wash off the dirt; her reasoning was that being clean would automatically make the sick person feel better. Dud did not object. He enjoyed having his baby sister fuss over him.

"Where's Fitz?"

"He's checking over the stock. He'll be back directly. I'm going across the run to the kitchen. I'll be right back."

"I ain't going nowhere."

He rested his head against the chair and shut his eyes, wondering how he should begin to explain the ideas he had in mind to his brother-in-law. And if he could keep Ponder out of it.

Callie returned, carrying a white mug of dark coffee with steam rising from the top.

Dud sat up and took it from her.

"Thank you, Sister."

She sat on a small stool near him while he blew on the coffee and took a sip of the scalding liquid. He nodded his head in approval. It was not real coffee. He did not know what it was, cotton seeds or something, but it was not too bad.

"How is Fitz?"

She looked away. "Better. He took me to church last Sunday. The first time he's been since he got back."

Her eyes returned to Dud. "He couldn't stay, though. He had to get up and walk outside to wait for me."

"Give him time, Sister."

"I know. Tell me what happened to you. And where is Beatrice?"

"She's in San Antonio. She filed for a divorce the minute I left to check on the ranch. When I got back, all my things were gone. She says she is going to tell people she is a widow because it sounds better than saying she is a divorcée."

Callie stared at him. "Dud . . ." she breathed.

Fitz and Ponder entered the room. "Well, Dud, I see you finally got a little of what's been coming to you," Fitz said, sitting in a nearby chair.

Despite his brother-in-law's habitual attitude of pretending he disliked his wife's family, Dud could see he was upset and concerned.

"I'll be all right. Women always make a fool out of me."

Ponder shook his head in disgust. "You must have got it from your mama's people."

"Uncle Ponder! Don't you start in on me."

Callie rose. "The water should be boiling," she said, and left for the kitchen.

Fitz got up from his chair. "Uncle Ponder, will you help Callie with the water while I see if I can't get this cripple over to the kitchen?"

Dud, thinking he could stand on his own, stumbled and almost fell. With Fitz's help, he made it across the dog run while Ponder and Callie went on ahead.

As they entered the kitchen, Ponder was telling Callie to leave, that he would handle it from there on. Callie nodded, gave Dud one more worried look, and left Ponder to empty the large kettles of steaming water into the washtub.

Callie had left a washrag, her best towel, and a fresh slab of soap next to the tub. Fitz lowered Dud into a chair and proceeded to remove his boots. As Ponder filled the tub, Fitz helped Dud remove the clothing that was covered in dust, filth, and dried blood sticking to his skin, causing him to brace against the pain of having them pulled away.

Fitz looked over Dud's cuts and bruises. "I don't know how you kept from getting any broken bones."

He helped lower Dud into the tub. The hot water and lye soap stung Dud's cuts, but soothed his battered muscles. He closed his eyes and relaxed.

"You got any turpentine?" Ponder asked. "And some old sheets? I think we ought to bind his ribs. They are probably cracked."

"Oh, God," Dud muttered.

Ponder rummaged around the kitchen until he found a pot with a handle. Dipping it into the bath water, he poured it over Dud's head.

"Uncle Ponder, I ain't five years old!" Dud sputtered and hollered.

"Hush your mouth. You can't raise your arms up, can you?" He didn't wait for an answer but took the soap and began scrubbing Dud's scalp with it.

Fitz threw back his head and laughed. Dud thought it was probably the first time he had laughed in months, maybe years.

With Ponder fussing over him, and Fitz worrying, Dud decided to hold off telling them of his plans. After his bath, Ponder insisted on rubbing him down with turpentine and wrapping his ribs. His sister fed him and made him go to bed in her and Fitz's room. Dud protested that he did not want to take her bed, but she would hear none of it.

The bed was wide and long, made especially by Fitz, according to him, soon after he first laid eyes on Callie. As Dud sank into the feather mattress, reveling in clean, crisp sheets, he looked at the rest of his brother-in-law's handiwork. A carved dresser, a chair, and a small table for a coal oil lamp that came all the way from New Orleans via Galveston.

Fitz had even built a special hidey-hole for Callie in the event they were ever threatened by Indians or bandits, and Dud's eyes searched the room until he thought he found where it was. He grew drowsy, wondering if the spring door still worked. Perhaps if he had shown as much concern for Beatrice's comfort and safety, she would still be with him. But her parents had already provided her with everything, he told himself, trying to justify his actions as his eyelids shut in a merciful release that would soon blot out all guilt and blame for hours to come.

A rooster crowing by his window awakened Dud the next morning. He tried to get up, but fell back on the bed. Turning his head, he saw where his sister had found his other pair of clothes and laid them out for him. It included a favorite black and gray check cassimere vest. He thought it distinctive with its large brass buttons, but Beatrice had disliked it, considering it too flashy, and he was surprised she had not discarded it.

With a monumental effort, he threw back the covers and sat up, trying to still his dizziness and the crickets chirping inside his head. Once he thought he could rise without falling down, he stumbled around, trying to put on his clothes.

He was interrupted when he heard what he first thought was thunder. Peering out the window, beyond the massive live oak trees, he saw a company of Union soldiers led by a stern-faced captain riding toward the cabin.

Turning away quickly, he looked about the room. Such a show of force could only mean they were searching for the sergeant and his men. Hurrying to the bed with unsteady feet, he began pulling up the quilt and smoothing it out almost as neatly as his sister would have.

Outside, the men had halted, and he could hear the captain's voice on the front veranda. Ponder responded in booming, clear words, much like a person who is hard of hearing might.

"Dud? He ain't here. His old lady divorced him, and he didn't want to have to face his sister, so we split up and he went on home."

Dud grabbed his shirt and pants, listening as he ran his fingers along the boards of the wall, looking for the door that should spring open.

"What do you mean, divorced?" Callie's voice shrieked. "Dud's wife divorced him? We've never had a divorce in our family!"

Dud's fingers poked and prodded the wall frantically while Ponder kept talking loudly, acting as if he was trying to calm Callie down but saying words that would lead her on. She, in turn, carried on hysterically about divorce bringing shame on the family. Meanwhile, the captain kept trying to get them to shut up. He finally managed to get a word in edgewise, sending Ponder off on another tear.

"What do you mean some woman said Dud and the soldiers got into a fight? He got into a bar fight before we left San Antonio. If she saw signs of a fight, that was what she was looking at. You just ask the sheriff there; he threw Dud in jail for fighting in a saloon. You just ask him."

Dud's fingers hit the right spot, and the secret door opened. He leaned down to get in, caught sight of his boots, and hobbled back to fetch them.

"What do you mean you want to search this place? Where's your warrant? Them soldiers is probably in Mexico, living it up with some pretty little señoritas right now."

Grabbing his boots, Dud almost laughed out loud. Nobody could argue with an old man and win. He shuttled into the hidey-hole and shut the door. Dark, full of cobwebs, and built barely tall enough to stand up in, Dud sank to its floor in exhaustion, his knees practically under his chin.

The captain would not be deterred, however, and when the sound of boots rushing into the room reached Dud's ears, he held his breath. But after a few seconds, they rushed out again, and he was able to take deep gulps of air. He had not been responsible for the soldiers' demise, but he was the army's strongest link to their disappearance, and he could rot in jail for a long time while they searched for the missing sergeant and his men. And sitting in jail was not part of his plans at the moment.

Dud's chin dropped, and he dozed. He dreamed his horse had a large eruption on his underbelly, and he lay still, allowing Dud to press on it until a surge of pus came out, a deep stream that seemed to go on forever. Even as he was dreaming it, he thought it was crazy. Pus coming out of a wound — what did that mean?

"Wake up, old man," Fitz's voice called to him.

Dud awakened, realizing where he was and what had happened. He shook the sleep from his head and allowed Fitz to help him clamber out of his hiding place. His knees still had a notion to give on him, but he forced them to stay locked, at least until he had to bend them to put his boots on.

"They've gone, have they?"

"They stayed a heck of a long time." Fitz shook his head. "You would have thought Callie and Ponder were actors putting on a play at the Casino Club in San Antonio, the way they were carrying on."

Callie peered around Fitz's shoulders, her eyes running over Dud to make sure he was all right. "Fitzy, we were just giving Dud time to hide, that's all. Come to the table, Dud, and eat some breakfast. We can talk later."

Callie fussed around him while he ate, but they did not engage in conversation. When he finished, she hovered behind him as he made his way across the dog run into the parlor with its big fireplace and comfortable chairs. Neither Fitz nor Callie were followers of fashion. Everything they had was built for comfort, something that used to irritate Beatrice, but in Dud's present condition, he found consummately satisfying as he sank into a cushioned chair.

Callie went out onto the veranda and called to Fitz and Ponder, telling them Dud wanted to speak to them. How she knew without him telling her was a mystery to Dud. Perhaps Fitz and Ponder wanted to talk, too, because it was only a moment or two later their boots hit the veranda, and they entered the parlor.

Callie had a pot of make-believe coffee boiling in the fireplace. Taking a potholder, she gripped the pot and began pouring it into cups, passing the steaming liquid around. Dud blew on his and waited for it to cool.

Fitz took his coffee, and likewise did not immediately drink, but in his blunt way, began speaking.

"You can hide out here until you're well, Dud, but that captain is going to have soldiers posted at every road leading away from this place."

"They'll send soldiers to our ranch," Ponder said. "And when you don't show up there, they'll be back. Hiding out is what you are going to have to do."

Ponder and Fitz got into a discussion over Dud's best recourse. Ponder said he knew of a cave on the ranch Dud could live in for a while. Fitz offered to let him stay on their ranch as long as he wanted, where there were just as many places to hide.

When Dud did not answer, letting them ramble on, Callie began giving him searching looks. Ponder was the most longwinded, and when he finally paused, Callie spoke in a quiet voice.

"If I know my older brother, he's already got a plan, and he's just waiting for us to shut up so he can tell it."

Six eyes turned and settled on him.

"Out with it, boy," Ponder demanded.

Dud scratched his neck, wondering where to start. At the beginning, he guessed.

"Fitz, I'd like you to round up as many cattle as you can down here, and Uncle Ponder to go back to our place to round up as many as he can there. They'll have to be branded, too. Because I'm taking them on a cattle drive."

"A cattle drive? Where in tarnation to?" Ponder demanded, not giving Dud a chance to respond. "The market's glutted in Californy. Every state that has a railway to ship cattle got a law against Texas fever. There ain't no place to take them."

"I heard Kansas is thinking about passing a law letting some of the cattle come through in the western part of the state," Fitz pointed out.

"Well, there ain't no law passed now. And them farmers up there is shooting people what try to drive them through. Even the Indians in Oklahoma Territory can't get nobody to buy their cattle because of the fever."

The fever, spread by ticks, did not affect Texas long-horns, but devastated cattle farther north that had no immunity to it. Ponder was right — they could try to slip the cattle through, but even then, they might not be able to sell them.

"If you'll shut up a minute, I'll tell you, Uncle Ponder," Dud said. "I'm not going north, so get that idea out of your head. I'm taking these cattle west to New Mexico. I'm selling them to the army at Fort Sumner to feed the Indians on the reservations."

Three faces paused and frowned. Ponder snorted just like an ornery old mule.

"There ain't nothing but a bunch of renegade Comanche between here and New Mexico."

"I know, Uncle Ponder."

Callie touched his shoulder. "Dud, this is too risky. I realize you faced death a thousand times in the army, but this could mean torture and mutilation. It's far too dangerous."

Dud looked up at her. "I'll have to risk it, Sister."

"It ain't just Indians," Ponder said. "It's a hell of a country to pass through. And ain't you had enough of the Union army? It will be just like consorting with the enemy. Besides, you're still wanted for questioning."

"War's over, Uncle Ponder. And those soldiers in New Mexico ain't going to know about or be concerned with a few soldiers over here."

Callie looked from Ponder to Fitz. Dud looked down at the coffee in his cup. He needed Fitz and Ponder. He looked back up, hoping they would agree with his plan.

Ponder rubbed his eyebrow and spit into the fireplace before starting in on him again. "And just what are you going to be doing while we're rounding up cattle? And what are we going to do for horses? We ain't got no money for horses. That poker game I was playing back yonder was for pennies. And you can't have a cattle drive without a lot of horses."

"That's what I'll be doing. Rounding up mustangs."

Ponder swelled up, crossed his arms and leaned back in his chair. "Even with horses, it will take five or six months to get there and back."

"That's right. And you can look after the ranch while I'm away."

"There ain't nothing left to look after. I'm going with you."

"The hell you are!" Dud said, forgetting Callie was present. "You're too old. This here kind of trip is only for young men. You are too dang old and stove up."

"I'm going to be the cook."

"You can't cook!" Dud yelled. "Your food tastes like boar hog with the hair still on."

Fitz was rubbing his top lip with his forefinger, trying to keep from laughing. "I'll round up as many cattle as I can, Dud," he said. "but I can't go with you. You can take my cattle and sell them on halves."

He rose and stood beside the chair Callie was sitting in, placing his hand on her shoulder. "I'm not leaving Callie that long. She's going to have a baby."

"Of course, you can't, not in her condition," Ponder agreed.

Dud felt stupefied. "A baby?"

"Dud, open your eyes; can't you see nothing?" Ponder asked.

Blood rushed to Dud's face. He had thought his sister had just gotten a little plump. He did not realize she was pregnant.

He gulped. "Halves it is, then."

It was disappointing, but Dud realized it was probably for the best. A big man and hard on horses, it would be a difficult trip for Fitz to make. Dud would need small, lightweight young men who would be easy on their horses and able to ride for miles without complaint.

"Where are you going to get these mustangs?" Ponder asked.

"They're out there running loose on the plains, Uncle Ponder."

"You better use a different name while you're out hunting for them, or the army will be rounding you up, too."

Dud nodded. Ponder and Fitz immediately began a discussion on what price the army might be willing to pay for beef. It was unspoken between the men, that no matter what it was, they were all so poor, it would be worth the gamble.

Ponder wanted to know what route Dud planned on using.

"We'll take them to San Antonio and pick up the old military trail west."

"Dud, you're going to need as much

firepower as you can get," his brother-in-law warned. "One little six-shooter ain't gonna do it."

"I still got Pa's old gun belt and holsters he had made before he passed," Ponder said. "He always wore two guns and a knife in each boot."

"Grandpa Ned had more grit than anybody I ever met," Dud said.

"That's right," Ponder said in grim satisfaction. "Not like this younger generation of hot house flowers, used to coal oil, fancy wood stoves, trains, and such as that to rush them wherever they want to go."

Fitz adroitly turned the conversation back to the matters at hand. Callie was in and out of the room. Dud realized she was worried about Ponder and him, but every time Fitz's lips moved, a look of relief would cross her face. He probably talked more that day than he had the entire time since he got back from the war.

Dud let the other men lead the discussion on details most of the time, content they had fallen in with his plans. Except the part about Ponder going along. That was going to be a sore spot for thousands of miles to come.

"Sister, can't you teach Uncle Ponder

anything about cooking before we leave?" Dud asked.

Chapter Three

Ponder intended on staying several days before going back to the home ranch. Or what was left of it. When Dud returned from the war, all he found was a burned-out shell. He and Ponder built a log cabin similar to the one Fitz had, without all the comforts, for Beatrice had made it plain from the very beginning she was never going to live there.

Fitz's two-bedroom cabin had withstood the war, however. Because every muscle Dud had ached, Ponder insisted on letting him have the bed while he slept on a pallet in the parlor, near the fireplace. Since Ponder's snores could drown out a Rebel yell, and he had elbows and feet as sharp as yucca leaves, Dud was grateful not to have to share a bed with him.

One night, though, soon after they arrived, the Yankees came for Dud. They had him surrounded, about to kill him. There was nowhere he could turn, no way he could escape. In desperation, he jumped out of bed and grabbed the Colt he kept on the nightstand.

"Dud! Dud! Wake up!" Ponder yelled.

"Dud!" Fitz said, reaching for the gun.

Dud blinked his eyes. Ponder stood in his long johns; Fitz was wearing his britches and nothing else, taking the pistol gently from his hand.

"I could have killed you," Dud said, so sick, he thought he might vomit.

Ponder grimaced, blowing it off with a wave of his hand. "I came in here earlier and unloaded the darn thing when I heard you muttering and tossing."

He turned and left the room, shaking his head. Fitz took the Colt and placed it back on the nightstand. Dud sank down on the edge of the bed.

"Why am I still living?"

Fitz put a big hand on his shoulder, giving him a reassuring pat. "We have to stay alive and thrive for the women of Texas, Dud."

Dud looked up. "There's no woman in Texas that needs me, Fitz."

"That's a lie, and you know it. Do you think it is easy for Callie? To have lost her parents and three of her brothers in the war? You and Ponder are the only close blood kin she has left, Dud. If anything happened to you, I don't know how she could stand it."

"Sometimes I think I'm still kicking just so Uncle Ponder can have somebody to yell at."

Fitz grinned. "There might be some truth in that."

"Is Callie really upset about me being divorced?"

"I may not be able to take her to San Antonio for a couple of years for fear she might look Beatrice up and give her a piece of her mind, but she thinks you being divorced is a sight better than your Uncle Finn being the town drunk or your cousin Horace getting hung for being a horse thief."

"Callie doesn't let anything bother her too long," Dud said with relief.

Fitz nodded and padded his bare feet out of the room, shutting the door behind him.

Dud let the back of his head sink into the feather pillow while his eyes searched the darkened ceiling. Would he be able lead men and hundreds of cattle on a long drive to an unknown destination without falling to pieces? He had seen too many brave men in the war, who after so long of being barraged by death and destruction, become unsure and irresolute, unable to make decisions. Or else they become mean, crazed killers who nobody could stand to be around and finally had to be stopped with a bullet or a hangman's noose.

"It is what it is," Dud murmured, closing his eyes and letting himself drift toward sleep. He would either succeed or fail. He had botched his marriage, but maybe he could put his life back together better than before without falling to pieces or turning into a bigger asshole than he already was.

Ponder left in a few days' time, while Dud stayed with his sister and brother-in-law long enough to let his bruises fade and his beard grow out, making him look less like someone soldiers had beaten pulpy. As soon as he was able, he was back in the saddle, helping Fitz round up cattle. They began branding everything in sight that was not nursing on someone else's branded cow. Fitz's ranch hands consisted of two old Negro men who could castrate a calf with a straight razor so fast, it was almost scary to watch. Dud had long before decided he never wanted to get crossways with them.

He was getting ready to leave, oiling his saddle with tallow and beeswax in the barn, when his cousin Audie arrived, sent by Ponder to warn him not to go back to the ranch just yet.

"They still have soldiers posted on different roads looking for you, Dud. When you leave here, you're gonna have to stick to the back trails."

"Much obliged," Dud said, glancing over his cousin as he continued to wipe down the saddle.

Audie was thirty or close to it, about the same height as Dud, but heavier, with a square jaw and a clunky build. His eyes were big and round, and they looked sad all the time.

"You been helping Ponder round up cattle?" Dud asked.

"Yep. You know Ponder. He's done been around to all the neighbors, mustering up teenage boys to help him, promising them twenty dollars a month if they help deliver the cattle. The parents are kicking a little about them going through dangerous territory, but they are all so poor, they know they need the money, and the boys are happy to get to go."

"They may not be so glad if they don't make it back."

"It's either that or possibly turning outlaw if they don't have some kind of work that pays them something, Dud," Audie said, rubbing his hand over the saddle, examining the intricate carvings on it made long before by one of the men who had worked for Dud's father.

Dud did not object to anything Audie told him. He had explained to Ponder what he wanted and how much he would be willing to pay. For some reason, people trusted Ponder, and he knew his uncle would succeed in getting help when a younger man might not.

"I want to go along, too, Dud," Audie said.

Dud did not answer right away. He left the saddle and turned to his horse, a dark bay with black points. Picking up a brush, he stroked the gelding's hair, trying to decide what to say to Audie.

"What happened to that slick gray you were so fond of?" Audie asked.

"He got shot out from beneath me at Chattanooga. Jax is a good horse, but I never have been able to cotton to him like I did the gray."

Dud paused and looked at his cousin. "What about your wife and children?"

All the color drained from Audie's face. "Dud, they died of cholera before I got home."

"Oh God, Audie," Dud said, feeling like a heel. "Uncle Ponder told me that when I first got back, and it slipped my mind with everything else that's been going on."

Audie walked closer, standing on the other side of the horse, looking over it at him.

"Dud, I can't stand to go back to that house. I'm about to go crazy with grief. I got to get away."

Dud forgot all about Audie's age, how slow he could be in making judgment calls, his heaviness. "If you'll help me handle Ponder, I'd be much obliged to you, Audie."

A slow grin spread over Audie's face. "I can do that, Cousin Dud."

Dud gave a wry smile in return.

"You going after those mustangs tomorrow? You need some help?"

"Yes, but you go back and help Ponder. I'll do this on my own."

Audie nodded. "I'm good with cattle and horses, but I ain't no count as a stealthy tracker, that is a fact. What you need is a horse-savvy Mexican to help you."

"Maybe, but I ain't got one right now."

As Dud prepared to leave the next day, Callie took him aside before he got in the saddle. Her eyelashes flicked at tears.

"Dud, you don't know what this means, with the baby coming and everything."

"Now, Sister, don't get to blubbering," Dud said.

She sniffed. "Dud, do take care. I'll be

praying for you every night."

Not a demonstrative man, he nevertheless pecked her cheek. He patted her shoulder and got on his bay.

"Don't worry, Sister. It's going to work out all right."

He and Audie left, riding through the woods and brush with a pack mule and an extra horse that Fitz could scarcely afford to lose, but insisted on loaning Dud anyway. Audie rode part of the way with him, branching off to go back to Ponder and Dud's ranch, while Dud headed for the open plains and what he hoped would be hundreds of mustangs roaming free. He wanted fifty of them.

Dud kept to the back trails, not seeing anyone for the first two days. In the early morning hours of the third day, he topped a hill and looked down on a small hacienda.

A Spanish pony stood tied to a small chapote tree underneath a second-story window, its white coat blending in with the ancient stucco walls of the hacienda. As Dud watched, a small man climbed out of the window. In one leap, he landed square in the saddle. A pretty young Mexican señorita leaned out the window and called, "Enrique!"

Enrique blew her a kiss just before she

disappeared into the house, yanked back by an angry father who leaned out the window, screaming curse words. Enrique spurred his horse just as the father pulled out an old pistol and fired at him.

Dud watched as Enrique disappeared over a hill on his swift little Spanish pony. Dud gave one last look at the angry *papá* waving his fist at the dust Enrique left behind. He turned his horse and headed in the direction the rider took.

He traveled reckless, not bothering to hide his tracks. Dud followed at a slower pace, knowing Enrique would find him when he got hungry.

Dud was not particularly ready to eat, but in the late afternoon he crossed the Atascosa River and decided it was as good a spot as any to make camp and give the horses a rest. He hoped the next day his hunt for mustangs would begin to bear fruit.

Throwing his rigging underneath a post oak, he staked the horses and mule with long ropes so they could feast on fresh grass, yet still be within sight. With them taken care of, he got a fire going. Removing a slab of fatback from his grub sack, he cut it into small chunks for bacon and soon had it frying in a skillet over his fire. His sister had cooked beans for him, later placing them on a rock in the sun to dry. He threw a few handfuls of beans in with the bacon and added enough water to rehydrate them.

By that time, it was getting dark, and he ran a picket line between two trees near his campfire, tying the horses and the mule to it where he could keep an eye and ear on them during the night. He gave each animal a reassuring pat before returning to his beans.

The edge of darkness passed; the stars in the night sky above him shown like sparkles on a dark lake with moonbeams shining at just the right angle. Four years of war had given Dud a sixth sense, and he knew the man he had been following had approached his camp.

"You better come closer and get some vittles, Enrique," he said.

The young Mexican walked forward. The flame from the campfire showed a slender, small *muchacho* dressed in striped pants and a black leather vest with silver conchos and latigo hanging from the front. He wore a black sombrero, with intricate gold embroidery and trim surrounding the high crown. A small goatee and dark mustache added to his rakish appearance. He couldn't have been more than nineteen.

"You may call me Henry, señor," he said

with a Spanish accent. "It is easier on the Anglo tongue."

"Have a seat, Henry," Dud said, and fetching another spoon and plate, he loaded it up with beans and the corn dodgers his sister had also sent along.

"You have no coffee, señor?" Henry asked as he crouched down and took the plate.

"Not this time."

Dud watched as the boy ate with abandonment, realizing it had probably been a long time since his last meal. His horse and riding skills had impressed Dud, but he was not ready to offer him money to help with the mustangs until he had a chance to see what he could do.

"But, of course, I will help you find mustangs tomorrow, Señor Dud," Henry said. "I know where one such herd waters near here, on the San Miguel Creek. They always go to the same spot."

Dud nodded, relieved that at least he knew that much. Dud spread out his bedroll near the fire, while Henry fetched his saddle and blanket. They stretched out; Henry almost instantly asleep. Dud put his Colt under his saddle, within easy reach.

Before dawn, Dud awakened, half expecting to see one, if not all, his horses gone, but Henry was still sleeping soundly, looking like an angelic choirboy. Dud thought about the girl in the window, and that made him think of Beatrice when she still liked him.

Forcing himself to put that aside, Dud kicked at the coals and added more wood to the fire. He began thinking about the elusive mustangs that haunted the prairies like otherworldly kings.

They staked out a spot near the creek where the mustangs came to water, but upwind and hidden from view.

"I think today is the day, Señor," Henry said. "But if not, they will be here tomorrow."

The morning air had a little bit of a bite in it, left over from winter, as if not yet ready to give in to spring. That it was still chilly was comforting to Dud, but at the same time, reminding him that time was slipping away, and they should be starting on the drive soon.

Herds would come to the spot they watered every two days. Dud hoped Henry had his days right. He shifted in the saddle and forced himself to stay calm, waiting.

When they arrived, the energy and power they possessed in those lithe bodies and muscled legs caused a catch in his breath as it always did. The mares came first. On their side, nearest Henry and him, ran a dark stallion, a slick, proud creature that looked to be four or five years old, the age Dud most desired.

At the water, the mares hung back until the stallion could taste and see it was safe. When he decided it was all right, the mares came forward. They drank heavily, until their bellies were bloated with water. One by one, they left the water and gathered under the trees to browse lazily in sleepy silence.

Henry moved so smoothly, Dud almost didn't catch what he was doing until he had spurred his little pony closer, a lasso in hand. Dud expected him to aim for the head of the stallion, but instead, Henry lassoed the feet, as smooth and as neat a throw as Dud had ever witnessed.

At the flick of the rope, the other horses began to flee in a mass of excited confusion. With the stallion down, Henry leaped from his saddle while his stout little pony held tight. With another loop of a rope, he had the horse choked down. The awful frenzied sound of an animal choking to death was equal to the cries of pain Dud had heard on the battlefield and just as tormenting.

Quicker than a slap from a mad mammy,

Henry tied the feet. He slackened the choke hold on the horse, and the animal came up, covered in lather and trembling.

Dud watched, knowing what Henry did next would tell the tale of just what kind of a horseman he was.

Henry walked up to the stallion, talking softly in Spanish, telling him what a magnificent creature he was. He stroked his ears and forehead, rubbing his nose and making gentle passes over his eyes with his hands. He drew closer and breathed into the frightened animal's nostrils.

Dud let out a sigh of relief. He had found his man. Now if he could just convince the amorous little devil to help him catch forty-nine more.

Henry, preening in justifiable pride, readily agreed to Dud's offer of employment.

"I will help you take the horses to your ranch, Señor Dud, but I cannot go into *La Bahía.* I am forbidden to go back."

As a wanted man himself, Dud had no qualms about that. And he was almost positive Henry's crime had been one involving an angry father, not murder or theft. He assured Henry there would be no need to go into the village of Goliad.

Henry, however, refused to contemplate going on the cattle drive.

"Not for me to aggravate some Indian into attacking this little Mexican. I am much too fond of my manhood to have it cut off and stuffed into my mouth by a bloodthirsty Comanche."

Dud nodded. He would like to have someone such as Henry on the drive, but he did not press him. Instead, he began to discuss ways they would catch a lot of mustangs at one time. As good as Henry was with a rope, it would still take too long amassing a herd of mustangs in a short amount of time using that method.

One stallion would ride with a herd of mares and fight off any other stallion that tried to join them. And Dud didn't want a bunch of mares. But the bachelors not allowed to join the herds with mares would group together, and this was what Dud wanted to find.

Henry knew of a little box canyon. After finding a herd, they would run with the mustangs, keeping them from food and water until they could turn them toward the canyon. But first, they would have to chop brush for a fence, being prepared to hold the mustangs in the canyon until they could be tamed enough to herd to Goliad.

Fence building was tedious and boring, but once completed, the catching of mustangs became dangerous and exciting enough to keep Henry from riding off in search of another señorita. That, and all the grub Callie had insisted Dud take along. They killed a deer for fresh meat, dragging it far from the canyon before butchering it. Nevertheless, the horses shivered and paced during the night to far-off screams of panthers fighting over the carcass, while Dud kept his gun handy, and Henry unsheathed a slender stiletto.

The mustangs were wild and excitable, and the best ones were also the most untamed and hard to handle. They had to keep them thirsty and half-starved in order to force the animals to trust them for food and water. Still, Dud could not stand cruelness, and it pleased him that while Henry could be firm, he knew how to keep from breaking a horse's spirit.

They culled the unsuitable ones and went after more. On their final foray, it began to drizzle. The weather grew colder, making them even more miserable. Henry flagged, and he stopped talking about girls and horses, riding with uncharacteristic gloom in the saddle. Dud wanted to quit but knew he would be running short on the drive if he stopped and went home.

They rode for hours, not sighting so much

as a jackrabbit. Dud was about to give up hope when they came upon a herd grazing in the rain in the middle of a meadow, and because the wind was not blowing, the horses did not immediately sense their presence.

On the outside of the herd stood a dun stallion with dark striping down its back and around its legs. They had already captured a few like him, but this one caught Dud's interest as none of the others had. Although he looked to be only five or six years old, his body already had many scars where he had fought with other stallions and probably panthers, too. Dud had no desire to own a foul-tempered stallion, but he sensed the mustang would fight, not out of meanness, but to hold his ground against all comers.

The stallion began herding his mares away from the enemy he had spied. Dud looked at Henry, nodding in the direction of the stallion he knew in the next heartbeat that he wanted very much for his own. Henry gave a slight nod, and they took out after the herd.

The stallion could have easily outrun them, but he would not leave his mares. Knowing Dud did not want more mares, Henry got his rope ready. Despite being numbed by cold drizzle and on the run, Henry made good his throw, around the neck this time, and soon had the horse thrown down. Dud dismounted, and it was he who talked gentle into the stallion's ear, and he who brought the quivering mustang up.

Dud took his time, and after a while, was able to tie the dun next to Jax, who did not put up with any nonsense. They started to ride again into the miserable weather. But they were rewarded when they came upon another group of stallions grazing near a shallow creek.

Henry hollered out praise Mary or something that Dud did not completely understand, and waving his hat, he took out after the mustangs with Dud and the dun following.

They kept after them, and with unremitting pressure between their hides and the leather of their saddles, the next day they finally got the herd, along with the dun, turned into their makeshift corral in the canyon. They had ridden all night in the thunder, lightning, and a rain that had been intermittently driving and drizzling, but always constant.

They quickly cut out what Dud did not want, and when finished, he counted forty-five good mustangs ranging between the ages of four and eight years old, including the dun stallion.

Exhausted, trembling, he allowed Dud to pet him and breathe into his nostrils.

"What are you going to name him, Señor Dud?" Henry asked, recognizing that Dud had chosen this magnificent creature to be his own.

Dud petted the dun, looking him over. "Oh, I reckon I'll call him Ned after my grandpappy."

"It is always good to honor one's ancestors, Señor Dud."

Dud hoped at least a few of Henry's descendants would even know who he was. He doubted they all would.

Chapter Four

When they started for Goliad, the mustangs were half-broke. Dud and Henry had worn the same clothes, not even changing so much as their socks, in order not to confuse the mustangs about their scent. They had ridden the horses, petted them, hand-fed and watered them, blown in their nostrils, everything they could think of to keep them calm and get them used to humans.

The mustangs were tough, but they would never be as easy to ride as horses that had milder blood from the east. But Dud was not looking for easy. He needed something with hooves of steel, a heart that would not quit, and a hide so resilient it could take the bony butt or saddle of any cowboy who had to ride for twenty-four hours straight if necessary.

They had just crossed Sarco Creek, nearing home, when two riders appeared on the level plain. Dud saw them and prepared himself to greet or fight the newcomers. He and Henry kept the herd together, although they smelled the two new men and had begun to snort in fear. Just as Dud reached down to put his hand on his Colt, the riders broke into a run, heading for them, intent on scattering the herd and cutting out some of the horses for themselves.

Dud rode straight at them, leaving Henry with the herd. He was riding Ned, and he thought it a good time to test the horse's mettle. He rode Ned in a direct line for the man he thought was the leader, the one who had broken into a charge first, a saddle tramp who was nothing more than a blur of old hat and ragged clothes. He raised his gun and fired. Dud heard the whistle of the bullet come close. Ned ran faster than any horse Dud had ever ridden, but he wanted to flee, and it took all Dud's strength and will to keep him heading in the direction of gunpowder. Raising his pistol, Dud aimed and fired, shooting his attacker in the chest. He let Ned swerve to the right, but reined him to turn around and go back.

The herd had not scattered, but ran past them. Henry was still with them. As the other outlaw approached him, Henry drew out his knife and let it fly.

It hit him so hard in the chest, he fell

backward off his horse. Dud stayed with the mustangs, letting Henry fall back to retrieve his knife and rob the dead of anything they might possibly have, which Dud figured was little of nothing.

Dud let them run off their fear, easing up on Ned gradually to set the pace. It took a while for Henry to catch up, but when he did, he wore a big grin.

"*Mucho emociones,* Señor Dud!"

"Si, amigo," Dud said, with a grin of his own.

Before Ponder had left Callie's, Dud had asked him to have a corral ready for the mustangs. Ponder had been more than a little skeptical of Dud's ability to round up enough horses. But he agreed they had better put them near the cabin because somebody was going to have to stay with them night and day to keep thieves away. They had not seen a bear in the area for years, but panthers and wolves readily ripped apart and feasted on calves, foals, along with unwary house cats and dogs. They would be more likely fending off the human kind of predator, however.

As Dud approached their cabin, he saw a brush corral. Ponder had driven in posts in a large circle and piled brush facing inward between the posts. The mustangs would avoid getting entangled in the brush, and Dud thought it would hold them for the short time he hoped to be there.

Vast herds of cattle grazed in the distance, but the place looked deserted. Dud had expected to see a beehive of activity, like what had been happening at Fitz's when he left. The barren scene did not feel right, but he did not have time to think about it. His main concern was getting the mustangs into Ponder's corral.

Jax, his bay, however, hadn't forgotten that when he went into a corral, no matter how crude, he would get a helping of oats, and he led the way. Dud had to press Ned and be firm with him, but the horse had begun to realize, out of this tribe, Dud was the head honcho, and he was the head honcho's horse. When that sunk home, he began pushing the other horses forward.

Once the horses were inside the corral, Henry leaped from his mustang and began putting logs across that would serve as a makeshift gate. Dud dismounted, removing his rigging and throwing it over the logs.

With the mustangs secure, Dud and Henry began watering the horses and feeding them a few oats, something the mustangs had never tasted and were suspicious of at first. Dud again tried to get Henry to go on the cattle drive with them, but he smilingly refused. Dud could not even talk him into staying for supper.

"I'm sorry I cannot stay, Señor Dud. I must vamoose. It is not healthy for me to be in this neighborhood."

Dud paid him and told him to pick out two of the mustangs to take with him. Henry already knew exactly the ones he wanted, two flashy little black horses that would do to impress a señorita or two.

As Henry rode away, Ponder and Audie rode in from another direction. Dud picked up his rigging and met them in the barn.

Ponder looked him up and down. "Great smokes, Dud, you look like a grizzly bear with all that hair, and you smell worse than a dead polecat."

"Nice to see you again, too, Uncle Ponder," Dud said as he threw his saddle over a bench. "Audie, I thought you told me you and Uncle Ponder had a bunch of boys rounding up cattle, cutting, and branding them."

Audie and Ponder looked at one another. Audie turned back to Dud.

"We did, Dud. We been working harder than bees on a mescal bean in bloom. Just when we thought we done rounded up every stray bovine in three counties, a fever swept through here and put down every hand we had."

Dud paused, not wanting to believe his ears. "What?"

Ponder grimaced. "It passed me and Audie by. Maybe it was something we already had and were immune to."

"You mean to tell me, there is no one in Goliad County who can help with this cattle drive?" Dud demanded.

"The whole countryside's down with it. Ten people have died already."

Dud leaned back against the wall of the barn and shut his eyes. Cattle everywhere, half-wild horses in the corral, and no cowboys to work them. All he could think of was to regret letting Henry leave without trying harder to get him to stay.

"Well, Mr. Bright Ideas, what in the Sam Hill are we supposed to do now?" Ponder asked.

Dud stood upright and took a deep breath. "I'm taking a bath, and I'm going to eat."

He turned and strode from the barn with Ponder and Audie following him.

"Did you get a wagon ready? Did you find any oxen trained to pull?" Dud asked Ponder.

"Yeah, I got the wagon ready, and Old Man Lackey said we could borrow his oxen if we'd let his gal Sal and her new husband live in the cabin for a couple of months until they get a place of their own."

"We'll probably have to end up throwing them out after a year's time, but that's all right," Dud said, glancing at the corral as he headed for the house. "Audie, I've already had to fight off two saddle bums looking for easy pickings with those mustangs. We'll have to take turns guarding them at night."

"But what are we going to do for cowhands, you chowderhead?" Ponder hollered.

"I don't know," Dud yelled back. "Start praying, I guess!"

Ponder cooked supper while Dud bathed in a washtub in the kitchen. After emptying the tub and putting on fresh clothes, he cut his beard short, considered keeping it, and in the end, shaved it off, all while Ponder threw pots around and grumbled. Audie wisely decided to stay outside until supper was on the table.

Dud gave himself one last look in the mirror.

"I sure need a haircut. Are those soldiers still after me?"

"Naw," Ponder said. "Somebody spread the rumor that sergeant and his men they was looking for was seen down at the border."

Dud turned and arched an eyebrow at his uncle. "Some old man named Ponder, you mean."

Audie grinned and helped himself to some of Ponder's beans. "Can't get a haircut, though. The barber is down with the fever, too."

"I'll cut it after supper. Sit down," Ponder ordered.

"I don't know how I can be in any worse of a fix," Dud said, taking a chair. "Having one of Ponder's haircuts just puts the flies on the horse . . ."

"Shut up and eat," Ponder said, interrupting.

It upset Dud, though, to think of all his neighbors being ill. Cholera and the like were always lurking, waiting to carry off friends and loved ones, so much so that one became almost immune to the grief, and that was sad, too.

"Who all died?" he asked.

Ponder rattled off a list of names. Most seemed to be the very old or the very young, as was almost always the case. Dud shook his head in sorrow. But he had to forget the past and think about the future.

"I think we ought to say adios to this place

before we all take sick," Dud said, taking a spoonful of the most unappetizing beans he had ever gazed upon and plopping them on his plate. They almost bounced.

"You've got to castrate those stallions first, Dud," Ponder said.

Dud felt his temper rising, and it took all he had to keep from lashing out at his uncle.

"No, *we* have to castrate those stallions first. Starting tomorrow."

"That ain't gonna give them much time to heal, Dud," Audie said.

"It's going to have to be get tough or die time on the Washburn Ranch.

"Audie, after that, ride to Fitz's but don't stop anywhere along the way. Tell him about the fever, and see if he can't rustle us up some hands. Come back here as quick as you can, and we'll begin herding cattle, picking up Fitz's as we go north."

"You want me to try to talk Fitz into going?"

"Hell, no," Dud said, shaking his head. "Don't let him."

The next day consisted of grueling hours of catching stallions, tying them up in enough rope to send half of Grant's army provisions by parcel post, and cutting them as fast as possible. Every muscle in Dud's body ached, and before the afternoon was over, Ponder looked like if the wind picked up, he might topple over.

A wagon on the horizon interrupted their work. They stopped to stare — afraid strangers might bring the dreaded fever to the ranch. An ancient mule pulled the wagon; an old man perched on the seat. Two boys rode in the back, their tow hair sticking out from hats that would have been an embarrassment to the oldest saddle tramp who roamed the prairie.

The wagon stopped, and the old man hollered toward them. "We ain't got the fever."

Dud did not recognize them, but they looked harmless. He walked up to the wagon with Ponder beside him. Audie stayed behind, watching and trying to catch his breath — the work was wearing him down, too.

Dud looked in the wagon bed and saw a woman who appeared to be in her forties lying in a pile of quilts, but she was so sickly pale, she might have been much younger.

"Ma'am," he said in greeting, removing his hat with a blood covered hand.

"It ain't the fever, Mr. Washburn," she said. "It's my heart. It's about to give out."

Dud looked up at the old man, but he was spitting out tobacco juice and saying nothing. He looked back to the woman. She knew him, but he did not know her.

"My husband fought with you early in the war," she said to his unasked question. "Brent." She paused, took a breath and forced herself to continue. "Brent Hollister."

The name meant nothing to Dud, but those first wild years were filled with young men who died early on and faded from his memory.

"My children have been staying home, taking care of me," the woman said, her face turning bluer by the second. "They haven't been exposed to the fever. But we 'uns heard about you and your uncle taking cattle on a drive."

"That's right, Mrs. Hollister," Dud said.

She reached her hand up, and Dud, wiping the blood from his hand on his pants first, took it, surprised by the strength of her grip.

"Mr. Washburn, you take my children with you. I be passing soon."

Surprised, Dud glanced at the boys. They appeared to be about eleven and nine years old, but it was hard to tell. The youngest had a haircut that looked like it had been hacked off with a butcher knife. He had the largest, most frightened blue eyes Dud had ever seen on a child. The eyes of the older boy were just as blue, but narrow and suspicious.

"Mrs. Hollister, any of your neighbors would take those fine boys. This cattle drive ain't gonna be no picnic. We may not be coming back here alive."

"No," she said, shaking his hand in her tight grasp. "Everybody around here is suffering from lack — lack of food, lack of clothes, lack of a decent place to live. I don't want my boy to turn outlaw like so many young'uns have. My husband used to speak highly of you. You take them with you."

Dud looked at Ponder. Ponder gave him a stare before turning back to the boys. His uncle's keen eyes swept over the oldest boy, but rested on the youngest for so long, Dud was about to say something when Ponder finally spoke.

"I'll be needing an assistant."

That settled it. Dud turned to the older boy. His jaw was set in belligerence, as if he was trying to be strong no matter what and hold back all tears. "Can you ride, boy?"

"Like a Comanche," he said, adding, "sir."

The grip on his hand loosened, and the sick woman let it fall back to her side in relief.

"They got saddles their pa made. He was one of the best saddlemakers around these here parts," she said, her voice filled with pride.

Dud looked at the saddles in the back. They were ancient affairs, with dry cracked leather. He motioned with his head for the boys to get out. He and Ponder removed the saddles and tossed them away from the wagon.

"I'll take care of them the best I can, Mrs. Hollister," Dud promised.

"Y'all best stay for the night," Ponder said.

"No!" Mrs. Hollister said. Calming, she added, "I'm afraid if I stay, I'll back down. And I don't want to do that. Come give mother a kiss, children."

They went to the wagon, climbing on the wheel to lean over to kiss their mother. The youngest boy buried his face in her breast and let out one sob.

"There, there. Remember, I'll be praying for you every day, and when the time comes for me to join Pa in heaven, I'll be looking down on you, watching over you."

The boy nodded, and his older brother pulled him down. They backed away, instinctively knowing it was time to let go.

Dud walked to the old man in the wagon seat and gave him an inquiring look.

He spat out another stream of tobacco juice. "I was just passing through on old

Felicity there," he said, nodding to the mule. "She told me I could have the wagon if I brung her and the young'uns over here, and take her back and bury her."

"She got anybody there to look after her?" Dud asked.

"Mister, she ain't gonna make it home. I'll bury her proper though."

Dud nodded and let him go. He was not getting much of a bargain. The wagon looked like it might not make it back either.

The old man nodded, popping the reins. "Hi-ya, mule," he said, and the wagon turned and left the ranch, the boys staring with stoicism after it, only the slight quivering of lips giving away their anguish.

Glancing at the saddles, Ponder spoke to the boys. "What's your handles?"

The oldest boy swallowed. "My name is William, but folks call me Will. This here is Jemmy, sir," he said, putting his hand on his brother's shoulder. Although polite, he said the words as if he was daring Ponder and Dud to refute them.

Ponder ignored his attitude and instructed them to take their saddles to the barn. "You'll need to saddle soap them and rub them down before we head out, so you might as well do it now."

The boys picked up their saddles and followed Ponder. Dud did not think they could look any more forlorn. Audie joined him. They stared at one another.

"Dud, we can't be dragging them dang kids with us."

"Well Audie, just what would you have done?" Audie didn't answer, and Dud began to walk toward the mustangs. Audie kept in step with him, and Dud added: "Don't worry. In no time, they will be so sick of picking up buffalo chips and being in the saddle, they'll be begging to stay at the first decent ranch house we come to."

"You did say you wanted some young ones."

"Yeah, well, next time, I'm going to be real specific in saying out loud what I want. Come on, let's finish. By this time two days from now, we'll be sick to death of eating fried *cojones,* but I'm not letting good food go to waste."

The next morning, Audie left for Fitz's, and Dud was not sorry to see him go. With Audie questioning every decision he made, and Ponder treating him like he was a shave-tail, Dud did not know how he was going to stand being on the trail with them for months.

Dud left the two boys with Ponder and

saddling his bay, went out to check on the cattle.

He rode for a long time, thinking about Beatrice, wondering just how much money he might make, worrying even then it might not be enough to satisfy her. He rode up to the edge of a low bluff and looked out over the river. In the bottom land on the other side, hundreds of cattle grazed on the fresh grass Ponder had put them on. He heard someone coming up behind him. He knew even before turning his head it would be Ponder.

Ponder joined him, and together they sat looking over their future.

"They are a sorry-looking bunch right now," Dud said. "But they'll fatten up on tall grass along the way."

"What are we going to do about cowboys?"

"I don't know. Hope Audie brings back some. Pick up a few along the way." He turned to Ponder. "What did you do with those boys?"

"Left them to clean up the kitchen and chop kindling. That little Jemmy knows a bit about cooking — said he used to help his ma when she got down."

"Well, thank God. Maybe he can teach you something."

Dud reined the horse away from the bluff and started back to the cabin with Ponder following.

As they neared the house, they saw a small pile of kindling, but no boys. They found them as they neared the corral, jumping on the backs of the mustangs, not bothering with blankets, saddles, or bridles, using their knees to guide the horses and their fingers to wind in the manes to hold on.

"Well, I'll be danged," Ponder said. "Them little Comanches do know how to ride."

Dud did not know who was more startled to hear Ponder's voice, the mustangs or the boys. The boys gaped at them and jumped from the horses, running to the corral fence.

"We just thought we'd ride them a little bit, Mr. Ponder," the oldest boy said.

"What's your name? Will? You think you could put bridles and saddles on them?" Dud asked. "I want them to get used to being saddled and unsaddled, and having the bridle put on them."

The brothers looked at one another. "Sure!" Will said.

"We can try with your horse, Mr. Dud," Jemmy said, those round blue eyes looking up into his. "But he won't let us get on him."

"Leave him be for now. Fetch your saddles and some bridles out of the barn and see if you can saddle some of the others. But don't try to lead those mustangs around by their bridles. You'll have to use rope."

"Yes, sir, Mr. Dud," Will said, and Jemmy nodded.

The boys ran to the barn and came out dragging their old saddles.

"Jemmy, you stand back and let Will go first," Dud said.

Conscious he was being watched, Will looked the mustangs over carefully, trying to decide which one might be the most obliging about being saddled. He finally picked a little roan about fourteen hands high. The horse shied from him, and it took him ten minutes to put the halter and rope on. He kept looking back at Dud and Ponder, but they sat on their horses, watching patiently. Once he realized they expected him to take his time, he grew in confidence. Working slowly with smooth motions, he talked to the little mustang, gentling him into letting him place the saddle on his back.

"Either Henry and I broke those horses better than I thought," Dud told Ponder, "or those boys have got the magic touch."

"I think the oldest boy does. I'd watch that little one for a while."

Jemmy had climbed on the gate and was craning his neck, looking at something off in the distance. Dud turned and saw a rider approaching the ranch.

"Now, who the devil can that be?"

Chapter Five

Whoever the rider was, he wore new clothes, a new hat, had dark skin, and looked uncomfortable.

As he neared, it became plain he was of mixed blood. Dud guessed by his heavy eyes and high cheekbones he was part Cherokee. His nose was straight and his reddish-brown skin had a paleness to it that denoted white blood. He was slender, but well built, and Dud could see how women might consider him handsome. Under the hat was thick, coarse, short hair held in place with a pomade preparation that Dud could smell even where he sat on his horse.

"Howdy," he said in greeting.

"Mr. Dudford Washburn? And Mr. Ponder Washburn?" the stranger asked.

"That's right."

"My name is David Sullivan. I heard you were planning on taking cattle on a drive to New Mexico to sell. I thought perhaps you might be needing help."

Dud did not know what to think of him. He talked like a man of education, and his appearance said tenderfoot.

"How is that?" Dud asked.

The young man blushed. "A friend of mine coming up from Matagorda stopped by your brother-in-law's ranch while they were rounding up cattle. He reported the news to me when he reached San Antonio."

Dud stared at him so hard, the blood rushing up turned Sullivan's neck almost as red as his new bandanna.

"Do you know anything about horses and cattle?"

"I know how to ride. But, frankly, no, I am unfamiliar with cattle."

He did not know anything about cattle, and Dud did not know what to think about him. He took in a deep breath of air and expelled it.

"Why do you want to go on a cattle drive?"

The young man straightened in the saddle. "Because I know of the Washburn reputation. I want to be a cowboy to prove that I am not just a misfit, half-breed attorney from the city. By participating in this drive, I hope to become a man people look up to."

Dud looked at Ponder, but Ponder looked just as bumfuzzled as he felt. One word caught his attention. "Attorney?"

"That's right, Mr. Washburn. I was your wife's attorney."

He saw the look of disbelief that Dud could not help showing.

"That is correct. Her father wanted an attorney no one in their social circle would ever run across."

"I'll say," Ponder muttered.

Dud shifted, crossing one hand over the other, trying to get his thoughts straight. He gave the young man a keen look. "What's her name?"

"Pardon?" the attorney asked in surprise.

"I said, what is her name? You must be trying to impress some little gal to go on this kind of a wild goose chase."

The young man gulped and spoke the name of a young lady from a wealthy and old San Antonio family. The father owned a large lumber mill in town, but despite his position in society at the moment, he had started out as poor as Job's turkey.

Dud thought for another minute. "Listen, Sullivan. You got Indian blood in you, don't you?"

"Yes. My mother was Cherokee. My father was a white man, an attorney in Georgia. I studied law under him, but they both passed away shortly after immigrating to Texas."

He had answered evenly enough, but Dud thought he detected a slight bristling.

"Well, I don't want to hurt your feelings none, but we're going to be traveling through some bad territory. And I don't want those horses over there getting used to smelling Indians. If an Indian comes around, wanting to steal my horses, I want them to raise a commotion."

David Sullivan was dogged if anything. "I can speak Cherokee and a smattering of Comanche, along with a few other dialects. I can be of great service to you in that department."

Ponder had been sitting quietly, listening to the exchange. Dud thought he would not have much use for a tenderfoot lawyer, and Ponder surprised him by interrupting.

"Wait, Dud. If he'll wear that smelly pomade on his hair the whole time he's with us, the horses will associate it with him and not with other Indians. He might be able to get us out of many a scrape."

Dud recognized the wisdom of his words. He turned to the lawyer. "All right, you lay in a good supply of that grease, and you're hired. You'll get the same pay as the rest of the men we hire on."

He nodded in relief. Dud turned to the boys in the corral. "Jemmy, you hop out of there and help Uncle Ponder get to cooking and making us some coffee. Will, you keep working with those mustangs. Lawyer, you feed and water your horse and come on in the house when you're finished. Uncle Ponder and I will try to explain how things are going to work on this drive."

Ponder shook his head and gave him a look of disgust. "I guess you can see who considers himself the onliest boss in this outfit."

"That's right, Uncle Ponder. You are the *segundo* and don't forget it." As soon as Dud spoke the words, he regretted sounding so harsh. But he did not apologize. He couldn't be telling the men one thing and have Ponder telling them something else. Somebody had to have the last word or turmoil would ensue.

Later that afternoon, Dud saddled Ned. Ponder left Jemmy in charge of the kitchen with instructions to stir the beans every so often, fill up the wood box, and make another pan of cornbread. He saddled one of the bigger mustangs and left with Dud to work the cattle. The lawyer and Will had instructions to work with the mustangs.

"Every hour you put in now will save you a heap of trouble later," Dud said. "Be thinking about what horses you'd like for your own. The best out of the bunch you chose will be your night horse."

"You planning on letting Will out there at night with that herd?" Ponder asked, still smarting for being regulated to second-in-command.

"Not by himself, although the Lord knows we need all the help we can get."

Dud was to regret his words the next day. They'd slept piled in the cabin the night before. Will, protective of Jemmy, made him a pallet next to his. Jemmy, shy and scared, did whatever his older brother said. Dud had been close to his brothers, but at that age, they had fought like wild heathens. If they were not arguing, they were pushing and shoving one another, but Jemmy did whatever Will said without complaint. Both were more than a little frightened, and when inside, watched the men with wary eyes. Dud supposed given the circumstances, it was only natural.

Dud, Ponder, and the lawyer took turns guarding the mustangs that night. Jemmy wanted to know why, and Will tried to hush him, but Dud told the boy the truth — they meant to keep away horse thieves and might be forced to kill someone who tried stealing those imperatively necessary horses.

The next morning at dawn, they had the

lawyer saddled on a splotched mustang, ready to take him out with the cattle. Will begged to go along, saying Jemmy would be all right at the cabin alone for a while.

Dud looked at Ponder. "What do you think?"

Ponder shrugged. "Better go ahead and get him started."

Ponder left Jemmy with a list of chores he hoped was long enough to keep the boy out of trouble. And Dud tried to remember to consult with Ponder and Audie and not act like the tyrant of the plains. Being boss of this outfit was going to be a lonely position; he could already see it coming.

Before Ponder's crew had taken ill, they had tamed the wild longhorns enough they did not charge at every rider they saw. There were still a few recalcitrant ones that were spooky or wanted to fight. These had to be lassoed and necked to a tree or a gentler cow until they calmed.

Ponder or Dud would lasso the unruly ones. It took a few times for the lawyer to catch on how to neck them, but he soon had it down, and that became his job. Will's was to head off any cow heading for the brush. A few slipped through, and those were tailed. Ponder had always been a master at it, riding alongside the animal, grabbing its tail, wrapping it around the saddle horn and giving it a yank, causing the cow to trip or somersault. He would dismount and hogtie the cloven hooves quick as a lick, leaving the cow tied long enough to take the fight out of it. But now, Dud did most of it, having been taught by Ponder and his father many years ago. Will and the lawyer were fascinated by it.

They soon wore Will and the lawyer out. The attorney was determined, however, and although exhausted, Will was clearly thrilled to be working with men.

They ended the day early. As they approached the cabin, they saw a wagon and rider at the corral being held at bay by little Jemmy Hollister holding a shotgun on them. Dud realized he must have dragged a chair over to the doorframe to reach the shotgun that hung above it.

As soon as Dud saw who was sitting in the wagon, he started cussing.

Ponder leaned forward and peered at the wagon. "Is that Florine and Shug?"

"You darn right it is," Dud said, spurring Ned to the corral with Ponder galloping behind him.

Dud jumped off his horse and stood by Jemmy. "Florine, what are you doing here?" he hollered.

"I'm being held at gunpoint by a midget, that's what."

Dud took the shotgun from Jemmy's hands and glared at his middle-aged cousin. Florine had a square jaw, eyes that could bore through the barrel of a rifle, and a voice that sounded like a rasp running across metal. She sat in a wagon seat wearing the clothes she always wore — a faded skirt, a long-sleeved blouse, and a man's hat with a flat top and a wide, floppy brim, all of them at least twenty-five years old.

"Florine," Ponder said. "I don't know what you want, but you can just turn around and go home right now."

Florine looked over at Ponder. "Is that you, Cousin Ponder? Still trying to meddle in everybody's affairs?"

"That doesn't explain what you are doing here, Florine," Dud said. For once, he and Ponder were in accord.

"We heared you and Ponder was going on a cattle drive, and we come to join you. Me and the boys got three hundred and fifty head about a mile north of here. Billy Sol's over there with them right now."

"No!" Dud and Ponder thundered at the same time.

"We're not taking you and your cattle on any drive with us, Florine," Dud added.

"Don't get your long johns in a crack, Dudford. They's all branded and ear cut. And from what I hear, you need Billy Sol and Shug right bad."

"That don't mean we need you, Florine," Ponder said. "You just turn that wagon around and go on home."

In answer to that, Florine got out of the wagon. Dud shot an angry look at Shug. Shug just stared at him with those heavy eyelids that turned down on the corners. He had a face like a hatchet and a nose like a chicken hawk's beak.

"Can't you do nothing with your mama?" Dud demanded. "She ain't got no business going on a cattle drive."

Shug shrugged. "Can't nobody do nothing with Ma, you know that, Cousin Dud."

"Florine!" Dud hollered. "Do you know where we're going? We're not headed up north. We're headed straight through Comanche raiding grounds, not to mention every other kind of hell God decided to put west of the Pecos."

"That's right, Florine," Ponder thundered. "You ain't too old to get raped by a gang of Comanche, but you're too old to become a squaw, so they'd probably just kill your old ugly hide."

In answer to that, Florine shrugged and

peered over the fence at the mustangs.

"You got some good-looking horses over there. I bet they've got bottom."

Shug dismounted, walking toward Dud. He stopped and looked at the lawyer.

"That there is an Injun. You taking an Injun on a cattle drive?"

"That's right," Dud snapped. "He's also my ex-wife's attorney, and I intend on wringing every ounce of flesh from him that he managed to get Beatrice to steal from me. And if you don't like it, you can get on that flea-bitten bag of bones you ride and head out of here right now."

Dud turned to the attorney. "She didn't get the ranch, too, did she?"

He shook his head. "I tried, but the judge wouldn't allow it."

"Dee-vorce!" Florine said. "Does Callie know about this?"

"Yes, Callie knows. But you know Callie — nothing holds her down long."

Florine gave Ponder a dirty look. "Cousin Ponder, I'm going in that cabin, and I'm making myself a pot of coffee. No doubt I'll have to fight the roaches and rats off to do it, but I'm worn to a frazzle."

Dud stared in impotent anger as Florine marched into the cabin. Shug tied his horse to the back of the wagon and began leading the mule to the barn. Suddenly conscious that Jemmy was still by his side, Dud looked down to see a mortified expression on the boy's face.

"Did I do wrong, Mr. Dud?" he stammered.

Dud grasped his shoulder. "No, son." He gave the boy's shoulder a squeeze. "You'll do to ride the river with any day, Jemmy."

He turned to Ponder who looked like he might be ready to spit every one of his teeth out in anger. "Uncle Ponder, can't you give this boy a decent haircut?"

Ponder shot Florine's back one more evil look, but when he turned to Dud and Jemmy, he was all right.

"Sure. Come on, boy. Fetch a chair and put it in the dog run. I'll find my scissors and see if I can summon up enough willpower to keep from stabbing Florine in the heart with them."

Jemmy looked scared, and Dud gave him another pat. "Don't pay any attention to Uncle Ponder, he's just flapping his jaws. You run along and fetch a chair like he said."

As Dud walked by the lawyer, he spoke. "Thank you, Mr. Washburn."

Dud stopped to look at the earnest young man. "Call me Boss or call me Mr. Dud. I don't want Uncle Ponder to get mixed up and think you are speaking to him."

Later, when Dud walked by Ponder and Jemmy in the dog run, he saw that Ponder had only evened out Jemmy's hair. He had expected him to do like his pa had always done — cut his hair short on top and shave the sides. When he raised one eyebrow at Ponder as Jemmy scooted off the chair, Ponder shrugged his shoulders.

"I left a little hair hanging to protect his ears from the wind. We don't need a couple of kids getting sick on us."

Jemmy had gone into the kitchen. "I hope they are not with us that long," Dud responded.

They threatened and cajoled, but could not talk Florine out of going. In the end, Ponder and his oxen would drive the main chuckwagon with Jemmy as a helper. They would add their mule to Florine's wagon and use it to hold anything else. Will would help her, and when not needed, be riding drag with the lawyer. Unfortunately, Florine was not any better of a cook than Ponder was.

"I know what you are thinking, Dudford," Florine said over the supper table. "But I can get up at three-thirty in the morning, and that's about the time Ponder usually goes to bed. He's going to have a hard time on this trip."

Ponder shot Florine a murderous look, and Dud coughed, trying to stifle a guffaw. To prove Florine wrong, Ponder would be up at three making coffee. Maybe having Florine along was not such a bad idea after all, if she could keep Ponder straight.

The next morning, Audie came riding in with three young'uns all under the age of sixteen. Dud had already been out to check on the cattle, had eaten his breakfast, and was in the process of double-checking to make sure the wagons held everything they might need. It bothered him they did not have rain jackets. Any extra money would have to be spent on more saddle blankets to make sure the horses had clean, dry pads between them and the saddle. Men would just have to suffer.

Earlier, he and Ponder had found some moth-eaten buffalo coats, but when they got wet, they would get so weighted down they would be impossible to ride in. Dud feared what the weather would be like. In those wide-open spaces, lightning was a lethal killer. It was springtime in Texas, but by the time they got to New Mexico Territory, it could be winter weather. He walked out of the barn, determined to strip every blanket and quilt out of the house and load it in Florine's wagon. They could cut holes in the middle and use them as ponchos.

That's when he saw Audie with his new help, standing at the corral looking over the mustangs. Audie looked up and hailed him. His smile was happy and almost reached his sad eyes.

"Dud! I brung you three more."

Dud met them, stopping to pause and look them up and down. They all looked like slender unripe grass and just as green. The smallest was a Negro with pocked skin left over from a bout with smallpox. The taller one, who was still shorter than Dud, had sandy hair and a smooth blank face. Dud wondered if he might not be all there. The last one, bigger boned than the others, had large droopy eyes, like a sad dog.

"Dud," Audie said. "This here is Darnell. His uncles are the ones who did the cutting at Fitz's place. And that there," he said, nodding to the one with blank expression, "that's Toomey, short for tombstone. The other one is his buddy Mutt."

Dud thought both boys came by their nicknames honestly. He glanced at the horses they rode in on. Two of them were a little rough, but the third looked like a good horse.

"You boys know where we are going?"

"Yes, sir," all three answered, looking serious.

"Y'all know anything about cattle?" he asked.

"I knows a little bit," Darnell said. "Not as much as my uncles, but some."

Dud nodded and looked at the other boys. "We don't know much, Mr. Dud," Toomey said, sounding like he might have more sense than his face let on. "But we're willing to learn."

"Whose horse is that over there? The chestnut with the star on his forehead?"

"That's my uncle's horse," Toomey said. "He said I could borrow him, but he said don't never try to tie him up. He goes loco. He'll stand in one spot all day if'n I drop his reins to the ground. I just got to remember not to tie him up."

"Well, horses will get ideas in their heads," Dud said. "You boys take your horses to the barn and leave them in the corral up yonder. Don't put them in with these mustangs just yet. If you've had breakfast, start in helping the lawyer there train these mustangs."

He looked around for the Hollister boys and found them near the back of the corral. "Will, Jemmy! You've messed with these mustangs enough to know a little something about them. Work with these new men to help them get used to them."

"Yes, sir, Mr. Dud," Will hollered.

Dud and Audie let the new hands go on ahead while they talked about Fitz and his cattle.

"Fitz said we better get a move on, Dud," Audie said. "He's got about four hundred and fifty head and only two old men to help hold them."

Dud nodded. "We've got six hundred, and Florine's got another three hundred and fifty Billy Sol's trying to handle. I don't know how these tenderfeet we've got will work out, but we'll find out soon enough."

"Florine? What's she doing here?"

Dud explained. "And that's that. Tell me about these boys."

"I think Darnell knows more than he lets on," Audie said as he watched the three boys return and climb over the brush corral gate. "I don't know about Toomey and Mutt. They may end up like Shug and Billy Sol. You know them two don't have a lick of sense when their boots are on the ground, but put them on a horse around cattle, and there ain't nobody better. As far as I'm concerned, it's worth putting up with Florine to have Shug and Billy Sol along."

"Yeah, that's what I keep telling myself. Come on, Audie. We'll tend to your horse and then find Uncle Ponder."

Before they made it to the barn, Ponder and Florine came out of the house arguing with one another.

"It's going to be like Cain and Abel all over again," Dud said. "I don't know if Ponder will kill Florine first or if she'll get him."

Dud called to his uncle. "Uncle Ponder! Go meet the new hands and come on out to the barn for a powwow. We got to make some decisions."

"Why? You've already decided!"

"Well, maybe I'm wrong, and you can tell me. That would make you happy, wouldn't it?"

Ponder threw his hands up and walked toward the corral.

"Don't try to ride Ned, you bonehead!" Ponder yelled at Darnell. "That horse won't let nobody but Dud on him. Jemmy, why didn't you warn him?"

Dud looked at Audie. "I hope you explained about Uncle Ponder to those new hands."

Chapter Six

Ponder, surprisingly enough, agreed with Dud's delegation of who would ride where on the drive. As the best cattlemen, Shug and Billy Sol would ride point. Audie would be the wrangler. Behind Shug and Billy Sol, Darnell would ride swing. Mutt and Toomey would ride flank, taking turns being behind Darnell. It would be Jemmy's job to help Ponder. Will was to assist Florine, and when he was not needed, to help Audie with the horses and ride drag with the lawyer. They were still a few men short for so many cattle, but it could not be helped.

Florine rang the dinner bell, and Dud let out a sigh. If this crew did not like the cooking, they could decide to up and leave. He walked with Ponder and Audie, joining the others. Dud led them around to the back of the house, to the back door that led into the kitchen.

"Go on in, get a plate and go outside to

eat," he instructed. "There ain't room inside for everybody to sit at the table."

He looked around. "Where's Shug?"

"He went to check on Billy Sol," Ponder said. "He'll be back directly."

That was not what worried Dud. He was going to have trouble with Shug and Billy Sol over Darnell. When they walked into the kitchen, it relieved him to find that Florine had stepped out for a while.

She or Ponder had set the table up buffet style, and Dud tried to hurry everyone through the line before Florine walked back in.

"Here, take a piece of cornbread. Here's a knife, take that," he said, pressing everything he could off on the men to hurry them up.

"What's the matter with you?" Ponder asked when Dud tried to shove a cup of coffee in his hand. "You got grasshoppers in your britches?"

Before Dud could answer, Shug walked in from the back door. He looked around the kitchen. Dud steeled himself, ready with a speech the minute Shug said one word about Darnell.

"I ain't going on no cattle drive with the likes of him," Shug said.

Dud opened his mouth and snapped it shut just as fast. Shug was looking daggers at Mutt, not Darnell.

"What the . . . ?" Dud asked.

Shug turned to him. "I ain't going nowhere with him. Us Higgins don't associate with the Clampits."

Florine walked in. "Who said Clampit?"

"Ma, we ain't going on this here cattle drive if a Clampit is going. I ain't having you feed no Clampit."

Dud stared. Vague recollections of some kind of family feud bobbed into his skull, but he could not get a handle on them. He looked at Mutt. His lips were pressed together and pointed downward, looking stubborn and unhappy, his big droopy dog eyes shooting hateful glares at Shug.

Florine turned to Ponder and Dud. "That's right. Us Higgins don't have nothing to do with them Clampits. We ain't going with y'all if that's the case."

Dud felt his stomach lurch. He had known all along Shug would back down over the lawyer, and had counted on him backing down over Darnell if he gave him a good talking to, but nothing would induce them to end a family feud of forty years.

Without Shug and Billy Sol, they might as well just stay home and starve. "I'm never going to make enough money to get Beatrice back," Dud muttered. He hadn't meant to say it out loud and was glad no one appeared to hear it with Florine and Shug carrying on about the murderous Clampits and how in 1826 one of them had killed a Higgins on purpose over a pig.

Feeling helpless to deal with his relatives, Dud turned to Ponder.

A look of glee had spread over Ponder's face. As soon as Shug and Florine stopped long enough to take a breath, Ponder butted in.

"Florine, I totally understand and agree with you. You can't possibly be expected to lower yourself to go anywhere with a Clampit. We'll help you get your things packed and be on your way."

Florine looked shocked down to her boots. "You old scallywag! You mean you are going to take a Clampit over your own kin?"

"We ain't got no choice," Ponder said. "Do we, Dud?"

Dud stood there feeling stupid. He did not know what Ponder was doing.

"We can't go against Fitz," Ponder continued. "Fitz done promised this here boy we'd take him on, and we got to do it."

"Fitz ain't blood. We is your blood, Ponder Washburn."

"Fitz ain't blood, but Callie is. And you

know how set Callie is on Fitz. If we went against Fitz, why Callie would just cut us off. Your boys got you, but it's different for me and Dud. We ain't got no womenfolk in this family except Callie. Every woman I get dies, and Dud runs his off."

Dud wanted to smack Ponder for that last statement. Instead, he glanced around the room, registering how scared Toomey looked, how shocked the lawyer appeared, and how quietly thrilled Darnell was by the exchange. He looked down and saw that the Hollister boys were hiding behind Ponder, watching. Audie just looked amused.

Florine was clearly having a fight with her feelings. It surprised Dud to see how badly she wanted to go on the drive. After several tics and blinks, Florine gave in.

"All right, you win, Ponder."

"Ma!" Shug said, shocked to his core.

"Shug, I got to think of you. We'uns need to swallow our pride long enough to get our cattle sold."

Shug gulped, but did not cross his mother. "Okay, Ma, but as soon as them cattle is sold, me and that there Clampit is going to fight to the death."

"Wait a minute!" Dud said. "You're bigger than he is by a foot and thirty pounds. That ain't a fair fight."

"All right. Billy Sol can fight him."

Billy Sol looked as dumb as Shug, except he was fair whereas Shug was dark, and his big round eyes didn't have folds over his eyelids. He was also a runt.

"I'll fight your brother to the death and be glad to do it," Mutt said, clinching his teeth in anger.

Dud turned to Ponder. "Uncle Ponder, do something. I don't want to ride a thousand miles with them three ganging up on one member of the drive."

Ponder looked at Florine. "He's right, Florine. There will be times when we'll be depending on one another for our very lives, and we can't have no constant discord disrupting this outfit. Since you can't do that, y'all might as well head on home."

Florine started breathing fire out her nostrils. "That's what you want, ain't it, Ponder Washburn? Well, you ain't getting rid of us so easy. From this moment on, we'll treat that sorry, no-good Clampit just like he was one of our own. But as soon as them cattle is sold, he's done for."

"Are you willing to that, Mutt?" Dud asked. "It means no pranks, or nothing like that, on one another." He turned to stare a hole in Florine. "And don't be trashing the Clampit name, either."

Dud looked back at Mutt and had to hand it to the stubborn little cur. He was willing.

"I accept them there terms," he said.

Dud turned to glare at Florine and Shug.

"No Clampit trashing," Florine said, agreeing with little grace. Shug nodded.

"All right, get something to eat," Dud instructed the others. "We'll be leaving in the morning."

They lined up at the table, and Dud had never seen anyone look as relieved and happy as Darnell, his even white teeth showing up brilliant against his lips. He piled food high on his plate, and Dud thought with a wry smile that he might not be so happy after he ate some of Ponder and Florine's cooking.

They filed out the back door to sit with their backs against trees just starting to bud. Dud followed Ponder, leaving Florine by herself in the kitchen. As soon as they were out the door and out of earshot, Dud muttered to his uncle.

"Were you working Florine like that on purpose?"

Ponder looked over his shoulder but said nothing.

Darnell was not the odd man out, the lawyer was. Darnell lived the outdoor life, and he did know a little about herding cattle. The lawyer looked as uncomfortable as a Baptist deacon at a hoedown. No one was rude to him; they just ignored him.

After eating, Dud wanted to check on cattle. Ponder, who declared he had had his fill of Florine, wanted to ride with him. Shug rode with them part of the way, splitting off to check on a herd in another pasture.

Dud and Ponder rode for some time, looking over cattle that calmly ignored them, happily chewing on fresh, verdant grass. Dud refused to be lulled into a false sense of security. Their wickedly long horns could kill a man in an instant, and the calmness they displayed at the moment could change in a heartbeat to a raging, irrational fear that could cause them to trample everything in their path.

Despite knowing all this, as he and Ponder stopped to watch the sight of hundreds of cattle eating contentedly, a sense of peace came over Dud. Whatever happened, he knew that this was the right thing to do.

Ponder spit out his wad of chewing tobacco, pausing to let his eyes sweep over the cattle once again before speaking.

"It's going to be aces or deuces, Dud. Win, lose, but no draw."

He was stopped from answering by the

sight of a small dark figure riding toward them on a white pony, leading two little black mustangs with him. Dud felt his spirits lift. He would have recognized that pointed black sombrero with all the fancy gold trim anywhere.

"Señor Dud!" Henry greeted him. "Is there still a place for me on this cattle drive?"

Dud assured him there was, and introduced Ponder to him. "We'll put Audie on swing and make Henry the wrangler."

They rode back to the ranch, discussing the drive and what Henry's duties would entail. Dud, however, was curious about the horses.

"I thought you had two pretty señoritas you planned on making those mustangs a present to."

Henry raised his shoulders philosophically. "Ah, Señor Dud, their father was unappreciative of my gifts."

Ponder gave Dud a hard stare under lowered brows. Dud took the hint.

"Henry, we got an old lady cousin who is insisting on going with us. She's as mean as Old Scratch, can't cook worth a lick, and has two sons always itching to duke it out with somebody. Don't be practicing your romancing skills on her just for the fun of it."

Henry made a show of looking shocked. "I would not dream of it, Señor Dud."

Dud turned to Ponder. "And while we are on the subject, since we are going to be isolated out of the trail for weeks at a time, I don't want you and Florine to decide you got an itch that needs scratching either."

Ponder raised up in the saddle. "Get thee behind me, Satan! I ought to knock you off your horse for even running that evil thought past my brain, and when this drive is over, I just might do it anyway."

"And no card playing unless we happen to get a chance to go into town," Dud said. "I don't want no fights breaking out over cards either."

"You're just full of orders, ain't you? Anybody would think, there goes God, he thinks he's Dud Washburn."

"Aw, hush," Dud said.

"And another thing. You're the one always getting into trouble with women."

Dud was about to respond when they came within view of the cabin. A small patrol of soldiers, along with a civilian in a buggy, were on the opposite side, heading in that direction. Ponder spoke first.

"Dud, you and your little amigo better

make a wide circle and come back up behind the barn. Let me talk to them."

Dud did not answer but reined Ned to his left, where his approach to the cabin would be hidden by a line of trees. Henry followed silently behind him.

When they edged to the back of the corral, they could hear the booming of Ponder's voice, but could not make out his words. Dud dismounted, and as furtive as if he intended on stealing a horse, opened the corral gate, easing Ned inside. Henry did the same with his mustangs. After shutting the gate as quietly as he could, Dud moved to the back door of the barn, and together, he and Henry sidled inside.

Dud paused, aware someone else was in the barn. He looked around but did not see anyone. Glancing at the loft, his eyes caught a movement. He motioned with his head to Henry, and they crept to the ladder, climbing it as softly as their boots and spurs would let them. When Dud reached the top, he paused. Will and Jemmy were in the hay loft, looking out the window down at the scene below. Will turned, caught sight of Dud and gave a start. Dud put his finger to his lips. Will nodded, and Jemmy, who had turned in time to see him, nodded, too.

Moving like two panthers, Dud and Henry

joined the two boys. They got down on their stomachs, removing their hats so they would not be easily seen, looking out over mounds of hay at the soldiers below.

Surprised, Dud recognized the civilian climbing from the buggy as the man who had cut in front of him in line at the stage-coach counter. A Mr. Karling. He moved his eyes to the Union captain, taking him in. It was not the stern-faced one who had made a show of force at Callie's. This man was just as much of a career soldier, but gave the appearance of someone wiser and more human.

"If it looks like they are about to start searching," Dud, staring at the soldiers, whispered to Henry, "burrow yourself in the hay."

He glanced at the boys. "You kids don't know us." Will nodded. Jemmy's eyes widened in terror.

Dud could not make out what Ponder was saying, but he seemed to be talking in earnest with the Union captain. He was dismissive of Karling, ignoring him to the point of rudeness.

The lawyer stood nearby, expressionless, but his intense eyes watched the exchange without wavering. Every once in a while, Dud would catch a soldier staring at Sullivan and turning away to spit, as if making a statement, but if the lawyer saw it and cared, he gave no sign.

The captain twisted in his saddle and said something to his men. They turned their horses and began riding away.

"He's sending them to the river to water their horses," Dud whispered.

The captain dismounted, handing his reins to an orderly who trailed behind the others to water. The captain followed Ponder to the house. Dud watched in surprise as Ponder put a chair for him in the dog run, placing it so the barn would be obscured from his view. Ponder took another chair and sat nearby.

"What is Señor Ponder doing?" Henry hissed.

"No telling," Dud said. He wondered the same thing.

They lay motionless in the hay. He was used to it, and evidently Henry was, too. He expected the boys to start squirming and wanting down from the loft, but they surprised Dud by remaining quiet.

Karling came back from the river and left his buggy in front of the cabin. He entered the dog run, but Ponder did not offer him a chair, and he remained standing, looking uncomfortable and impatient. The lawyer had quietly taken a horse and tied it near the dog run where he would not be noticed as he brushed it down, but Dud was sure he was eavesdropping on every word spoken. Mutt, Toomey, and Darnell remained with the mustangs, riding first one, then another, but Florine had disappeared, no doubt with her ear against the kitchen door. Audie and Shug were supposed to be out working cattle.

The soldiers came back and loitered underneath a tree in view of the house. Dud feared they would get bored, let their eyes roam, and catch sight of them hiding in the barn. But as soon as it became apparent the little lieutenant's eyes were looking only in the captain's direction, waiting for a signal from him, they grouped behind their horses and soon had a crap game going.

A good hour later, the captain stepped down from the veranda. The crap game ceased, and the lieutenant stood stiffly, waiting for orders. The captain motioned him to bring his horse. He turned to Ponder and spoke a few more words before mounting. Karling stalked to the buggy and with the impatience of a landlord denied his rent money, climbed in.

They left, with Ponder watching them go. Henry made a motion of impetuousness, but Dud stopped him. "Wait for Uncle Ponder's signal."

Ponder spoke to the lawyer. He nodded, getting on the horse he had been brushing and following the soldiers. In ten minutes, he was back, shaking his head. Ponder looked up at the window in the barn and motioned for them to come down.

The boys had not made a sound or movement until then. When Jemmy got up, his head bowed in shame because he had wet his pants. Dud pretended not to notice.

"You boys go take a swim," Dud said. "It might be the last bit of fun you have for a long time. Take a cake of soap with you and see if you can't wash your hair and a layer of dirt off, too." The water would be cold, but that had not bothered him when he was their age.

They scatted down the ladder, running off to the river, while Henry followed Dud downward and to the cabin where Ponder stood waiting.

Dud, knowing his uncle well, realized by the set of his jaw and look in his eyes the captain had given him disturbing news.

"Does everybody need to hear this?" Dud asked.

Ponder nodded. "I reckon so, since it concerns them."

Dud stood on the front veranda, and putting his fingers in his mouth, emitted a sharp whistle. Mutt and Toomey looked up from the corral, and Dud motioned for them and Darnell to come. Shug and Audie came from around the house, and Florine stepped out of the kitchen into the dog run. They looked Henry over, and he did the same. His eyes met with Darnell's and paused, narrowing slightly.

"Where are those kids?" Ponder asked Dud.

"I sent them down to the river to swim."

Ponder nodded and took a seat on the steps. "You better hear about the powwow I had with the captain."

"First, I want to know what that city slicker was doing with them," Dud asked as the others began to crowd around.

Ponder grimaced and waved one hand in impatience, sweeping aside any importance that might be attached to that. "He was just here looking for runaway orphans. I told him any children we had were brought here by their mama, two boys, not a boy and a girl, and they weren't orphans. It might have just been an excuse to spy out the countryside for all I know. He acted suspicious enough to me. Nosy as all get-out."

"All right, why was the captain here?"

Ponder gave a hard look at Henry. "Some high-tone rich Mexican family in San Antone complained about a peon who seduced their two daughters, and they have enough political clout to send the army out looking for him. Naturally, we don't know nothing about that."

"Did he ask about me?" Dud said.

Ponder rolled his eyes. "Only because he had to go through the motions. He don't give a hoot about you. Evidently, them was the sorriest soldiers in the army, and he is glad to get shut of them. He's more than willing to believe they deserted. I told him you was stung because your old lady divorced you, so you decided to go to Louisiana and ask my second wife's cousin to marry you."

It smarted that Ponder felt like he had to tell the whole world his wife had divorced him.

"Your second wife was an orphan who didn't have any family," Dud said, feeling a little petulant.

"Everybody in Louisiana has cousins, even orphans with no families. Now shut up and pay attention."

Despite his aggravation at Ponder, it relieved Dud to hear he had dropped so far down on the list as a person of interest to the army. He listened as Ponder began describing his conversation to the captain, how he had told him he and Audie planned on taking cattle to sell to the army in New Mexico.

"He said the government contractors let out for bids in the summer, and just about every jack one of them is as crooked as they come, so be special careful in dealing with them. He heard through the grapevine that a big rancher in the Panhandle is heading for Fort Sumner. He said for us to stop at Fort Bliss in El Paso first. That's the big hub of all them forts out there. They might send us anywhere — Fort Stanton, Fort Craig, no telling. They is all trying to round up the Mescalero Apaches. He said they have totally destroyed crops, livestock, everything, trying to subdue the Indians, and now they is all starving, including the soldiers."

Audie unexpectedly broke in. "I don't know if I want to feed the Indians or Union soldiers. It's hard to get past seeing your kinfolks with arrows in them and their heads scalped, not to mention other kinds of torture that drive a man insane thinking too much about. And Yankee soldiers killed my brothers and yours, Dud."

Chapter Seven

Dud looked from Audie to the others. Mutt was looking at him with his solemn dog eyes, while Toomey stared with that flat vacant face turned to him. The lawyer gazed at him without expression. Henry and Darnell did not try to hide a lively interest in his response. Florine watched him with anxious eyes, and even Shug looked unexpectedly apprehensive. Ponder leaned his head back and stared at him, waiting for an answer.

"We don't have to like them, Audie," Dud said. "And I'm not going to sit here starving out of some false sense of honor or loyalty. Besides, it's no sin to feed somebody who is hungry, even if you do hate their guts."

Audie accepted his reasoning, but he still grumbled. "Some of your neighbors and friends ain't gonna feel that a way."

"Then they can lump it." Dud turned to

Ponder. "What else did he say? And how come a Union officer was being so helpful to us?"

Ponder looked at him with sharp eyes. "He joined the Union army, but his brother fought with me and Big Foot Wallace." Ponder did not elaborate, but spit out more tobacco juice and continued. "He said to take the Lower Military Road going out there. It's longer, but safer. He said sometimes the Indians . . ." Ponder paused to look around.

"I'm talking about the Comanche, the Kiowa, and the Apache, not none of the lawyer's kinfolks. Anyway, sometimes they let people pass with nothing more than demanding a few beeves. Most times, they try to steal horses. Other times, they attack. It just depends on how they feel when they get up in the morning."

"And coming back?"

"He said they'll be waiting for us to return on the lower road, so take the high road coming back and travel only at night." Ponder paused again to emphasize the importance of his next words. "He said take as many guns and as much ammunition as we can get our hands on. Not to be thinking we might be able to squeeze through without getting attacked, because we will be."

Dud looked at his motley cattle hands. Shug and Billy Sol would be well armed, and Florine never went anywhere without a shotgun. The lawyer had a pistol, but Dud was not sure he even knew how to use it. Henry carried only a knife, and the three others, Darnell, Mutt, and Toomey had nothing.

Dud and Ponder exchanged glances. They both knew what they were up against. But would these boys understand?

"Do you see how dangerous it is going to be?" Dud asked. "Now is the time to back out, not a few hundred miles down the trail when we need every man."

Shug looked at his mother. Mutt and Toomey exchanged glances. The lawyer unexpectedly blinked. Dud looked at Henry, the wild card. But it was Darnell who spoke.

"I wants to go," he said.

The others nodded in agreement. Dud spoke to Henry.

"Henry, you see where this puts you. It will take every piece of cunning you ever had to outwit the Indians to keep them from stealing our horses. The rest of us will be depending on you to see to it that we don't get put afoot in the middle of no man's land. If you want to back out now, none of us will hold it against you. But we'll curse you till our dying breath if you desert us later on."

Henry drew himself up to his full four feet ten inches. "Señor Dud, if I stay here, I am a dead man. I never should have seduced two women in the same family. It was not two sisters; it was *la mamá* and *la hijita.* Now, Señor Hidalgo wants to assassinate me. I will die with honor among men, not in dishonor in an alley off a backstreet."

Ponder shot Dud a "what did I tell you?" look. He pushed back his hat and scratched his head. "Between Dud and Henry, it will probably be woman troubles that are the death of us."

He got up and rose to go back into the cabin.

"Where are you going?" Dud asked.

Ponder turned. "I'm leaving for San Antonio to buy supplies. When you get there, send one of the boys into the Blue Horn Saloon to fetch me. You know the one — close to the army garrison."

"Make sure you buy supplies before stepping foot in a saloon, Uncle Ponder," Dud said. "And buy real coffee if you can manage it."

"You just make sure you don't get led

astray by some ole whore before we get these cattle sold," Ponder retorted. "Most of the time you are as cunning as a fox with the courage of a panther, but when it comes to women, you ain't got a lick of sense, boy."

Dud turned to the people who would now be depending on him for their lives and addressed them.

"Cuss all you want to, but no drinking or card playing on the trail. You can do plenty of that when you get to go to town." Except that towns would be few and far between. "And Henry, you're going to have to lose that pretty sombrero. Everybody seeing it will know who it belongs to. I've got an old hat you can wear."

"Mr. Dud," Darnell said. "I gots me an old fiddle, can I brings it along?"

"Sure, you can put it in the wagon," Dud said. "You'll be too tired to play it, but by all means, bring it."

They dispersed to examine their private thoughts and feelings about the danger they were facing. Dud stopped the lawyer.

"Are you sure you still want to go? There is no love lost between the Comanche and the Cherokee. They will kill you as easily as they will kill us."

The attorney stared at him. "I am ready,"

he said, and turned to go back to his mustangs.

Before Ponder left, Dud tied two mustang mares to the oxen leading the wagon. He gave instructions on selling them — he especially wanted one of the new improved Henry rifles, but Ponder was to buy as many supplies, including guns and ammunition as he could. Henry said one of his little black mustangs was broke enough it could be tied to the back of the wagon and sold, too. His weapon of choice was a sharp knife, but he also wanted a pistol and for the gringos with him to have as much gun power as possible.

Before going to bed, Dud gave a myriad of instructions. He threatened to kill anybody who fired a gun unless it was to save a life. No unnecessary shouting and rough horseplay — they were to sing softly to the cattle, keeping them as calm as possible. Even the striking of a match at night could set a herd off into a stampede. Luckily, nobody smoked cigarettes. The rest of the men except himself, the lawyer, and Henry chewed tobacco. Florine dipped snuff occasionally and sometimes smoked a corncob pipe. The Hollister boys had not taken up any bad habits yet, but they had to be included in all the warnings. Dud hoped to find a ranch house on the outskirts of San

Antonio with nice people to take them in, but in the meantime, he had to treat them more or less like the others.

He went to bed that evening worrying he had forgotten something. That night, the soldiers came for him again, except this time, they turned into Indians. They surrounded him, and one came after him with a knife. He kicked the knife out of his hand and began to wrestle him, trying to kill him before he was killed.

"Dud! Dud! Stop!" Florine was hollering.

Dud kept struggling, his hands around someone's throat, while other hands tried to pull him off. He blinked his eyes, realizing it was not an Indian he was strangling, but Toomey, and it was Shug and Audie trying to pull him away. His hands instantly loosened, and he stared at Toomey in horror.

Toomey stepped back, falling and catching himself, gasping and holding on to his throat.

"Dud!"

"It's all right. I'm all right," he said. "Toomey, I'm sorry. I'm sorry, Toomey."

They loosened their hold on him, and he stood upright and panting.

Toomey was trying to catch his breath. The others stood silent. Dud did not know what else to say or do. They all thought he was a maniac. He had never felt so alone in the world.

"Mr. Dud," Toomey croaked, "I'll . . ." he stuttered, "I'll put my money on you against an Indian any day in a wrestling match."

Dud relaxed his shoulders and went back to bed.

He was back up at three the next morning. They were all nervy, but the younger men were more excited than anything else. Florine's wagon carried enough supplies to see them to San Antonio. Dud knew the way to San Antonio like he knew the curve of his ex-wife's breasts, but once they started west from there, it would be a different matter.

They were clumsy with the cattle at first, even Shug who rode left point. But the longhorns started to string out naturally, and things were beginning to shape up when they came upon Billy Sol with the Higginses' three hundred head. Billy Sol came charging up to Dud, glad to see a human face.

"Cousin Dud!"

Dud returned his greeting, thinking Billy Sol and his brother were two of the plainest and most simpleminded looking, if not downright ugly, cowboys who ever hit the trail. Billy Sol was slight, with moony eyes set in a face that looked like a flatiron. While he talked with Billy Sol about the state of the cattle, Darnell rode up to ask if Mutt was to ride in front of him or behind.

"Behind," Dud said. "You're riding swing and Mutt's riding flank. I'll tell him again."

Billy Sol rode away to begin moving the Higgins cattle in with Dud and Ponder's. Darnell paused to look after him.

"Is that man all there in the head, Mr. Dud?"

Dud grunted. "Yes, I know he looks like a halfwit. Before it's all over with, you'll realize he's no fool when it comes to cattle. Just with everything else.

"Now, get back there and keep those cattle moving."

"Yes, sir, Mr. Dud," Darnell said, swinging his horse around smartly.

Will and Jemmy had asked to ride drag with the lawyer, and Dud rode back to check on them. Will had a kerchief to cover his face but Jemmy did not. Dud removed the blue one from his neck and handed it to Jemmy.

It looked more like a circus in the rear, with the attorney and the two boys darting horses back and forth, trying to keep stragglers in line, but Dud knew they would get the hang of it soon enough.

"Keep these cattle moving," he said through the dust and above the noise. "The cattle in the drag is what sets the pace."

Several hours later, it became unpleasantly apparent that Darnell and Henry weren't getting along. They hollered at one another to stay out of the way and slurs regarding color and the marital state of mothers were tossed back and forth. After a while, Dud had enough and sent Darnell around to the other side of the herd, ordering him to trade places with Audie.

When they made camp, Darnell and Henry stayed on opposite ends of the grub line and sat as far apart around the campfire as they could from one another without getting out of hearing range of the others.

"Audie's taking the first watch with me. Shug and Billy Sol take the second. Darnell and the lawyer will take the third, and Mutt, you and Toomey will take the last guard. I want Henry to stay with the horses at all times."

"Mr. Dud, what about me and Jemmy?" Will asked.

Dud nodded. "You can ride with me, and I'll see how you do."

Although the lawyer was still treated like an unwanted stepchild, Darnell did not object to taking night watch with him. He was, however, nervous about failing on the job.

"Will you repeat your instructions to me again, Mr. Dud?"

"One of you rides clockwise, the other counterclockwise. Watch for rustlers or varmints or anything else that might threaten the herd. Be especially watchful for wildfires. Sing to the herd to keep them calm and yourself awake."

The lawyer swallowed and nodded his head in understanding. Dud did not know how long he would be able to take it. He expected him to give notice when they reached San Antonio.

The two boys circled the herd with Dud. As they rode together in the dark, he gave them instructions about what to do if the herd stampeded — they were to stay on their horses and ride out of the way.

"Uncle Ponder swears that longhorns aren't like other cattle, and they won't step on a man down, they'll go around him, but I don't want to put it to the test."

"Have you ever been in a stampede, Mr. Dud?" Will asked.

He had, many times, and it helped while away the night hours of endless riding in circles to tell them cowman stories that were far away from war and divorce. Nevertheless, by the time the shift was over, their heads were nodding. Dud took them back to Florine's wagon and told her to find a place in the wagon for them to sleep.

"Let them sleep a little later in the morning."

Florine did not like that. "I need them to help me gather firewood and water in the morning."

"All right, then," Dud agreed. "But tell them if they want to be nighthawks with me in the evening, they'll have to sleep a little after dinner. They're still kids, Florine."

"They'll grow up fast if they stay with this outfit," Florine said. "I already feel ten years older."

"Nobody asked you to come along," Dud retorted.

Florine grew silent, and Dud left her alone to find his own place to bed down for the night. He threw down his bedroll near Jax and Ned. As he put his head down on his saddle, he could hear the croaking of the bullfrogs in the creek near where they had bedded the cattle. He heard Billy Sol's voice getting stronger, singing a comic tale about a gal named Bet, before fading into the night. Dud shut his eyes and slept without dreaming.

The next day as Dud watched the great stream of cattle plod by, kicking up dust, he knew he was going to regret trailing a mixed herd for the next several months, if not the rest of his life. The steers were more powerful than the cows and had a stronger stride. Throw calves into the mix, and the pace that was already broken and awkward would be worse. It meant a thousand miles of struggle to keep the herd together in one continuous line.

They had crossed the creek without incident. The Hollister boys were all over the place — helping the lawyer ride drag, fetching firewood for Florine and washing dishes from the wreck pan, tying horses to a string line for Henry.

Audie rode up to Dud as he sat on Jax to momentarily watch the boys help the attorney.

"Things are shaping up, Dud," Audie said. "That's a good omen."

Dud grunted. He was not sure he believed in omens. It could turn bad in a heartbeat.

Audie observed the boys as they chased after an errant yearling. "I never seen two kids work so hard. I guess if I was an orphan afraid of getting dumped somewhere, I'd be scared, too."

Dud turned his head to look at Audie.

"We can't take them where we are going, Audie."

"You don't think Callie and Fitz would take them in?"

Dud sat silent for a minute. "I thought about it," he finally said. "But Callie's already lost one baby, and she's pregnant again. Fitz isn't going to want to put anything on her right now. I'm not even going to mention it to him."

It surprised Dud, how hard the Hollister boys were trying. Between all the work they were doing and Florine's sharp words, he thought they would be raring to get away.

"Florine ain't exactly the motherly type," Audie said as if reading his mind.

"She sure is not," Dud agreed.

"What happened to her husband anyway?"

"Oh, he disappeared a long time ago," Dud said. "Ponder said he was pretty worthless."

Audie turned to go back to his place with the herd. Dud rode with him, Jax seeming to know every move he wanted to make almost in advance.

"Jax and Ned are shaping up to be good cow horses," Audie commented as they passed the plodding cattle.

Dud agreed. "You'd think going through war together we would have developed some kind of a rapport. Instead, Jax waits until we are trailing cattle to become responsive. I wonder if it is that way with women?"

"Dud, you are asking the wrong person. I got married when I was nothing but a pup, and I never learned a darn thing about women. Ask Ponder, he's had plenty of experience."

"Oh, shoot," Dud said. "Ponder just picks one, says 'let's get married,' and they agree. I never have figured out what women see in that old fart."

Audie laughed. They rode past Mutt, nodding their greetings. He smiled at them, looking as contented as an old drunk with a full jug, just happy to be riding along with a slow-moving herd of cattle.

"He's found his calling," Audie said.

Dud grunted, looking the cattle over, not even sure yet what he should be watching for. Mutt, Toomey, and Darnell had placed their faith in him without question. The lawyer was trusting in the Washburn reputation, whatever that was. The work he did with Henry with the mustangs had laid the foundation for their relationship. The others were kinfolks who knew his strengths and his failings.

His eyes swept across the landscape. As soon as they left San Antonio, scouting would take priority. Between there and the borderland they would be traveling, it would be outlaws and bandits threatening them. And everywhere, there would always be the threat of Indians who had done what they pleased for a thousand years and would not be willing to give that up to the white man's sense of law and order.

They could hear Darnell's melodious voice singing something that would have been banned even in a saloon, it was so filthy. Dud grinned and Audie chuckled.

"He changes the words and tones it down when he gets around Florine and those kids, and at night, it's strictly gospel," Dud said.

Darnell gave them a big smile as they went by, and they nodded their greetings. When they were well past him, Audie spoke.

"He's got the best voice of the whole bunch."

"Have you heard Shug and Billy Sol?" Dud said. "It's enjoyable as long as you don't have to look at them."

"That poor lawyer is so self-conscious, he barely makes a whisper."

"If he's going to practice law in Texas, he'd better learn how to use that voice," Dud said. "But that's his lookout, not mine."

Chapter Eight

On the third day, Dud saw improvements. The cows were developing their following. In a few weeks, all the muleys would find one another and keep separate from the horned ones.

Every man, down to the two boys, knew better than to complain about the cook's food. But it seemed to have gotten better. It was becoming apparent that Jemmy Hollister could produce a mean batch of biscuits in a dutch oven.

Toward the end of the day, they reached Fitz's ranch. They had a creek to cross before tying in with Fitz's herd, and Dud wanted to get that over with before settling the cattle down for the night. It was so shallow in most places; a man could stand up in it and not get his knees wet. Dud sat on Jax, waiting on the other bank for the herd to cross. They had gotten everything across except the drags when the lawyer's horse stepped into a sinkhole. It spooked the animal, and he threw his rider into the creek. The horse swam, gained his footing, and came across to the other side. Dud caught his reins and held them, watching the water, waiting for the lawyer to come up.

Dud was contemplating jumping in when his head finally bobbed up. He splashed and sputtered, making his way out of the sinkhole with awkward swimming strokes. He stood up, hatless, and breathing heavily.

Audie reined up next to Dud. "What happened to him?"

"Fell in a sinkhole, I reckon."

His dark hair streaming down on either side of his face, the lawyer hobbled out of the creek.

"Next time, ease up on the reins and hold on to the mane," Dud said.

Barefoot, he nodded. "I lost my boots."

Dud looked down at his bare feet and could not help laughing. Audie smiled.

"Well, Mr. Barefoot Lawyer," Audie teased, "you best rest a spell before going back in to look for them."

Toomey and Mutt rode up. "What happened?" Toomey asked. Mutt, looking at the lawyer, added, "Look at them big ole bare feet."

The other men arrived to see what was wrong. Amidst much laughter and ribbing, everyone except Dud and Audie stripped off to take turns going into the sinkhole to search for the lawyer's boots.

After one fruitless dive after another, they quit at dusk. The hat was found downstream, but the boots never turned up. David Sullivan, however, now had a nickname. Every man in the outfit took to calling him Barefoot.

A cheerful group sat around the campfire that night, and even Henry and Darnell left off shooting hateful glances at one another. Mutt offered to make Barefoot a pair of moccasins, but the spare leather was in Ponder's wagon. Billy Sol gave him a pair of socks since he'd lost those, too. Shug had the oldest leggings, so he cut pieces of leather and strips of latigo to tie to the bottom of Barefoot's feet.

The attorney gave his thanks, but otherwise, he remained quiet, as if overcome by the events. He had ceased to be David Sullivan, lawyer, and had become Barefoot Sullivan, cowboy.

Dud took the first watch by himself, having sent Audie to the ranch house to tell Fitz to have his cattle ready to join theirs and move out in the morning. He did not want to put Callie through the torment of goodbyes again, and he was reluctant to leave his new responsibilities in any case. The Hollister boys, who had joined in plunging for Barefoot's boots, had fallen asleep around the campfire, their plates untouched. He had carried them to Florine's wagon, putting them inside.

She was mad because they had fallen asleep before they could wash the supper dishes.

"Ain't you got any womanly feelings at all, Florine?" Dud hissed.

She had thrown a dishrag in the wreck pan as hard as she could. "Don't you be talking to me about womanly feelings, Dud Washburn. You're just like Ponder."

He had left before a screaming match could start.

Now, as he rode on Ned in a wide circle around the sleeping cattle, he wondered why Florine had not gone with Audie to visit Callie. But Callie would question Florine, asking her why she was willing to make such an arduous journey. Florine would cuss him and Ponder rather than tell them her reasons, but she would not, or could not, do that with Callie.

Thoughts of Beatrice began to occupy him, and he could not get her out of his mind. He wondered if he should sneak over to her parents' house when they reached San Antonio. He ached to hold her in his arms, Union soldiers and divorce decree be hanged. Or he could use the excuse of the Hollister boys, saying he needed her help in finding them a home. He would use whatever means he could to get close enough to her to try to convince her to let him touch her.

The yipping of coyotes filled the night air. He looked around uneasily, even though knowing they had the ability to sound as if they were right under a person's nose when a mile away. The cattle were not bothered; they were used to such sounds.

Billy Sol and Shug met him, ready to take over the watch. They muttered a few words about the coyotes and separated to make their rounds. Dud rode to the remuda to check on the horses. Henry appeared, as quiet as a cat and looking more like a shadow than a flesh and blood man.

Dud spoke in soft tones. "Everything okay?"

"*Sí,* Señor."

Dud started to ride away when Henry stopped him with a word.

"Señor."

Dud pulled lightly on the reins. "What is it?"

"Señor, when we get to San Antonio, I think the man who is after me will know, and he will send men to kill me. Will you stand with me, Señor Dud?"

It would mean kissing goodbye to his plans of sneaking into his ex-wife's bedroom. "Yes," he answered, suppressing a sigh.

After tying Ned near his bedding, Dud tried to sleep, but thoughts of San Antonio kept running through his head. Shug and Billy Sol's watch ended, and he still could not sleep. He knew the sound of Barefoot's horse, and he could hear them coming toward him. He rose, scaring Barefoot by stepping into the dark in front of him.

"You going into San Antonio to buy a new pair of boots when we get there?"

In the faint light by the stars, he saw Barefoot shake his head.

"I gave all the money I had to Mr. Ponder to buy a rifle and more ammunition for me."

But Barefoot had not said he was leaving the outfit, as Dud thought he would. Maybe he did intend to stick it out.

"You any good with a knife?"

It was Barefoot's turn to hesitate. "How do you mean?"

"I mean like protecting yourself and killing somebody."

"I've never killed anybody. I joined up with Stand Watie but got sick with the measles. And then I came down with the mumps. After that I was wounded. I spent almost the entire war in the infirmary. Why do you ask?"

"There's going to be trouble over Henry in San Antonio. I don't want to start a gun battle around a jumpy herd of longhorns if I can help it. But I need a good man to stand watch with me and Henry. Shug and Billy Sol can fight, but they'd do better looking after the cattle. Audie's steady as a rock, and he fought like a bearcat in the war, but he's beginning to slow down. Those other boys are too young and unpredictable. I don't know why I'm trusting you, lawyer, but I am."

Barefoot said nothing, and Dud was about to leave when he paused.

"Ponder's got big feet, too. Maybe he'll have an extra pair of boots for you."

Dud left Barefoot to continue his rounds, no doubt to ruminate about stabbing someone with a knife.

Fitz and Audie rode into camp at daybreak the next morning. Dud wanted to know how Callie was and if she was angry at him for not coming to the house.

"Sick as a poisoned dog. She looks at food and wants to throw up, but no, she understands, and she's not mad. But she is a little miffed Florine didn't bother to visit her."

Dud, standing with the other men around the coffee pot, looked in Florine's direction as she threw pots and pans back into her wagon.

"She doesn't want to have to explain herself to Callie, I reckon," Dud answered.

The Hollister boys came from around the wagon, carrying a bucket of water from the creek to throw on the campfire.

"Whoa, what's this?" Fitz said.

Dud introduced him to the boys and explained their presence.

"Rinse out the coffee pot and the cups, boys, and put out the fire," Dud said. "We'll be heading out here directly."

They nodded, keeping their heads down. Dud had never seen two more modest and retiring boys. As soon as they finished the chores Dud gave them, they made for the remuda. When they were out of earshot, Dud explained his plan of finding homes for them on the trail.

"I promised their ma I'd take care of them, but I can't take those boys where we are going."

Fitz looked after them. "Callie would kill me if I didn't bring them home."

"Then don't tell her," Dud said. "I don't want to put no extra burden on her right now. I'll find some good folks somewhere."

Fitz, looking a little sad, gazed again in the direction the boys had taken, but he gave a reluctant nod. He turned back to Dud.

"I've got a brindle steer with a black stripe down its back that is always wanting to be at the head of a herd. Shug and Billy Sol might as well put him on point now, because he's going to pass everything in sight eventually to get there. And he's good about going where you want him to."

"Dang," Dud said, impressed. "He got a name?"

"General Sherman," Fitz said with a laugh. "Because he can find his way through any thicket and cross any river, marching his way through Georgia, if he's a mind to."

"Fitz, you've given me your best horse, and now you've given me your best steer."

"I want you to bring both of them back, Brother Dud, along with your and Ponder's ole sorry hides."

Before Dud could answer, Florine screeched out his name. "Dudford! When are we going to get this cattle drive going?

Are you going to stand there jawing all day? Time's a wasting."

Dud looked at Fitz. "I can't promise I'll bring her back," he said, pointing his head in Florine's direction.

Fitz grinned, but Dud left to get Jax, knowing Florine was right.

Darnell's two uncles and Fitz stayed to help with the drive at least part of the way. Fitz planned on leaving before making camp, but Darnell's uncles wanted to go to San Antonio to visit relatives in Ellis Alley they had not seen in years.

Florine grumbled about the extra mouths to feed, but Dud was glad to have them. They were experienced cattlemen, and every night, Darnell played his fiddle for them. The old men would lead the singing, and everyone except Henry and Florine joined in. Mutt and Toomey would dance jigs, and Mutt, who shuffled like a loose-boned hound, gave the best performance.

Henry stayed with his horses. Whenever Dud went to check on him, Henry would find some way of expressing his displeasure, snubbing his nose, complaining of the noise, whatever it took to let Dud know how he felt about Darnell and his family. Dud did not chastise him — the only thing he was concerned about was the smooth running of the drive. As long as Henry took care of the horses, and Darnell took care of the cattle, Dud did not care how they felt about one another.

Darnell and his uncles were not blameless. But the snide remarks they made about Henry and the Mexican race in general were not loud enough or bothersome enough for Dud to step in either.

On the evening before they were to reach San Antonio, before he and Audie began their watch, Dud stood at the campfire while the others crouched on their haunches and ate. The men ate in a steady, silent rhythm, and it was only when they finished that the discussions about the day would begin. The hoorawing — that jabbing, teasing, and joking with one another — started afterward.

Dud addressed them while they ate, knowing he would have a minute or two of silence, anyway.

"Somebody's going to have to fetch Ponder, and I know you boys want to cut loose in town."

No one said anything. Shug and Billy Sol did not look up, but kept shoveling food in their mouths as fast as they could. Dud reckoned they had learned a long time before not to try to savor it.

"Darnell's uncles," he said, giving them a nod, "are leaving us. Barefoot and I are going to stay with Henry and the horses. You can take turns going into San Antonio. Darnell can go with his uncles and come back. Audie, you can go at the same time. When they return, Billy Sol and Shug can go."

Shug looked up from his plate. "Me and Billy Sol will stay here with the cattle."

Billy Sol nodded in agreement. It took Dud by surprise, but he did not question their reasons.

Audie spoke up. "I don't want to go either. Send Mutt and Toomey after Ponder."

There was no reticence about Mutt and Toomey. They were as anxious as girls putting up their hair for their first dance. They began pumping Dud about saloons to visit.

"Hold on, there," Dud said. "The first thing you have to do is find Uncle Ponder and send him to camp. Then you can live it up." Dud reckoned they probably only had about fifteen cents between them.

He turned to his cousins. "When do you want these hell-raisers back?"

They looked at one another and shrugged. Shug turned to Dud.

"Don't matter. I reckon we can look after the herd for one night."

"All right, then," Dud agreed. He looked

at Toomey and Mutt. "As soon as we get the herd settled for the night, you can take out. Be back at camp before sunup."

Ned already had his routine down pat. He would stand, looking like a patient prophet waiting on the Lord. If Dud was a few minutes late, he started getting antsy. That evening, Toomey and Mutt would not shut up, driving everybody crazy talking about San Antonio, the sights they were going to see, the girls they were going to talk to. Dud got so tired of it he did not give Ned any cause to get agitated, but jumped on his back early.

It seemed every hope Dud had involving San Antonio had crashed into dust. He would not be able to even try to have one more night with Beatrice. And what was he to do with the Hollister boys? The best he could think of would be to send Ponder around with them and listen to Florine scream bloody murder because she had to do all the cooking herself.

He and Audie exchanged a few words as they met on their rounds. Audie approved of his plans to have Ponder find a place for the boys.

"Ponder will have better luck than you anyway," Audie said.

"Thanks a lot, Cousin," Dud said. "I'd be

mad except I know you're right."

When Dud's watch ended, Mutt and Toomey had stopped talking long enough to catch some sleep, but they started again first thing in the morning.

Having agreed to push the herd hard for the first couple of weeks to get the cattle trail broke, they were making good time. But that afternoon cows started dropping calves. They would not leave their babies, and the calves could not keep up with the herd.

Dud waved at Shug, giving him the signal to ride back to the drag.

Shug met him at the rear with Barefoot, Will, and Jemmy.

Dud reined his horse closer to Shug.

"I don't want to have to shoot them." That was the only way Dud knew to force the cows to move on. Calves would only slow them down and were not worth any money. "You got any ideas?"

Shug stared at the calves from under slanted lids. Dud figured he would offer to kill them, although he hoped Shug knew of an alternative.

"When Cousin Ponder comes back, we can load them in his wagon to ride in daytime, then turn them loose to go back to their mamas at night. Ma ain't gonna let us put them in her wagon."

Dud sighed. "Yeah, but Ponder ain't here right now."

Will came closer. "Mr. Dud, I can hold that calf across my saddle. Jemmy can hold the other one."

Dud looked at Shug, and he nodded. "Them kids can tote them. But you can't let them calves get to mixing with one another, or their mama won't recognize their scent come nightfall."

"How the heck are we going to keep them separated in a wagon then?" Dud demanded.

Shug stared back at Dud. "Put them in a tote sack with a number marked in tar, Cousin Dud, and mark the mama with the same number."

Shug said it like he could not believe Dud did not know to do that. Dud rolled his eyes and sighed, thanking God, that despite Florine, He had sent Shug and Billy Sol.

"All right, that's what we'll do." Dud nodded to Will and Jemmy. Without any help, the two of them wrestled the calves and got them thrown over their saddles. Dud realized with a start how much he was going to miss them. They were the most obliging cowhands he had.

He left to scout out a good place for the

herd to bed for the night and found one about a mile south of town. He rode back to the herd to tell Shug and Billy Sol.

As he neared, he waved his arm to Billy Sol, motioning him to join Shug. Billy Sol rode a sorry-looking brown gelding with a big head, but he was about the best cow horse Dud had ever seen. They met up with Shug on a favorite gray at the same time. Audie saw them and cantered his horse to join them.

"It's at a bend in the river close to town," Dud said. "I'm expecting trouble tonight because of Henry. I don't think anybody will try to stampede the herd that close to town, but if they do, I think the herd will move straight west instead of crossing the river to go into town."

"You're taking a big chance," Audie warned, "be easy for someone to sneak a few head off. And what if they do stampede and head straight for downtown San Antonio? We'll never gather them."

"No, Dud's right. If these here cattle stampede, they'll make a run for the west," Billy Sol argued. "Ain't that right, Shug?"

Shug nodded. "If they head west, best to let them run it out. With three men short, we might have a passel of unnecessary trouble trying to circle them."

"I'm hoping Uncle Ponder hires on a couple more men in San Antonio."

Audie shook his head. "I'm just hoping he bought supplies before he started playing poker."

"You don't have to worry about Cousin Ponder, Audie," Billy Sol said. "He's the best dang poker player I ever did see, and he don't cheat neither. Ain't that right, Shug?"

Shug nodded and turned to Dud. "You think Barefoot's got it in him not to run in a fight?"

Dud let the air flow out of his lungs. "This is a good place to find out."

Chapter Nine

Dud sent Mutt, Toomey, and Darnell, along with Darnell's uncles, into town with instructions to send Ponder back and not tell a soul they knew anybody named Enrique or Henry, or any handsome Mexican by any other name.

Florine was happy that she had three less men to cook for. Her joy did not last long when Ponder came rattling up to camp just as the rest of them had finished eating. Instead of two oxen, Ponder had six and another wagon hitched behind the one he left with.

Audie, standing near Dud, was the first to comment.

"Jumping Jehoshaphat. Would you look at that."

"We don't know what's in those wagons yet," Dud said, unwilling to take anything for granted.

The Hollister boys ran to greet Ponder.

He got down from the wagon and patted the boys on the back. Reaching into his pocket, he took out two sticks of candy, handing it to them.

"After you unhitch my wagon."

The boys gave enthused thanks and ran to do Ponder's bidding, delighted in their unexpected treat. Ponder raised tired eyes to the men.

"I'm hungry, and I am so dang wore out, I'm close to falling down to make an acquaintance with the earth in front of my feet."

"Come sit down, drink some coffee, and eat one of Jemmy's biscuits," Dud said. "That will soothe your stomach enough it can take some of Florine's cooking afterward."

Ponder took a campstool and sat down near the fire ring. He poured himself coffee and grabbed a biscuit while Jemmy and Will unhitched the wagon. Florine shoved a plate in his hand none too graciously, mad because she had to wait until Ponder finished eating before she could be done with cleaning since the boys had deserted her.

Dud crouched down on one knee near Ponder. The sun was setting on the horizon, a ball of orange fire, leaving a pinkish sky. Audie, Shug, and Billy Sol stood near

Ponder. Barefoot, his eyes anxious and drawn, had taken a place near Henry and the horses.

"Did you get any extra hands?" Dud asked.

"Nope," Ponder said, sopping up beans with his biscuit. "As soon as they found out where we was headed, they all backed off going."

"What? All of them?"

"That's right. The Comanche have been raiding something fierce north of Uvalde. A couple of weeks ago, they killed a young woman, raping and disemboweling her. They bashed her baby's head against a tree. Another girl was raped and left for dead, but she lived to tell the tale. Said a white boy with red hair was riding with them.

"When I told them we were headed through that, they said not 'no,' but 'hell, no.' "

Dud exchanged glances with the others. They were unsure of what to do or say next. All eyes turned to Ponder, waiting for what he advised.

Ponder took his time and gulped the last of his coffee down. He wiped his mouth with the back of his hand and handed his empty plate and cup to Audie, who threw them in Florine's wreck pan.

"I bought supplies first off and had the store keep them for me. After that, I had a good run with the cards. Some Comancheros was hanging around, and I could see they was talking among themselves, looking at me every so often."

"Comancheros? In San Antonio?" Dud asked in surprise.

"Dud, don't be such a knucklehead. Everybody goes through San Antonio sooner or later."

Dud could not fault that logic. He shut up and let Ponder continue.

"They sidled up next to me, saying they heared where I was going, and did I want to buy some guns and ammunition. The whole back of that second wagon is full of crates of Henry rifles and brand-new Army Model Colts. And with enough ammunition to start the War Between the States all over again."

Dud did not know at first what to say. "Uncle Ponder, those things are as expensive as a mouthful of gold teeth and just as hard to come by. How did some poor old Comancheros passing through San Antonio get a hold of them?"

Ponder glared at him. "Dud, I never knowed you to question any woman who offered you a free poke, so excuse me for not asking where this gift from God came from."

Audie burst out laughing.

Ponder was not finished showing off what he had accomplished. He went to his wagon and pulled out a roll of leather. "Lookee here what four deuces got me."

They crowded around as he unrolled it. Inside was a map showing every watering hole along the military road between San Antonio and El Paso. Dud was pretty sure it belonged to the military and wasn't for civilian use, but like the rifles, the less he knew of its origins, the better off he would be. It was a godsend, wherever it came from.

"Dang, Cousin Ponder," Billy Sol said in awe, echoing everyone's admiration.

Dud glanced at the extra wagon. "I think we'd better unload those crates and put them in Florine's wagon."

"You ain't just gonna leave that other wagon here, are you?" Ponder asked.

"No, we'll use it to put baby calves in." Dud turned to the others. "As soon as it gets dark, Shug, you and Billy Sol move those guns. I don't trust those Comancheros not to come and try to steal those guns back. Throw all those quilts and blankets I brought in the empty wagon, like we was trying to hide something."

Dud walked away to fetch Ned. Audie followed him to get his horse. Will and Jemmy appeared.

"You boys stick with Uncle Ponder tonight," Dud said.

They nodded, turning and running to find Ponder.

As Dud untied Ned, Audie gave a low laugh.

"Ain't nobody but Ponder could have accomplished that with a few hands of cards."

"A few hands my foot," Dud said. "He's probably been playing cards nonstop since he got to San Antonio. I bet he got down to three dollars and a wad of chewing tobacco at least ten times. I'd have given up or gone bust just to get it over with. That old man has nerves of steel, I'll say that for him."

"I'm glad of it," Audie said.

"Yeah, well, he'll use that as an excuse to lord it over me for the next five hundred miles."

Audie got on his horse. "We couldn't have asked for a worse night. Enough light for bandits to find their way here and shadowy enough to hide from one place to the next."

Dud did not answer, and Audie left to make his rounds. Dud saddled Ned, but staked him nearby to let him graze with the rest of the remuda. He joined Henry and

Barefoot.

"Everything look okay?" Dud asked.

"*Sí,* Señor Dud."

A half-moon emerged, but clouds kept passing over it, obscuring the faint light it gave.

The horses grazed on an open plain, and the only place anyone could hide would be in the trees near the river. Dud examined the lay of the land, the river winding around them, the trees near the river, the horses grazing, the cattle sleeping nearby, the wagons where Florine, Ponder, and the boys lie sleeping. He saw a shadow pass in the moonlight and heard Audie singing to the herd, the sound rising and lowering.

Dud realized they could end up fighting a battle on two fronts — assassins after Henry, and Comancheros hoping to steal back the guns.

"Henry, get your saddle and lay down on it in full view. Barefoot, you lie as flat as you can nearby where you can keep your eye on Henry. Ned and I will be guarding the other side of the remuda. We'll switch places later on."

The men nodded and followed Dud's instructions. He took Ned off the stake. The mustang tensed, as if sensing something unusual was happening. Dud stroked him and talked low, and Ned calmed.

For the next hour, Dud and Ned watched over the horses. The bullfrogs came out, and their croaking sounded louder than if a polka band had been playing near the river. Dud listened to every noise, examined every shadow as he and Ned made their rounds.

When Dud returned to Henry, he was lying as he left him, as tense as a steel spring in a gold pocket watch. Barefoot saw Dud and rose to his feet. Henry jumped up.

"I don't like being *el blanco facilísimo,*" Henry said. "I want to fight, but my enemy is invisible."

Dud opened his mouth to answer but stopped when he heard an unexpected noise. He put his hand up to shush them and strained to listen, peering into the darkness as the men around him did the same, aware that something or someone was heading their way. It sounded like a horse walking in their direction.

A cloud had covered the sky, making it impossible to see more than a few feet in front of them. The head of a horse came at them, and they all jumped. Henry noticed the star on the horse's forehead first.

"It is the ghostly white boy's horse, Señor Dud. El Toomey's horse."

The riderless horse approached Henry

and nickered. While Henry petted him, Dud grasped the reins, holding them up so he could examine them.

"He's broken his reins. Toomey must have forgotten what his uncle told him about the horse and tied him. I'm surprised he came back here instead of galloping all the way back to DeWitt County."

The tension that had gripped them loosened. Dud smiled and started to grunt in laughter. He heard a splash, and the frogs stopped croaking. He froze; the clouds parted, the moon shone, and in the few seconds between the time he began to grunt and when the light brightened, he saw they were about to be jumped by five men.

He did not wait, but pulled his knife and charged, ramming the blade into the gut of the first man he reached. A brawl broke out, and the swipe of a blade behind him cut his shirt, grazing his skin. He whipped around and with his free hand caught an upraised knife as it was about to crash down upon him. With his other hand, he drove the blade of his home. Jerking the blade out, he looked over to see Henry holding off three men as they danced in front of him, waving their knives. Wasting no time, Dud pushed his knife in the back of one. The others charged Henry, and Barefoot appeared, cut and bleeding, but with enough strength to throw himself in front of the attackers and send his knife into one of them. With one vicious swipe, Henry cut a slash across the throat of his opponent, who had let himself be distracted by the attack from Dud and Barefoot.

The three men whirled around, but there was no one else there. They stood breathing in heavy gasps.

A sound pierced the darkness — the cry of a child. In an instant, the longhorns that had been sleeping so lazily jumped to their feet in unison, raised their tails, and began to race in one crazed, thundering mass of motion.

"Stay with the horses," Dud yelled above the noise. He dashed to Ned and jumped on him. There was no way he could make his way across the hurtling cattle; he would have to ride around them to get to the Hollister boys.

The sound of thousands of hoofbeats deafened him to everything else. He could see the shadows of Shug, Billy Sol, and Audie racing beside the herd, letting them run as Shug advised, hurtling west as he had hoped. But the cry of the Hollister boy had scared Dud into religion and action, and he began to pray as he urged Ned forward.

Before he could make his way around to the back of the herd, gunfire could be heard over the rumbling. He could barely see through the dark and the dust to make out the wagons. As he got closer, he saw Florine leaning out the back of her wagon, holding a shotgun. She let go with both barrels, and a roar of buckshot tore through the night. One rider on a horse fell, and more shots could be heard coming from Ponder's wagon. A horse racing toward town caught Dud's eye, and his stomach lurched. Whoever it was looked to be holding onto a struggling boy.

Dud put the spurs to Ned, and he leaped forward. In a matter of seconds, they were racing next to the fleeing rider. Jemmy was fighting the man in the saddle, struggling to get free and jump from the speeding horse. The man turned and saw Dud, his face etched with raw fear and determination. He couldn't reach for a gun to fire at Dud as long as he had a hold on Jemmy, and Dud didn't want to give him an opportunity to decide to throw the boy off. He pushed Ned closer, running neck and neck until he could grab the reins of the other horse. He pulled on them, at the same time, eased on Ned to slow down. As the horses slowed, the other rider threw Jemmy off and went for a gun tucked into his waistband.

Dud was so close, he grabbed the other rider's arm and jerked him from his horse. He pulled out his Colt and shot him in the chest before he could regain his balance.

He halted Ned and dismounted. Jemmy, crying, ran to him and threw his arms around his leg, holding on as tight as he could.

Dud looked up, his eyes searching in the dark. The sounds of gunfire from the wagons had ceased. He could not see any movement. He looked down at Jemmy.

"Are you all right?" he asked.

Jemmy, unable to talk, nodded his head. Dud rubbed his hair.

"It's okay," he murmured.

"Jemmy!" Will called.

Jemmy let go of Dud's leg and ran to his brother.

The herd of longhorns was long gone, and the frogs started to croak again. Dud leaned over the body of the man he had shot. He went through his pockets, looking for the money Ponder had paid them.

"Dud," Ponder's voice came, cutting through the night.

"Over here, Uncle Ponder," Dud said.

Ponder appeared and looked down at the

slain outlaw. "Take his belt and his gun. And take off his boots to see if anything is in them."

There was not anything in his boots, and they were not big enough for Barefoot's feet. Dud pulled off the belt, gathering the loose change he had found in the Comanchero's pockets, his gun, and his knife.

"How many were there?" he asked as he stood up.

"Three," Ponder said. "I killed one and Florine blasted the boogers out of the nose of another one."

"We've got five dead Mexicans over yonder. Should we fetch the law?"

Ponder shook his head. "Law ain't gonna care about no dead banditos or Comancheros neither one. All the law we have now cares about is putting as many ex-Confederates as they can behind bars. I think we ought to get the wagon, load them up and toss them in the river."

"I reckon you are right. Everybody okay?"

"Yeah. I don't know why he grabbed Jemmy. I was fighting off one of them, and this hombre reached in the wagon, going straight for Jemmy. That don't make no sense."

"They're dead now and can't tell us."

Ponder went back to get his wagons. He

had tied his oxen earlier, so they had not stampeded with the rest of the herd. Dud gathered the horses of the Comancheros. In the dark, they didn't look like much, but he led them to the other horses that Barefoot and Henry were guarding.

Ponder helped Dud load the bodies in the wagon. They found the Mexican horses tied near the river. Dud was not sure what to do with the captured horses. The Comanchero horses had about three different brands on each of them already, so adding his and Ponder's wouldn't hurt. But the Mexican horses all carried the same brand. He did not want to be arrested for horse stealing. That could get him in more trouble than killing their attackers.

"If you will permit me, Señor Dud," Henry said. "I think the touch of an artist with a hot iron, and those brands could turn into something else."

Dud shook his head. "Let's just leave them. We've fought our way out of one mess of trouble — we don't need more."

Florine said she was all right, but it was obvious Ponder was on the brink of giving way. He had played cards for days with little sleep and came back to a gun battle. Dud tied Ned to the rear of his wagon and insisted Ponder get in the back with the

Hollister boys.

"I'm driving this wagon. I'm tired of being in the saddle anyway. My legs are starting to bow."

The tracks of the cattle were easy to follow, even in the dark, but they had to travel a slow six or seven miles before they caught up with the herd. By that time, Audie, Shug, and Billy Sol had them calmed and bedded near a creek.

Billy Sol rode out to meet the wagon, still in the throes of excitement. "Cousin Dud, that was some kind of ride. They weren't slowing down for nothing. Me and Shug spied that creek yonder and knew they'd go barreling in there, getting bogged and trample each other to death. It took everything we had to get that herd turned and milling before they reached that there creek."

"Y'all did good, Billy Sol," Dud replied. "Did we lose the mama cows with the two calves?"

"Yeah, but I think that's all we lost, Dud. That's all. That's not bad for a stampede, Dud. That's not bad."

Dud assured Billy Sol he was right. "You better check on your ma. She's had a rough time of it."

It appeared none of them would get much

rest that night. Ponder woke up long enough to insist on helping Dud unhitch the wagon. Shug and Billy Sol unhitched Florine's for her. The Hollister boys were dead to the world. Barefoot had his forearm slashed — his shirtsleeve was soaked in blood. Ponder cleaned and bandaged it for him. Henry, who had been on a high rush since the fight, crashed down hard, so exhausted he could hardly stand upright. Dud ordered Henry and Barefoot back to the remuda, telling them to take turns on guard and try to stay alert. Dud asked Audie if he would take the first guard with him. Audie readily agreed — Dud had forgotten that although Audie might be slow, he had incredible endurance.

Darnell rode back into camp, singing a bawdy song about three encounters in one evening, so Dud guessed he had a good time. It relieved him to have Darnell back, but he worried about Mutt and Toomey. Ordinarily, they would be on their own, but being short of men had Dud wondering if he should send somebody back to town to look for them. There just was not anybody capable of going at the moment.

Dud sent Darnell to spell Henry and Barefoot with the horses, while he and Audie stayed guard before turning the watch over to Billy Sol and Shug. After the intense fracas of the first part of the night, the rest of it passed without incidence.

Chapter Ten

Each man got about three hours of sleep before dawn. Florine was up before then getting breakfast ready. Ponder, not to be outdone by Florine, also rose early, but his eyes were bleary and his temper sharp. After their excited run of the night before, the cattle were docile. Ponder, at Shug's suggestion, put a bell around General Sherman's neck so the other cattle would follow the sound. Henry said perhaps they should put a bell around the neck of one of the older compliant mares. "That's a good i-dee," Ponder said, adding with a touch of malice: "Maybe I ought to put one around Florine's neck, too, since she is always raring to go and forge ahead."

"Cousin Ponder, you ought to be nicer to Ma, ain't that right, Shug?" Billy Sol said.

Ponder frowned. "I don't see no need to. And can't you say one sentence without asking Shug if it's right?"

Dud was about to step in and tell them it was time to get moving. According to the map, they would have to push the cattle another eighteen miles to reach water. Before he could say anything, Mutt came riding into view with Toomey behind him on the saddle.

They dismounted on shaky legs, looking so bedraggled Dud wanted to laugh at them.

"I'm sorry we're late, Boss," Mutt said. "But . . ."

Dud cut in. "Go change mounts. We're about to move out. Toomey, your horse rode into camp last night."

Toomey almost wept with relief. "Man alive, I'm so glad. My uncle would have skinned me when I got home."

"Get moving. You can tell us everything after supper."

Dud tried to talk to Ponder about searching for a home for Will and Jemmy as he climbed into his wagon.

Ponder sat down, taking the reins in hand. "I ain't searching for nothing right now. It's going to be all I can do to sit upright in this wagon and follow this here herd."

"I told you that you were too old to be going on this drive," Dud said.

"Oh, thank you very much, Uncle Ponder, for winning all that money at poker and bringing in all those supplies," Ponder mimicked.

"I reckon you'll be expecting me to kiss your behind all the way to New Mexico and back for it, too," Dud said. "All right, I'll go look my own dang self."

"You do that. Giddyup, you boneheaded oxen, before Florine reaches El Paso ahead of us."

Ponder and Florine went ahead of the herd. The next camp would be near a little village founded by Alsatians on the Medina River. Dud rode back and told the others to keep going — he would meet them when they neared the town to show them where to bed the herd.

He made his way to several different ranches scattered along the way. Everywhere he went, people were kind and hungry for news. He was unable to stay long in any place he stopped, and it disappointed him that they all proved unsuitable.

It would be a family who already had a passel of hungry-looking kids. Or two old bachelors. Or a widow woman who had enough children to feed as it was. Nothing proved suitable.

The water in the Medina River ran clear with a greenish cast from overhanging cypresses. The grass near it stood stirrup high already. Dud rode back to report to Ponder and Florine where to set up the wagons. Ponder had Will at the reins, and Florine was mad because Jemmy had deserted her to help Barefoot with the drags. Dud promised to go to the back and tell Jemmy to ride forward to help Florine. It was easier to comply with Florine than to fight with her, especially since she had proved herself so handy with a shotgun the night before.

When they did make camp, they swapped stories about the previous evening. Several women in Ellis Alley were impressed that Darnell was going on a cattle drive that would bring him home with money in his pockets, and they wanted to make sure he remembered them when he returned. Mutt and Toomey, not nearly as lucky, but just as happy, repeated in great detail what every woman they saw looked like. One had accidently fallen and shown her petticoats to passersby on Commerce Street, and Dud thought Mutt would never tire of describing her stockinged ankles.

When Ponder got up to put his frying spider back into his wagon, Dud followed him.

"Uncle Ponder, did you see Beatrice?"

Ponder did not look at him as he shoved

the spider into the wagon bed. "Now why would I see Beatrice when I was in a saloon playing cards?"

"I didn't ask you that. I asked you if you saw her."

Ponder refused to look him in the face. Instead, he tightened the rope holding the bonnet over the wagon. "Yeah, I saw her walking on the street when I went to buy supplies."

"Was she alone?"

Ponder stopped fiddling with the wagon and turned to Dud.

"No. She was strolling down the street with a dude in a suit. He looked like some kind of a banker or something."

He added in a kinder tone. "Leave it be, Dud."

Dud looked away, feeling ill in his stomach.

Ponder squeezed his arm and walked back to the campfire. Dud followed him, but he was sick of listening to Darnell's yarns and Mutt and Toomey's adventures.

"Audie, if you think you can handle the first watch by yourself, I'm going into town and see if I can't find a home for these here boys."

Jemmy did not cry, but tears began down his cheeks. Will's fists clinched in anger.

"You promised our ma you'd take us with you."

"I promised your ma I'd take care of you the best way I could. And that means not taking you into the devil's den that we are headed for. Don't sass me, boy."

Will backed down, and Jemmy wiped the tears from his eyes with the back of his hand. Audie spoke.

"Go on, Dud. I can handle the first watch. I think all our excitement is over for the time being."

Dud turned to Ponder and caught him mouthing "don't worry" to the boys. He looked up and returned Dud's stare with eyes as innocent as a choirboy's on Sunday morning. Dud wanted to knock his hat off.

"If you're bent on going to town, see if you can't find Barefoot some boots," Ponder said. "I ain't got nothing that will fit him."

Dud turned to Barefoot. "What size?"

Barefoot told him, but added with embarrassment. "I don't have money to pay for them."

"I'll dock your wages." He looked around. "Anybody else?"

They shook their heads in silence. Mad because he was cast in the role of bad guy when he was just trying to do what was right, he stomped off to the remuda to saddle Ned.

Henry petted Ned while Dud saddled him, but he was in a bad mood, too.

"Big mouth *negrito,* always bragging about women." Henry stopped muttering long enough to spit.

Dud thought it was a case of the pot calling the kettle black, but he did not feel like getting into it with Henry.

"Henry, I forgot to tell the others to get as much rest as they can tonight. Tomorrow, we'll have to push the herd even farther to get to the next watering hole. Will you pass the word?"

"*Sí,* Señor Dud," Henry said. He paused and looked up at Dud.

"I won't forget, señor boss man, that when I needed you, you were there for me."

Dud put his foot into his stirrup and swung on top of Ned. He looked down at Henry.

"And I won't forget that you have been here for me, Henry. *Adios.*"

Dud left camp feeling better, and when he entered the little town founded by Alsatians, his spirits lifted further. Like other German towns in Texas, it looked neater and cleaner than average with well-built rock houses and little square yards surrounded by white picket fences. Dud found the mercantile still open, and he entered, a bell tinkling above his head. Rows of orderly stacked merchandise were laid out in front of him, and a round jolly merchant with a walrus mustache greeted him.

When Dud told him what he was looking for, a smile crossed his face.

"I have just the thing," he said in a heavily accented voice. He went to the back of the store, entering a door and disappearing. Dud looked around and wondered if he should buy some sardines and crackers or just take a chance that somebody in town would feed him.

Before he could make up his mind, the storekeeper was back holding a pair of boots that looked as if someone had hastily dusted them.

"Someone ordered these big boots and died before they arrived. So, they have been waiting here for you, *ja.*"

Dud took the boots — the leather was still supple. When the storekeeper told him how much he wanted for them, Dud thought he was mighty proud of his merchandise, but he did not haggle. He needed information and agreed to the price. While paying, he asked if he knew of anyone who might be willing to take on a couple of orphan boys, explaining the circumstances.

For the next thirty minutes, the storekeeper described every house in town, who lived there, and their history. At the end of the conversation, Dud was not any better off than before. For one reason or another, there was not a person in town who could or would be willing to take care of two orphans. There was no minister since the town was Catholic, and the priest was away on business; otherwise, he would have helped.

Disappointed, Dud bought his sardines and crackers and left. He stuffed the boots in his saddlebag and found a place to sit on the veranda of the store to eat. Exhaustion caught up with him, and he leaned his head against a post and shut his eyes.

A dog barked, and Dud's eyes flew open. He shook his head awake, looking up and down the dusky streets. It would be dark soon. He stood up and turned to see the store clerk had already put up the closed sign. Holding his rubbish in one hand, he untied Ned and swung into the saddle. Reining the horse behind the store, he threw the sardine can into a pile of trash.

He had long made a habit of riding into a town one way and leaving it another, even if he had to circle back. Consequently, he had only descriptions of the houses he passed.

The storekeeper said the one with the pretty pink flowers was a widow woman over eighty. On the other side of her with the brown shutters was a woman with eight children and a sick husband. It was the same with every house, until he reached the last one out of town. He looked it over — a stucco house with timbering, an unusual gabled roof, and a large barn to one side. He frowned. The storekeeper had not said anything about this house. A woman opened the door, letting out a large orange tabby. Dud removed his hat.

"Howdy, ma'am."

She was a looker all right — blonde, blue-eyed, and a figure that was neither too skinny nor too chubby.

She gave him a big smile. "Hello, there," she called in the same accent the store clerk used. "We don't get very many visitors passing this way."

"I'm with a trail drive. Our cattle are over yonder about a mile north of here."

She walked closer to him, still smiling.

"And I bet you haven't had a decent meal," she said. "Why don't you come in? My husband and I were just about to eat supper."

Dud got a little disappointed when he heard the word husband, but the word supper cheered him right back up again. He hadn't eaten that many sardines.

"Thank you kindly, ma'am. I sure don't mind if I do."

She smiled and nodded. "Put your horse in the barn. There is feed in there and water next to it."

Dud nodded and gave his thanks again. He rode Ned to the barn, dismounting at the water trough to let him drink. He looked around while Ned got his fill. The house, even though still in town, had an isolated feel to it, as if they were there, but not there.

Dud shrugged and opened one of the wide, solid barn doors. The interior replicated the outside of the property, swept out, every item hanging neatly in place. He had never been in a barn so orderly looking. It almost scared him. Up the ladder was a hay loft, and Dud climbed the rungs, taking another gander. Instead of having his nostrils attacked with the usual musty odor, the loft was filled with fresh, sweet smelling hay.

He fed Ned and left him in a stall. Walking outside, he closed the door and went up to the front of the house.

The same pretty woman opened the door almost as soon as his knuckles left the wood.

"Come in, come in," she said, standing aside to let him enter.

Dud stood hat in hand, trying to take everything in without appearing rudely curious. The ceilings were so low, they felt almost claustrophobic. The furniture wasn't the fancy Victorian stuff he frequently saw in homes of the moderately well-to-do. It was chunkier, with beautiful hand carvings. His hostess led him to the dining table covered in a tablecloth embroidered in bright colors. It was laden with dishes containing meat swimming in gravy, noodles, and at least four different kinds of pickles and relishes.

"And here is my husband," his pleasant hostess said, placing her hand on the shoulder of a man already sitting at the table.

Dud smiled and nodded, introducing himself and trying not to look shocked that this beautiful woman had a husband old enough to be her grandfather. He was stooped, with white hair and glasses. He welcomed Dud in a loud voice.

"*Ja, ja,* sit. Anna, sit," her husband said. "Our guest is probably starving."

She smiled and sat down, bidding Dud to take a place in the middle of the table while she and her husband sat on either end.

Now that he had a closer look, Dud estimated her to be a little shy of thirty years old. Her nose crinkled in amusement, as if she knew everything he was thinking.

As they ate, she treated her husband with a jolly, slightly chiding respect. The food tasted delicious, and there was an abundance of it. The discreet glances Dud made as he ate told him that Anna was as good a housekeeper as she was a cook.

"Mrs., er . . ." he had forgotten her name.

"Anna, call me just Anna."

"Yes, ma'am, Miss Anna," Dud nodded. "Do you and your husband have children?"

"Alas, no, we have been robbed of that pleasure."

Since Anna always raised her voice a little when speaking to her husband, Dud assumed he was a little deaf, even though he appeared to hear whatever Dud said well enough. Other than that, he seemed to have all his facilities and be of sound mind. Anna talked pleasantly and asked intelligent questions about news from the outside world. Dud figured they would be good foster parents. He wondered how to introduce the subject. As soon as he had thought of his opening sentence, Anna insisted on putting another helping of meat and gravy on his plate, and he did not want to be rude by not digging in right away.

They lingered over the meal, and Anna appeared pleased that Dud had just about wiped out her pickle and relish tray. When it grew late, Anna rose from the table. Dud jumped up.

"Would you mind if I caught a few hours of sleep in your barn before I headed back to my herd?"

"Nein, nein," they both cried.

"We have a spare bedroom upstairs," Anna said.

"I wouldn't want to be stomping down your stairs at three o'clock in the morning, ma'am," Dud said.

"Nonsense. Besides, the stairs are on the outside of the house."

Dud nodded, familiar with the German architecture that frequently had steps on the outside of the house leading up to a second-story room to save space on the inside — like the thrifty people they were. He took a deep breath, opened his mouth, about to describe Will and Jemmy when Anna interrupted.

"Here, you come, and I'll show you."

Dud hesitated, but instead of asking her to wait, he gave his thanks to her husband and followed, feeling meek and somewhat overwhelmed by their kindness. He decided he would discuss it with Anna. It might be better that way. She could make up her mind before broaching her husband with the subject.

As Dud followed Anna up the stairs, trying not to stare at her swaying backside, he looked down at the little town with its twinkling coal oil lamps in the windows. Why hadn't the storekeeper mentioned this house and the people who lived here? It made no sense to Dud that he would go on so purposely about every house in town and stay silent about this one.

Anna opened the door and led him into a small room, again with low ceilings. The window was cracked, and setting down her lantern, Anna opened it wider to let fresh air in. She walked to a small homemade table by the bed and lit a candle. Backing out of the room smiling, without saying another word, she shut the door behind her.

Dud cursed himself for acting like a tongue-tied schoolboy and missing his chance to say something to her about the boys. In frustration, he ripped back the quilt and top sheet of the bed, knowing the bottom sheet would be clean and tucked under the mattress so tight, a two-bit piece would bounce if he threw it on the bed.

He undressed, almost, but not quite, feeling guilty that he had such a fine room to sleep in while his men were lying on bedrolls on hard ground. He threw himself on the bed, thanking God for clean sheets and pretty women. The room was hot, and there was no need to cover himself, and he fell asleep that way, ordering his internal clock to awaken at three.

Less than an hour later, the sound of soft footsteps coming up the steps outside the door aroused him. He reached for his pistol. The door opened slowly, with so little noise he realized the hinges must have been oiled, and the person outside the stairs came into the room.

He knew by her smell and the shadow of the outline it was Anna. She must have been wearing the sheerest of nightgowns. Dud placed his pistol back in its holster. A thrill of excitement ran through him, and on its heels, a terrible fear.

The next thing he knew, she was on top of him, and her lips were pressing against his. Her hands were doing things that had him so excited, if he had a brain, he could not remember where it was.

"Miss Anna, your husband is downstairs," he managed to gasp. He looked toward the door and gulped, thinking of that old man busting in with a shotgun.

Anna stopped kissing his chest long enough to gasp close to his face, "Don't worry; he can't hear a thing."

Dud was not so sure about that. He felt guilty for betraying a man whose hospitality he accepted just an hour before, but he could not stop the other feelings Anna had summoned.

He tried to sit up, but she pushed him down. It was like wrestling with a big beautiful cat, and the cat was winning. Her fingernails clawed his skin. She kissed him, thrusting her tongue into his mouth and biting on him until she drew blood. She withdrew, and grasping his shoulders so hard with fingers firm from kneading dough, she brought up bruises.

Dud took a deep breath and tried once again to get up. "Honey, things are getting a little rough," but it was hard to talk because his tongue and lips were bleeding.

In answer to that, she shoved him down on the bed, her fingernails clawing at him in a frenzy of excitement. Baring her teeth, she bit him up and down his arms. It took a massive amount of willpower not to yelp when she almost took a hunk out of his chest.

There came a sound from below, something like a thud. Dud bolted upright, and tangling with arms and legs, managed to push Anna away. He began pulling on clothes as fast as he could.

Anna kept trying to interfere, purring to him that it was nothing. Grabbing his gun belt, Dud strapped it on with shaking fingers. He had to keep stopping to push Anna's hands away from the buttons on his shirt.

Grabbing his hat, he took a deep breath. "Thank you for your hospitality, ma'am," Dud said in a hoarse whisper. He headed for the door, paused, came back and gave Anna a swift peck on the cheek.

He heard another noise coming from below, and when he left the room, he did not worry about the stairs creaking; he slid down the railing.

Dud crossed the yard so fast; he left no imprint in the dew. Once inside the barn, he went straight for Ned. The horse had never been saddled so swiftly and probably never would be again. When Dud left the barn, he did not bother to stop and shut the door.

Chapter Eleven

Despite the darkness, Dud let Ned cut loose, and they raced across fields and gullies back to camp like a lynch mob was on their tails. He shuddered at how close he had come to leaving Will in the hands of a woman who might initiate him into her bizarre idea of lovemaking. Not to mention how narrowly he had escaped dying by the hands of an old German with a rusty shotgun. No wonder the shopkeeper had omitted Anna and her husband.

He rode up to the remuda, frightening Henry who jumped and stood staring at them with knife drawn.

"Señor Dud?" he questioned. After ascertaining it was Dud and Ned, he asked, "Are the bandits after you?"

"No," Dud said, pulling up short on the reins. "Just maybe an irate husband."

Henry stifled his laughter.

"Is everything all right?"

"*Sí,* Señor, it is quiet tonight."

Dud nodded and left, making his way to Ponder's wagon where he would tie Ned nearby and try to sleep for another hour before rising. He did not think he would be able to, but once he had his bedroll down, heard his uncle's snores and saw the Hollister boys sleeping under the wagon bed, he had no trouble collapsing into a dreamless sleep.

Dud arose when Ponder began banging his pots. There wasn't enough daylight for Ponder to get a good look at him until Dud got near the campfire to pour himself a cup of coffee.

"What in tarnation happened to you?"

"I can't tell nobody just yet, or Mutt will take off for town. We might not ever see him again."

He finished his coffee and went for Jax.

They would have to push the cattle to reach the watering hole, but it was more of an inconvenience than a danger. They were far enough away now from San Antonio that Dud did not perceive threats coming from soldiers angry because Ponder had won all their pay, or husbands/fathers who Henry had enraged, or friends of the Comancheros they killed, if they had any. They were still far enough away from the Mexican border that the likelihood of bandits trying to stampede their herd so they could steal horses and beeves was slim. But now they were entering territory that Indians like to raid, and Dud was not sure if he met the perfect family to foster the Hollister boys that he would feel easy about leaving them. They might be safer with a soldier and his family at Fort Inge or Fort Clarke. The incident with Anna had spooked him. He would have to be careful where he left the boys.

With Jax saddled, Dud rode to the front of the drowsy herd where General Sherman was already up and ready to go. Billy Sol was too busy removing the latigo that held the clapper still on the bell around the General's sturdy neck at night to be interested in Dud. Shug could see the scratches on Dud's cheek, and maybe even the bruises and bite mark on his lip, but he said nothing as Dud gave instructions, talking with a thick tongue.

"It's twenty-five miles to Seco Creek, so we need to get moving. Just follow the road. The markings are faint, but you can see them. I'm going ahead to scout, but I don't foresee anything but a long, boring ride to D'Hanis."

"What's D'Hanis?" Shug asked.

"Some wide spot in the road," Dud said. "They've got a Catholic church there if you think you need to go to confession and tell a priest how pretty some of these little heifers are starting to look to you."

"You've always had a smart mouth, Cousin Dud," Shug said, his deadpan expression never changing.

Billy Sol joined them. "Ma always said she didn't know how you and Ponder managed to stay alive this long. Ain't that right, Shug?"

Dud had at least five retorts on his swollen tongue, but he said instead: "It sure hasn't been due to Ponder's cooking."

He left them, riding to scout the lay of the land. The rolling plains would present few problems, or so he hoped. He rode back to check with Billy Sol and Shug, avoiding the others. He asked Billy Sol to fetch him some jerky, which he did without comment.

Dud found a good spot near D'Hanis to bed the herd, but he did not venture into town. The night before had rattled and, to a certain extent, embarrassed him. Instead, he went back to tell Shug and Billy Sol where to point the herd and to lead Florine and Ponder to the ground they would spend the night.

Florine gave him a dirty look, but said

nothing. Ponder only nodded.

Once the drovers had the cattle settled, Audie came around to Dud.

He blinked and did a double take. "What happened to you? Ponder finally had enough?"

"No, mister smart mouth. I'm only going to tell this story once after I get some coffee and some supper. So, come on if you want to hear it."

They were all sitting or standing around the campfire, drinking coffee, talking, and waiting for Ponder and Florine to set out the grub. They stopped when they saw Dud and stared.

"I'm hungry," Dud told Ponder. "You got supper ready?"

"Can't you see me putting it out, knucklehead, or are your eyeballs bruised, too?"

Dud didn't reply, but took a plate and let Ponder ladle food into it. The rest of the men followed, eating in steady silence. When they finished, Ponder spoke.

"You better tell us what happened before we all bust a gut wondering, Dud."

Dud put his plate in the wreck pan and looked at the Hollister boys.

"You know any bird calls, like a hoot owl?"

They both nodded.

"Yes, sir, Mr. Dud, we know how to make

hoot owl calls," Will said.

"All right, show me."

They looked at one another, silently agreeing Will would go first. He raised one hand to his mouth, lifted his head and made the call. He looked at Dud for approval, and Dud nodded his head.

"Our grandpa always told us if we heard an echo, it wasn't a real owl," Will said. "He said that's how a man could tell an Indian was making the call, not a real owl, because an animal hardly ever makes an echo."

"Your grandpa sounds like a right smart man. All right, Jemmy, let's see what you can do."

Jemmy cleared his throat and repeated what his brother had done. It struck Dud that his voice had a different ring to it, and he thought it funny that two brothers could be so alike, and yet so different.

"That was good. I want you boys to go to the remuda and stay there until I fetch you. We probably won't be bothered tonight, but if you see anything unusual, you give that signal."

They both said, "Yes, sir," and left to stay with the horses.

"All right," Ponder demanded. "Let's have it."

Dud took a deep breath. "Last night, a

wildcat jumped me with her husband in the house right underneath the bed. I've never been so scared in my life."

Every mouth opened and gaped at him.

As he told the story, he watched their faces — disbelief, excitement, awe — they did not know whether he was telling the truth or pulling their legs. As he suspected, Mutt believed every word and was ready to desert the cattle drive and ride back to town to find out for himself. He finally relented after Ponder threatened to tie him to a wagon wheel.

Florine stood up, hands on hips. "Dudford Washburn, you're the biggest liar that ever rode a horse through San Antone."

"Florine, I swear on the Bible I'm telling the truth."

Darnell and the others could not stop laughing and grinning, But Florine would not be satisfied until Ponder fetched a Bible out of his wagon and made Dud swear he was not lying, and even then she was suspicious.

"I'm telling you, it's a sorry world when a man's own kinfolks won't believe him," Dud said. "Come on, Audie, we better start our watch."

"Aw shucks, Boss," Mutt begged. "Tell it again, please, just one more time."

"Don't worry," Ponder said. "He'll be telling that story all the way to New Mexico and back."

"No, I won't," Dud called as he went for Ned, not bothering to turn around. "I get the shakes just thinking about it."

They passed through D'Hanis without incident. Despite misgivings, Dud rode ahead and checked it out, almost relieved that it told the same story Anna's town had, nowhere really suitable to leave two boys. Arriving back, Shug remarked that the herd was shaping up nicely. It was so out of character, Dud stopped to give him a second look. Billy Sol echoed Shug's comment, and Dud guessed it was their way of apologizing for calling him a saucebox.

The next morning at breakfast, just when Dud was beginning to feel complacent, thinking things were finally running smoothly, Ponder announced it was going to rain.

"My back tooth is aching, and it never fails me."

"Aw, fiddle," Dud said. "It rained two weeks ago, and you never mentioned your tooth hurting beforehand."

"That's because it wasn't much of a rain. This here is a powerful ache, meaning we got fierce weather coming."

Dud wanted to argue but stopped. He did not have time.

"Laugh if you want to," Ponder said at his back as he rode away. "The tooth never lies."

That afternoon, it grew so hot and sultry, Dud wanted to remove all his clothes and ride naked, he was so miserable. They had crossed one creek, and the cattle had been moody and balky. They had taken them across in batches, with each group being harder to handle than the previous one. Barefoot had his boots, but he was determined not to lose them. He stuffed them in his saddlebags and brought the drag through the creek, fighting to get every wayward old cow and stubborn steer across. Dud and the Hollister boys stayed behind to help him. As soon as the last of the hardheaded ones had been brought across, Dud rode back to the front of the herd.

The cattle had spread out, not so close they would build up too much heat from one another, and not so far away they would be trotting in leaps and bounds trying to catch up. Dud looked up at the sky. A nasty green cast filled the air, with dark clouds building in the west. The cattle began to bellow, butt, and kick one another, exhibiting as much tension as the cowboys herding them felt.

When the thunder began to roll in deafening booms, pounding the ground, and lightning crackled clear across the sky, Dud and the rest of his drovers began to wonder if hell had broken loose from the nether regions. Hail the size of large marbles began to pelt them, and they were certain the cattle would stampede.

For some reason Dud was never to fathom, they did not. He rode back to the Hollister boys and hollered at them to ride ahead and get in Ponder's wagon. He halted Jax near Barefoot, getting off and removing his saddle to put over his head, yelling at Barefoot to do the same. He got back on Jax, trying to balance the saddle, and rode ahead. He passed Mutt, and as soon as Mutt could see him through the storm of hail and rain, he stopped to remove his saddle. Darnell was in the process of taking his off when Dud rode by, and by the time he reached Billy Sol, he found him fighting his way through the storm with a saddle over his head.

Dud still did not understand why the herd had not stampeded; except they were lucky enough to have bad weather in daytime instead of at night. General Sherman had kept the lead, determined to push through the balls of ice bombarding him and keep his troops in order. Dud decided then and there that even if it killed him, he was seeing to it that the General made it back to his home in DeWitt County.

The hail stopped in less than ten minutes, but it lasted long enough to cover every cowboy with bruises. Dud put his saddle back on Jax. As he rode by the wagons, Ponder turned and seeing him, hollered out, "I told you so!"

Dud rode ahead with rain lashing in his face. There was no use in wasting time wishing they had rain slickers. There was a narrow river to cross before they reached Comanche Creek, where the map indicated plentiful water.

The river Dud found was already swelling over its banks. Dud sat staring at its roiling waters, trying to decide if they should cross it or wait. He did not know how long the rain would last. He did not want to get caught on flooded land between a river and a creek. After finding the best place to cross, he rode onward to Comanche Creek.

He rode up and down its banks, realizing if they could get the cattle across, they would be on high enough ground flooding would not be a problem. The grass would not be as lush, though. As Dud sat staring with the rain pelting him, he weighed the options. He could stop the cattle and wait it out, hoping the storm would pass. If night fell, and the cattle did decide to stampede, they could kill each other piling into the waters ahead before the men could stop them. If they were going to cross, it might be better to do it in daytime when they did have some control over the herd. Besides, old-timers had always said the thin grass in the high country was so rich in minerals, cattle thrived on it, even though it did not look like much.

With his decision made, Dud rode back to tell Shug and Billy Sol the bad news. They would have to get over a thousand cantankerous, nervous cattle to cross two waterways already on the rise.

Billy Sol and Shug accepted what he told them and consented to Dud's decision with calm. He had never met two men who had more courage dealing with cattle. It was a challenge they welcomed. Dud left to pass the word they were to push the cattle harder. Audie, as he expected, faunched and questioned, but in the end, accepted it.

Florine, when she heard, set her jaw in determination. "Go tell the others and then get back up here and lead me and Ponder where you think we ought to cross ahead," she yelled above the rain.

Dud did not have time to be aggravated with her, but hollered "all right" and left. Ponder agreed with a nod of his head, water pouring into his lap when his hat brim dipped. The others, not wise enough to know any better anyway, accepted his judgment. Or else they did not feel like arguing with sheets of rain falling from their hat brims, too.

Ponder, with the Hollister boys watching from the back of the wagon, and Florine made it across the river without too much difficulty. Worried that by the time they approached the next creek it would present more of a problem, Dud raced back to fetch Audie to help him.

With Audie beside him, Dud rode back to Ponder and Florine. When they reached the spot Dud thought would be the best place to cross, Ponder went in without a problem. Dud and Audie rode beside his oxen, with ropes around the singletree to help pull them along. Ponder and his oxen made it across on sure, steady hooves.

Florine refused to wait for assistance. She hollered, "Hiya! Get going you hardheaded, stubborn old fools," and gave hard pops on the reins. Her mules went in, lost their footing and began to panic. Taking their ropes, Dud and Audie dropped loops over the mules, dallied the rope around their saddle horns and pulled, helping the mules along until they reached the other bank and climbed upon solid ground.

Sopping wet from creek water, they gathered their lariats and returned to the herd in quick time. The hard rain washed away any river silt left on them by the time they got back. Audie went back to his place on swing, while Dud rode up and down, urging them to press forward.

Again, they took the herd in batches across the river. They were so high-strung; the constant fear of another stampede was on everyone's mind. It was growing late, but Dud had them slow the half-mile long string of cattle as they drew near Comanche Creek. He feared they would bolt, falling on one another as they crossed and drown. The cattle were so skittish, Dud gave the word to bring them across the water in a continuous line. He did not think they would be able to hold them back to go in batches.

Once in the water, they tried to mill, and it took every cowhand to get them across. Even Ponder saddled a horse and helped, leaving Florine and the two Hollister boys to build a fire under a tarp and cook the best they could, with instructions to make sure there was plenty of hot coffee available.

By the time they did get every animal across, the rain had slowed to an intermittent drizzle, just enough to keep up the misery. Dud always had Henry put his remuda between the herd and whatever river or creek they were near when they bedded down for the night. The Plains Indians who raided in the area would only eat fish if they were starving, and horses were their conveyance of choice, not canoes. Dud did not think they would risk splashing through water to get to the remuda from that direction.

In the growing dark, Dud checked on Henry. He and his mustangs were all right — like the cattle, exhausted from being pushed so hard and from their own nervousness. While Henry talked about the state of the horses and which ones swam the best, Dud raised his hand to silence him. Henry grew quiet, listening to the sounds at dusk. A distant roaring sound could be heard from far away.

"Señor Dud, I think we should move these mustangs to a little higher ground."

Dud concurred, and they began herding the remuda farther away from the creek. The roar grew louder, and in the dim light,

Dud turned and saw an incredible wall of water heading toward them from upstream.

"Hi-ya," he called, slapping and waving his lariat. The mustangs ran to escape the water, and again Dud thought the cattle would stampede, but they ignored the sounds and sights of the mustangs coming toward them.

The wall of water pushed its way downstream, leaving a flood where the horses had been. Relieved to be on higher ground, Dud nevertheless thought the miserable night would never end.

Chapter Twelve

The next morning, the world looked like a different place. The sun shone bright, while water droplets glistened on fresh grass and rocky soil. Animals and people were spent from the day before, and they debated whether to stay where they were or resume the drive. It was not the best spot for grazing, but it was the spot they were in, and in the end, they all agreed it would be better to recuperate before moving on.

There was no rest for Dud, however. After breakfast, he saddled a little buckskin that had not been ridden the night before. The Rio Frio was about eight miles from camp, and he expected to find it flooded. But after searching, he found a spot where the clear, cold water ran shallow over rocks with large cypress trees hanging overhead. It was one of the prettiest spots he had ever seen, and he had to remind himself it might be the most dangerous, too. The abundance of game and brush to hide in would make it attractive to outlaws and Indians. He pressed on to find a good place to bed the herd. When he thought he had, he returned to the Frio and shot a deer for supper.

With the deer across the back of the mustang, who took some convincing to allow it, Dud rode into camp. The cattle grazed lazily, while Henry, ever vigilant, rested with his beloved horses. Mutt saw the buck and offered to dress it.

"Me and Pa was known as the best butchers in DeWitt County."

After Mutt and Toomey removed the deer from the back of the mustang, Dud returned it to the remuda. He took the saddle from the mustang and put it on Ned, riding him back to Ponder's wagon, where he would be tied nearby as he was every evening.

They feasted on roasted and stewed venison with all parts thrown into the pot except the hide and hoof. Everything should have been serene and pleasant after the nightmare of the day before. The clear weather felt cool against their roughened skin. The cattle were peaceful, the horses calm. Florine had not thrown any dishes around, and she had kept her snappish words to a minimum. The drovers had full bellies of something besides salt pork. When they finished eating, there was still daylight enough that it was not yet time for the nighthawks to begin their constant circling of the herd. All seemed right.

Dud did not know how the argument got started. He had been squatted on one knee near the campfire, listening to Billy Sol and Shug discuss the events of the previous day and had not been paying attention to Henry or Darnell.

Voices got angry, and Dud looked up. Darnell and Henry were standing, facing one another. Racial slurs were exchanged, and in the next instant, Henry had his knife out, and Darnell had pulled a razor from his pocket. They stopped talking and began to crouch, staring at one another in hatred and circling, preparing to strike.

Henry made the first swipe, but Darnell jumped back enough to be missed. He lashed at Henry with the razor, but Henry, also, was too quick on his feet to allow the blade to land.

Despite being absorbed in the drama in front of him, a feeling came over Dud, the one that had been so keenly developed during the war. They were not alone.

His eyes darted about and stopped by Ponder's wagon. Four Indians stood watching the fight, their eyes keen, black, without lashes against their reddish-brown skin. Erect, graceful, they were naked except for small, colorful and tasseled aprons hanging from belts of narrow leather from their waists. One of them had his coarse hair shaved off on one side of his head while the other hung in a braid almost to the ground. They all had arrows on their backs and were carrying bows, but they were not drawn. Dud stood up and walked toward them.

One man's eyes after another left the brawlers to see why Dud had turned his back on them. They started when they caught sight of the Indians, so much so that Henry and Darnell paused to see what was wrong. Dud looked over his shoulder at Henry and motioned with his eyes for Henry to return to the remuda. He gave the same look to Darnell, and Darnell slipped away after Henry to make sure the horses were not disturbed. The sight of Indians scaring the fight out of them.

Dud looked to Barefoot. "Ask them what they want."

Barefoot's face flushed, and he walked forward. Standing by Dud, he gave some kind of hesitant greeting to the Indians, who had begun to frown. They evidently had wanted the fight to continue to find out who the winner would be.

Barefoot muttered to Dud from the corner of his mouth. "They are Comanche, and the Comanche always invite strangers into their camps to eat. They will think we are rude if we don't."

"Ask them if they would like to sit down and share our venison."

Florine opened her mouth. "You ain't . . ."

"Hush, Florine," Dud said, interrupting her without turning his head.

Barefoot spoke to the Indians, and they nodded.

Dud led them to the campfire. Ponder piled venison stew on plates for them while Shug hustled his mother into her wagon. The Indians ate hungrily, grunting when they wanted more. Ponder again loaded their plates. Mutt's and Toomey's eyes were so round and full of fear, they looked as if they might defecate in their pants at any minute. Audie just stared, watching and waiting.

After the Comanche finished eating, they demanded tobacco. Ponder took a square of tobacco out of his pocket. He cut it into four chaws and handed them to the men. They did not put it in their mouths, but placed the bits inside bags that hung around their necks.

They refused to look Barefoot in the face,

and the next time they spoke, they looked directly at Dud.

Barefoot translated. "They want four beeves to feed their families in exchange for letting us pass peacefully."

Dud stared. They had a wild and reckless splendor, but they were also dirty and wore none of the fancy beadwork Indian tribes were known for. All they seemed to possess were the clothes across their privates and the small pouches around their necks, along with their bows and arrows.

"Tell them I would be happy to give them four beeves to feed their families, but I would like a token of their goodwill. I would like two of their arrows in exchange for the four beeves."

Barefoot translated, the Indians again refusing to look at him, but watching Dud's face instead. When Barefoot finished his speech, they looked at one another and nodded. Two men removed arrows from their quivers, after first rejecting one and exchanging it for another. Dud realized they were keeping the best ones back. They handed him the arrows, and he took them, giving his thanks.

He turned to Audie. "You and Billy Sol cull out four of the weakest cows we have and bring them back here."

Barefoot spoke to them and turned to translate to Dud. "I told them to wait, the men would bring them the cattle."

Dud nodded as Billy Sol and Audie rode away. While they were gone, the Comanche waited patiently. Led by Dud's example, the drovers did the same.

Audie and Billy Sol returned. The Indians took the cattle, but before they left, the one with half his head shaved looked at Barefoot and spat on the ground. Barefoot's face did not change expression. One of the other Comanche glanced over Ned, and Dud caught a gleam of covertness flit across his face. But that flicker, like the Indians, disappeared.

Only then did the drovers let out a collective sigh of relief, and even that was tempered with reservations. Dud walked over to the Hollister boys who had been hiding behind Ponder. He handed them the arrows.

"A souvenir of your first cattle drive," he said.

Barefoot came up behind Dud and spoke. "The one with half his hair cut off — that means he showed cowardice in battle. He'll try to make up for it by some daring deed."

Dud nodded and turned to the other men. "I want four men on every watch. Two to ride together. We're not going to get much sleep tonight." And Ned was going to stay close beside him the entire night. Toomey refused to part with his uncle's horse, even for a minute, so fearful of facing the old man's wrath if it got stolen.

The Comanche did not return, however, and there was no more drama that night. Henry and Darnell put aside their differences to protect the horses. Whether the extra guards deterred the Indians, or they had decided to keep their promise, did not matter much to Dud except that they had not come back bringing trouble.

Early the next morning, Shug rode out with Dud so he could show him where they were to cross the Frio, describing the spot a mile or two from the fort where he wanted the cattle bedded. Shug went back to the herd, while Dud rode on.

Fort Inge sat in a protected spot between the Leona, a modest river with sluggish water, and a small mountain, its square parade grounds surrounded by a low dry stacked stone wall. A dozen limestone buildings and a few more that were little more than mud huts made up the barracks, hospital, and quarters. Soldiers in blue came out to stare at him, and he guessed they did not receive many visitors. He had little fear they knew anything about the soldiers east of San Antonio looking for him.

He halted Jax in front of the headquarters. A young private came forward.

"Are you here to see the captain?"

"That's right."

A door opened and a tall man with graying hair stepped out. He looked Dud up and down.

"Did the hail get you, or did you pay a visit to Anna?"

The private sniggered, and the captain turned to him.

"Take care of his horse, soldier," he ordered. Turning to Dud, he bade him to come inside.

The room was large with a framed map on one wall, an American flag on a stand behind the captain's desk, and beside it, an opened window, letting in a small breeze. It was neither nicer than Dud thought it would be nor worse.

"Have a seat," the captain said.

Dud did. "I reckon Anna must be pretty well known around these parts."

The captain snorted. "I spend more time sending men over to Anna's to fetch errant soldiers than I do chasing Indians." He gave Dud a keen look.

"She likes them young and handsome, so

I imagine you were her type." He added in a dry voice, "I have not had the pleasure."

"I don't know how much of a pleasure it was," Dud said. "It scared five years' growth out of me. But I did get caught in the hailstorm, too."

He looked around the room and from long habit, noted every escape route or surprise entrance. "The army still brand soldiers for going AWOL?"

"No, I believe Lee put a stop to that while he was out here." The captain leaned back in his chair. "What's your business?"

"Driving cattle. We've got over a thousand head coming this way. You interested in buying any?"

The captain kept him occupied for hours, dickering over the price of a few head of cattle, discussing the incident with the Indians of the previous night.

"The Comanche hate the Cherokee ever since President Jackson sent them west to Oklahoma territory. They see them as encroachers and hate them almost as much as they hate us."

Dud thought of the hatred Southerners had for the Northerners swarming down South since the end of the war and could empathize, but he kept those thoughts to himself.

The captain wanted to know the news from San Antonio. Afterward, when Dud explained about the Hollister boys, he discussed the few people who lived in the area surrounding the fort. There were no wives among the fifty or so soldiers stationed there and only a smattering of settlers. The rest was riffraff consisting of desperados, smugglers, rustlers, and thieves.

"You've reached the point where it is just as dangerous to leave the boys here as it is to take them with you," the captain told Dud as they ate dinner in his quarters.

Dud sighed. Fate seemed to have placed the Hollister boys in his care for the time being. He did not want to linger after eating, although he realized the captain wanted him to stay — it was a lonely life. To be polite, he continued talking about Indians and relations with Mexico for some time before rising and giving his thanks.

"Are the men riding with you former Confederates?" the captain asked as he stood up.

Dud nodded. "All but two."

"Don't have your men come here. I'll have to send a couple of soldiers with you to fetch the beeves," the captain said as they walked to the door. He opened it, and Dud stepped onto the veranda. "I have a couple of diehard Yankees here who think there is still a war on."

"I know a lot of Confederates like that," Dud said, putting on his hat.

A private fetched his horse, and as Dud put his foot in the stirrup and swung his leg over the saddle, the captain gave some final advice.

"Once you leave Fort Clark, it's a long stretch to Fort Lancaster. Try to move through the territory around San Felipe Springs as quickly as you can — you'll be closest to the Mexico border then, and desperados on both sides of the river will try to steal your horses and any cattle they can, usually by stampeding. After that, you'll find yourself cursing the Pecos River just like everybody else who has the bad luck to face it. You'll have plenty of water around Fort Davis, but it will be rough traveling. Good luck."

"Much obliged," Dud said. He turned and left the fort with two privates trailing along beside him. Young, strapping soldiers with broad shoulders, they were eager to share their experiences with Anna, and as they talked, Dud realized Anna must have been having an off day with him. He got off light compared to what happened to them.

His drovers had followed his instructions,

and the cattle were moving in a long slow line to the spot Dud had picked out for the night. Dud invited the soldiers to stay for supper, but they said they best get the cattle and head back. They were clearly uneasy at the prospect of being away from the fort after dark. A couple of cows had dropped calves, and Dud culled those out for the soldiers, telling them to take the calves, too. Audie joined them, but said little to the soldiers and watched them in silence while Dud bid them goodbye.

When they were out of hearing, Audie spoke. "Longhorns are running everywhere hereabouts. How come they buying cattle from us?"

"I reckon they are paid to chase Indians, not cattle," Dud said.

"Looks to me like they ain't doing neither one," Audie said.

Dud made no comment, but reined Jax around and headed for the remuda to trade him for Ned.

They were still four days from Fort Clark and the Las Moras Springs. However, the Nueces River was broader and deeper than the Frio, and Dud had a difficult time finding a place to cross the herd. He settled on what looked like stable land near a pecan bottom. It was still deep enough that once he got Florine and her wagon across and settled in camp west of the river, the cowboys stripped off their clothes to ride through it naked. A cottonmouth bit Mutt's mustang as it climbed onto the bank, and it had to be put down. It was the first horse they had lost, and while Dud was sad to see it go, he was grateful the fangs of the snake had landed on it and not Mutt. It shook Mutt up, and Dud knew he would be talking about it for the next three weeks or until another incident occurred to take its place.

Two riders came into camp that evening, white men in their thirties. There was a sloppy look about them, and their horses were ill-shod with dirty blankets on their backs. But it was not the custom of cowmen to deny any visitor to camp food or a welcome unless they proved themselves unworthy of either. Dud and the others ate with them and listened as they talked at length about the countryside around them.

"You don't want to follow the road to Turkey Creek," one of them said. "It's too dangerous — too many bad outlaws hang around that area."

"What do you suggest?" Dud asked.

"There's a trail that goes up through the hills that's easy enough on cattle. Only local folks know about it, and won't nobody be expecting you to take your herd up yonder way. It's just as easy of a route and only a mile or two longer. It will save you a heap of trouble in the long run."

They sounded as if they knew what they were talking about. There was not anything wrong about them other than the odor of sorry white trash, and that was not a sin. Nevertheless, Dud did not have to warn every man to be on guard with strangers in the camp — they knew it as instinctively as he did. The night passed without incident, however, and the next morning at breakfast, their visitors were laughing and joking about local characters who inhabited the region. Before leaving, they again reminded Dud of the safer route.

He made noncommittal replies. When the two strangers had ridden away after breakfast, knowing full well if they stayed, Dud would put them to work, Audie, Shug, and Billy Sol crowded around Dud.

"We gonna follow the trail they told us about?" Shug asked.

Dud shrugged. "Stick to the road till I get back. I'm going to see where they are headed."

"They acted like they knew butter from lard," Audie said.

"Maybe, but I'm following them for a

while, just the same." Dud took the reins of Ned, intending on trading him for Jax, but changed his mind. Audie caught his actions.

"You want us to come looking for you if you don't come back?"

Dud got in the saddle. "Yeah. If I'm still missing midafternoon, start looking."

Dud stayed well behind the riders, using every tactic he had ever learned to keep from being discovered. But as time wore on, he began to believe they gave no thought he might be behind them. They followed the trail they had laid out for him, going over rocky ground that eventually led into a box canyon. Dud worked his way up on higher ground and looked down on a shack with a smoking chimney at the end of the canyon. The two outlaws entered the shack, and Dud guessed there were more men waiting for them inside.

He had no call to start a commotion with the would-be robbers and set off down the hill to warn his drovers to keep moving down the original road. Making the mistake of thinking about the outlaws in the cabin, he was not as aware of his surroundings as he should have been. He came upon Indians, and he did not know who was more surprised, them or him. It was the same group who had asked for beeves. The one with the half-shaved head gave a Comanche yell and started for him.

Dud gave Ned the spurs and urged him down the hill, letting him find his own way on the sure, hard hooves that characterized the tough Texas mustangs. Arrows whizzed by them, one of them sticking in Dud's saddle. He did not look behind him, but hollered, encouraging Ned to flight.

With nostrils flared and almost breathing fire, Ned flew, never stumbling. An arrow ripped through the sleeve of Dud's shirt, but he did not pause to even look down to see if it had drawn blood. Ned reached open ground and cut loose, tearing up dirt.

After a minute, it seemed the arrows around them were falling short, and then there were no arrows. Ned did not want to ease up, and Dud let him have his head. When the herd came in sight, Dud had to make him slow down so they would not frighten the cattle. Gasping, trying to catch his breath, he halted by Shug.

"Push the herd harder," he instructed. "I've got to change horses."

Shug nodded, raising up in the saddle and making hand signals to his brother. Dud left him and headed for the remuda.

"Señor Dud, the Comanche were chasing you!" Henry said when he saw the arrow in the saddle.

Dud nodded, but did not waste time in conversation while he switched his saddle over to Jax. Henry took charge of Ned, who pranced about, proud he had beaten the Comanche horses. Jax knew it was his turn to show his stuff — Dud and horse rode away to find a spot to cross Turkey Creek. There would be no hiding a thousand head of cattle, but these robbers did not want a large herd of cattle. They were after horses.

Dud, riding several miles northwest of the Military Road, found a grassy field perfect for feeding the hungry cattle. More importantly, a devilish briar thicket nearby encircled an open glade. When he returned to the herd, he found Shug and Billy Sol had gotten them almost to the creek. The arrow in his saddle had evidently told them the same story it told Henry.

Dud gave directions to Shug on where to cross and went back to scatter the birds roosting in the trees around the creek so they did not fly upward and spook the cattle as they approached. Every cowboy sat on his horse as tense as a prisoner waiting for the gallows. Dud helped Ponder and Florine across, leading them through a narrow path that would take them to a wide meadow hidden by a line of trees. The thicket was too impenetrable for them to get their wagons through, and they had to stop at its edge.

When Dud returned, Shug and Billy Sol were castigating the jittery drovers in even more colorful language than usual for pushing the cattle too hard through the creek. Dud told the brothers to follow the wagon tracks — he would see that all the cattle got across.

They had to lead the horses into the thicket one by one. Two men were posted at the narrow entrance to the meadow while two more circled the herd. On Dud's turn at watch, he was forced to shoot at a moving shadow. The other shadows scattered into the blackness. They had no more trouble that night, and the exhausted cattle ignored the popping noise and the smell of gun smoke.

The next morning, they found the body of one of the strangers who had tried to lead them into the trap. Dud disliked leaving any man's body in the open for buzzards and coyotes to ravage. Plus, if his friends came back looking for him, it would be healthier if they believed he had escaped.

"Better to feed him to the fishes in the creek," Ponder said.

Chapter Thirteen

They went without sleep for the next two nights, crossing Elm Creek the next day and being cautious where they bedded the herd. Ponder and Florine were not required to take a turn at watch, but Florine slept with her shotgun by her side, and Ponder was up half the night, prodding sleepy cowboys to stay awake and keep their eyes peeled for trouble.

As they neared Fort Clark, everyone began to breathe easier and eat heartier.

"I never thought I'd be so goldarned happy to be around a bunch of Union soldiers in my life," Audie said.

Dud scouted ahead, finding an abandoned stagecoach station with an old bearded desert rat in residence. He was eager to talk, and Dud had a hard time getting away from him.

"War's over, old-timer," Dud said, ribbing the old fellow a little. "What are you going to do when someone opens up the stage run again?"

He pretended shock. "You mean the war's over? Well, I'll be ding-danged. Who won?"

Dud laughed and bid him farewell. He had already told Dud about the untamed town of Brackett that had sprung up next to the fort. There would be saloons, gambling, and brothels — all the things Mutt and Toomey dreamed about, anyway.

Dud returned to the drive to tell the others. "I think we'll be safe enough to leave a skeleton crew on guard," he explained to Ponder and Audie. "I've already told Shug and Billy Sol where to point the herd. I'm going back to inform the fort commander we're here."

"They ain't no law there?" Ponder asked.

Dud shrugged. "I don't think so. That doesn't mean our boys might not get into trouble shooting up the town after what they've been through, but pass the word around to them. They'll soon be having a big time. I'll be back directly."

The grunginess of Brackett at the foot of the fort grounds did not surprise Dud, but the fort was bigger and more impressive than the ones he had previously seen. He felt so happy and relieved to have finally made it there, he decided to leave Jax at a livery stable and head for a barbershop. A shave, a haircut, and a bath would be more relaxing to him than walking into a saloon for the time being. To ease his conscience, he promised himself he would take first watch and let the others have their night on the town without waiting. Ladies of the night did not keep banker's hours anyway.

The Mexican barber asked if he wanted his beard and hair candled, but Dud told him no. He'd had it done in South Texas a few times, but his beard was so bushy, he was afraid his face would go up in smoke if the man did not know what he was doing. The barber was proficient enough with a razor, however, and talkative. Luckily, he liked to listen to the sound of his own voice, because Dud had already decided he was not advertising to the whole world he had a herd of cattle and a remuda of fifty horses a few miles away.

But the barber did not seem to mind that Dud talked about San Antonio and nothing else. And Dud rubbed his face in pleasure when he was done. The bath in the narrow tin tub felt even better, and Dud dunked his head repeatedly, feeling like a self-satisfied duck. When he got out, he picked up a towel that was crusty from use. Not wishing to rub too hard with it, he was still a little wet when he put on the fresh clothes he had taken from his saddlebags. He hesitated over the check cassimere vest with its flashy brass buttons. It seemed out of place in a backwater like Brackett. Would El Paso be any better? He doubted it and put the vest on. Maybe some pretty woman would see it and admire it.

When he exited the barbershop, a young man about his height and build bumped into him.

"Where do you think you are going?" the young man demanded, slurring his words. He smelled of whiskey and was having a hard time standing upright.

"I'm going to see the captain of that fort yonder," Dud said, having no wish to get in a brawl with a drunk.

"Well, you just better watch where you are going."

Dud looked down at the young man's gun belt. "Well, you just better watch your mouth, mister, because you ain't carrying a gun to back up anything you say."

The drunk looked down at his empty holster, trying to focus his eyes.

"Flank me down 'til the sun sees the bottom of my moccasins. Somebody done stole my pistol."

Dud walked around the confused

would-be desperado and went to fetch Jax. As he looked up the little hill, and the small spring that bubbled into a creek in front of it, on a whim, he decided to walk it. He crossed over a narrow bridge and entered, searching for the headquarters.

This time, the captain did not come out onto the veranda, and Dud had to walk inside and tell a young corporal sitting at a desk that he had business with the captain. The corporal rose, knocked on a door and opened it when the command came to enter. He shut the door behind him.

Dud went to the window and glanced out, deciding Fort Clark must be the hub of the other forts along the Military Road. The corporal opened the door and bid Dud to enter.

More money had been spent on the Fort Clark office judging by the furniture, the flags, and the picture of Lincoln on the wall. The captain sitting behind the desk looked like a disillusioned replica of General Burnside with all the accompanying facial hair.

"Captain, my name is Dudford Washburn, and I'm . . ."

Before he could finish, the captain rose from his chair and walked to the door, opening it and calling to the corporal. "Bring the guards."

"Guards? What the . . . ?"

Two muscle-bound soldiers who looked like they had been baked in the sun too long entered the room and stood on either side of him. The captain returned to his chair. He picked up a piece of paper on his desk. Tapping it for emphasis, he spoke.

"This came by special courier. It says I'm to hold you for questioning about a kidnapping until a special Board of Inquiry can get here."

"Kidnapping!" Dud was so flabbergasted; he couldn't even form a good curse word in his mouth.

The captain did not give him time to say anything, but ordered the guards to take him to the stockade.

The guards took his guns and rifle away, and taking him by the arms, manhandled him outside to a small rock building with a door made of iron bars. They threw him inside and locked the door. Dud put his hands on the bars and looked out.

"Can you tell me what in blazes is going on?"

"Shut up," one of them growled. They proceeded to have a dispute over who would take the first watch. The bigger and meaner one won, leaving the other to sit in a chair sulking by the door, refusing to look at Dud or answer any of his questions.

Giving up, Dud went to the cot and sat down.

"Karling!" he mumbled. That had to be it. But why chase him this far? Karling must have some kind of political clout to get the army after him. None of it made any sense.

Dud sat on the dirt floor beside the door hoping to catch sight of Audie or Ponder who would surely come looking for him. But the jail was off to itself, and darkness fell too quickly. He listened to every sound, hoping for a familiar voice, but all he heard was an out of tune piano, raucous shouting and laughter, along with the occasional strumming of a Spanish guitar. One surly guard was replaced by another, and every jack one of them refused to talk or let him speak without being threatened.

In the morning Dud was given stale bread and rancid sow belly. He ate it without complaint and waited. At nine o'clock, he heard the corporal's voice telling the guard to bring him to the captain's office.

Dud jumped up. The guard reached for a large keyring hanging on the outside wall, and rattling it in the keyhole, turned the big iron key and opened the door. Dud did not have to be told to get a move on. He was anxious to talk to the captain again and get the mess he was in straightened out.

The guard, rifle in hand, followed him to the headquarters. The corporal opened the door for Dud and motioned him to come inside. He stopped the guard.

"Wait out here."

The guard frowned, and Dud guessed no love was lost between the two men. The corporal led Dud to the office and opened the door, motioning him inside. He followed and closed the door behind him.

Ponder, along with the two Hollister boys and Barefoot turned to face him. With one look, Ponder warned Dud to keep his mouth shut. Ponder turned to the captain and started in on him.

"As you can see, these here is two boys, and their own mama begged us to take them because she was dying."

On and on Ponder went, repeating the story until the captain's eyes began to glaze. He held up his hand for Ponder to cease talking, looking at the boys as he did.

"Is what this man is saying true?" the captain asked.

"Yes, sir," Will said. And he began parroting Ponder's words, bold as the brass buttons on Dud's vest.

As soon as Will stopped to take a breath,

Barefoot jumped in. He started spouting a lot of legal mumbo jumbo, citing precedent after precedent, telling the captain what he was doing was illegal as all get-out according to the laws of the United States government, making such a moving speech about the rights of the individual that Dud was ready to stick his chest out and salute the flag.

Again, the captain raised his hand to stop Barefoot's flow of words.

"I will remind you that Texas is under martial law."

He looked at the corporal.

"Step outside for a minute, Corporal."

He threw out his chest and saluted. "Yes, sir!" he barked and turned on his heels, leaving the room.

"He wants my job," the captain muttered as soon as the door was shut. He stood up and went behind his chair to stare out the window.

"My sister sent me a bushel of persimmons just before the battle of Chickamauga. I ate too many and got so constipated, I was late arriving to the front. For my sin of gluttony and being late to battle, I was assigned to this hellhole. And George Thomas got named 'The Rock of Chickamauga,' not me."

He turned to face them.

"Because of persimmons, I am stuck here. I detest the thought of having any kind of Board of Inquiry here making my life even more intolerable than it is. However, gentlemen, although I agree this whole thing is a farce, I am not going to let anything jeopardize my ticket out of here."

He looked at Dud, but Ponder had moved in front of him, partially obstructing the captain's line of vision. He did not care enough to tell Ponder to move his ass, but pronounced his verdict.

"Dudford Washburn, you will remain in the stockade until the special Board of Inquiry arrives and decides what to do with you."

Dud opened his mouth to protest, but Ponder shot him another look to silence him. Dud shut his mouth.

"Corporal!" the captain called. "Bring the guards and escort the prisoner back to the stockade."

Out of the corner of his mouth, Ponder whispered to Dud. "Keep your head down."

Dud gave Ponder a look like he thought the older man had lost his mind, but he did what he was told. As the guards came in to take him away, he could hear the captain questioning the lawyer.

"What did you say your name was again?"

"Barefoot Sullivan, sir."

"A catchy name for a Texas lawyer. Well, Mr. Sullivan, if I am ever in need of a civilian attorney, I know who to go looking for."

Nevertheless, Dud fumed, with his head down, all the way to the stockade.

This time when he was thrown in, he went back into the shadows and stayed there. Ponder was up to something; he just did not know what. In the meantime, he tried to reason out why the Karling fellow might have it in for him to make such outrageous claims. It must have something to do with Beatrice. It had to be because of Beatrice.

One monotonous hour after another passed. The guards brought Dud his supper, and he took it with his head down, trying to stay in the shadows. They paid no attention to him in any case — arguing with one another, mostly over a woman. She did not sound like she was worth two cents, but Dud supposed any woman to argue over would be worth it to break the monotony.

Darkness came. Midnight passed. The guard outside in his chair dozed, then awakened, growing cranky and restless. Dud peered repeatedly into the darkness, wondering what was happening with the herd, wondering what Ponder had planned. The moon, not yet full, still cast enough light to see somewhat. But there was nothing to see but the shadow of cottonwood trees and nothing to hear but the slight rustling of their leaves.

Sometime after two in the morning, Dud caught sight of a figure making its way up the hill to the stockade. As it drew closer, he could see it was a woman. She was short and a little dumpy, but her humongous breasts jutted out in front of her, casting a long shadow. She wore a little bonnet tied with a big ribbon under her chin and was carrying a small handbag. Dud watched with interest as she approached the guard. He caught sight of her and jumped up from his chair.

"Ma'am," he said as she neared.

She spoke in a slightly breathless voice, full of Southern sweetness. "Hello, soldier. That's my cousin in there, and I thought maybe you would let me go inside and talk to him in private for a while."

Dud leaned forward, leaned back in shock, and leaned forward again, unable to believe his eyes or his ears. Mutt!

"I can't let you in there, ma'am," the soldier was saying. "You can speak to him through the bars."

"Oh," Mutt cried in a falsetto. "It's just

that my husband has been gone for over a week, and he's not due back for another week. And I was a little lonely. And I just thought, well, you know." And he simpered.

The soldier knew. He gave a low chuckle. "You don't need him, ma'am. He's just a little squirt. What you need is a big strong man."

"Well," Mutt said with a giggle, patting his cheek and batting his eyes. "Maybe you're right. But where would I find a big strong man this time of night?"

"You got one, honey," the soldier said. He took Mutt by the arm and began leading him away.

Mutt let him take him a few steps, but stopped. "Oh, I dropped my handkerchief. Would you pick it up? It's right by my leg, big boy."

The soldier grinned and leaned down. Mutt whacked him over the head with the handbag, and the guard went down like a cannonball. Which might have been what was in Mutt's bag.

Everything seemed to be happening at once. Mutt was bending down, going through the guard's pockets. Ponder appeared, grabbed the keys from the wall and opened the door. Audie and Toomey came from around the corner carrying a slender young man who looked and smelled as if he had passed out from bad alcohol.

Ponder pulled Dud out of the cell while Audie and Toomey took the other man inside. Ponder began unbuttoning Dud's vest.

"What are you doing?" Dud hissed.

"Hush," Ponder said in a low voice and jerked the vest off Dud. He entered the cell and put it on the other man, the one Dud now recognized as the drunk who accosted him when he came out of the barbershop. Ponder stuffed a letter into the inside pocket of the vest.

"Is that one of the letters Beatrice wrote to me while I was in the war?"

"Shut up, knucklehead," Ponder whispered, exiting the cell.

Audie and Toomey laid the drunk on the cot, placing a full bottle of whiskey in the crook of his arm. He began to snort and snore with his mouth open, but never opened his eyes.

They came out of the cell, and Ponder locked the door, replacing the key on the outside wall.

"Jax," Dud said, remembering. "Jax is at the stable."

"We've got him, here's a pistol, now come on."

They crept out the back, going over the wall using a ladder left carelessly leaning near a storage hut. The sounds of crude music and vulgar laughter from Brackett filtered through the night. Dud followed the others to a group of trees where their horses stood, almost walking into Darnell before realizing he was there.

As they rode away with the quiet stealth of coyotes from Fort Clark and Brackett, Mutt kept removing female clothing, bundling them into a ball. They traveled a mile before Dud thought it safe to speak.

"They'll know that's not me."

"No, they won't," Ponder replied. "He'll lay there in a drunken stupor for a couple of days, and all they will remember is that flashy vest. If they have doubts, they'll search him and find a letter addressed to Dudford Washburn, and that will allay all suspicions."

"You ought not of gone through my things," Dud said.

"You ought not be saving those letters, Dud. Keeping them is a constant prick against an open wound. Accept it — that horse has run its last race."

A bullet of fury shot through Dud.

"Shut up about that Ponder. It's not over yet and these cattle are going to help me win Beatrice back, so put that in your pipe and smoke it."

Ponder shook his head in disgust, but his shoulders gave a shrug of resignation.

"The way things are going, we ain't gonna live long enough to get back to San Antonio."

Dud, feeling guilty over his anger, changed the subject.

"They'll know the guard got knocked in the head."

"They won't know that either, because he won't tell. All he knows is that some señorita came up to him, thumped him and stole his money. He ain't gonna tell that story."

Forcing himself to forget about Beatrice, Dud thought instead of Mutt's masquerade, and before he knew it, he was chuckling over it, and the rest of the way back to the herd, they all laughed and hoorawed Mutt for making such a fine-looking woman with the help of a couple of flour sacks.

When they reached the remuda, Henry and Barefoot met them to take their horses.

"We'll have to move out, Dud," Ponder said. "It didn't sound to us like you told anybody in town we was driving cattle, and when that captain asked what we were doing and where we was headed, we told him we was going to Californy. But we can't take no chances. We'll have to avoid the road and go in a different direction for a good piece."

"Uncle Ponder! I don't know where there is water out here. All I have is the road map."

Barefoot cleared his throat. "I may not have done such a good job for you as an attorney, Boss, but my grandmother taught me many animal signs. I think I can help you."

Dud hesitated only a second. "Who's going to ride drag?"

"I will," Ponder said. "Will can handle the wagon by hisself, I been teaching him. And that Jemmy makes a right smart cook."

"All right," Dud agreed, and turned to fetch Ned. Ponder stopped him.

"Here," he said, holding out Grandpa Ned's gun belt. "I begged it off the post commander. I wasn't about to leave it behind."

Dud took it. "Uncle Ponder . . ." He stopped and swallowed.

Chapter Fourteen

Mutt appeared and turned over his costume to Ponder. He pushed the money he took off the soldier into Dud's hand.

Dud tried to give it back. "That's yours, Mutt. You earned it."

But Mutt would have none of it. "I know Mr. Ponder said I had to take it to make it look like a robbery, but keeping it would be too much like stealing. I ain't no thief."

"I feel guilty about leaving that poor sot locked up in my place," Dud said.

"Dud!" Ponder said. "We did the young man a favor. It will give him a couple of weeks to dry out and maybe turn his life around. Ain't you got no sense of Christian duty?"

Dud did not even try to understand that logic.

Florine could not have cared less about Ponder and his sense of Christian duty. The incident and the delay it caused infuriated her. "This is all your fault, Dudford. And I'll bet you any amount of money all this trouble is because of that stuck-up snob you were married to."

"Ma," Billy Sol interjected, unexpectedly taking up for Dud. "She was a mighty good-looking gal, and you know Cousin Dud ain't got no willpower when it comes to pretty gals. He turns into calf's foot jelly when he gets around them."

Dud gritted his teeth. Florine would not shut up, predicting all kinds of dire difficulties they would be facing because of him and his women.

"Florine, shut up. You're upsetting the Hollister boys. Now come on, let's get this herd out of here."

"At night, when we can't see nothing?"

"Florine!"

While Billy Sol removed the rawhide holding the clapper on General Sherman's bell, Dud instructed the drovers to sing the softest, sweetest songs they knew to the cattle. With General Sherman leading the way, the cattle rose with gentle prodding to follow in the darkness. For the time being, Ponder stayed with his wagon, and Barefoot kept to the drag. Dud rode ahead of the others, trusting in Ned's eyesight and instinct to keep them from falling off an unexpected cliff.

They traveled northwest, away from the Mexican border and the springs of San Felipe that every traveler going through Southwest Texas stopped at to get water. At one point, Ned balked and refused to go any farther. Dud got down and walked a few steps forward. They were at the edge of a precipice. He got back on Ned and turned around, warning Billy Sol and Shug to turn the herd to the right.

Before dawn, Dud had to ride back again and tell the men to turn the herd again. As soon as it became light enough for him to see, he rode miles ahead, keeping in a northwesterly direction.

This time, there were no craggy cliffs, only a sea of grass. He rode back to fetch Barefoot and inform Shug and Billy Sol to stop and make camp when they reached the tall grass.

"It was touch and go there for a while, weren't it, Dud?" Billy Sol said. "I told Shug, we must have come mighty close to losing the herd there once or twice."

Dud did not give him a direct answer, only saying if he was offered ten thousand dollars for Ned, he would refuse it without hesitation.

He traded Ned for Jax while Barefoot

switched out mustangs. By that time, Ponder had the coffee going. Dud was so nervy about traveling through territory they knew nothing about, and so anxious to get started, that he had to force himself to wait for Florine and Jemmy to finish cooking a late breakfast, early supper.

Mutt was full of talk, as usual. Dud apologized that his troubles had kept them from having a night on the town in Brackett.

"That's all right, Boss. Mr. Ponder let us take turns going in for a few hours. But you know them people there, Boss, them people still had the bark on they was so rough."

"They weren't much fun to be around anyway," Toomey mourned.

Audie grinned. "That corporal told us they were keeping you, Dud, but he wouldn't let us talk to the captain until morning anyhow. So, we had all night to plan."

"Me and Toomey went shopping for the female wrappings," Mutt said. "But they kept a smirking at us like I was buying that finery for myself."

"Well, you kept telling them your sister was the same size as you, and you were trying on the hats to see what would fit," Audie said.

Dud laughed along with the others. He spoke low to Audie so the others could not hear him.

"How come they didn't use Florine's clothes?"

Audie grinned. "They wanted to attract a man, not send him running for the hills."

Dud laughed. "Where did Uncle Ponder get the money to pay for them?"

"He sold one of them Henry rifles. Made enough off of it to load up on more supplies, too."

"I hope he was careful who he sold it to." That's all he needed, some outlaw carrying a rifle they sold him to use it to rob them.

Audie nodded. "He sold it to some old geezer who scouted for the army."

Dud looked over to Barefoot, whose eyes were bleary with lack of sleep. Dud had rested more than he wanted to in the stockade, but decided a catnap would not hurt either one of them.

"Barefoot, go stretch your bones somewhere. We'll sleep for thirty minutes before heading out."

The lawyer gave him a grateful nod and went around Ponder's wagon. Dud reckoned thirty minutes of napping was not much of a repayment for being so vigorously defended in front of a US Army captain, but it was the best he could do.

But they did not have any trouble finding water. It was early enough in the season the creeks that might normally go dry during summer droughts were running full. What disturbed them were all the abandoned Indian campgrounds. They were months old, but told of possible returns at any time.

At night the waxing moon shone, and Dud gave orders for two men to be on guard every night with the remuda. If Indians stampeded the cattle, Shug, Billy Sol, and Audie were to see what they could do to keep the herd together. Otherwise, every man was to protect the horses. They could live without cattle in this wild desolate country, but men afoot would mean disaster.

One month into the drive, Dud and Barefoot approached Devil's River and heard the sound of a waterfall. They could also hear the sound of men's voices, a rough mixture of English and Spanish. Dud looked at Barefoot and shook his head — giving the signal they were not going to approach the men until they had a good look at them first.

Hiding in the brush above the falls, the sound of the rushing water covering any noise they might make, Dud and Barefoot looked down upon the rudest of shanties. Several men sat on stumps in front of the shanty drinking out of bota bags. Mexicans and whites mingled together, armed with rifles, pistolas, and knives. They talked loud in English and Spanish with much boasting about their many raids. Dud turned to Barefoot and motioned they should leave.

Leading their horses, they crept away through the brush. As soon as they could safely mount, they rode far away, looking downstream for a place to cross the Devil's River, a waterway as wild and rough as the country they were traveling through.

The desolateness of the area started to get on everyone's nerves. That evening after supper, Mutt and Toomey began to tell stories about home. Dud interrupted them and asked Darnell to play his fiddle. It soothed them for a while.

The only place Dud and Barefoot could find water was near an abandoned army camp on the Military Road farther up the Devil's River. The camp sat near a creek, a tributary of the river. They could stay at the deserted camp by the road, or move the cattle across the creek and up to the river. Dud could see no sense in crossing the creek to get to the river, only to have to turn around and cross the creek again to head west. After a heated discussion with Ponder and Audie, they decided to take their chances on the Military Road.

"From what I've heard, Fort Lancaster ain't exactly a beehive of activity," Ponder said. "I can't see them following us this far. You can't be that important."

"He's right, Audie," Dud said. "We've got to take the chance. We're heading deeper west and will be moving away from these springs and creeks."

It took two days, traveling through flat plains and rolling hills, to reach what had once been Camp Hudson. The captain at Fort Inge had explained to Dud that it had been established to protect the stagecoaches carrying the mail on the San Antonio-El Paso Mail Line between Fort Clark and Fort Lancaster. However, it had been vacated at the beginning of the war, and the army had not yet decided what to do with it, if anything. There was talk of establishing the stage route again, but nothing had come of it yet. On an elevated spot away from the main road, it sat in deserted and eerie silence next to a small creek.

Dud went ahead of the herd to flush out any game that might spook the thirsty herd into stampeding. As he rode by the wooden pickets surrounding the camp, he saw the gates were opened and some of the posts had been forced down. Apprehensive, with the herd almost on his heels, Dud hurried ahead to the creek to scatter the birds roosting in the trees. They flew upward in one swoop, their wings fluttering, breaking the silence. Dud turned Jax and went back to the camp. Will and Florine had reached it, halting their wagons on the outside of the pickets. Dud motioned for them to wait.

He rode inside. Lying in the doorways of primitive buildings made of lime and gravel were bodies of dead men covered in arrows, their mutilated remains bloating in the sun. Dud rode closer, looking from man to man, building to building.

Barefoot rode up and joined him. He stared at the dead men.

"It's the banditos who were camped at the waterfall."

Dud nodded. "They must have seen the herd and decided to ride ahead here to ambush us. The Indians got them instead."

Barefoot dismounted and examined the arrows. "It was the Comanche."

He did not have to say there would be a full moon that night, the Comanche's favorite time to raid. Nor was it necessary to add that the bodies had been stripped of every weapon.

"What are we going to do? The pickets around this camp are already falling down."

Dud looked around. "We're going to empty these buildings. This evening, we are going to hide fifty horses in them. They will stampede the herd sometime tonight to try to distract us from the horses."

Florine got tired of waiting and drove her wagon inside the camp fence. She stopped, looking at the massacre without speaking, her jaws working before setting in a hard line.

"Pull up over yonder," Dud said. "You can make camp in here."

Dud rode outside, stopping at Will's wagon. "Take the wagon down to the creek and fill up your water barrels." Jemmy sat beside him, staring with wide eyes. They gave solemn nods, knowing by Dud's manner there was trouble.

While the other drovers were getting the herd watered and settled, Dud and Barefoot carried the bodies, throwing them into a pile in the back corner of the camp. Once they finished, Dud said a few words over the deceased, apologizing for not having time to bury them.

Dud and Barefoot left them — Dud to walk the grounds with Ponder while Barefoot went to help with the horses.

The walls of the buildings were somewhat crumbly, but built stout enough to withstand an attack. Most had windows front and back.

"Once they realize we've hidden the horses inside, they will attack wherever they see gunfire," Ponder said. "Every rifle we have has to be loaded and ready."

"Can we get most of the horses in the mess hall?"

Ponder agreed, and gathering some of the men, they began moving what little furniture was left up against the windows, leaving small spaces to fire from. They did the same in the blockhouse next door. Ponder left a large wardrobe lying on its back against a side wall, as if it had been casually pushed out of the way. Dud did not question him, but left it where Ponder had placed it.

When it came time for supper, they ate in silence and stayed that way while Ponder handed out extra rifles, pistols, and ammunition. Shug and Billy Sol had brought General Sherman into the camp, and no one said a word when they hand-fed him bits of food. The General with his long horns could not stay locked up with the horses, but Shug commandeered a small building once used as an armory for him.

Because whoever had to remain outside

with the stampeding herd would be much more vulnerable than those staying within the protection of the buildings, Dud had asked for volunteers instead of laying it all on Billy Sol and Shug. They had been offended, however, and insisted it was their job. Audie volunteered without hesitation to help them.

Dud was not sure if he should stay with the herd or with the men who would be fighting off the bulk of the Indians. Ponder, however, made that decision for him.

"Dud, me and you is the only experienced fighters left. These other young 'uns barely tapped their feet into battle, if at all. It's up to us to steady them."

Dud agreed. Afterward, they sat waiting, letting the horses graze, hoping Indians would not attack until the moon was up.

At sundown, just as the light was almost gone, the men herded the horses into the large mess hall. Henry and Barefoot would stay with them. The others took their night horses and piled into the blockhouse, along with all their extra rifles, ammunition, and supplies. Dud and Darnell took the first watch. Dud ordered Shug, Billy Sol, and Audie to rest if they could.

"They probably won't cause a stampede and attack until the moon is higher. Darnell and I will stay out a little longer than usual, because you three will probably be up all night." If he was wrong, and they struck sooner, Darnell with his dark skin would make less of a target than the others and stand a better chance. At least Dud hoped that was the case.

As Dud and Darnell led their horses to the door, Ponder took the Hollister boys aside and told them when the shooting started to hide in the wardrobe and not come out until they were sure one way or another the Indians were gone.

Dud and Darnell left to start the repetitive circling of the herd, although Dud wondered if it would be better to leave them to their own devices. There was no singing that night. Dud and Darnell exchanged only the briefest of words as they passed one another — neither one willing to break the strain of listening for the enemy. Dud made sure he slowed Ned or urged him forward enough so he and Darnell never met in the same spot. Ned knew exactly how long the usual watch was supposed to last and headed for the direction of camp when he thought the time was up. But tonight, the mustang sensed something was different, and he did not try to go back to camp until Dud reined him in that direction.

Shug, Billy Sol, and Audie were ready when Dud knocked on the door of the blockhouse. They came out with their horses. Without exchanging words, Dud went inside, stepping in horse manure and not caring. It was the least of his worries.

As soon as he shut the door behind him, Florine spoke in a low voice.

"Dud Washburn, if anything happens to my boys out there, I'm holding you personally responsible."

After a second's pause, Dud answered her. "You have two boys in here, Florine, who need you. You might try looking after them."

She refused to answer, and Dud turned to Ponder.

"If the Comanche caught sight of us putting the horses in the mess hall, they will concentrate on getting in there. You stay here, and I'll help Barefoot and Henry."

The moon was so bright, the night looked more like a day when a dark cloud had momentarily covered the sun. Dud gave a soft knock on the door of the mess hall, and Henry let him in.

Dud turned Ned loose with the other mustangs, none of them happy at being cooped up in a strange building. Henry did his best to calm them and keep them from kicking the furniture that had been piled against the back window.

Dud and Barefoot waited in silence by the window. Dud watched through the cracks, looking for shadows and occasionally thinking about Beatrice. For some reason, he could not remember her face. It aggravated him that when he could be facing death and breathing his last breath, the only faces he could see in his mind's eye were those of his mother and sister, not his ex-wife. He was grateful Fitz had not wanted to come along. He found himself glad that Ponder was with him.

They heard the sound of the hoot owl. And then the echo.

"Get ready," Dud said.

The Comanche yells, although expected, still made them jump. In the next second came the rumbling of a thousand cattle jumping to their feet. The building shook with the roar, causing dirt from the rafters to fall on their heads as the yells continued.

It seemed as if a thousand screaming Comanches poured into the fort. Dud fired at one holding a torch as he prepared to pitch it on the wagon. A hundred arrows flew in their direction, and the rumble of the stampeding cattle was replaced with the booms of gun fire.

The repeating rifles played havoc on the

Indians. As soon as the men ran out of ammunition, they picked up another and fired again. The Comanches attacking them panicked at the repeating rifles they had not come into contact with before, and their horses ran over each other trying to escape the fort.

Dud, along with all the men in the mess hall and blockhouse, mowed down everything without mercy. If a Comanche was wounded, crawling on the ground to safety, he was fired upon. If he leaned to one side of his horse to escape, his horse was shot down. The screams were horrific. It was a barrage of bullets that did not end until every living creature within firing distance was dead.

It took a minute for them to stop firing, to realize the silence and that there was nothing left alive to shoot. Dud turned to his men. Henry and Barefoot stood with rifles ready, tense and waiting, still full of fury and afraid to relax. Dud unbolted the door and pulled it open. A pile of dead Indians blocked his way. He had to climb over them to get out.

To his left, he passed by a tangle of legs and arms. One hand moved, and when it pushed away the body of another brave from its face and chest, a head with half the hair shaved off became visible. He stared at Dud, his mouth remained closed and silent while his eyes shouted to Dud to kill him and let him die an honorable death.

Dud aimed and fired his rifle, walking away and calling to his uncle.

The door to the blockhouse shook and opened. "Dud!"

Dud took in a deep breath and let it out. He stepped over more Comanche and horses to get into the blockhouse. Florine was sitting on the wardrobe with a shotgun in her hand, still protecting the children inside. Ponder was all right. Mutt, Toomey, and Darnell stood looking as edgy and frightened as Henry and Barefoot had.

"Reload!" Dud ordered and called to the men in the mess hall to do the same. The men fumbled with their rifles and ammunition until every rifle and pistol was reloaded.

"Uncle Ponder, you stay here," Dud said. "Come on, boys, we've got to catch that herd." Henry and Barefoot came to the door, and Dud called for them to stay with the horses.

"The night is not over yet."

"I'm going with you," Ponder said.

"No, you ain't. You've got to stay here and take care of women and children."

Ponder looked at Florine and frowned.

"Dudford, you are a killjoy."

"I'm glad you're alive, too, Uncle Ponder."

Outside, the doors to the armory rattled and shuddered. With a bang, General Sherman busted out. He shook his long horns to clear his head and trotted for the gate. Before they could realize what he was doing, he was headed down the path of the stampede to join his herd and take his place as their leader once again.

"Come on, let's go!" Dud said, unwilling to let General Sherman get away from them.

As Ned worked his way around the dead bodies of men and horses, Dud muttered a quiet prayer.

"I hope you rest in peace, because I don't think I ever will again."

Chapter Fifteen

Being in the rear of battle did not suit General Sherman, and he hurried to catch the herd and move to what he considered his rightful place in front. Dud, along with Mutt, Toomey, and Darnell, stayed with him, rounding up lost strays along the way. The moon shone on the rolling land they traveled, and Dud expected to be attacked again at any time. Or to find the remains of Shug, Billy Sol, and Audie lying scalped by the wayside.

To make matters even more tense, the clapper on General Sherman's bell had worked its way loose, and now they were following a ringing cow bell that in the clear night sounded like somebody beating on a church bell with a sledge hammer.

Dud reined Ned closer, intending on roping the steer to get him to stop long enough so he could tie the clapper down, but he changed his mind. After the thundering herd of cattle went through, any Indian within a hundred miles would know about it anyway. And it might help slow down any cattle who heard the bell and would pause to respond to the General's leadership.

They kept running across more and more strays and smaller groups of cattle that had stopped to wait for the General to pass. Nevertheless, they traveled for many more miles. When Dud sighted a group of cows bedded down for the night and three cowboys circling them on horses, it was like a fifty-pound weight lifting from his chest.

They herded their stray cattle in with the others. The three men joined them, looking as if they had just survived a hurricane.

"Get some shut-eye," Dud said, after assuring them everyone else was all right. "Toomey, you and Mutt do the same. Darnell and I will guard the herd for a while."

Thirty minutes later, Dud heard the hoof beat of many horses. He tensed in the saddle, straining his eyes. There was another sound — the creak of wagon wheels. In a minute, he could make out the wagons coming toward them, along with their remuda of horses. He and Darnell rode out to meet them.

Ponder pulled his wagon to a stop. Jemmy and Will poked their heads from around

Ponder, while Barefoot rode up beside them.

"I thought I told you to stay put, Uncle Ponder!" Dud said.

"Bottle it and put a cork in it, knucklehead," Ponder said. "One of them dying Indians was bragging to Barefoot that a band of a hundred or more Comanche would be coming through Fort Lancaster and Camp Hudson any time on their way to their old raiding grounds, and they would wipe us out. We thought it best to hightail it out of there while the getting was good."

Dud felt his heart give a lurch. "Why would he tell us that?" he asked, hoping it was all a made-up story.

"It was the redheaded white boy," Barefoot said. "When they are captured as children, they become indoctrinated in the Comanche ways, and they spend the rest of their lives trying to prove they belong by being braver and badder than the rest."

It took Dud a second to remember who Barefoot was talking about — the kidnapped young man the people in San Antonio had told Ponder about. Even in the dark, it looked as if Jemmy's and Will's ears grew larger as they listened.

"The others wanted to wait, but he and another brave were dead set on attacking tonight."

The brave with the half shaven head. Dud paused for a second or two. Exhaustion was beginning to take its toll. "Come on and make camp. We'll figure out what to do in the morning."

Darnell reined his mustang closer.

"Mr. Dud," he said. "I wants to go warn them people at the fort that the Indians is coming. I heared they got buffalo soldiers at that fort, Mr. Dud. I got to warn my people."

"Darnell, it's a hundred miles from Camp Hudson to Fort Lancaster. You may not make it in time."

"I got to try, Mr. Dud."

"Darnell . . ." Dud began and stopped.

"I catch up with you later, I promise, Mr. Dud."

Dud nodded. "All right. Get a fresh horse." It would take Darnell two days of hard riding to make it to the fort.

Darnell grinned, but before he could ride away, Dud stopped him. He dug in his pocket and brought out a five-dollar gold piece. He rode closer and handed it to Darnell.

"Here, they might have some good-looking laundresses at that fort."

"Thank you, Mr. Dud, thank you." Darnell grinned and rode away to fetch a fresh mount.

"We'll probably never see him alive again," Ponder said after he left.

"I know," Dud said. "But he's man enough now to know that, too."

When dawn cleared the shadows away, Dud, Shug, Billy Sol, and Audie rode a short distance in front of the herd. The horses halted. Billy Sol's mouth dropped open, and Shug's followed. Audie gasped. Dud stared. What had looked like a shadow across the land now made itself known. Because of the sound of General Sherman's cowbell, Shug and Billy Sol had been able to mill the herd and stop it only a few feet from a deep chasm.

The men turned their heads, twisting in the saddle, taking in the broken landscape. The cattle had stampeded onto a finger of land surrounded on three sides by canyons that dropped off without warning.

Audie let a low stream of curse words. "Them cattle done landed us in perdition."

"They may have saved us from being attacked by a hundred Comanche," Dud said. He turned his horse and headed back to the wagons where Florine and the two Hollister boys were preparing breakfast. Jemmy had made biscuits, and Florine had made something that was supposed to pass as gravy. The men dismounted and ate standing up, sopping the gravy with their biscuits so Florine would not have to wash utensils. When they finished, they stood silent, looking at one another.

"What are we going to do now?" Ponder demanded.

"We're getting out of here and heading west. That's what we are going to do," Florine said.

"If we do that, we'll run smack dab into the Pecos River. It ain't nothing but steep banks, salty water, and quicksand for miles," Ponder retorted.

Florine had a one-track mind and was not giving up on heading west. "Them there people in Brackett told Toomey and Mutt that there was a crossing due west hereabouts. I heard Toomey and Mutt talking about it."

Ponder gave her a look of disgust. "What you didn't hear, you old eavesdropper, was me and Toomey and Mutt talking about later. The old scout I sold a rifle to told me not to listen to them lying windbags. He said the onliest crossings within hundreds of miles was Indian Ford close to Fort Lancaster and Horsehead Crossing way up above Comanche Springs."

The wind blew Florine's hair from around the bottom of her hat, making her look even angrier than she sounded, which was plenty cross.

"We can't go to Fort Lancaster. That's where the Indians are attacking. Why should we believe that old rusty gut anyway? And besides, Dud can't go there, he'll be arrested again."

"He'll have to chance it."

They both stared at Dud, looking to him to make the decision. Dud turned to Toomey and Mutt.

"You think them men in Brackett was lying, like that old-timer said?" he asked.

Toomey spoke in his usual deadpan way, face expressionless, eyes wide and unblinking.

"It tallies. Most of them people was lying no-accounts."

Mutt nodded in solemn accord.

Dud addressed the others.

"Keep the herd grazing here as peaceful as you can. Barefoot and I are going to look for a way out of here and toward water. We'll try to avoid the road until the Comanche have passed."

Florine did not like it, and she took it out on Will and Jemmy, screeching at them to clean up so they could get moving. She muttered under her breath that if a priest threw holy water on Ponder, he'd spontaneously combust. Dud was surprised she knew what spontaneously combust meant.

Dud and Barefoot saddled fresh mustangs. Dud left Jax behind, knowing the mustangs could go longer without water on rougher ground. Backtracking until they could get away from the rough, broken landscape, they set out toward the north, hoping Darnell would make it to the fort in time.

Now, as they rode, neither man said much — that Darnell might die tortured and scalped hung in the air but remained an unspoken thought. Barefoot's eyes raked the sky, the ground, and the horizon, always on the lookout. After going ten miles or more, they came across a brackish pool of water, surprising Barefoot because he had not seen the signs he had searched for with such care. Dud dismounted, walking to the water's edge, knowing as he got closer what it would be. The mustang did not try to drink. Dud dipped his fingers into the water and tasted it. He spit it out and stood up.

"It's gyp. We drink this and we'll have dysentery for the next year, if we live that long."

They rode on, the sun rising behind them, a gigantic ball of fire. Their shirts became wet with sweat, and although neither man said so, they wished for at least a small breeze. No trees and nothing but scrub brush everywhere. There did not seem to be any living creatures about except rattlesnakes. Dud counted ten of them in one two-mile stretch. After that, he stopped counting. They dare not shoot and risk giving themselves away to any desperados, whatever the race or color, who might be in the area. Instead, they were forced to depend upon the instincts of the mustangs to deal with the snakes.

The ten miles stretched into thirty, and still no sign of water. Just about the time Dud decided they were all dead and wandering around in hades, Barefoot spotted a mesquite tree and got excited. Which for him meant that he blinked his eyes twice.

"The mustangs bring the mesquite beans up from Mexico. There must be mustangs around."

Dud agreed. Where there were mustangs, there was water. In South Texas, they rarely roamed more than three miles from water, but out here, it might be twenty-five. Dud and Barefoot approached the mesquite, eyeing the ground. The earth was awash with tiny purple, red, and yellow wildflowers, like pretty rosy cheeks on an ugly woman's face, but they were too intent to appreciate them as they cut for sign. Dud looked up and pointed silently at the distance. A line of mustangs, one after the other, were walking east, intent on slaking their thirst. Had they been meandering about, eating here and there as they went along, it would have meant they had already left the watering hole.

The men sat without talking, waiting until the mustangs were almost out of sight before following them, grateful now there was no breeze. As they watched the mustangs from a safe distance, they seemed to drop off the face of the earth, disappearing into an unknown chasm.

Riding closer, they came upon a creek bank that plunged down ten feet or more, lined with shinnery and brush. The mustangs drank from its shallow flow in indolent pleasure.

Barefoot's mustang pawed the ground, anxious to get to water. A scruffy gray stallion raised his head, spied them, and giving a loud snort, raced from the creek bed, the others following. Dud watched them go, following Barefoot and his thirsty little mustang to the water.

They dismounted, letting the horses drink, while they did the same, filling their canteens. The water was not the best Dud had ever tasted, but it was not gypped either. His eyes scanned up and down the creek.

"What are you looking for?" Barefoot asked.

"Signs of Indians. Old campfires, bones. This may be a dry creek that only runs at certain times in off years."

"Do you think there is enough water here for the whole herd?" Barefoot asked as the horses continued to drink.

"It will have to be."

After riding up and down in the creek, searching for sinkholes and quicksand, Dud and Barefoot turned and headed back. Dud long ago realized he had been fortunate to be born with a compass in his head that naturally knew which direction to take. As he watched the way Barefoot rode, in unison, going in the same direction and never following because he was lost, Dud realized he had been born with one, too. It wasn't something a man learned. He either had it, or he didn't.

Dusk did not last long. The moon shone larger and brighter than Dud had seen it in all his travels. As the moon began its rise, Barefoot questioned Dud.

"Why is Miss Florine so determined to get to New Mexico as quickly as possible?"

Dud thought for a minute. "I don't know. I don't why she was so bent on going in the first place. Right now, she's probably just scared and wants it over with."

"I didn't think Miss Florine was scared of anything."

"We all are," Dud said. "One way or another." He thought about Darnell and wished him back.

Billy Sol and Shug were changing watches with Toomey and Mutt when they rode back into camp. Barefoot parted to exchange his horse while Dud rode up to Billy Sol and Shug.

"I wish we could move these cattle out of here tonight."

Shug paused before saying, "One stampede and they'd fall right off these here cliffs."

Billy Sol agreed. "It's too dangerous, ain't that right, Shug?"

Shug gave a solemn nod. "Sometimes when cattle start stampeding, they won't stop. I was on a trail drive once to Missouri when them cattle stampeded ever night."

Before Billy Sol could say anything, Dud agreed. The timing was too dangerous. Let the cattle calm first.

Audie rode up. "I thought I heard you come in. Did you find any water?"

"Yeah, about thirty miles northeast of here. There's a gyp waterhole we'll have to make an arc around to keep the cattle away from, but we should be all right."

They discussed the best way to handle it — to push the cattle hard the next day or not. Shug and Billy Sol wanted to know what the creek was like. When Dud told them, Shug had expressed fears about the cattle getting close enough to the water to smell it, running over and maiming each other falling down the banks.

"We'll have to really be holding them, spreading them out thin along that bank."

"That's right, Shug, that's right."

Dud felt ready to drop from exhaustion, but he held off sharp words over Billy Sol's constant deference to his older brother.

"We'll work to keep the cattle away from the gyp water, pushing the cattle hard until ten miles or so away from the creek so they can't smell the water," Dud said. "Then we'll have to herd them in bunches to keep them from killing each other trying to get to it."

Billy Sol and Shug agreed, but Audie worried they would not be able to control the cattle.

Dud did not answer, but left to trade his mustang for Ned, just to have on hand nearby. He exchanged a few words with Henry about making sure no cowboy rode any one horse too long. They were going to be doing some hard riding, and he wanted every cowhand to trade off in order to keep from riding a favorite horse down. After he left Henry, Ponder heard Dud approaching and stirred on his pallet. As Dud threw down a bedroll, he thought about the snakes he had seen.

"Uncle Ponder, did you buy any of them fangled mothball things?"

Ponder's voice came through the dark. "Did we have money for mothballs?"

"Guess not. Too cool for snakes at night anyway."

"Yeah, they'll be looking for a warm spot. Right next to you," Ponder said.

Daylight came too soon. Ponder snapped at Florine. She snapped back. Toomey and Mutt were the most good-natured of cowhands, but when Henry informed Toomey he couldn't ride his best horse all night, he began to sulk.

"You cannot, the boss say so."

"Toomey," Dud said. "It's just barely daylight. Don't be borrowing on worry and trouble. Get through today first, and then think about tonight."

Dud helped lead the cattle off their peninsula, but once they were on safer ground, he scouted ahead to make sure they did not run into a war party. Ponder and Florine followed him at a safe distance. Barefoot stayed back to help Shug and Billy Sol point the cattle in the right direction.

When Dud reached the gyp hole, he rode back, telling them to move the cattle farther west until they could get around it. He had Will and Jemmy riding drag, with Audie, Toomey, and Mutt riding swing and flank on the gyp side until they could get around it. Barefoot rode the long line of cattle back and forth between Shug and Henry.

"Press them in, press them in," Dud ordered Toomey and Mutt. "They are starting to spread out."

The cowboys began complaining about the snakes, and Dud had the ones who were not riding mustangs to dismount and trade horses.

"Watch the cattle, not the ground. Let your mustang work his way around them," Dud advised and hoped he was right.

It did not seem to bother the longhorns much; nevertheless, by the end of the day, one mama cow had been lost after a snake bit her udder.

"Do you think her calf will make it?" Jemmy fretted when Dud rode to the back to check on them.

"I don't know, Jemmy. We're going to have some bawling calves tonight, because we aren't stopping until late."

Dud rode ahead, the stars twinkling above his head as if the worries and cares of mortals were of no importance. As soon as his mustang paused, raised his head with nostrils flaring, seeming to smell water, Dud turned back and had them halt the herd.

They ate, craving sleep but chary of snakes. Ponder made Will and Jemmy get into the wagon to sleep immediately after eating, making Florine mad because she had no help. Without a word, Dud tossed his plate into the wreck pan and washed it himself. Florine grabbed it and told him he wasn't doing it right. He left her to it and began his watch with Audie. By the time Shug and Billy Sol were ready to take his place, he was so tired he would have curled up next to a rattlesnake to get some sleep.

Ponder insisted on taking Darnell's watch with Barefoot. Dud got up just before Toomey and Mutt took their places, his ability to think and plan better since he had food and sleep. Leading Ned, he walked to where Shug and Billy Sol slept, speaking to them softly.

"Get your horses. We're going to cut a

hundred or so head out and take them to water."

The two men did not question him, but rose and got into their saddles. Ponder joined them, looking like he was about to drop from the saddle. Dud explained what they were about to do.

"Uncle Ponder, let Florine cook breakfast. You've got to rest."

Ponder looked about to protest, but he glanced at Florine's sons and left without speaking.

General Sherman rose, not to be left behind, but they left his clapper tied. The cattle closest to him, the ones that always like to be in front, rose with him, and cutting them out and taking them to water in the dark proved easier than Dud thought it would.

By dawn, they had taken over three hundred head to the creek. Shug tried to get the General to stay behind with Billy Sol, but he wouldn't do it, leading each group to water. They stopped long enough to eat breakfast before continuing to take the cattle in bunches. Ponder and Florine creaked their wagons to the creek to set up camp once again, this time Audie traveling with Henry to take the remuda to water. They stayed behind while Dud went to fetch another batch.

By midafternoon, Dud looked out over the animals, pleased they had all the cattle watered and spread out to graze. Shug rode up next to him. Dud glanced at him.

"Looks good."

"Yep, but I don't want to move the General just yet. He's getting footsore."

Dud nodded. "Barefoot and I are going to use what daylight is left to scout anyway." The creek they had found wasn't a tributary of a river they could follow, but had erupted from a small spring. They could only hope they would find another one. Giving the pastoral scene in front of him one last look of satisfaction, Dud turned his horse to find Barefoot.

Only a short distance away, the land Dud and Barefoot traveled became less broken, the grass lusher and greener. Barefoot found water forty miles from camp by backtracking the flight of birds with mud in their mouths. But when they rode upon it, it was little more than a faint bubbling from the ground, holding barely enough to water their horses and fill canteens. They rode on, but when darkness made looking for signs impossible, they had to turn and go back.

The next morning before dawn they rode out again, mindful that the other drovers were restless and worried about a possible Indian attack at such a fortuitous watering spot. Dud and Barefoot covered the first forty miles faster, keeping an eye out, but knowing it unlikely they would find something to lead them to a spot they had missed the day before.

A herd of antelope crossed the rolling plains, and although Dud wanted to shoot one to take back to camp, he didn't dare fire a rifle and give away their presence. Since antelope could go weeks without water, there was no sense in following them.

They were about to give up and turn back when they ran across Indian tracks.

"Ten riders," Dud said, examining the hoof prints. He got down from his horse and examined them. "I'd say they passed by here recently."

"How can you tell?"

Dud stood up and examined the horizon. The small rolling hills could hide an army of Indians. He replied to Barefoot's question without taking his eyes from the landscape around them. "The bent grass hasn't had a chance to wither much."

"Do you think they are on their way to water?" Barefoot asked.

"I don't know." Dud weighed all the possibilities. Were the Indians riding toward water? Could they follow them without being detected? He looked at the tracks again.

"I think one of these horses was being led. See how the tracks parallel without a break."

That could mean a variety of things, but the one that came closest to mind was that they were leading a prisoner on a horse. Still, it wasn't his lookout. It could be an Apache with a Kickapoo captive or vice versa. The Plains Indians were notorious warriors, only occasionally forming alliances. Dud's eyes followed the tracks as they led off into the distance. If he and Barefoot followed them, they could be riding into a trap.

He made up his mind to let the Indians go their way, and he and Barefoot would go theirs. Something caused him to get back down on his haunches and look at the grass again — a glint of something in the blades.

At first glance, Dud took the strands for short, dark threads. He stooped to pick them up. Rubbing them between his fingers, he realized what they were — not thread, but short, curling black hairs.

He stood up. "Come on," he said to Barefoot, and got back on his horse.

Chapter Sixteen

They followed the tracks without speaking, every sense heightened as much as a human body could allow without overloading and snapping. Out on that vast prairie, they felt as exposed as a newborn without a diaper — and almost as helpless.

A small rise of smoke coming from the other side of a ridge gave the Indians away. Catching sight of it at the same time, Dud and Barefoot eased their horses toward it. Riding as close as he dared, Dud dismounted, indicating to Barefoot to do the same. With eyes watching in the direction of the smoke, they put rawhide hobbles on their mustangs, hoping they would have enough time to cut them and escape if they had to. Armed with rifles and every intention of blasting somebody to Comanche hades if necessary, they did not want to be left stranded by horses frightened away with gunfire.

Sounds of stifled moans and groans removed any doubts of what to do. Crouching, they crept forward until they could look down on the other side of the ridge.

Darnell lay naked, tied to stakes driven in the ground. One Comanche had a burning stick in his hand. He placed it in the fire and brought it back to Darnell, waving it in his face to taunt him before poking his arm with it.

Dud scanned the Indians for weapons, seeing arrows, a few rifles, and knives.

Darnell groaned, struggling against the latigo that held him down. Another Indian held a knife over him, and he was moving toward Darnell's scrotum. Dud nodded to Barefoot. They raised their rifles and began firing.

Horses snorted with terror, stomping and struggling against their hobbles. Startled, the Indians went for their weapons, but they were not fast enough for Ponder's repeating rifles.

When the smoke cleared, Darnell lay staring at them with eyes as wide as the saucers the captain at the fort had served Dud's coffee on. He shook with uncontrollable fear, but his mouth was as mute as if it had been sewn shut.

Dud and Barefoot went to him, making a

fast check to make sure the Indians were dead. Cutting Darnell's bonds, they stared to see what damage had been done.

Darnell had random shallow cuts made across his body, along with several burns on his arms, chest, and thighs. A deeper cut between his thigh and scrotum was bleeding profusely.

Dud glanced at the dead Indians, but they were practically naked. He unbuttoned his shirt, taking it off and tying it around Darnell the best he could to staunch the flow of blood.

"Darnell, listen to me. Do you think you can ride?"

Darnell stared at him. His mouth opened but no words came out. Dud looked at the horses, spotting the mustang Darnell had ridden when he left camp.

Barefoot tore his eyes away from Darnell long enough to give Dud a look of helpless agony.

"Rope their horses together. We're taking them back. Leave that little sorrel out with the saddle on it for Darnell to ride."

Barefoot nodded and went for rope.

They got a shaky Darnell on his mustang, but the palms of his hands had been burned. Dud was about to give him his gloves when he realized Darnell was so shook up, he probably would not be able to concentrate enough to hold the reins.

They headed back to camp as fast as they could, with Dud leading Darnell's horse, and Barefoot leading the captured horses. Stopping long enough at the little spring to water the horses and pour some over Darnell's wounds, Dud managed to get a coherent narrative after several abortive tries.

Evidently some of the Comanche had escaped the gun fight and warned the others about the rifles the drovers were carrying. They thought the soldiers at the fort might be similarly armed and decided to give them a wide berth. At least, that was what the soldiers figured when they didn't attack.

"Who were the ones that got you?"

"They was just a hunting party. I was trying to get back to you, Mr. Dud, just like I promised. They sprung up on me."

Darnell looked about to weep. Dud interrupted.

"What happened to your rifle?"

"I lost it to the soldiers in a poker game."

"Well, thank God," Dud said. "It can't be used against us. Mount up, we need to hurry."

They had to get Darnell back to camp before he bled to death. The shirt Dud had wrapped around his cut dripped with blood.

They rode through the darkness without speaking, every nerve taut. Dud had to glance at Darnell every few minutes to make sure he had not fallen out of the saddle.

The others were waiting for them. They rushed forward to help Darnell. They tried to get him to lie down, but he refused and leaned against Ponder's wagon instead, the light from the campfire crackling nearby. Henry took over the horses, but he stood holding the reins and rope, his eyes staring at Darnell like he was seeing a nightmare in motion. Mutt gaped openmouthed; Toomey's face grew even more solemn than Dud would have thought possible. Audie's face drooped in shock and sadness.

Ponder took charge, bringing a lantern closer. He unwrapped Dud's makeshift bandage, staring at the wound with grim lips pressed together.

"Darnell, I'll have to sew you up. You best lay down."

Darnell, weak with shock, shook his head. "I can't, Mr. Ponder. Don't make me. I can't stand nobody leaning over me ever again."

Ponder paused. "All right." He turned around and spied Will.

"Fetch my sewing kit and the jug of

whiskey out of my wagon."

Will and Jemmy clambered into the back of the wagon while Ponder continued to give instructions.

"Audie, find a piece of rawhide for Darnell to bite on. Y'all got to hold him."

With Darnell full of whiskey and the wound splashed with it, Shug and Audie held Darnell's arms, while Mutt and Toomey grasped his legs. Florine stood in the background, not wanting to watch, but unable to turn her head. As Ponder stitched, Darnell trembled and twitched despite his efforts to be still. He bit on the rawhide to keep from screaming, but he began to sob, tears streaming down his cheeks.

When Ponder finished sewing the slash of the knife that almost robbed Darnell of his manhood, he washed the rest of his wounds and rubbed his burns with bacon grease.

"Get him in the back of my wagon," Ponder said when he finished.

That night, Ponder stayed up with Darnell while the rest of the drovers went about their work silent and withdrawn. The songs they sang to the cattle as they took turns on their watches were full of subdued sadness and touched with fear.

The next morning as Ponder puttered around, helping a silent Florine get breakfast, Dud asked him how Darnell was.

"He'll live. He's young and healthy. It will take a lot to kill him."

Dud went inside the cramped wagon where makeshift bedding had been put down. Crouching next to Darnell, he spoke his name. Darnell turned his head and opened his eyes. The lively interest that had always shown from those brown eyes was gone, and the look he gave Dud was dull and somber.

"Darnell, is there any water between where we found you and the Pecos crossing at Fort Lancaster?"

Darnell gave a shallow shake of his head.

"Are the soldiers there looking for me?"

Darnell again gave a shake of his head.

Dud gave Darnell's shoulder a pat and left the wagon, announcing to the others they would be pushing the cattle hard to get to Fort Lancaster and water. It came as no surprise to anyone.

They began the punishing drive. At midnight, Dud found the drovers a wide valley to stop in, letting the cattle graze while they ate before starting again. They were kept moving until daylight, with another brief stop for breakfast.

Dud scouted ahead, looking for signs of Indians. When he came to the spot where they had rescued Darnell, all traces of the fight had disappeared. Dud kept it to himself, and only Barefoot, when he passed by, realized that other Indians had whisked the bodies away.

Shug and Billy Sol did not want Florine to ride ahead with her mules, so she stayed with the herd while Ponder and his wagon followed closer to Dud. On the second day, Darnell wanted up. Ponder said he could ride in the wagon with Will, and he would take his place with the herd. All of Darnell's clothing had disappeared, including his boots. Florine unexpectedly loaned him one of her shirts. Barefoot let him wear a pair of his best pants, the bottoms rolled up in wide cuffs, and a rope put around the waist to hold them up. Darnell's hat had been lost, too. Henry rode up to the wagon, and with a solemn face, took his hat off and offered it to Darnell. Darnell stared at him.

"But that's yore hat, Henry."

"Take it, *amigo.* No bad men will recognize my sombrero out here; perhaps Mr. Dud will let me wear it once again."

Dud nodded, and Ponder found Henry's hat, returning it to him a little smushed, but still serviceable. Darnell stared at the ground, overcome with emotion. Whatever hard feelings Darnell and Henry had for one another melted.

But letting Darnell replace Ponder in the wagon presented other difficulties. Will could handle the team of oxen most of the time, but he was too young and inexperienced to fight off an unexpected attack. Darnell was still clumsy with a gun and would only be capable of handling the reins for short periods.

Dud ordered them to stay back with Florine. When it came time to set up camp, the drovers would just have to wait on fresh coffee and grub. In the meantime, he told Jemmy to jump from Florine's wagon and gather firewood whenever he could, throwing it into the possum belly underneath the wagon to have ready when they stopped.

When Dud found the road that led to Fort Lancaster, everyone drew easier breaths. Being on the loose in a vast area that seemed deserted of all human life except a strange warlike people who could strike any minute at whim had taken more of a toll on them than they realized. They were still at the mercy of an unseen and unfathomable people, but at least they were on a road where others had trod before them.

The landscape grew mountainous — in some places the road became a narrow trail only wide enough for three longhorns at a time. Dangerous during the daytime, it became treacherous at night with only the stars to guide them.

Florine disliked anyone handling her mules, but she finally let Jemmy take the reins long enough she could catch a little sleep. There were times when Dud rode back to the wagon to find both of them with eyes shut and the mules plodding along on their own. He often found Toomey and Mutt asleep in their saddles. Only fear or incredible endurance kept the others awake, including Ponder.

By the time they neared Fort Lancaster, the cattle were moving so fast, they had to be slowed so the weaker ones could keep up. Darnell said there was a creek with good water nearby with enough of a flow the cattle would not have to be led to it in batches, the Pecos crossing being about a mile from the fort. Dud, knowing when the cattle smelled water, there would be no stopping them, rode ahead to warn the soldiers they were coming.

Dud and Jax rode upward, stopping on a high bluff of limestone to look down at Fort Lancaster. Surrounded by low lying mountains, the fort looked like a small wrecked village of falling down stone and adobe in the middle of a beautiful, grassy prairie. All the structures predated the war; since then, it had been abandoned and now only held a few buffalo soldiers and a handful of white officers on a temporary basis.

Dud gave a slight squeeze of his thighs, and Jax began down a snaky, rocky path to the fort. Stones as big as water barrels had been shoved aside — a road so rough, the only cattle breed Dud would have trusted to tread on it were the sure-footed longhorn.

Soldiers in dusty blue, having spotted him, gathered on the grounds, watching his descent. As he grew closer, he estimated about forty buffalo soldiers stood waiting for him, along with a few white officers.

He hadn't thought about what he looked like until he got close enough to see their reaction to him. Eyes widened, some in disgust, others in pity. He looked down at his clothes, ragged and dirty. His face hadn't been shaved since they left Brackett. He'd lost weight, and he realized his eyes were probably sunken dark pits in his face because of lack of food and sleep. His ears were crusty with sunburned skin.

He reined Jax in front of the captain and dismounted. The captain, a man of about thirty with straight dark brows and flared nostrils, made a motion for one of the soldiers to take Dud's horse. He examined

Dud while the soldier took Jax to be watered.

"I didn't think I'd ever see another scarecrow Confederate again."

"We don't die; we just get skinnier and skinnier until we turn into mesquite thorns."

"And just as prickly. Will you join me in my quarters?"

Dud shook his head. "No time. We got a herd of over a thousand head south of here. They're thirsty, and I just came to warn you they'll run over anybody that gets in their way."

Surprise showed on the captain's face. "I thought you'd be . . ." He stopped and started again. "Let me send some of my men to help you."

Dud looked over the curious faces of the soldiers. They were probably so bored, they'd be grateful for anything to break the monotony. Nevertheless, he shook his head.

"I've got some good men who can handle them. They're going to be wild enough as it is. They see strange men in strange clothes, they'll liable to become totally uncontrollable. Much obliged, though."

Dud went for Jax, putting a foot in the stirrup and throwing a leg over the saddle. He paused long enough to tell the captain, "My men are tired and hungry. They would sure appreciate some good grub."

He rode away before the captain could respond.

Once back with the herd, Dud had Shug and Billy Sol hold the cattle back, telling Florine, Darnell, and the Hollister boys to take the wagons ahead into the fort. The soldiers would help them unhitch the teams. If the captain had been shocked to learn that the drovers and their cattle were still living after listening to Darnell's story, he would probably really be overcome at the sight of Florine and the Hollister boys. But then, Darnell had probably told him about them, too. Darnell wasn't one to keep secrets.

Dud helped Henry herd the remuda to the fort where they could be put in a separate corral from the soldiers' mules. The fort, built for almost two hundred men and fifty mules, had the room to hold them, despite its derelict condition.

Henry, suspicious of the *negrito* soldiers, stayed with the horses to make sure they were fed and watered the way he thought they should be, while Dud rode back to the herd.

Despite being deprived of sleep and food, the drovers controlled the cattle with renewed vigor. It helped that the narrowness of the road had kept them strung out to begin with. Dud realized the cowboys waving their hats and cracking the loose ends of their ropes might be showing off a little bit, too.

It took a while to get the herd watered and spread out to graze. There was always the possibility that after being without water for so long, they might overdrink and become waterlogged. Despite the rough treatment they had suffered, they looked none the worse for it.

With the cattle quiet and contented, the drovers crowded around Dud.

"Take care of your horses, then find some shade and go to sleep," he ordered.

They left with gratitude, even Shug and Billy Sol. Henry rode up on a little mustang and halted next to Dud. He twisted in the saddle, looking in a circle at the low mountains surrounding them. He turned to Dud.

"I don't like this place, Señor Dud. I feel eyes upon us."

Dud nodded. He felt it, too.

The soldiers, knowing they were exhausted, fed them and left them alone. Later, the captain ordered extra guards, but once the drovers had the cattle bedded, they began their usual watches. Henry slept as near the horses as he could without getting stomped on. When Dud finished his watch, he joined Henry's vigil. He didn't trust the eyes he felt were watching them either.

The night passed without incident, however. The lush green grass at Fort Lancaster grew tall; the nearby creek ran pure and clean. The cattle weren't footsore, but they had gone many punishing miles. It seemed contrary to good sense not to stay one more day, especially when the captain introduced his pretty little wife and sister-in-law to them.

Two sisters never looked more unlike. While the captain's wife was small and dark with friendly, darting gestures, her sister was heavy, with nondescript sandy hair and an expression that would freeze butter in July. They were women, nevertheless, and along with the two Negro laundresses, enough to stir up a man's blood to gallantry.

"We'll have a little party this evening," the captain told Dud and Ponder in the morning on the veranda of his office. "Mrs. Higgins can be our guest of honor, Mr. er, I don't think I caught your last name?"

He hadn't caught it because Dud hadn't given it. As he opened his mouth to reply, Ponder snorted at the thought of Florine being anyone's guest of honor.

"Fitz Callahan," Dud said, giving his

brother-in-law's name. "This here is my uncle, P.D. Callahan."

The captain's eyebrows drew together in puzzlement. "I thought the young Negro cowboy said when he was here the first time that he was working for some people named Washburn."

Ponder jumped in. "That's just a little mix-up. We had a cowboy by that name, but he was wanted for questioning about something that happened in San Antonio. We had to leave him at Fort Clark. Darnell probably had his stories running together."

The captain accepted Ponder's explanation, and Dud hoped his drovers remembered to refer to him as "Boss" and Ponder as "Mr. Callahan" while they were at the fort.

Aware they were ex-Confederates, the captain drew himself up, and looking a little pompous, pointed out that he had never commanded such a brave, hardworking group of soldiers.

Dud nodded. "I'm glad to hear it." And he meant it. While the captain expounded, Dud thought about Darnell's bravery. He wondered what he would have done without the help of Darnell's uncles. When the captain finally realized Dud and Ponder had no desire to argue with him, he stopped.

Barefoot didn't escape later on either. But not for being an ex-Confederate.

At the creek, while Barefoot washed his clothes along with the other men, he was subjected to scrutiny from the junior officers.

"Injun, are you the scout of this outfit? We could use a good scout. Can you speak English?"

Barefoot paused with the pants he had loaned Darnell in his hands. Darnell had been completely reoutfitted by the enlisted men who treated him as something of a hero. Barefoot let his face turn stone like.

"Me heap big lousy scout."

The officers looked confused. Dud gave a short laugh.

"He's an attorney. The only reason he is on this drive is to try to impress a pretty little gal back in San Antonio."

Barefoot gave a shrug and slight smirk before continuing to wash blood from his pants as the abashed soldiers tried to think of something to say.

"Don't let him fool you," Dud said. "He's becoming a darn good scout."

Dud turned to his own blood-soaked shirt and began scrubbing, all the while knowing the stain would never come out. It didn't matter anyway.

Chapter Seventeen

Although the women disappeared from view, the drovers knew they were there and responded accordingly. The creek filled with soap, razors were brought out, and the one mirror from Ponder's wagon was fought over.

"I don't want to be no guest of honor to no Yankee women," Florine declared at her wagon.

"And I don't want to claim her as kin while we're here," Ponder said to the universe at large.

"Florine, keep your trap shut and just show up for a little while," Dud ordered.

Shug and Billy Sol cleaned up, but not with the same vigor as the rest of the drovers. Late in the afternoon, they tromped to the arbor near a pit where the soldiers roasted one of Dud's donated beeves. He and the captain had done a bit of perfunctory haggling earlier, with the captain end-ing up buying more of Dud's beeves than he probably needed.

The genteel party the captain's wife and sister had planned did not quite come off. Florine refused to be drawn into conversation. She and the sister-in-law sat exchanging dark looks. Shug and Billy Sol were equally and just as painfully ignorant about how to behave in polite society. Shug stared and said nothing. Billy Sol broke out in hysterical giggles at all the wrong times. Dud felt sorry for them and yet aggravated, too.

Darnell did not ask for his fiddle. Despite his elevated status among the soldiers and fawning of the laundresses, he went off to himself, alone and silent. Henry had unbent a little. Barefoot observed from the sidelines. Mutt, dragging Toomey with him, fitted in, singing and clapping, dancing jigs for the enjoyment of the soldiers and the women. Florine left as soon as she ate, returning to her wagon. When Shug said he was leaving to check on the cattle, Billy Sol gave up and joined him. Audie watched some of Mutt and Toomey's antics, but he, too, made to leave.

Dud stopped him. "You don't have to leave. Shug and Billy Sol have it under control."

Audie stared at him, his face a mask of sadness.

"I can't enjoy myself thinking that I'll never be able to picnic with my wife and children again. If I had been with them instead of rushing off to join the war, maybe they'd still be alive. I should have been there, Dud."

"You know you can't live life looking back like that."

Audie shrugged and walked away.

Not long after Audie left, Darnell offered to guard the horses with Henry. He admitted he would not be much good with a rifle for a while yet, but he could sound the alarm if he spotted trouble. Dud nodded his permission, and Darnell, too, left the party.

As boss and *segundo,* Dud and Ponder felt obligated to turn their attentions to their host and hostesses. Dud knew Ponder well enough to read the signs of dislike for the sister-in-law, but he hid it well enough.

They all knew Mutt was a clown, but Toomey surprised them with his courtly manners. He bowed to the captain's wife and asked her permission to join him in a round of dancing. She obliged, and while the soldiers called out a reel, Toomey, with light, nimble feet, promenaded and do-sidoed as if he had been born into high Virginia society.

Dud and Ponder felt it only their duty to do their share of promenading, too.

Many dances later, Mutt, in an expansive mood, proposed to the sister-in-law, telling her that it didn't make no difference to him how old she was. She huffed and frowned, and shortly thereafter, the party broke up.

Later that evening, after the ladies had retired, Dud and Ponder were entertained in the captain's bare-walled quarters. Serviceable lamps, a stark table and chairs provided little comforts of home. The captain, however, was in a generous and somewhat pontifying mood.

"Comanche rule to the east, but you'll be entering Mescalero territory. You'll still run across a few Comanche, but most of the Indians you'll meet will be the Apache."

"I thought they were putting them on the reservations in New Mexico," Ponder said.

The captain shook his head. "There is no such thing as one Apache nation. They are various groups that split off from one another all the time."

"Sounds like the Baptists," Pondered muttered.

"One Apache clan agrees to a treaty, but the other one does not," the captain said, ignoring Ponder. He continued to explain.

Before the war, the fort's only duty had been to escort wagon trains and stagecoaches to Fort Davis. Fort Stockton, situated between the two, had been added later. During the war, the forts had been abandoned, and Indians had taken advantage of the absence of soldiers to reclaim what they considered theirs — attacking, robbing, and looting anyone who got in their way. That included Mexicans and other tribes, not just Anglos.

"There is no proof, but many people believe the Mexican government is actively encouraging the Kickapoos to raid farther and farther north."

Dud nodded. The captain took another sip of wine.

"The good news is, the Apache rarely rape their women captives as the Comanche do. If they capture Mrs. Higgins, they will make her a slave. If she is not keeping up, they will use torture to prod her. If that doesn't work, they'll kill her."

"If that's the good news, what's the bad news?" Dud asked.

"They will try to snatch the children traveling with you. Because they are children, if captured, they will be treated fairly well. Naturally, you and your men won't be captured. You'll be killed. And you hope instantly."

"And the Kickapoo?"

"They'd probably trade the children to another tribe for horses. You and your men would still be just as dead."

Dud looked around the captain's spartan quarters. Would it be better to leave the Hollister boys at the post? He turned back to the captain and explained how the boys had come to be traveling with them.

Although he had not asked, the captain must have read his mind. "When we saw the children, my sister-in-law immediately put her foot down over the possibility of the boys staying here with us. Despite appearances, my wife's health is not good. Her nerves are not what they should be, and my sister-in-law tries to shield her as much as possible from stress and responsibility.

"And the few people who do come through here now are usually desperados, or the desperately poor. The boys wouldn't stand any better chance with them. On the contrary, they'd probably be much worse off."

"We're not leaving them no how," Ponder said.

Dud shot him a look and frowned. Ponder spoke with such firmness Dud wondered if he knew something he didn't.

"Right now, General Sherman thinks the Indian threats in Texas are greatly exaggerated."

Dud grimaced. If General Sherman was ever convinced otherwise, it would mean the same total war he had practiced on the South. Dud could see the handwriting on the wall for the Apache. They had pushed lesser tribes around plenty, and soon their time would be coming. It had already started. Nevertheless, Dud intended on moving his cattle to New Mexico. He had no desire to kill or rob anyone of anything. All he wanted was to push through and hopefully make a profit selling cattle to the army.

The captain tried to talk them into a poker game. Dud knew he was not going to, but expected Ponder to agree. Ponder surprised him again by declining.

Once outside and alone, while walking to the barrack they were allowed to bunk in, Dud questioned Ponder.

"Why did you turn down a chance at a poker game?"

Ponder looked back over his shoulder at the captain's quarters, the flickering lamp lighting the window.

"Because he won Darnell's rifle, and now

he wants to win the rest of ours."

That night, Dud walked in the starlight through tall grass. The Apache with their painted faces, spears, and knives appeared out of the darkness, surrounding him. He broke out in a sweat, fear blowing out of his nostrils like a frightened horse. They advanced upon him. His only recourse was to fight his way through them. He gave a Rebel yell and threw himself at them.

From a distant place, he could hear Ponder's voice, loud and commanding.

"Get back! Leave him alone! He'll come out of it in a minute."

Dud heard boots pounding, getting closer. He paused, shaking his head. He wasn't walking in the starlight; he was standing in the barracks, fist raised, teeth bared. Someone had put a match to a lantern. Soldiers and officers were asking what was wrong.

"Leave him be, he'll come out of it. It was just a nightmare."

Dud took a deep breath and exhaled, relaxing. One of the officers shook his head.

"That scream! I'll be having nightmares I'm back at Shiloh tonight."

Dud watched the soldiers file out. Shiloh — he might have been the Yankee who killed Milford or Bradford.

When they left, Ponder turned to him.

"Dudford, this is the last time on this trip I'm letting you sleep with a roof over your head. You're all right as long as you got the sky above you."

Dud swallowed, grateful for Ponder's excuse. "I'm okay now," he said. "It won't happen again tonight." He went back to his cot.

He could not worry about the Yankee from Shiloh. Maybe he had killed one of his brothers or maybe he hadn't. It was war and didn't matter anymore. What mattered was much more pressing. Forts Stockton and Davis had been abandoned during the war — there wouldn't be another settlement for the next three hundred miles until they reached El Paso. How was he going to lead this ragtag group through that kind of hell?

Always before, it had been his pappy who made decisions on the trail, and he had been the one who learned how to ride point and follow directions. But this would be much worse than even the awful drive to Louisiana when they were almost eaten alive by giant mosquitoes and had to fight off alligators. Everyone would be counting on him to lead them.

What was it his pa had always said when things got rough? The words came back to him in his pappy's voice, deep and forceful.

Dud repeated them out loud, just as his pappy had done.

"Uncle Ponder, you best get praying."

The next morning, Dud felt calm, with a plan of action that gave assurance to his walk and cool confidence to his speech. He and Audie rode to the Pecos crossing looking for the steep drop-offs and quicksand the river was known for. Leaving Audie to show the other drovers where the river would cause them treachery, Dud rode on to check the lay of the land at the next waterhole. After Ponder's comment about the rifles, Dud had been careful not to let the acquisitive captain know he had a map. But the captain, in spite of any faults he may have had, was free with information.

Pecos Springs, about six miles northwest, would be the last of the good water and grass for a long time. The road would touch again with the Pecos River nearly forty miles away, its water brackish and foul, but drinkable.

Finding the captain's description of the springs true, Dud rode back to the fort. Shug and Billy Sol were waiting for him. Henry saw Dud approach the two brothers, and he joined them.

"Cousin Dud, it would be best for these here cattle to graze right here a couple of days before heading on."

Henry spoke up. "As much as I dislike this spooky place, the horses need to be reshod, Señor Dud."

Dud nodded in agreement. For the next two nights, Dud and Ponder ate supper with the captain, his wife, and sister-in-law. The women were gracious but did not attempt another party. The rest of the drovers lazed around, doing as little as possible. Henry had to say a few choice words in Spanish to get them to help with the horseshoeing. Ponder wiggled out of playing poker, although the captain tried hard. Dud told the others in a few choice words of English what would happen to them if they lost any more rifles or ammunition to the soldiers in any poker games.

At a powwow the night before they left, they decided it was too dangerous to let the wagons go ahead. They would have to travel with the herd. Knowing of the lack of fuel ahead, the soldiers had volunteered to load their possum bellies with firewood in addition to filling water barrels. Dud thought it was probably the first and only time he would see soldiers volunteering to do anything on their journey, such was their regard for Darnell and his traveling companions.

Dud rode up just as several soldiers were

begging Darnell to stay behind and join the army.

"You's be a lot safer here with us than out there with them vile Apache. They tie you upside down, cut you up and build a fire underneath your ole black hide."

The other drovers gathered round, appreciating the soldiers' colorful language that went on to become a lot baser and coarser. All eyes watched Darnell to see what he would do. None of them would blame Darnell for staying behind.

At first, Darnell looked confused. After a minute or two, he seemed to make up his mind. His eyes searched until he found Dud.

"Boss, I be healing up, if you and Mr. Pon . . . Callahan, be agreeable, I'll handle the wagon for a day or two before getting back to the cattle."

Dud gave Darnell a steady stare. "That would be up to Mr. Callahan." Usually when a drover was injured, he was immediately let go. The other drovers would not tolerate the hard work while one man remained idle, no matter what sympathies they might feel for him. But this was no ordinary drive.

Ponder must have thought so, too. "I'm agreeable."

"All right," Dud said. "Come on, men, I want to talk to you before we leave."

The men included Florine, but Dud did not correct himself. They separated from the soldiers, the cattle grazing unconcernedly in the meadow in front of them.

Dud explained what lie ahead while they listened, watching his face, their own mirroring his stoic resolve. They were about to embark on the grueling second half of their journey.

"I want whoever is riding swing and flank to switch out each morning. And trade sides, too." The men and horses who rode closest to point had the easier of the jobs. It would spread out the labor between man and horses and keep one group from eating dust from the blowing wind every single day.

"I want the ones who are on flank to ride far enough back in their circling to assist with the drag, too, just like you've been doing.

"We won't be stopping until we get to Pecos Spring. We don't want to give the cattle a chance to run back to the river.

"When we bed the cattle, I want the horses and the wagons to be in the middle of them every night from now on."

Audie immediately protested. "The stench is going to be awful, and even though it ain't hot at night now, it will be with all them cattle giving off heat."

When Dud did not answer, Audie threw in another concern. "And what if two steers get to fighting? They could tear the wagons to pieces in nothing flat."

"We'll take that chance," Dud said, dismissing Audie's fears. "Now, we've got to figure out what to do with the Hollister boys to keep them from getting kidnapped."

They argued back and forth many minutes about that. Dud wanted them in the wagons. Everyone seemed to have an idea about where would be the safest place for them.

Ponder ended the disagreements by holding up his hand, marking off fingers one by one.

"Apaches is going to be after our horses first," he said, hitting one forefinger against the other. "Then whatever they can loot from the wagons. Then the cattle. Snatching children is only something they'll do after they done satisfied their lust for the first three. Didn't you hear that captain say they done got smart about not taking the drag cattle in any kind of parley? They'll try to stampede the lead cattle. Riding drag is the best place for them young 'uns to be."

Dud had not tried to shield the boys from knowledge of what might happen to them.

They watched him now, their eyes wide and solemn.

"I want you kids in those wagons at night, though. No walking off for any reason."

They nodded. "Yes, sir."

Dud patted Jemmy's shoulder. "You'll be all right. You know if something happened to you, Mr. Ponder wouldn't give me a moment's peace until I found you and brought you back."

They tried to smile. Dud turned to Barefoot.

"Barefoot, you not only have the worst job riding drag, you'll have the responsibility of protecting two children."

Barefoot took it without turning a hair. "The boys are a big help to me."

Dud dismissed them, and the group dispersed. Ponder walked up beside Dud, watching Barefoot walk away.

"It's almost gives me a shiver, Dudford, thinking how close we came to leaving that man behind."

Dud gazed at Ponder, thinking Barefoot was not the only one he had been foolish enough to almost leave behind.

They gave thanks to the captain, his wife and sister-in-law, and to his men, bidding them goodbye with bows to the women, hats flourishing downward. Dud rode up on a rise, turned Jax quickly in a circle, stopped and faced the direction of Pecos Springs. He waved his hat forward, indicating the drive was to begin. With General Sherman in the lead, the cattle began down the road leading them to unimaginable horrors or welcomed riches.

Despite the harshness of the territory ahead, many of the soldiers wanted to accompany them to Comanche Springs, but their job was to escort travelers, not cattle drovers. They went with them as far as the river, where despite the precautions taken, cattle still bogged down in the Pecos. The soldiers did not hesitate to help pull them out. They stood on the banks waving, their skins glistening in sweat and saline water. Dud wondered if they would ever see them again.

Chapter Eighteen

They made camp at Pecos Spring, the last good water for almost forty miles. It consisted of a burned-out cabin and corrals, remnants of a stagecoach station that Indians had destroyed in an effort to stem the ever-encroaching westward tide. As long as soldiers and stage line owners had continued to bring horses and mules to steal, the buildings were allowed to stand. But once the war ended that, the Indians burned the stations as grim reminders that interlopers were not wanted. The soldiers at Fort Lancaster told the drovers they could expect to see the same thing at every watering hole they stopped at along the Military Road.

The next day, the cattlemen followed the brackish river on the dry and barren west bank. Again, they pushed the cattle to reach a spot in the Pecos the cattle could get to water, but it was so full of minerals, they dared not let the cattle or horses drink too much. Even so, it loosened the bowels of man and beast to the point Audie's prediction of overwhelming odors came all too true.

Glad to escape the Pecos, they followed the road as it turned directly west into a wide plain with broken ridges on either side. The grass became even more sterile. They made it to an arroyo with scattered pools, some of them deep, just before sundown. Grass hardly fit for fodder grew thick and marshy. The water was clear, but only slightly better than the Pecos. The cowboys had a rough time getting the cattle bedded — it seemed that at least a quarter of the cattle bogged in the marshes and had to be roped and pulled out. The skeletons of man and beast they had to work around unnerved the younger drovers. Even Audie, who had witnessed worse in the war, seemed affected by the boneyard and the eerie blackened shell of a stagecoach station occupied now only by the unceasing winds.

"I hate this place," Mutt said as he tried to pull a braying steer out of the mud. "I thought DeWitt County was the butt end of civilization, but this here country is like knocking on the devil's door."

"Aw, shut up," Audie said, dismounting from his horse and wading into the water.

Dud threw another loop around its horns, and with two mustangs pulling and Audie pushing, they at last got the frightened and bawling animal out. By then, the wind had died down, a mugginess taking its place that had the drovers covered in as much sweat as the bogged down steer and Audie dripping with water. Ponder rode by on his way to rope another steer out of the mud and complained that all his teeth were hurting.

That night, the wind began to blow again, bringing with it crashing thunder and blinding strikes of blue lightning that seemed impossibly long and wide. None of them had ever witnessed such a spectacular show of force by Mother Nature. The vast emptiness of the land and sky made the bolts of lightning seem like a personal condemnation of their presence there. Horrendous thunder deafened other noises — in an instant, the rain swooping down in sheets drenched everything.

It took all drovers rounding the herd, pushing them back into a circle, to keep the cattle from stampeding. Lightning would land on the tips of their horns, jumping from steer to steer, scaring the younger cowhands who had never seen it before. Above the howling wind and thunder, Dud heard Audie calling.

"Mutt's been hit!"

Dud spurred Ned in the direction of Audie's voice. He found Audie down on his knees, next to a crumpled Mutt on the ground. Dud jumped from Ned's back, dragging Mutt away from the frightened herd.

"Stretch him out!" Dud hollered above the wind. They pulled on Mutt until they had him lying flat on his back. Dud removed Mutt's hat and opened his clothes before standing back. He shouted at Audie above the howling, "Let the rain wet him down!"

Mutt remained ominously still as Dud and Audie watched and waited. Cascades of water poured over his body, running over his unkempt brown hair in rivulets. In a minute, he shook his head and opened his eyes. Dud and Audie helped him to stand.

"You gonna be all right?" Dud yelled.

Mutt looked dazed, but he nodded. Dud stuck his hat back on his head. Audie handed him his reins, and they got back on their own mounts, turning to keep the herd from trampling over one another in a frantic race that might end at the bottom of a canyon.

After a night that seemed to last an eternity, all was calm in the morning. The sun glistened on the wet grass; otherwise, the hard ground looked untouched by water. The drovers teased Mutt, saying he had mocked God, and God had let the devil knock on his door. Mutt wholeheartedly agreed, but other than shaking his head and blinking his eyes every once in a while, he was back to his normal self. Except for the bodies of three dead heifers with black streaks on their hides, it was as if the night before had been nothing but a bad dream.

Surviving the night without a stampede put the drovers in a good mood at breakfast, despite their lack of sleep. While most women would have wanted to linger in the safety of the fort, Florine gave every appearance of being glad to be away from it. Nonetheless, she stayed in a foul mood because all she had was Jemmy helping her cook, and she shot Darnell looks of disgust when his back was turned, as if leaving, being captured, and wounded had all been part of a diabolical plan to cause her more work. Much to Dud's relief, the other drovers did not share her feelings, never appearing to resent Darnell's forced inactivity.

Dud's eyes were getting so accustomed to scanning the far-reaching horizon, he found himself blinking like Mutt when he had to read the map. Escondido Spring looked to be about nine miles or so away. He rolled up the map in leather to leave in Ponder's care while he prepared to scout out the lay of the land.

"Escondido Spring is where Bigfoot had to fight off an Indian attack, probably, nigh on ten years or so ago," Ponder said, taking the map for safekeeping.

"Where has Bigfoot Wallace been that he didn't have to fight off an Indian attack?" Dud said, not too interested in the exploits of Ponder's friends.

"Just saying," Ponder shrugged.

Dud left on Jax without responding. Beside the faint road was nothing but chaparral, poor grazing, and prickly pears. Squawteat Peak appeared in the distance, giving him forlorn thoughts of his ex-wife. The land around it was flatter, however, and would present no problem to the longhorns. Dud soon found its evenness deceptive. Undulating terrain hid low spots deep enough for men to hide in. By the time he approached the spring, it had become hilly. He rode, always wary that someone might be secreted in a gully or behind a hill. Nevertheless, he reached the spring without incident.

The water flowed from under the shelf of a limestone bluff. Surrounded by barren ground and rocks, the gushing spring nevertheless ran clear and beautiful into a creek. Not a good place for grazing cattle, but perfect for watering.

Dud rode closer, letting Jax put his lips into the water to drink. As in the last place, bones of unfortunate humans and animals littered the ground. Dud, his eyes scanning the scattering of grasses growing farther down the creek, at first did not see anything unusual. He was about to dismount when he paused, Ponder's warning coming back to him.

Dud turned his eyes away, glancing around. When he turned back to the rushes, he let his eyes bore into the grasses while at the same time trying to appear casual. It was then he noticed brown humps that should not have been there.

He looked around again as if he had not seen anything. With slow deliberate motions, he turned Jax around. They left the campgrounds just as they would have under ordinary circumstances.

Tense, ready to be attacked at any moment, he forced himself to relax. Even though he figured the Indians were waiting for him to bring the horses to them, he half expected to have an arrow put in his back at any moment.

He controlled his movements until he was

well out of sight of the spring. When he thought there was no possibility of being seen, he put the spurs to Jax.

Ponder was the first one to catch sight of Dud dashing for camp. He turned and said something to the others, and they went for their rifles. Dud pulled up to Ponder, stopping Jax short, both of them winded.

"Indians are there waiting to attack."

He dismounted from Jax, removing his saddle.

"Do you want Ned, Señor Dud?"

"Si." Dud replied and Henry led Jax away to exchange him for Ned.

They held a conference, Dud and Ponder getting into it as Dud expected.

"We can't both go. You've got to stay here, Uncle Ponder. Somebody's got to lead the drive if I get kilt. What if they kill both of us?"

Ponder would not be left out of this fight.

"Shug and Billy Sol are capable of leading these here cattle anywhere."

After another few more minutes of arguing, Dud gave in.

"All right, you old hard head." He turned to Henry and Barefoot. "I'm not going to order you to ride into a trap. But I need to leave half the horses here and take the other half with us to fool them into believing we are bringing all of them. Will you herd them?"

"It will be an honor, Señor Dud."

Dud stared at the young man. Of all the crew, he had been the most honest about his fear of Indians, and after seeing what had nearly happened to Darnell, for him to go along took a tremendous amount of courage.

"I'll go," Barefoot said.

Dud had ceased to be surprised by Barefoot's willingness to do anything. He nodded in gratitude.

"Henry and Barefoot will be with the horses. Ponder will be driving the wagon. I'll be riding beside him. We need two men inside the wagon."

Toomey and Mutt immediately volunteered.

"No, you won't," Audie said. "I will."

Before anyone could say anything else, Florine spoke.

"I'm going."

They were so shocked, no one could speak. They all stared at Florine.

"I can shoot as good as any man, shotgun or rifle. If you think I'm going to let those savages get to my boys, you got another thing coming."

"Ma!" Shug and Billy Sol protested together.

"I have spoken," Florine said. "Dudford's right. You got to stay with the herd."

Dud turned to Ponder, expecting an outburst. But even Ponder looked dumbfounded.

"What happened to Darnell must have pushed Florine over the edge," Ponder said out of the corner of his mouth.

"I'm just glad she's on our side and not theirs," Dud said out of the corner of his.

They gave in with helpless shrugs, dispersing to divide the horses and prepare the wagon.

The group started back to the spring, Audie and Florine hiding inside the wagon. Dud led the way, riding slightly in front of Ponder as he sat at the reins. Barefoot and Henry had half the remuda behind them, pretending they were going to let the horses drink first before the others brought in the cattle. The rush of energy and fear that had sent Dud flying back to camp had disappeared. All he felt now was the unnatural calmness that came just before the train wrecked.

When they drew closer, Dud did not know if their ruse had fooled the Indians or not. The air around them was so peaceful, he wondered if he had imagined seeing the brown humps of Indians lying low.

That thought had no sooner passed through his mind when arising out of the grasses came terrifying yells, and with guns firing, arrows singing, and black hair flying behind them, the Mescalero Apaches attacked.

Dud began firing — Ponder immediately turned the wagon up a hill, with Dud following and shooting as he rode. Waves of Apaches swept forward, more than Dud had imagined. The cover of the wagon flew up. Audie and Florine began return fire. From the hill, they rained devastating flames upon the advancing Apache. Surprised by the repeating rifles, they broke into a confused run, mowed down by the smoking guns.

In less than two minutes, it was over. Dud looked down upon the bodies of the braves. He shook his head and looked to make sure none of his people were hurt. Ponder sat in the wagon, biting off a chaw of tobacco. Audie climbed out of the wagon and stood next to Ponder. Florine stayed rooted, staring with expressionless eyes at the bodies of the blood-soaked Apaches.

Without a word, Dud reined Ned back to camp to fetch the others. Henry and Barefoot had taken off with the remuda in that direction as soon as the firing started.

That night, knowing the Apache were superstitious about angry spirits arising from the dead who hadn't been buried immediately, Ponder had the bodies placed in strategic spots where Indians might try to sneak up. They were still there the next morning when Dud left to scout what lie ahead.

He rode out of a long draw from the lowlands into a world of weird windswept mesas and sugarloaf mountains. He traveled the road, winding in and out of the increasingly soaring and turreted mesas and peaked hills. The loneliness of the landscape was overwhelming. Because of the Indian attack the previous day, Audie had wanted to ride with him. But Dud knew that big boned Audie would have a hard time outracing Indians, and he had refused to let him ride along. Instead, his eyes scanned the outlying country sharper than they had ever done before. The cunning Apache and Comanche were a thousand times more proficient at the quick hit and disappearance into the landscape than any Yankee he had ever fought.

To Dud's relief, the grass became thicker. The captain had said there was a creek to the north, but the water was salty and rank.

He avoided it, keeping to the west on gravelly soil and riding almost upon Comanche Springs before realizing it was there. The springs caused him to blink — it was like finding an oasis in the desert. He rode up and down the stream created by six large springs — finding the water as clear and pure as had been described. Dud got down to drink — it tasted of minerals, but not the strong alkaline of the Pecos. Despite his pleasure, he remained wary. The springs flowed in the crossroads of the Military Road and an ancient trail used by the Plains Indians of the north on their raids down into Mexico. While there, Dud found the nearby remains of Fort Stockton, burned to a rubble, and came across five skeletons lying near the water where they had been attacked as they drank.

Dud, on a feisty little copper dun, headed back to the Escondido. Indians liked to lie in wait on a man's return trip, and he was doubly on guard, but had no problem reaching the herd.

Returning to the springs, Dud ordered the wagons ahead of the herd so they could have fresh water before the cattle entered. Nobody had to be reminded to stay on guard.

The younger cowboys were both impressed and disconcerted by the eerie landscape.

"Man alive, we ain't gotten nothing like this in DeWitt County," Mutt said, craning his neck in all directions.

"Move along, Mutt," Dud said. "We got a hard fifteen more miles to go before dark."

Once the cattle smelled water, they rushed forward. There was enough time to let them graze before bedding them down, and the cowboys took full advantage of it.

With Florine's wagon behind a mott of small trees, the men stripped and jumped in the water. Dud and Audie said they would guard the horses, and as they rode by Florine's wagon, they could hear her fussing at the boys.

"You boys stay here and help with supper," Florine ordered Will and Jemmy.

Will looked crestfallen. Jemmy stared at the water longingly.

Before Dud could intervene, Ponder appeared by the wagon.

"I'll help you, you old bat. Will, you go on up the creek with the men-folks. Jemmy, you go jump in over yonder for a minute or two and then run back here to help us."

The children appeared satisfied with that, but to Dud, it did not seem fair.

"Let . . ." he began, but Florine interrupted.

"You just mind your own business, Dudford, and get on out of here."

Ponder motioned for Dud to leave. With a shrug, he reined his horse toward the remuda. Audie followed with a chuckle.

"What are you laughing at?"

"Ponder and Florine, side by side shooting up Indians to save their lives, and now it's all over, they still hate one another."

Dud turned to Audie. "You better be glad. Because if they ever team up, they'll be no handling them."

When it came time to bed the cattle down for the night, Audie questioned Dud's judgment.

"Why not just keep the wagons where they are? We ain't gonna have no more troubles out of Indians tonight."

It was tempting to leave the wagons beside the springs. Dud thought about it and shook his head. "No, let's get away from this tall grass where anybody could hide. One slip in this country, and a man's dead."

Audie shrugged and let it drop.

Chapter Nineteen

Leon Holes, nine miles away, consisted of deep blue pools in a valley in the middle of a vast plain. There, Dud came upon a herd of antelope drinking from clear water in a green oasis. Three little hills to the west kept watch over them. Tired of salt pork, on impulse Dud raised his rifle and fired. The antelope scattered.

More careful now than ever that he had given himself away with a rifle shot, Dud circled the springs, making his way to the fallen antelope like a prudent old maid walking down a disreputable alley, but he could see no signs of fresh horse manure or recent hoof prints. Not taking any chances, he dismounted, skinning the antelope with one eye on the flesh and the other on his surroundings, expecting Indians to come swooping down from the hills at any minute. He dunked the meat in the water to cool it down, washing the hide. The water tasted of sulfur, but was drinkable. He circled again, evaluating the site before going back to the antelope, wrapping it in the hide and tying it to Jax's back. The horse did not faunch; he had plenty of experience carrying wild, and not so wild, game — whatever Dud could find to eat during the war.

Dud rode back to the camp at Comanche Springs without incident. Darnell, Will, and Florine were waiting for him next to the wagons and watched as he threw the antelope in the back of one of them. Ponder, along with Mutt and Toomey, rode their horses into camp to see what Dud had brought.

"It ain't quail eggs, but it ain't bad."

"You don't expect me to butcher that, do you?" Florine fumed. "I've got enough on my hands with Ponder off on a horse instead of helping me cook."

Darnell ducked his head in embarrassment. He had tried to help Florine and been rebuffed. With every word and movement, she made him feel guilty for being wounded.

"I'll take care of it, Miss Florine," Mutt said. "Do we have time to do it this morning, Boss? The quicker antelope is dressed the better the meat."

He wasn't telling Dud anything he didn't already know. "Do it. The grazing is better here than up yonder anyway." He looked around for Will and Jemmy.

"You boys gather as much firewood as you can. We'll be getting into some mighty poor country."

With wet burlap sacks keeping the butchered antelope cool, and as much firewood as the possum bellies under the wagons could hold, Will climbed in next to Darnell. Florine, still sputtering, climbed into her wagon and took the reins of her mules. Darnell and Will followed Dud, while Florine stayed back.

On that level land, with no rise to climb so all the cowhands could see him, Dud had to suffice with a wave of his hand, motioning for Shug and Billy Sol to get the cattle moving. He rode back to urge the others onward.

The trip to Leon Holes proved uneventful. The antelope had left, and there was no indication of anyone else having been there. Will and Jemmy, when Florine wasn't hollering at them or Ponder sending them on errands, stood at the edge of the pools dropping rocks in, trying to decipher how deep the water was. Florine muttered something about not signing on to work in an orphanage or a hospital.

"Where's a Comanche when you need

one?" Audie said, giving her a dirty look as he poured himself a cup of coffee.

As soon as the Hollister boys finished their chores, they asked to explore the nearby stagecoach station. The rock walls had partially fallen and only a few charred rafters of the roof remained. After being cautioned about snakes, the boys headed out with the ever-handy shovel they used to pop snakes on the head and otherwise mutilate them into death.

The boys had not been gone long when they came running back to camp, their faces bright with excitement.

"Mr. Dud! Mr. Ponder! We found buried treasure! Come look!"

Dud exchanged glances with Ponder. Ponder, who had been cornered into helping Florine cook, looked down at a pot of beans bubbling on the campfire. He shifted his eyes to Florine.

"Take over, Florine," he said.

She retorted with a few choice words, but Ponder ignored her, letting the Hollister boys lead him to the burned-out shell. Dud followed, wondering what they could have found in a broken-down shanty station-house in the heart of no-man's-land.

Kicking aside rocks and charred timbers, they entered. A blackened trap door had been dug up and tossed aside. The four of them stood at the edge of a large square hole, peering down into a darkened cellar.

"There's stuff down there," Will said.

"Let me have the shovel," Dud said.

Will handed it to him, and Dud, after testing the sinew-tied ladder leading downward, descended. He stood motionless, letting his eyes accustom to the darkness. His ears strained for the sound of rattlers, but heard nothing. A table stood in the middle of the room, and on it, a candle. He lit the candle, and grasping it in one hand and the shovel in the other, he looked around the small room. Shelf after shelf contained jugs. There didn't seem to be anything else. He searched the cobwebbed cellar for snakes, but found none.

Going to the opening, he looked up and called. "You can come on now."

The boys scampered down; their eyes wide. Moving slower, Ponder made his way down, being careful of his head so he didn't knock his hat off. He looked around the room.

"What is it?" Jemmy asked.

Ponder took one of the jugs, blew some dust off and uncorked it. He took a whiff.

"Moonshine," he said, looking at Dud.

"Can we keep it? We found it. The jugs

are nice."

They looked like ordinary clay pottery, but Dud did not want to dampen the boys' enthusiasm over their find. He turned to Ponder.

"What do you think? We got room?"

Ponder stared at the jug in his hand. "We can make room. Might come in handy sometimes."

"I don't see how. Might cause nothing but trouble, but I reckon we'll deal with it."

That evening, they feasted on son-of-a-gun stew made with the entrails and roasted meat. Strips of flesh seasoned with salt and pepper hung over a low fire to make into jerky. Because Mutt had done the butchering, they allowed him the entire tongue. He sighed like a happy puppy.

There were no secrets in camp. They talked of nothing but the jugs in the wagon — how long they had been there, who had made it, was it mescal made from the maguey plants dotting the West Texas landscape?

"If I see any of you sneaking over there for a snort, I'm taking a knotted rope to you," Dud warned. "We'll save it for a celebration." He looked at Will. "And that includes you, pardner."

Will blushed, and Dud suppressed a grin,

knowing the boy had been thinking of trying to filch a sip. Dud's thoughts turned, resulting in a smothered sigh. The antelope meat and jugs of liquor had taken their minds off Indian depredations for a while, but none of them could afford to relax their vigil. The awe-inspiring mountains in the distance hid a thousand shadows.

In the morning, Dud found the next watering spot little more than muddy pools of sulfur water. Enough to survive on and that was all. The cattle were restless; the grazing was poor. They had left the semi-paradise of Comanche Springs with its heightened danger of attack behind. Leon Holes had been good. But the dirty, brackish water of Hackberry Ponds had more of a laxative effect than they realized, and camped in the middle of a herd of runny cow shit with cowboys who could barely stay in the saddle a couple of hours before jumping off to take care of their own business made for an unpleasant night. When Billy Sol and Shug complained to Florine, she got up and browned flour in a skillet, telling the cowboys to eat a spoonful. It helped somewhat, but there was nothing they could do for the cattle.

The next morning, Dud headed in the direction of Limpia Creek, rumored to have clear water and good grass. According to the map, the road would follow the creek to Fort Davis, thirty-something miles away. Dud had heard at Fort Lancaster the army had plans to revive Fort Davis, bringing in more buffalo soldiers. They might even be in route if the captain at Fort Lancaster had his information correct. That did little to help Dud and his crew, who knew they would be on their own in a land that harkened back to prehistoric times.

Despite the treachery the mountains surrounding it contained, the captain said Fort Davis had been a favored spot for soldiers before the war. He claimed the views were supposedly magnificent, the water pure, and unlike the rest of Texas, blessed with a moderate climate. As Dud rode in that direction with rifle in hand, he tried not to let his senses be lulled by the peaceful surroundings. Unbidden thoughts of his ex-wife began to creep into his mind, and he began to wonder about the girl in San Antonio Barefoot was in love with.

Sounds of shots being fired woke him from his reverie. He twisted, looking around, but could see nothing. Pausing to listen, he could tell the shots were not coming from the direction of the herd, so they would not be from the guns of his drovers.

The sounds came in furious pops, signaling it was not hunters.

Whatever it was, it wasn't his fight. He had a responsibility to the men under him and the cattle and horses they were charged with. Whoever it was would have to do without his interference. The Washburns did not get involved in fights they had no dog in.

On the other hand, the Washburns often succumbed to the irresistible urge to put their dog into the fight. Dud turned the little mustang, not toward the herd, but in the direction of the gunfire.

He rode onward, hiding in scrubby brush as he neared the sounds. Approaching an abandoned stagecoach stop, he saw Indians surrounding it, and by the looks of them, Mescalero Apache. About fifty braves were shooting a barrage of arrows, along with bullets from a few heavy caliber rifles, toward the rock walls of what remained of the station. From behind the walls, rifle fire was returned, but it became clear as Dud watched and listened that the men on the outside greatly outnumbered the men on the inside.

For all Dud knew, the men on the inside could be a few Comanche who had wandered too far into Mescalero territory.

"But I dislike the odds," he muttered under his breath and raised his rifle.

The Apache were surprised by the rapid fire from his rifle as Dud picked off one by one. The addition of his fire brought renewed vigor and stronger rounds from behind the walls. In only a few seconds, the remaining Apache, unsure of the number of men they were now dealing with, decided they had enough and with much yelling and screeching to hide the indignity of retreat, beat it out of there.

Dud remained partially hidden by the trees. The men inside were just as reluctant to show themselves. Seconds ticked away. Dud shifted on the mustang he dared not dismount, prepared to wait.

"Quién va allá?" a voice called out.

"Amigo gringo."

Two men came out from behind the wall, hesitant and unsure who their rescuer would be. They were both young Mexican men, dressed not as peasants, or bandits, not even vaqueros, but as caballeros — proud horsemen. Their flat top hats were covered in dust and ashes, as were the black jackets and pants they wore. They still wore red sashes around their waist, but the color had faded to something indescribable. Dirt, however, could not hide the aurora of dash and style clinging to them. In his faded torn clothes, sweat and blood-stained hat, Dud knew he must look like poor Texas trash to them.

As they spoke in Spanish, Dud recognized the dialect of interior Mexico, not the border Tex-Mex he was used to. He responded in Spanish, asking if they spoke English.

"*Si.* Yes, we speak English."

Thereafter the conversation took place in English. Dud explained about the cattle drive and invited them back to camp.

They exchanged glances. They clearly wanted to accept, but each gave a slight negative shake of the head before refusing Dud with polite phrases and thanking him for coming to their aid.

"We are on a quest, looking for a young woman," the taller one said. He swallowed, as if in pain. "My fiancée — his sister. She was kidnapped on her way to our wedding. We were to be married at her cousin's hacienda in Las Cruces. All the men with her were killed. We have been searching for weeks."

The shorter one looked down at the fallen Apache around them. "I must see if any of these *demonios salvajes* are still alive and can be made to talk."

He left Dud and his would-be brother-in-law to pick up various bodies by the scalp to see if they were still breathing. He had put his knife against the throat of one when Dud spoke to the tragic bridegroom.

"Is there anything we can do to help you find the young lady, besides keeping our eyes out for her?"

He shook his head. "No, señor."

Dud turned to go, when the young man stopped him.

"The mountain road goes high and there is no water to speak of on the pass. As long as there is no rain, you would do better to take your cattle into the canyon and follow the creek. It is rough, narrow, and you will have to cross many times, but your cattle will fare better, and you will be somewhat safer from the Apache who will be looking down on you the entire time. There they can only attack you from the front or the rear."

Dud stared at him a second. "Much obliged."

He wanted to ask more questions. Had they started out with many men? What was the territory farther west like? But they would not want to interrupt their search long enough to answer his questions. Dud left the caballeros to their desperate hunt and wished them well.

Chapter Twenty

Unable to feel otherwise, Dud returned to camp tense and unhappy. He found the others the same, standing around the wagons looking strained and on edge, as if instinctively knowing the trouble that lie before them.

Dud dismounted, removing his saddle from the little mustang he rode. Henry arrived, standing next to him. He handed the reins to Henry who attached a lead rope, taking the horse back to the remuda. Dud put his saddle down. He leaned over, grasped the coffee pot and poured himself a cup. He blew on it, swirling it in the tin cup to cool before taking a sip.

"Speak up, boy," Ponder said. "Tell us if we is facing Comanches, Apaches, or Kickapoos next."

"I ran into some Apaches," Dud said and explained about the caballeros.

The men grew silent, thinking about the

young woman.

"Interior Mexico?" Audie said with a shake of his head. "They'll never find her. But I admire their grit."

Dud nodded. He wanted to get their mind off the woman and wasn't ready to go into detail about the canyon until he had scouted it. Instead, he concentrated on the hurdle immediately before them.

"It's going to be rough — mountainous, narrow trails, almost no grass for the next twenty or so miles."

"We going to push the cattle through?"

Shug and Billy Sol had joined them. They listened, watching Dud through narrowed eyes.

"It's rugged. It will be hard on the herd."

"It's going to be hard holding cattle through the night with no food or water for two days," Audie said, always stating the obvious when it was bad news. "And they're already dehydrated because of this briny water. And what about the horses?"

With a grimace, Dud downed the last of his coffee before setting the cup down.

"There's a spring with enough water for the horses, but not the cattle. If something stampedes the cattle at night when we are on the move, it will take us weeks of searching through hills and valleys. And then we'll never find all of them."

"Dud's right, Cousin Audie," Billy Sol said. "These here longhorns are tough; they can take it. Ain't that right, Shug?"

Shug nodded. "Thunderstorm come up out here at night with them moving, we won't have much of a chance of holding them. As long as we got water for us and the horses, we'll make it."

With that agreed upon, they made preparations to gather the herd. Darnell took Dud aside when all the others except Ponder had left.

"Boss, you think those Injuns going to come back and attack us?"

"There is always that chance, Darnell. All you can see out here is old bones around burned and wrecked stagecoach stops."

Darnell nodded. There was nothing to be done about it. He would have to face his fears.

"I's be ready to start cowboying again. That riding in that wagon, that don't set with me too well."

Dud suppressed a grin. Darnell was a true cowboy. "If you think you can handle it, go ahead. Ponder here will take over wagon duties again."

Darnell strode away with a happy lilt to his shoulders. Indians may attack him, but at least he would be on the back of a horse and not stuck with a wagon. Ponder looked after him.

"And here I was thinking I was free of Florine for a while."

With that, Ponder turned to go back to his wagon, while Dud went to fetch a fresh mount of his own, shaking his head as he did.

By the time Dud reached the remuda, Henry had gotten wind of the caballeros and their story of the beautiful kidnapped bride-to-be. His hands shook in repressed anger as he held the lead rope of a spotted mustang, and his face had paled.

"Is it true, Señor Dud? About the young señorita?"

Dud nodded as he threw his blanket and saddle over the back of the mustang. "Yes, Henry."

Henry stood motionless as Dud slipped the bridle in the horse's mouth and patted him.

"We'll do what we can, Henry, but she could be a thousand miles from here, or dead."

Henry's fist clinched, and Dud cut him off before he could speak.

"I know you want to catch up with the caballeros and help them in their search.

But that is their job, and your job is here with us. It may be that we are able to learn something about the señorita as we go on our way."

Henry swallowed. "*Si,* Señor Dud." But it was hard for him to accept, and Dud left him alone with his musings.

The two wagons stayed in front of the herd, but within sight. Will and Jemmy, happy to escape Florine's caustic tongue, went back to riding drag with Barefoot.

Their happiness was short-lived when they passed a buffalo hollow, and Dud made them get down and pick up chips for the campfire. But they did it without grumbling.

For two days they wound their way through intermittent rolling plains, mountain passes, and canyons, all of them made dismal by the continual bawling of hungry, thirsty cattle. On the first night, Dud slept lightly, listening to the sounds of the drovers making their rounds. He heard the sound of Darnell's favorite night horse, but not Darnell. He rose from his pallet, and walking past sleeping cattle in the dark, he softly called Darnell's name.

"What is it, Boss?" Darnell asked, mirroring Dud's low tones. "You spooked me."

"You're not singing to the cattle, Darnell."

Darnell did not speak right away. In the

darkness, Dud could barely make out his form or that of the horse.

"Boss, I can't. I opens my mouth, but I gets choked up, and I can't sing nothing." He ended with a strangled sob, and Dud knew he was struggling to keep from crying. It cut Dud to the quick, but he had no choice.

"Darnell, I'm ordering you to sing to these here cattle. Do you hear me?"

"Yessir," Darnell said. He began to sing, almost imperceptive at first, a mournful gospel that would have brought tears to the church choir back home. His voice wobbled, but as he urged his horse forward, it began to come out steadier.

Dud looked after him and sighed. Darnell would be like Fitz and the rest of them, on the outside okay, but on the inside, full of cracks and fissures that might not ever heal. Dud turned back to his bedroll determined to move on and not dwell on it.

On the afternoon of the second day, Dud scouted out the small spring a few miles off the Military Road where he had encountered the Mescalero. Uneasy, but unable to find anything untoward, he went back for the remuda so the horses could drink. Ponder could outshoot anybody, even on horseback, and turning the reins of the oxen over to Will, he joined Dud and Henry on the trek back to the springs. Despite the stone ruins of the nearby stagecoach station that had witnessed several Indian attacks, trees hung over the springs unperturbed by violence. That it was pretty and peaceful did not stop three pairs of eyes from continually scanning the horizon. It was with relief when they began driving the horses back to the herd.

They were not more than a quarter of a mile along the trail when they heard the cry of the Apache. A swarm of Apaches on horseback came down the canyon, yelling, screaming, waving spears and rifles, and heading straight for them. A running battle ensued until the repeated fire of the Henry rifles convinced the Apaches to fall back.

Toomey rode to meet them as they came within view of the herd. His eyes scanned the horses until he located the one belonging to his uncle. Blood drained from his sunburned face as he listened to Dud's account of the shots exchanged as they raced with the horses back to camp.

"I never should have let you take my uncle's horse," Toomey said. "I should have gone with you. I should have gone with him."

"He's all right, Toomey. He's not hurt,"

Ponder said. But nothing any of them said could console Toomey.

"I can't let him out of my sight again like that," Toomey repeated over and over. "My uncle, he'll kill me if anything happens to that horse."

Dud shook his head, giving up. Toomey had bundled every worry and anxiety of the trail and placed it on the apparition of a foul-tempered uncle back home.

Later, when discussing the clash around the campfire, Dud admitted he did not know why the Apache had waited to attack, unless they were hoping on the element of surprise.

"Yeah, being attacked from the rear flank always threw the Yanks off, too," Audie said. "Do you think it was the same ones you had the run-in with earlier?"

Dud thought for a minute. "I don't know."

Nobody got any sleep that night. The restlessness of the cattle, the fear of Apaches and a stampede, kept all eyes open. At breakfast, Mutt spoke what everyone was feeling.

"I never was so glad to see sunrise in my whole life."

They twisted their way through rough, hilly country, trying to keep the cattle far enough upwind of the springs they didn't smell the water and trample one another trying to reach it. The cattle grew recalcitrant, stopping, refusing to move and trying to make fight with each other and anything else that got in their way. The cracks of slapping ropes filled the air, along with curses that would have made a hog ranch pimp blush. It drove thoughts of a beautiful young Mexican maiden held captive by a band of Mescalero from their minds, and it seemed to Dud that he was the only one left on the lookout for a surprise attack.

Leaving the cattle and riding ahead, Dud entered a valley surrounded by sheer mountains — so striking it almost took his breath away. He did not know if it really was as stunning as he thought, or if the relief of seeing verdant grass and a shallow creek rushing madly over craggy rocks made it that way.

He went back to tell the others, and their enthusiasm at being in such close reach of grazing land and water conveyed itself to the cattle. They perked up, eager to move ahead. The horses began stepping livelier as the prospect of deliverance flooded the faces of their riders.

When they reached the valley, some of the cattle hurried to the water. Others felt content to slow down their pace long enough to pull at the tall grass. The cowboys whooped with joy at the sight of something clear and wet.

After watering, Dud helped spread the cattle out over the lush pasture. Ponder rode up beside him, his hat wet where he had dipped it into the creek.

"Resilient critters, ain't they?"

Dud nodded, staring at the welcome sight. "Don't know if the rest of us will be in as good a shape when we get to New Mexico. Even Mutt and Audie are starting to look poorly. If anybody was to come up on us sideways, we'd be almost invisible."

The cooler night air held nothing but the sounds of peaceful sleep as they bedded down. Ponder and Florine had not argued. Billy Sol and Shug had looked relieved and hand-fed General Sherman before beginning their watch. Henry, Darnell, Toomey, and Mutt ate with ravenous abandonment.

In the early morning hours, Barefoot met Dud at the remuda. Barefoot still wore his hair slicked back with smelly pomade, but it now hung below collar. His dark eyes sank into his skull like two unfathomable dark pits.

"May I explore the canyon with you?"

"If you want," Dud said, surprised that after the past few hard days, Barefoot did not want to rest at camp with the others while the cattle grazed.

Dud did not question him, however, but set out to investigate the canyon, their sure-footed mustangs stepping lightly over rocks of varying sizes and shapes. Iron pyrite covered one section; other than that, they all had one thing in common — they looked as if they had been there since time began.

They came in sight of what seemed to be a miniature forest.

"What the devil is that?" Dud asked.

Riding closer, they found a vast bed of cholla cactus reaching up eight to twelve feet, and all of them covered in spines.

"Everything in this country has a thorn on it," Barefoot said, his moody eyes glancing with disdain at the "forest" they had found.

Dud gave him a sideways glance, relieved in a way that Barefoot no longer felt the need to hide every emotion. The two men urged their horses leftward and continued, giving the cactus a wide berth.

Once found, the canyon was just as the caballeros described. Good grass, shallow, fastmoving water that was more of a tortuous winding creek than a river. The imposing columnar walls of the surrounding canyon rose eight hundred feet in some places. There were places in the canyon so narrow, only three of four longhorns could get through at a time. And they would be crisscrossing the creek constantly to stay on grassy ground. Despite the black walls of the canyon that seemed to hover over them frowning, the bed of the Limpia covered itself with a variety of showy stones in multiple colors.

When Dud figured they had ridden far enough in the canyon for one day, he and Barefoot dismounted to let the horses drink once more before heading back to camp. They picked up a few of the stones and pocketed them to show the others.

Barefoot stopped to raise his head, stretching his neck, staring at the sheer rock walls. "If a hard rain comes, it will flood this canyon and kill us."

"If we go on high ground, it will wear the cattle down even more trying to climb those flinty mountains with almost no grass and very little water," Dud said.

Barefoot nodded. "We are stuck between a rock and a hard place, but then we have been almost since the beginning of this trip."

Dud agreed. They stood silent watching their surroundings. Dud felt Barefoot wanted to say something more, so he did not rush to get back into the saddle.

Barefoot began, looking as if he was casting about for the right words to express himself.

"I know you wanted this trip to make enough money to entice your wife back. I wanted to earn a reputation as a tough man in order to impress a girl into marriage." He paused and looked Dud in the eye.

"Do you think there is any possibility she will want me? Or have I been risking my life for a foolish dream?"

Dud thought for a moment before speaking, turning his eyes upward to the ridgeline above them. He looked back to Barefoot.

"There is no telling what a woman will do. But a man has to have dreams, doesn't he?"

Barefoot nodded. "If I am honest, I will admit there are days I no longer care if I live or die out here in this vast wilderness."

"We all feel that way from time to time. But we have other people and animals depending on us, so we have to go on regardless of how we feel."

Barefoot nodded. Dud went to Jax, gathering the reins, and Barefoot did the same. They got back on their horses and with a squeeze of a thigh and a gentle cluck, headed back to camp.

The others had just finished eating supper when Dud and Barefoot returned. Will and Jemmy took their horses while Dud and Barefoot went to the campfire to get the scrapings from the bottom of the pan for their supper.

"What do you think?" Ponder asked.

Dud, crouched and eating with one knee on the ground and the other propped up, looked at Ponder.

"Your tooth been hurting?"

"Nope. What do you want to know for?"

Dud explained about the advice of the caballeros. He pulled the small stones from his pocket to show them.

Audie rubbed one that resembled a garnet between his fingers. "You think we can trust them caballeros?"

"Don't see why not. I did them a good turn; they was just returning the favor."

When it came to cattle, nobody thought about how ugly Shug was or how dumb Billy Sol looked. While the men discussed it, every eye kept glancing to the two brothers to see what they would say.

"Well, Billy Sol, Shug," Dud said. "I vote for the canyon. We don't know if there will be another blade of grass between here and New Mexico. What do you say?"

Billy Sol looked at Shug, unwilling to

voice his opinion until Shug had said his piece.

"You say your tooth ain't been a bothering you, Cousin Ponder?" Shug said.

"Nope, but that don't mean it won't start hurting powerful bad when we get about midway inside that canyon."

Shug nodded. He thought for a moment, every eye on him and every mouth silent while he considered their choices. Mutt, as much or more than the others, held Shug's cow sense in the highest esteem.

"I'm with Cousin Dud, take the grass and water while we can."

Mutt nodded. Even Audie did not object.

That night, when the others had drifted to sleep, Dud stirred the coals of the campfire. Under that vast sky with its brilliant stars, he felt like a small and helpless speck of humanity. As the coals caught and blazed red once more, he removed his ex-wife's letters from his pocket. He took one out and opening the envelope, held the letter near the light of the fire so he could reread it once again. Were the words of love she wrote for him, or just some ideal of love she had? He sighed, putting the letter back and replacing it with the others. The flames leaped and danced in front of him. He wasn't ready to give up just yet.

No one said anything to Dud the next morning, but every quick glance holding the hint of pity told him they all knew about the letters and his late-night reading. He ignored the looks and called the drovers around him for a powwow.

"There will be places Indians could swoop down on us from the top of the canyon, but it would be rough going for them and not to their advantage. Instead, a bigger threat would be an attack from the rear."

He let that sink in, his eyes going from man to man.

"But I imagine they will let us reach the head of the canyon where they'll be waiting for us."

Dud laid out his plans. The wagons would travel in the middle of the herd along with the horses. The dust, heretofore miserable, would be minimal in the rocky canyon. Shug and Billy Sol would stay on point; Audie and Barefoot would ride drag. Nobody complained.

CHAPTER TWENTY-ONE

They traveled the canyon four days, the cattle spread out in a long line. The canyon was so winding, most of the time when Dud and the drovers looked back, they could only see a dozen longhorns at a time. The weather remained calm, although the wind blew cooler down the walls of the canyon. Any man who had a jacket wore it. The rest of them cut holes in the old blankets and quilts brought along for that purpose and poked their heads through to make serapes. The walls of the canyon, the sound of rushing water tumbling over river rocks, the cool weather, combined with the thick grass to bring a sense of peace and contentment to the cattle. There was no heightened fear of a sudden stampede other than the normal attentiveness a cowboy carried with a herd.

The same could not be said of the Apaches. The drovers knew they were never truly out of their sight. Sometimes they would see a line of Indians containing one chief made obvious by his many feathers with forty to fifty braves staring down at them from atop the canyon. Other times, it would only be two or three. Only a fool would believe others were not lurking and waiting. Nevertheless, a calm came over the men, too. It was not a lack of alertness or apathy, but a sense of acceptance. They watched and waited, too. In the meantime, they herded the cattle down the creek, back and forth, stopping to pick up unusually pretty and colorful rocks along the way to take home, all the while knowing they might not ever reach home.

Dud rode up and down the long thin line. He relieved Audie and Barefoot, staying with the drag so they could ride to the middle of the herd and eat whatever Ponder and Florine had prepared. Sometimes Dud was able to ride ahead and flush out game, and they ate venison and turkey, along with wild watercress that grew in abundance. Dud did not have to worry about the herd stampeding at the sound of rifle fire — they were too strung out. One memorable early morning, Dud came upon a bear, and they were able to feast upon the delectable fat before it turned rancid.

They paused long enough to butcher the

game, eat what they wanted, and save the rest for the cool weather to age.

Dud scouted ahead, finding a draw that led to Fort Davis. He sat overlooking the abandoned fort, realizing how thick the grass was in the valley around it — perfect for cattle. He sat for a long time, watching. There were no visible signs of Indians, but the twitching hackles on the back of his neck told him they were there. He eased forward, keeping away from the fort itself.

He rode on, away from Fort Davis, scouting the Military Road. He didn't know why he wasn't attacked, for he knew they were watching him, except that perhaps they were waiting for a bigger paycheck. He found a beautiful grove of live oak trees, and although ancient, had never and would never reach the heights of the ones back home. The head of the canyon began there, and he followed it back to his herd.

He returned to find Ponder and Mutt in a long discussion over the campfire on the best way to preserve the bear meat.

"If I was at the ranch, I'd cut it in chunks and soak it in water so salty, it'd float a tater."

"Nah, Mr. Ponder, Pa just salted it down. He didn't go to all that trouble."

Dud stood in the dusk, watching and

listening for movements and sounds in the increasing darkness, listening with only half an ear to Ponder and Mutt's palaver. Nearby, Audie threw the dredges of his coffee away and set the cup down by the campfire for someone else to refill and drink from. He walked into the shadows. Dud acknowledged his presence with a nod and waited for Audie to speak.

"How many do you think are out there?"

Dud paused. "We saw fifty. I'd say seventy-five or a hundred."

"They'll be waiting for us at the head of the canyon."

"I know."

Audie opened his mouth to say more, but stopped. When the lines were drawn, and all the soldiers were in place, you didn't ask a man right before the battle commenced what he intended to do. Audie turned and left, leaving Dud to his thoughts.

Audie wouldn't have been surprised to learn that Dud had put everything from his mind except how to best complete the task he had begun. Before beginning his watch, he explained the decision he made to Ponder and Audie.

"There is sloping draw we could take the cattle down to Fort Davis and let them pasture on some good grass in that valley.

Once they've eaten, we could put them back on the road and continue from there."

"What's this 'could' business?" Ponder demanded.

"Apaches will probably be waiting for us at Fort Davis. The canyon ends in a grove of trees where it rejoins the road. They will be waiting for us there, too, but they will have to regroup and move on to catch up with us."

Ponder thought about it for a minute, while Audie remained silent.

"So, you are saying you want to go where the canyon comes out, hoping they will attack us there, and if they do, the cattle won't scatter far, instead of all over creation."

"That's right."

Audie, surprisingly enough, did not argue the point. Dud guessed he figured their goose was going to be cooked one way or another. With a nod, Dud left them and began his watch. When Dud checked on the drag later that night, Audie muttered something about feeling he was being watched, but he did not question or argue Dud's decision to bypass Fort Davis.

They arose the next morning without the usual horseplay, Ponder and Audie having told the others of Dud's plan. They passed by the sloping canyon that led to Fort Davis in silence.

The following morning, Dud arose even earlier than usual.

He had purposely held the herd back so they would arrive at the end of the canyon early in the day. He wanted every man to be as rested and ready as possible before any encounter with the Mescalero. Before Ponder and Florine had arisen to prepare breakfast, he rode to the drag and many miles beyond to make sure they weren't being followed. When satisfied they were not, he rode back to camp, and equipping Florine's wagon with guns and ammunition, he instructed Billy Sol to take Florine and the Hollister boys to bring up the drag, sending Audie and Barefoot to the front. Like so many small men, Billy Sol was a scrappy fighter who did not know fear. He would protect Florine and the Hollister boys with everything he had, saving his last bullet to put into his mother's head so she did not suffer torture before being killed.

Ponder moved his oxen and wagon to the front of the herd — Dud did not try to stop him. Audie, Shug, and Barefoot joined them, leaving the four younger men to push the cattle and horses along. Every man had been armed with as much firepower as he could carry, and no one whispered why.

Despite knowing what was waiting for them, when Dud and his four men arrived at the canyon's end in a high mountain valley set among a beautiful grove of live oak trees, they were still taken aback by the wild and horrific splendor that met them. They halted to face a line of seventy-five braves. Dud took a deep breath as the two sides sat staring at one another. The Apaches had gone all out in warpaint, various beads and feathers, holding spears with multiple scalps. They carried bows and arrows on their backs — many held old pistols and heavy rifles. The headdress of the chief contained intricate beadwork and enough feathers to reach the ground, had he dismounted. Even the horses had been decorated with warpaint, and Dud supposed he should be impressed that they thought the cowboys a formidable enough enemy to go to such lengths.

Looking at the scalps hanging from wickedly pointed spears was enough to lurch his stomach. He blinked, remembering something long forgotten. He remembered his pa saying how the pioneers had to build fires over graves to hide where people were freshly buried so the Indians didn't dig them up and take their scalps. That knowledge, that some of those scalps had been obtained in a somewhat cowardly way, put a dent in the daunting sight.

He half turned to Barefoot. "Ask them what they want."

Barefoot addressed the chief. The chief did not answer directly, but indicated with a tap of his spear that one of the braves was to speak for him. The brave on his right, already rigid, seemed to straighten his back even more while he spoke a few sentences to Barefoot.

"They want half our beef and all the horses that we are not riding."

Dud looked at the spectacle before him. He figured they knew of the firepower he and his drovers had. This magnificent display of ferociousness was intended to scare them into turning over their beef and horses without a fight. The Apache were capable of great violence and cruelty, but they were not stupid.

"Tell him I said no."

Barefoot looked at Dud. He turned back to the chief, and instead of repeating a long sentence explaining what Dud said, he responded with one word.

"Dah."

Everything Dud and Barefoot had wanted so badly in San Antonio fell away. All that was left was grit and determination to complete the drive. Dud did not turn his head, but every sense told him Ponder, Audie, and Shug were of the same mind. They were ready to kill anyone who blocked their path.

There followed a long pause when no one spoke, when no one moved. Dud broke the standoff by tightening his hand on his rifle a fraction of an inch.

The chief turned to the brave on his left and barked out a few words. He left, disappearing into the wooded grove. For fifteen minutes, no one spoke, no one moved a muscle. When the brave came back in sight, he was holding something in front of him. It became horrifyingly apparent that whatever he held had a mass of dark hair.

To the shock of the drovers, they realized it was a woman — a beaten, slashed young woman wearing what was left of a filthy red and white silk dress.

The brave threw the woman down and dismounted. He picked up her crumpled form, holding her up by the arms in front of him. There was no way she was capable of standing on her own.

A beautiful mouth with battered red lips drooped. Her eyes were so swollen with bruises they were unseeing slits. One cheek and jaw were twice the size of the other. In addition to the bruises and slash marks, there were blackened burn marks on her arms, ears, and nose.

Dud had been so stunned; he had not realized the younger drovers had joined them until he became aware that Toomey was holding an enraged Henry back. Although no one said anything, the contained fury of the other drovers rose in the air like a palpable cloud.

It was the missing fiancée, of course.

The chief spoke a few words to the brave on his right, and he in turn spoke to Barefoot.

"He said they got her from some traveling Kickapoo."

Dud didn't care if the story was true or not. The girl was almost dead. She would die soon no matter what they did for her. Cunning. Cunning like a fox Ponder had said. He didn't feel cunning.

"Tell him I said she is useless to us."

Barefoot hesitated only half a second. He returned to the chief, translating Dud's words.

The chief was cunning, too. He said a few words, and the brave threw the girl over the back of the horse and got on behind her. Before he could turn and leave, Dud spoke again.

"Tell the chief he can leave her and take something of better value than a few mangy longhorns and some worn out mustangs."

Barefoot nodded, pausing to remember the right words before he spoke. This time, the chief lost his nonchalant air and listened intently when Barefoot spoke.

Dud turned to Ponder. "Bring out those jugs of moonshine."

Ponder turned, rummaged in the wagon and brought out a jug. Audie rode over, taking it from Ponder. He rode to the Indians, and keeping his eyes on them, placed the jug on the ground in front of them. This was repeated multiple times, until almost all the jugs they had collected were in a line before the Apache.

The chief made a sign to one of the braves, and he rode forward, sweeping up a jug with one smooth movement. He opened it, smelled it, and took a swallow. He spoke to the chief, and faster than Dud would have thought possible, braves rushed forward to grab the jugs. With yells screeching in their throats, they turned and headed for the mountains. The brave with the girl rode forward and swept her off with one contemptuous shove. He turned and rode away, shrieking and joining his fellow warriors.

"Get that girl into the wagon," Ponder said.

Audie had already swooped her in his arms before Ponder could finish the sentence. He carried her to Dud.

"Dud, you have to let me take care of her."

Dud nodded and followed them to Ponder's wagon. Ponder worked to make a place inside for the young woman.

Henry, itching for revenge, wanted to follow the Apache, and it took some minutes for Dud to convince him of that folly. Ponder came out of the cramped wagon, and Audie gently put the girl inside. He sat down beside her, taking hold of her hand.

"I need a washcloth and a bucket of water," he said without looking at the men outside who crowded around the back end of the wagon. Ponder motioned for Toomey to fetch the water. He told Audie where in the wagon to find a clean cloth.

The girl looked as if she had no idea where she was. If she was aware of Audie and the rest of them, she gave no sign of it. She mumbled and gave faint moans, staring off into another world.

Dud stepped away from the wagon, and Ponder joined him.

"Do you reckon we should take her back to Fort Davis?"

Ponder shook his head. "It ain't gonna make no difference where that poor little gal dies. I say let's get the hell out of here before we have to face a bunch of drunken Apaches."

Dud agreed. He called to Shug.

"Let's get these cattle moving."

It took a while to get them out of the canyon and spaced along the Military Road. The rocks that resembled chunks of charcoal on the dark mountains around them added to the gloom they felt over the girl. There was no thrill of victory — only a surety that when the Apaches sobered, they would try another method to get the horses and beef they wanted.

Dud, as always, had to be everywhere, scouting the front, checking on the drag. Since Audie wasn't riding with the herd, Ponder turned the reins over to Will and took his place. After a while, he rode up beside Dud.

"This here is part of the Old Spanish Trail. Think about four or five drovers took a few thousand head through here to Californy during the Gold Rush."

"And your point being?" Dud said as he spied a herd of antelope. He dismissed the antelope. They still had bear meat.

"My point being we ain't the first ones to

pass through here, and we won't be the last."

Dud knew what Ponder was trying to say — don't feel sorry for yourself because others had to face the same things before you.

"I ain't much in the mood for philosophizing at the moment," Dud said and rode away.

They found the grazing along the way fair at best, and the cattle had to be led to the next spring in bunches. It took longer to get them settled, and the men worked in almost silence, their minds on the young woman in the wagon and the Apaches they left behind.

Afterward, they gathered near the wagons as Florine prepared supper. Audie had stayed with the girl all day, refusing to leave the wagon or let anyone take his place. Florine made muttering sounds. "All this fuss over a Mexican gal."

But the men stood silent and still, listening to the sounds of soft moaning and crying coming through the canvas bonnet.

Toomey was the first to break the circle. He fetched his razor and a bar of soap, and despite the coolness of the fading day, headed for the spring.

Dud took a deep breath and exhaled. He went in search of his razor and another slab of soap.

Thereafter, the rest of the men, except

Audie, went to the spring in twos, to bathe, shave their beards, and try to clean up the best they could for the frail young woman in the wagon, despite knowing she would never live to see them. Audie remained to hold her hand and bathe her feverish face.

That evening, they sat around a campfire without talking, mindful of the girl.

In the morning, Dud found good grass for the cattle, passing by another grove of live oaks. He reached Dead Man's Hole — a small spring located in a grassy valley at the foot of a dramatic bluff. He dismounted, letting his sturdy coon tail mustang drink. Although an oasis in a sterile land, to his disgust, Dead Man's Hole proved to have only enough water for horses. Dud supposed he should be grateful for that at least.

Indians had made colorful drawings on the face of the bluff. Always aware of a possible attack, he did not take time to give them more than a fleeting glance. He put his foot in the stirrup and swung a leg over the mustang to begin traveling in an ever-widening arc, looking for water. If he couldn't find water, he'd have to go back to fetch Barefoot, leaving the drovers even more shorthanded.

Dud and the mustang climbed up in the mountains, going through narrow passes, until accidentally coming upon a small Apache encampment. They did not spot him, and he was about to nudge the mustang to turn around, but the movement of children playing caught his eye. They were almost naked with little ribs sticking out, but they were laughing and running, full of unbridled joy. He watched for a few seconds more, his eyes scanning the pitiful encampment and the rest of its inhabitants. They were probably hiding from other, stronger Apache tribes who would attack the men and take the women and children.

He made his way back through the narrow passes and down the mountain, returning to the herd. He cut two beeves out of the drag.

Barefoot rode up to him, halting his horse. "Boss?"

Dud did not feel like explaining. "I'll be back."

He herded the two cows, following his way back to the encampment. He left the cattle close enough where they would be found and rode away.

Chapter Twenty-Two

Again, Dud searched for water, this time finding waterholes nine miles west of the Deadman's Hole. Not much, but it would do. It began to shower. They had been traveling for two months now, picking up two children and one battered and wounded woman along the way. Dud counted himself fortunate that he had not lost a man and was down only one horse. That in itself was miraculous.

While Shug and Billy Sol led the cattle in batches to the waterholes, Dud had Ponder and Mutt take the boys to the oak grove to gather firewood. Audie and the girl went with them, staying in the wagon. Henry and Toomey took the horses to Deadman's Hole. Since the most likely place for an attack would be there, Dud escorted them. He stood guard with water dripping from his hat while Henry and Toomey watered the stock.

They met up with the herd near the waterholes. No one, not even the boys, complained about the rain. They congregated near Ponder's wagon. Dud went to the back of the wagon bed and peeked in. The young woman slept quietly. Audie sat by her, gazing into space.

"Audie?"

Audie turned his head and looked at Dud. He gave a barely perceptible shake and turned away, to stare without seeing, waiting for death.

Dud returned to the men. Their eyes hung on him, and he gave them the same negative sign Audie had given him. The rain stopped, and they ate their food in silence. A pall cast over them, oppressive and growing more stifling as every minute passed. Will and Jemmy washed the dishes in the wreck pan with a carelessness unusual for them. They slopped so much water, Ponder had to growl at them. After finishing and looking somewhat sullen, they began to follow Henry to the remuda as he disappeared into the ever-increasing dusk. Dud had to call to them to get back to Ponder's wagon and stay there.

Mutt was the first to break.

"Them boys ain't right. I ain't never seen brothers act like them." Before he could begin to enumerate, Ponder interrupted.

"Shut your puddin'head mouth and leave those young 'uns alone."

"Mutt's right, Mr. Ponder, they be something wrong with them there boys," Darnell said unexpectedly.

Toomey took a step forward, his right hand curled into a fist by his side. "Don't neither one of y'all be picking on those children."

Mutt stood up and stuck his chin out. "Don't you be telling me what to do."

To Dud's surprise, Toomey hauled his fist back and hit Mutt, turning it on Darnell before either man had a chance to register what was happening. Ponder waded in, and instead of stopping the fight, entered into it, along with Shug and Billy Sol. Florine stood back, ready to swing a frying pan at anybody who hurt her boys, but the fight became so intense so fast, and there seemed to be no sides being taken, just fists flying in every direction, that she couldn't jump in and be sure of not smacking one of her own sons. Dud and Barefoot stood back and watched.

Through the din of the ruckus, Dud heard another sound — the noise of whinnying and snorting.

"Indians!" he shouted. The word had no sooner left his mouth than the sound of gunfire came from the remuda.

Dud ran for Ned. The cattle, now trail worn, had not leaped up in one unit to race away, but they were rising in alarm. With rifle pulled from his scabbard, Dud issued orders as the others raced for their horses.

"Shug, Billy Sol, get these cattle moving westward. Uncle Ponder, you and Florine take the wagons and go with them."

Shug and Billy Sol gave terse nods before whipping their horses around. If there was a gunfight, it was better to get the cattle moving along the trail than it was to have them scattered all over the rough hills in the dark.

When Dud reached the remuda, he found Henry trying to calm and hold what horses he could. About a dozen Apaches were leading terrified mustangs away. Amidst the pawing, snorting and frightened horses, the sound of a thousand cattle hooves stomping by them almost drowned them out. Dud and his men went after the Apache, firing at them, and in Henry's case, slashing at them, without remorse. One brave almost made it into the hills with two mustangs when Dud's slug tore into his back and stopped him. Still others gave up their plunder and tried to ride away as swiftly as possible. Darnell chased one down, firing at his side and taking the reins of the horse he fell from in one swift movement. Barefoot fought methodically, picking them off with intense and perfect aim. Mutt fired with wild abandon, but managed to hit a target sooner or later.

The horses the drovers rode whirled, but there were no more Apache — they had fought them off. It crossed Dud's mind they were very likely the same Indians he had left the beeves for, but he couldn't bring himself to be bitter. The remembrance of little ribs of children refused to let that happen. He had no time to dwell on it, regardless.

"Round these horses up," Dud yelled, his voice hoarse above the din. He looked around. "Where's Toomey?"

Barefoot spoke. "I saw him go after a brave who was leading his uncle's horse."

Dud cursed under his breath. Toomey would follow the Apache straight into hell to get that horse back.

"I'm going after him," Mutt called.

"No! You help Henry, then get back to the herd. I'll go after him."

Barefoot pointed Dud in the direction he saw Toomey go before turning his mustang to chase after the scattering horses.

Dud trailed blindly, climbing into the darkened hills that could hide the signs of a hundred Apache. Dud let Ned pick his own way up through the sotol and cactus while he strained to see clues on the ground, searching for Indians behind every shadow. He began to despair of ever finding a trace of Toomey when he heard a shrill whistle. He halted Ned. He was not sure, but he thought most Indians had a superstition against whistling at night. He decided it had to be Toomey calling for his horse, and he reined Ned in that direction.

Out of the shadows came a mustang with its rider holding onto the reins of another horse, barreling down the hill. The shape of a hat made Dud think the dark streak was Toomey, and the Apache were chasing him. They fired upon Toomey, the crack of their rifles splitting open the still night air. Toomey was in such a wild hurry; he did not take time to fire back.

Dud urged Ned down the hill, and putting the reins in his teeth, fired at the Apaches chasing Toomey. With Ned's hooves flying downward and the reins flapping against his cheek, Dud managed to shoot two of the pursuers off their horses. The other two gave up the chase, slowing down, turning, and fading back into the hills.

By the time Dud and Toomey made it back to the camp, it was deserted, and they wasted no words in catching up with the herd. The longhorns had left the hills and entered onto a flat, almost grassless, prairie. The two men found Henry and exchanged horses.

"How many did we lose, Henry?"

"Only two, Señor, but we captured two little Indian ponies. Not as good as what we lost, but they will keep a man from getting sand in his boots."

Dud nodded and rode away to find Shug. He took a head count of all the drovers along the way to make sure everyone had made it without injury. With relief, he found every man intact.

"I say we keep moving them, Cousin Dud," Shug said when Dud found him. "This here cool night air is better for the herd than hot sun beating on them after these showers."

Dud nodded in agreement. Shug's main concern was, and always would be, for the comfort of the herd. That it might also be more comfortable for the drovers didn't come into it.

In the morning, Dud found the next spring and stared at it in disappointment. At the foot of a mountain, Van Horn's Wells were nothing more than slight depressions in the ground, round and deep, surrounded by rushes. They would sustain the horses but nothing more. The sterile barrenness brought a lump of disgust in Dud's chest. He had prepared himself in the beginning for what was to come, and now that it was here, he had a hard time reconciling to it.

"Tell Shug to keep them moving," he instructed Billy Sol when he returned to the herd. "If I'm not back, stop them at noon. If there's no good grass, rest a while and then head out again."

Billy Sol nodded. He, too, knew what was coming.

Dud led the wagons, along with Henry and his remuda to the spring. Fetching Barefoot, they went in search of water.

Instead of water, they found that the road led through a canyon on the north side of ominous mountains that nevertheless possessed a wild and reckless splendor. As they rode through what seemed utter desolation, the silence was broken only once by the flutter of a bird they surprised in a clump of agarita. He came up holding a snake in his mouth, flying away with his prize to some unknown crevice.

"This is an unsettling place," Barefoot said.

"Yes, and made for another Apache attack."

After that, they remained silent.

The bones of dead animals lined the trail, and Eagles Springs told almost the same story that Van Horn's Wells did. Filthy water oozing at the foot of the mountains and collecting in numerous holes that looked dug for that purpose. Again, it would be enough for the horses but not the longhorns.

They returned to tell the others that despite their searching, there would probably be no water for the cattle until they reached the Rio Grande, a torturous thirty-something miles away.

Shug and Billy Sol had found good grazing about seven miles west of the Van Horn's Wells. The wagons, as usual, had been set up in the middle of the herd. As the cattle grazed peacefully around them, Florine had set about cooking on the shady side of the wagon with the Hollister boys to help her.

When it came time to eat, they did so in silence, knowing that in a few hours, they would be heading out again. Toomey, who had remembered to express his gratitude to Dud in the politest of terms as usual, fell asleep holding a spoon in his hand. Mutt had to poke him before his face fell into his plate.

Audie stepped down from the wagon and

stood beside it, breathing heavily. The men were at first so lethargic, they did not immediately grasp what it meant. Dud rose.

"Is she?"

Audie nodded.

Mutt began to cry. He was ashamed of his tears and turned away. Henry wiped his eyes with the back of his hand repeatedly. Shug and Billy Sol remained expressionless, but they stared, their breath coming out harsher than usual, and everyone understood they were just as affected by the girl's death as the others.

Ponder rose, sighing heavily. "We best bury her here, so we can set a fire over her grave."

They took turns digging the hard ground next to the campfire. When at last the hole was deep enough, Audie brought her out wrapped in a quilt. He had cut a piece of her hair and a swatch of silk from her dress, asking Ponder to wash the patch of material for him. Despite their shortage of water, Ponder did as he requested while the others covered her body with dirt. When finished, they packed the soil down as hard as they could, using precious fuel to build another fire over the grave, in hopes it would give the appearance of just a large campfire, so her body would go undisturbed.

Ponder, as always, said a few words over the grave. It came to Dud what a religious man Ponder was. He hadn't really thought about it before. Ponder didn't mind kicking the snot out of anybody, was the best man to be standing with in a fight, and he could win any cursing contest, but he had an unshakable belief in a heavenly hereafter.

They stood around the grave, hats in hand while Ponder said his piece. When he finished, Henry made the sign of the cross over his heart. He looked at Darnell.

"Would you play a song for the señorita before we leave her, *mi amigo?*"

Distress came over Darnell's face. He had not wanted to play his fiddle in a long time. But he nodded his head. Ponder fetched the instrument out of his wagon and handed it to him.

Darnell played hesitantly at first, the sounds coming out as mild squawks. But he bit his lip in determination and soon had the fiddle playing a sorrowful farewell to the nameless young woman.

After the last note faded away, Dud waited for a respectful pause. He put his hat back on and spoke.

"We best get these cattle moving. It's better to travel at night in this hot flat land. Once we get into the mountains again, we'll go back to herding them by day."

Nobody disagreed. Darnell handed the fiddle back to Ponder. The others put their hats on, mounted up, and did what they had to do.

Audie, back in the saddle, stopped to speak to Dud around midnight.

"Thank you, my cousin and my friend, for allowing me to take care of that girl."

No comments were necessary. Dud gave a nod, and Audie rode on.

They traveled all night and into the next day without stopping. Of all the men who should have been the most torn by the death of the young woman, it was Audie. Yet he approached his duties with renewed vigor, determined to make up for the time he had taken off.

"It's like he's a new man," Ponder told Dud in one of their rare meetings.

Dud nodded but it passed through his mind without making a stop. He had too many other things to worry about. They entered the canyon with its air of evil menace that seemed to seep into the bones of every man and animal. Every eye narrowed; every nerve tightened, waiting for an Indian attack. As they neared Eagle Springs, Dud instructed Shug and Billy Sol to keep the cattle moving — they would take the horses in batches. If Indians attacked, maybe they would not get off with the entire remuda.

Barefoot rode up to Dud from the drag, so covered in dust and dirt the only way Dud recognized him was by the way he sat in his saddle, as if man and beast were one. Barefoot may have been half-white, but mounted, the Indian's natural affinity for horseflesh had taken over as the trail drive lengthened.

"We have half a dozen lame cattle in the rear."

"Cut them out and leave them at the springs." Perhaps any marauders would be content with them and leave the rest of the animals alone.

Barefoot nodded and rode back to the drag. When Dud took his turn taking horses to the springs, the cattle were there. He hoped Indians would find them and take them for food, and they wouldn't be left to become yet another foul, stinking pile of bones, killed by starvation or wild animals.

About seven miles west of Eagle Springs, they found grazing that could only be described as better than nothing, and they slowed the cattle to take advantage of it. Dud hated to leave it and go back into the mountains, but they had to reach water soon. The weather grew colder as they climbed higher.

"We is either getting scalded or getting close to frostbit," Mutt said. He shut his mouth with a snap to avoid being labeled a crybaby, but Dud, understanding how he felt, said nothing.

The road wound around the northwest side of Eagle Mountain. When the north wind began to blow harder, Mutt's prediction of getting close to frostbit came true. It became particularly fierce on Devil's Ridge where men huddled in jackets and wore rags tied around their heads to keep their ears warm. Dud could only hope that the foul weather would keep any Mescalero in the vicinity close to their teepees.

They made it across the Devil's Ridge only to be faced with another, rockier ridge. Dud rode ahead, taking Barefoot with him. But it became a fruitless effort.

"What's up ahead?" Ponder asked when they returned.

"A sand wash you are going to have to invent a few new cuss words trying to get through without bogging down. After that, it levels out a little." He did not tell him the next pass they had to go through would be a nightmare of rocks, twists, turns, and a boneyard that would send chills up their spines.

They rested briefly at the bottom of Rocky Ridge, deciding to herd the cattle that night until they could reach the gorge at the foot of the Quitman Mountains known as "Calamity Pass."

At dawn, Audie, on top of the biggest mustang he could find as usual, stared with the others at the rugged and rocky gorge bristling with seemingly every plant known to man with a thorn on it. As they eyed the gravelly arroyo they would have to follow, Audie let out a mild curse.

"How long is it?"

"About three, maybe four miles."

"It will take us all day to get through that mess. That is, if we live to reach the other side."

Shug and Billy Sol sat frowning in their saddles, as if unwilling to lead the animals they had so faithfully tended into the desolate corridor.

"We best get going then," Dud said, and gave the signal to start the herd moving.

Audie was not far off in his estimation — it took eleven tortuous hours to traverse what Dud thought had to be the worst landscape God ever put on the earth. Every rock they passed looked stained with blood.

Rotting human skeletons mingled with the remains of animal bones. The men became so edgy, when Dud rode up to Toomey, the younger man whirled with gun in hand only barely stopping himself in time from firing.

The cattle became footsore, bawling for water. The noise reverberated off the silent cliffs around them giving them a double dose of agony they could do nothing about. Passing a large round rock covered in Indian signs, Dud wondered why they weren't already being attacked. When he scouted ahead, he came across the bodies of twenty Mescalero. Although buzzards were picking their eyes out, the bodies were stiff and not bloated, telling him death had been recent.

Passing them, Dud reached a spot he could look down on the valley rolling into the Rio Grande, a wide muddy river that had no redeeming features to it other than it was water and it was wet. He stayed for a long time, still without moving, watching and waiting to see some sign of life — living beings who had snuffed out the Mescalero behind him. But he saw nothing, and eventually, turned back to the herd.

The men passed the dead Mescalero in grim silence. Dud approached Shug and Billy Sol, telling them of the Rio Grande ahead.

"Once they start running down that incline, there won't be any way to hold them. They'll kill each other getting to the river."

"When we'ens get close, send some men up here from the back, Cousin Dud, and we'll do our darndest to slow them down."

Dud agreed, leaving them to tell the others what was ahead. Ponder questioned him about the river.

"Those Mescalero had bullets in them, not arrows. Ain't nothing but bandits on both sides of the river down yonder."

"I know it, Uncle Ponder. But we ain't got much choice. It ain't like we can turn around and go a different way."

"I'm just telling you, boy, be prepared."

Dud sighed and rode away. He checked on the drag. The Hollister boys were with Barefoot. The heavy, oppressive air and relentless toil made Florine's already vile temper and razor-sharp tongue even worse — it was almost impossible to be around her longer than thirty seconds. There was no firewood to collect, no water to put in barrels, no dishes to wash because they hadn't eaten, so the boys were better off with Barefoot anyway.

As the neared the end of Calamity Pass, Dud rode ahead to inform the other drovers to help Shug and Billy Sol hold the cattle in trickles if possible so they didn't kill one another getting to the water.

"I hope once I'm through this, I don't ever have to piss in that vile cauldron of evil again," Audie said.

"Don't count your blessings just yet. Somebody killed those Mescalero back yonder."

Audie nodded, leaving Dud and stopping to talk to each drover along the way. No doubt warning them to be on the lookout. Dud knew he should have done that. His only excuse was the exhaustion seeping so deep into his bones it made straight thinking almost an impossibility.

With lungs bawling and udders flapping, the cattle tried to race to the Rio Grande once they smelled the water. Dud joined the others in holding back the mad torrent the best they could. Four longhorns went loco, stampeding not into the water, but back into the mountains. They had no choice but to let them go.

Chapter Twenty-Three

Once at the Rio Grande, the cowboys had trouble keeping the longhorns from drinking so much they'd bloat. While they attempted to herd cattle onto poor-looking grass, Will and Jemmy gathered firewood. The pickings were slim, and they had to range from one sorry-looking tree to the next, but they found enough to get supper going and more for breakfast the next morning.

Ponder and Florine set up camp on higher ground and began cooking. Dud found it impossible to settle down to any one job. Instead, he switched horses to Ned and began to climb the rocky mountain, his eyes scanning in every direction he could see, his ears sharpened to danger that seemed to be lurking only in his mind.

His senses had not lied to him, though. A small cloud of dust from across the river became larger and larger until it revealed a group of riders. A dozen men wearing a hodgepodge of Mexican sombreros and ragged felt cowboy hats came into view — a combination of men that reminded Dud of scraps thrown together in a slop bucket. Whatever they were, they were bad.

Dud gave Ned a sharp nudge, and together they fled down the hill to warn the others.

"Men coming across the river," he hollered.

Every man stopped what he was doing, going for a horse if he was afoot, reaching for a rifle if he was unarmed. Dud rode to the edge of the shallow, sloping river and waited with Ned — rifle in hand. Ponder rode up beside him. The other men formed a line on each side, all armed and ready.

The strangers crossed the river, their horses splashing forward without caution or hesitation. In the center was a gray-haired older man in tattered, mismatched clothes, smiling at the drovers and appearing as carefree as a colt. But the lines on his filthy face were so deep they looked like furrows of muddy rivers. White men with the same hard faces rode with him, along with a few Indians and the most callous-looking Mexican banditos Dud had ever seen.

"Comancheros," Audie breathed on the

other side of him.

The old man greeted them. "Howdy, folks. Whereabouts y'all be headed?"

It was none of his business, and Dud did not answer. His eyes swept over the other men.

The old man shifted in his saddle to better reach his gun. "Well now, you ain't got no call . . ."

Dud pulled up his rifle and shot him between the eyes in one smooth motion. He turned the rifle on the other men and began firing. It took only a second for the others to begin firing. Water splashed as men went down in a hail of bullets, horses and men screaming. The Comancheros fired back, but the drovers had the element of surprise over them and never stopped pumping bullets in their direction.

In fifteen seconds, it was over. Dud's eyes scanned the bodies of the men floating in the river, but none of them appeared to have a breath of life left. He looked over his men. All were in the saddle, but Mutt was holding his arm, blood oozing from around his fingers.

"Mutt, you hit?"

Mutt nodded. The men dismounted and crowded around him. Ponder took Mutt's hand from the wound and examined it.

"It don't look like it hit bone."

"Get back — get out of my way," Florine said, pushing the men crowding around Mutt aside. She barely glanced at Ponder. "You don't know what you are doing, Ponder. Let me look at it."

Ponder stepped back in shock. Mutt's already large eyes opened wider, and the boy's mouth sagged in fear when Florine began examining the wound.

"Come with me, I'll fix you up."

The men opened up a path for Florine and Mutt, too stunned to speak. They looked at one another and at Florine's sons.

Shug spoke as if he didn't quite believe what he was saying.

"When one of them there banditos charged me, my rifle jammed. Mutt pushed his horse in front of me and fired at him."

They were too in awe to speak. Billy Sol shuddered and looked at Dud. "Pa used to say Ponder had more sand than anybody he ever knew, and that you was gonna be just like him, Cousin Dud."

Uncomfortable with praise and comparisons to Ponder, Dud said, "I think your pa would have been proud of your grit, Billy Sol. Now let's see if we can round up their horses without too much trouble."

Shaken, the others nodded and returned

to their mounts. Only Toomey stayed behind.

"Boss, they were going to kill us, weren't they?"

Dud gave a nod. What kind of man had he become who shot men without provocation just because he didn't like their looks? But he knew he'd been right.

"They slaughtered the Mescalero back yonder and would have killed us, too, after they had a little fun toying with us."

Toomey nodded, and Dud added: "Thanks for standing with me, Toomey."

A look of surprise came over Toomey's face. "It was an honor."

It took Dud aback for a second or two. "You go on now and help the others. In a little while, we'll have full bellies and rest."

They set up guards as usual that night, but they had a peaceful camp, the first in a long time.

Now that they were nearing El Paso and Fort Bliss, there was an almost overwhelming desire to push on. The grazing was poor around the Rio Grande, and even though the river wasn't as rank as the Pecos, it lacked the charm of the Limpia and so many others they had crossed. But the cattle were footsore and the men, including Florine, were exhausted. The horses, the life-blood of the drive, had to rest to be able to go on. The drovers washed and brushed the horses, and one day was spent in reshoeing them. After that, the men bathed and those who felt like it shaved beards and tried to cut one another's hair. Men, horses, and cattle were open to threats from across the border and all other points, but the general feeling was they were safe for the time being. Their only trouble was keeping the longhorns and horses from swimming across the river.

On the fourth day, they pointed the herd northwest to El Paso, following the muddy river. Sand blew around them, and flies continuously bothered the horses. For a long while all they could see were mountains and rocks. They passed the abandoned Fort Quitman, the sorriest excuse for a fort Dud had ever seen, despite the cottonwoods with their cool fluttering leaves around it. The fort consisted of a few rat-infested houses, so poorly built the adobe was falling from the walls in chunks. No one had any desire to stop and sleep in one, least of all Dud who feared the mother of all nightmares would visit him if he did. They continued westward, camping near a small lake.

Moving the herd, they passed inhabitants of the region, glad to see faces other than their own. Villages consisted of two or three small huts and a larger population of chickens than of people. Mexican men in wide sombreros would come to their camp, bringing onions, peppers, and whatever else they had for sale. They wore the simplest of clothes — long shirts without pants, short drawers, or sometimes just a cloth draped around their middle. They presented a happy, carefree people who enjoyed a little haggling over their produce with Ponder. They never failed to seek out Henry for a congenial conversation in Spanish.

As the drovers neared one village, an older man with skin like leather arrived in camp carrying a basket of eggs, which Ponder promptly bought.

"It was you who killed El Escorpion and his men," he said, looking at Dud.

Dud understood he meant the Comancheros and so did Ponder.

"Why? Was he some of your kin?"

"No, no, señor! He was a bad hombre. Not as bad as the Mescalero. They come down and kill us, but El Escorpion, he only sting us, keeping us alive to steal from another day."

While the talkative old man proceeded to give them a recitation of the tribulations his people had received from El Escorpion's hands, a fat older woman waddled up carrying a jug. She handed it to Ponder.

"*Cariño,* for you."

Ponder reached in his pocket and pulled out some change, but she waved it aside.

"El Escorpion killed her son when he tried to stop him from taking his woman," the old man explained.

Dud and Ponder looked at one another in restrained relief. If her son had been one of El Escorpion's men, the jug of honey would have contained arsenic.

"Muchas gracias, señora," Ponder said with a deep bow.

The old woman flushed with pleasure and smiled, showing a row of brilliant white teeth with only one or two missing gaps between them. Ponder smiled back and Dud suppressed a sigh of irritation. All the women loved Ponder.

"We better get moving," Dud said, adding under his breath, "before we get into trouble."

An argument broke out later among the men on whether to eat the eggs fried or scrambled. Ponder settled it by saying if Dud could kill an antelope, they would scramble the brains with some of the eggs and make a "cake" from the others, pouring honey on it. The cake would be made with mostly cornmeal, and Dud had a pretty good idea Jemmy would probably be cooking it, but he did not object.

The pleasure at seeing villages, even as small as the ones they passed by, became somewhat soured, however, after a time.

"I think they is keeping the señoritas hid in the houses," Mutt grumbled. Complaining about being uncomfortable was one thing, griping about women, or lack of them, was entirely acceptable.

"Do you blame them?" Dud laughed.

Dud scouted, but did not find any antelope. Because he thought a celebration would lift their spirits after the previous harrowing leg of their journey, he ended up buying a goat, and that night, they feasted on scrambled eggs with the brains, cornmeal cake with honey, and cabrito.

They begged Darnell to play his fiddle, promising him extra helpings of honey. Darnell, with his tremendous sweet tooth, didn't have to be asked twice, and they danced jigs around the fire. Audie surprised everyone by joining in, and like many heavy men, he proved as light on his feet as a leprechaun.

But celebrating with barbequed goat and music did not make up for the merciless heat radiating off the pale sand or the flies.

After a few hours sleep, they began their journey again, traveling in the cooler night air and dodging the mesquites that studded the area.

By morning, they had herded the cattle again within sight of the Rio Grande, passing a few huts with irrigated corn crops they were careful to keep the longhorns from trampling. Dud scouted ahead, coming upon a small community on the river consisting of three adobe huts and a sign that read Birchville. Directly across was a sleepy looking little Mexican village. The hut on the American side with the Birchville sign also had one that read Supplies. Dud dismounted and went inside.

Looking around, Dud was surprised at the variety of stock. A coating of dust covered everything, but Dud didn't see how it could be otherwise, given the country they were in. A middle-aged man with a sandy mustache and wearing a large faded and stained silk bandanna around his neck walked forward from the back, greeting him in an unnatural gravelly voice.

Dud exchanged howdies and explained about the cattle that would be coming through. He dickered a while over coffee and flour, but it was a good thirty minutes of talking before the storeowner let down his guard.

"You're the man who killed El Escorpion."

"Is that going to be a problem?"

The storeowner shook his head. "Mister, life is too cheap out here for anybody to bother about a grudge."

Dud invited the storeowner to visit their camp, and he took him up on it fast enough. Indian raids and sudden hair-triggered killings notwithstanding, life apparently could be somewhat monotonous on the Rio Grande.

When the store owner rode into camp later, he eyed Florine but did not question her presence. She in turn ignored him and disappeared into the background. Dud knew from experience she was eavesdropping on every word.

"What made you decide to come west?" the storekeeper asked, enjoying the coffee they had paid him so dearly for.

Dud explained about the northern and eastern routes being closed, along with hearing the army was having a hard time feeding itself and the Mescalero on the reservation.

"You gonna try Fort Bliss first?"

Dud nodded.

"Well, you may sell some. Trouble is, there

is a group of men who came out here to build empires, and they ain't gonna take too kindly to strangers bringing cattle into their territory, whether they is needed or not."

"We fought off Indians for five hundred miles, I reckon we can fight off a few empire builders for another hundred or so."

Even as he said the words with an offhand confidence, Dud felt uneasy. He exchanged glances with Ponder. Ponder raised his eyebrows, but said nothing.

Before he left, the storekeeper paused to watch Mutt, still favoring his hurt arm, do an animated imitation of an ornery steer that had the other drovers laughing. Keeping his eyes on Mutt, the storekeeper spoke to Dud without turning his head. Dud wondered if his throat hadn't been injured in some way, he kept his voice so hoarse and low.

"If you let your men go into San Elizario, tell them not to dance with the Mexican girls unless they want to wake up with a knife in their back. It's a matter of pride to some of them señoritas to see how many men they can get killed fighting over them." He pulled his neckerchief down to show a deep scar.

"How many people live there, anyway? I

thought El Paso was the big city out here."

"Oh, about a thousand. El Paso barely beats it. They sell an excellent local wine there, by the way."

"Wine we don't need," Dud said. "Just cattle buyers."

"And another thing. Keep an eye on those two kids. There are people deep in Mexico that will pay a high price for blond-headed children like that. Sometimes they will adopt them, but most often they are used as slaves."

Dud blanched, but nodded. Ponder's face grew stern.

As soon as the raspy-voiced shopkeeper left, Florine appeared.

"You ain't aiming to sell all these here cattle in Fort Bliss, are you?"

Dud turned to her in surprise. "I'm selling them wherever we can get a good price for them, Florine."

"You said we were going to New Mexico. You said." Florine wrapped her arms around her middle and squeezed her arms together.

"Florine! Go to bed," Ponder said. "It's too late to be ah arguing about anything."

Florine, clutching herself as in some internal struggle, opened her mouth, thought better of it, and left them instead.

"That woman drives me insane."

"Get some shut-eye yourself, Uncle Ponder. We are going to have our work cut out for us, keeping these young bucks out of trouble in San Elizario."

Ponder scoffed. "You just worry about your own self, Dudford Washburn. We've already had to rescue you once."

"And I guess I'll never live that down either," Dud muttered on his way to his bedroll.

For the next two days, Dud cautioned the drovers about their behavior in San Elizario. He rode ahead, stopping only long enough to scope out the edge of the hilly town before reporting back to the men.

"It's on this side of the Rio Grande, but it looks like a Mexican adobe village. Some small houses and several big fine ones. The parts that are irrigated are right nice looking. Lots of cantinas and cafés. And lots of people. Some whites, lots of Mexicans. Some look Spanish. I don't know. Just lots of people."

Darnell wanted to know if any of them were of his color, and Dud said he had seen a few. Henry preened, cutting his mustache and combing it with precision. Audie was amused, almost happy. Barefoot appeared pleased at the prospect of seeing something that at least passed for civilization. Shug and Billy Sol said they were staying with the herd.

"We didn't come this far to lose it now, Cousin Dud."

Dud didn't argue with them — social interaction in mixed company was difficult for Billy Sol and might near impossible for Shug. He wasn't going to push any man into being something he didn't want to be.

Mutt and Toomey surprised him by their lack of enthusiasm.

"What's with you two? We finally get close to a town with pretty women, and you aren't foaming at the mouth in excitement?"

Mutt shrugged. He looked downward, rubbing his boot in the ground as if embarrassed. Toomey spoke.

"We decided to stay with the remuda. We figured Henry always gets stuck with the horses, so we ought to let him cut loose. These here are Henry's people anyway."

Dud stared at them. A flush came over Mutt's cheeks, and Toomey's eyes widened in anguish.

"Well, it's like this, Boss," Mutt said. "Toomey here, he's got this idee in his head that if his uncle's horse gets this close to the border without him keeping a close eye on it, it might end up in Mexico, and he'd never see it again."

Toomey nodded in earnest agreement. He turned his somber eyes on Mutt, causing him to fidget in even more discomfit.

"And well, me and Toomey, we didn't want to tell you, but we 'uns got throwed in jail in San Antone. That's the reason we was late getting back to the herd."

Dud did not comment, but waited.

"Aw shucks, Boss, I ain't got no sense in no big towns," Mutt said, throwing up his hands. "We saw these women dressed up, and we thought they was sporting gals cause they was dressed so funny. I said something bold to them. I didn't know they was just a going to some fancy dress up ball."

Dud coughed to stifle the chuckles coming up in his throat.

"They told the law on us and got us arrested," Toomey added. "I never was sure what the charges were, but they kept us for a few hours and then let us go."

"It wasn't like being at Brackett, where everybody was rough and lowdown any hows," Mutt said to defend himself. "And you kept a talking about us being careful in San Elizario, so we figured we would stay out of trouble this time."

"Did you tell Henry?"

"Yes, sir. He promised if he had any adventures, he'd spill every detail."

"Well, knowing Henry, he'll have a lot to tell you."

Chapter Twenty-Four

Toomey and Mutt made solemn vows they wouldn't let anything happen to the Hollister boys. Florine didn't vow anything, except to kill Dud if he got tangled up in any trouble and slowed the herd from reaching New Mexico.

Dud allowed Henry and Darnell to go into San Elizario while the rest of them settled the herd about a mile north of town. Dud had told Shug to stop them south of town, but Ponder insisted they get the herd on the other side.

"We might have to hightail it out of here in a hurry." He gave Dud a frown. "Like usual."

Dud grimaced but was stopped by further comment by the appearance of three riders heading into camp. Shug and Billy Sol disappeared into the mass of cattle. Mutt and Toomey gaped until Dud gave them a nod of his head to get out and guard the herd.

Audie, Ponder, and Barefoot stood with him, watching the riders approach.

They were on good horses with expensive saddles and tack. The one in the middle rode with the assurance of a leader, a tall, fine-boned man with ginger hair and a clipped mustache. His gray jacket, tweed britches and soft gray planter's hat looked as though no expense had been spared. The rider to one side of him looked like some kind of Spanish don rigged out in black pants with fancy embroidery on the sides and a flowing red sash tied around a white shirt. The rider on the other side, however, wore slouchy cowboy clothes, a man with a hard jaw and a look in his eyes that said they might have seen the world through prison bars more than once.

They halted their horses, and the ginger-haired man in the gray jacket smiled engagingly, introducing himself.

"Charles McHugh. These are my men, Delgado and Smith."

The drovers nodded in greeting, but there was something about the men that reminded them of the Comancheros who met them at the river, only a shade more civilized. They could get away with shooting men whose every appearance and gesture screamed banditos, but Charles McHugh and his men would have to be handled a different way.

"You're on McHugh ranchland, you know."

Dud watched the face with its benign smile. "We're just traveling through. We'll be off of it in a day or two."

McHugh did not answer, but sat waiting, looking around expectantly. It was the universal rule to invite visitors into camp. Dud issued the invitation for them to get down and have coffee.

McHugh, in the friendliest of ways, agreed. He and his men dismounted, and standing with coffee cups, let their eyes scan the camp and the cattle without any awkwardness over their curiosity.

Delgado and Smith never spoke, never gave any indication they knew how to talk. McHugh did it all. After a few desultory comments about the horses and cattle, what kind of trouble they had come across on the trail, McHugh asked where they planned on taking the cattle.

"Wherever we can find a buyer," Dud said.

"The market at Fort Bliss is already flooded with McHugh cattle," he said with a laugh.

Dud shrugged.

"Why don't you come to my house tonight for a small dinner party? I'll have a few of the local ranchers there, and maybe you can dicker with them."

McHugh glanced at the other men. "Bring your uncle and your cousin," he said, his gay tone covering over the snub to Barefoot.

Dud did not trust the man and did not want to go. He looked at Ponder and Audie, but their faces were masked. Feeling he was again stuck between a rock and a hard place, Dud assented.

"We are much obliged."

"Good, it's settled then." McHugh threw the remains of his coffee into the fire, and his men did the same. "We'll see you at eight. Just ask anybody in town; they can direct you to the McHugh villa."

They watched the men ride away. When they were out of hearing range, Dud turned to Barefoot.

"Ride into town and see what kind of talk there is about this McHugh fellow. And try to get some kind of idea of where Henry and Darnell are in case we have to leave town without saying our goodbyes."

Ponder leaned forward, shaking his finger at the ground and glaring at Dud. "And if there is a pretty woman in the house of that snake in the grass, you stay away from her, you hear?"

"All right, Uncle Ponder," Dud said, aggravated at being treated like a baby cub that didn't know any better. "Let's get these cattle moved north of town. Gosh dang it, I'll be starving by eight o'clock."

"Something ain't natural about a man who wants folks to come to his house so late," Ponder grumbled.

After getting the cattle settled, Dud, Ponder, and Audie headed for the heart of San Elizario. Small adobe houses crowded on hilly, crooked streets that had no rhyme or reason.

"All this open land, and these here houses are bunched together like lucifers in a box," Ponder said.

"I think an alcoholic surveyor in a drunken haze laid out these streets," Audie said as they turned their horses after reaching an unexpected dead end.

After stopping several times for directions, they finally reached the McHugh house. It was more of a mansion, with tall stucco walls and a bright tiled roof. A servant appeared in front to take their horses, but after exchanging glances with his companions, Dud insisted on going to the barn, too. He didn't like the idea of not knowing where Jax was.

The servant shrugged but said nothing as

they dismounted in a stable full of spirited horses.

"I'll say this for him, that ginger-headed dandy knows horseflesh," Ponder said, eyeing the horses.

"Come on," Dud said. "It's getting dark, and we're late."

The servant led them to the house and opened the door for them to pass through. Tile on the floor, black wrought iron fixtures, and expensive furniture greeted them. Another servant in a white coat appeared. He took their hats, placing them on a long metal rack next to others that made their hats look like refugees from a burn pile. The silent servant beckoned them to follow him into a parlor.

The room looked like someone had taken the advertisements for Victorian furniture in a mail order catalog to heart. Heavy furniture, thick drapes over the windows, and expensive lanterns gracing lace covered tables filled the room. The three drovers took stock of their surroundings. Cigar smoke rose from a cluster of middle-aged men talking in the center of the room. To one side, sitting in a chair, was the lone woman, and her loveliness took Dud's breath away. Lustrous dark hair parted down the middle and pulled back in wings framed a face with almost perfect features. Her mouth was plump and as dark as a red apple, and the eyes above were large and smoked with a sultry fire. Dud found himself gulping.

"Ah, you found us," his host said, coming forward. He pointed to the woman. "My wife, Conchita."

Dud and his companions nodded, but their host made them drag their eyes away by introducing them to the other men. A small, stocky Mexican girl wound her way through, gathering empty glasses and frowning at discarded cigar stubs. One of the men turned and glanced at her as she picked up an empty glass near him.

"What are you looking at?" she said, her voice harsh and uncompromising.

"That's enough, San Juanita," the woman reprimanded. "Go see if the chef is ready for us."

McHugh turned to Dud and smiled. "One has to take what one finds in these outposts from civilization."

McHugh was beckoned away by one of the men, and Ponder used the opportunity to hiss into Dud's ear. "That there little gal was the only real person in this here room."

Audie grinned. "Present company excepted."

McHugh called to them, and they joined a conversation about cattle that continued as they were called into the dining room. A long table with candelabras, china, and silver gleaming atop a white cloth awaited them. Open French doors on one side of the room led to a darkened walled garden. The feisty little San Juanita filled glasses with wine, but this time she said nothing.

While the men continued to talk about cattle, the woman of the house sat silent at the foot of the table nearest the garden, watching, listening, and on rare occasions, injecting a bit of conversation if she thought it was called for and giving terse commands in Spanish to San Juanita on occasion. Dud had a terrible time keeping his eyes off her.

The food alone could have occupied him, but as appetizing as it was, Dud was more interested in selling cattle. He ate with appreciation in an abstract way, but listened closely to the conversation, answering the questions put to him.

As the meal ended with a soggy milk cake he disliked, but ate anyway, he found himself disappointed not only with the dessert, but with constant talk of cattle that circled around like the streets of the town and ended nowhere. He had the distinct feeling they were being played, and no offer to buy was forthcoming. He rose with the other men, intending on pleading exhaustion as an excuse to leave early.

Intended on walking out of the dining room, he somehow found himself alone with the mistress of the house near the garden doors.

"Did you enjoy your supper, Señor Washburn?"

He looked down into her smoldering dark eyes and thought how easily it would be for a man to toss away everything he held dear just to keep staring into them. She continued the conversation, talking in a desultory way about nothing important. With the hot blood she engendered pumping through his veins — it was all Dud could do to concentrate on her words.

"Would you like to stroll into the garden with me?" she asked. "It's very beautiful at night."

Dud looked up, catching Ponder's eyes. The two rapid blinks Ponder gave told Dud if he walked into the garden with Conchita McHugh, Ponder would never let him live it down, no matter how innocent or guilty the outcome.

Dud looked back to Conchita. "You are so lovely, I could never trust myself alone in a darkened garden with you, señora."

Her eyes fluttered downward. "Perhaps you would feel safer meeting me later tonight in the presidio gardens," she said in an almost whisper, her voice fading away enticingly.

"Perhaps," Dud said in a heavy breath.

She reached down and gave his hand a discreet squeeze. "At midnight."

She left, leaving a trail of some intoxicating smell behind her.

The men, who had been standing to one side talking, began following her out. San Juanita approached Dud.

"The chef, he saw how much you like his cake. He wants to give you some to take back."

Dud paused. What did the girl want?

"That would be right nice of him. I'd like to give him my compliments."

San Juanita indicated he was to follow her. Ponder whispered something in Audie's ear before turning to the men, catching up and speaking loudly.

"I'd like to hear some more about this winemaking operation you got here."

Audie blended into the shadows of the room and stayed behind, watching Dud as he passed on his way to the kitchen.

San Juanita opened the door, going through and shutting it behind Dud. He found himself in a covered walkway. The kitchen was in its own building, some distance away from them. Barefoot and Henry emerged from the shadows.

"What is it?" Dud asked.

"The señora who gave Señor Ponder the honey is San Juanita's grandmother," Henry said.

"They want to trap you at the presidio. Locking you up in the jail, keeping you here so they can steal your cattle," San Juanita explained. "They are bad men."

"Where's Darnell?" Dud asked Henry and Barefoot.

"With the horses."

"Can you find your way back to the herd in the dark?"

They nodded and Dud continued. "Get going and move the herd northwest toward El Paso as fast as Shug and Billy Sol think is safe. We'll stay here for a little while longer and follow you."

Henry and Barefoot disappeared into the darkness. Dud looked down into the straightforward little square face of San Juanita.

"Can you get us out of town quickly?"

She nodded. "The *mozo de cuadra,* he will bring your horses. When you leave, turn right. I'll be on the corner, waiting for you."

"Thank you, señorita. God bless you."

Dud turned to go back in, but San Juanita stopped him.

"Wait, the cake," and she placed a paper wrapped package in his hands.

"To be safe, I should thank the *cocinero.*"

"*Si.* Go there."

Dud walked to the kitchen, opened the door, and seeing a fat man with a stained apron tied around his middle, called out in Spanish that the food was *muy delicioso.* He shut the door behind him, but San Juanita had disappeared. He paused, weighing the best options to get out of San Elizario alive and with all the cattle. He left to fetch Audie.

Ponder knew by the look on his face when Dud reentered the parlor that something was up, and he went along with staying for almost another hour while Dud walked the line trying to lead his hostess to believe he would meet her in the presidio garden while trying not to be too obvious about it.

When Dud felt it safe to leave, McHugh followed them to the door as they gave their thanks.

"Oh, I see the chef did give you some cake to take with you. He does that occasionally when he is pleased with someone's appetite for his food. It's amazing how thin he stays cooking all these delicacies."

Dud allowed himself a puzzled look. "Thin? The one I said thank you to was fat as a hog."

McHugh gave a short laugh of satisfaction. "That was probably Ramon, his helper."

Dud suppressed a snort, and with as much innocence as he could muster expressed his appreciation again. He bowed and kissed the hand of his hostess, holding it a second longer than good manners allowed. She took pains to cover her feelings, but Dud caught the brief, fleeting expression of triumph in her eyes.

They left the McHugh mansion, reining the horses right as instructed. At the corner, San Juanita appeared out of the shadows, covered in a black shawl and barely visible. She took Jax by the cheek strap and led him down a dark and confusing maze of byways with Ponder and Audie trailing behind. Dud could do nothing but hope Henry's faith in San Juanita was well founded.

At last, they were on the edge of the town, and Dud was able to breathe easier.

"You can find your way now," San Juanita said, making to disappear after giving Jax a pat.

"Wait," Dud said. "Would you be offended, señorita, if I paid you something for your trouble?"

"Shut up! I do it because I want to. Get away from me, you animal."

"I apologize, señorita. And hope I won't offend you again by telling you what a beautiful, virtuous young woman you are. Because if you weren't, I would sweep you in my arms and kiss you."

"Dud!" Ponder said.

San Juanita laughed. She blew Dud a kiss and faded into the night.

"Let's get our tails out of here before you get carried away, Dudford," Ponder said.

They caught up with the herd, took a head count of man and beast and found them all accounted for. At dawn they stopped, and Dud fed his soggy milk cake to General Sherman with Shug's and Billy Sol's blessings.

Eager to reach El Paso and Fort Bliss, they pushed onward. There was water in the Rio Grande, but for the most part the grass on the sandy soil was sparse and poor in nutrition. On the flat land where one could see for miles, Ponder and Dud rode into the small town of Ysleta to buy fruit while the others herded the cattle within sight of the few adobe houses, staying well away from their irrigation canals.

The farmers put their fruit in burlap sacks, handing the fruit to Dud and Ponder who tied the bags around their saddle horns. Ponder paid the men, and as soon as the money hit their palms, they disappeared. Without looking at one another, Dud and Ponder raised their rifles.

Men with pistols and rifles aimed at them appeared from behind houses, and Dud and Ponder did not stop to wait to see who fired the first shot. A volley of fire was exchanged, and Dud's horse went down. He was able to jump free, his first thought was gratefulness that he hadn't been riding Ned or Jax that morning. Using the fallen mustang as a shield, Dud picked off one shooter, then another. From his side, Ponder, still mounted, did the same. Another man stepped out from around a corner of the house, and as Dud fired the shot that would smash his breastbone, he recognized the McHugh man called Smith.

From behind them, they could hear more rifle shots and knew there were other men trying to stampede the herd into another direction — one that would lead them into the McHugh stronghold.

The barrage stopped. Ponder and Dud looked at one another. Dud gave a jerk of his head; motioning Ponder to ride back to the herd to help them. Dud gave one last look to make sure the men who jumped them were dead. He had to shoot the poor mustang whose fate it had been that morning to be in a gun battle. Removing his saddle and tack, Dud turned and walked.

The trail-weary herd, now used to Indian attacks, had not stampeded as expected. Instead, the McHugh men found themselves facing the bullets of drovers who had lived through much worse. A couple of the cattle thieves tried to escape, but Mutt and Toomey, almost blinded with rage, raced after them, halting to stop and take aim, firing with unexpected accuracy. The men, shot in the back fleeing, fell off their horses. The horses raced on, never looking back.

Dud walked on, and after a while, Henry rode to him, leading Jax.

Chapter Twenty-Five

El Paso had the reputation of being a haven for outlaws. It lay somewhat isolated in a valley between mountains and the Rio Grande, and its full name, El Paso del Norte, meant Passage Way to the North. It was a desert, but irrigation canals from the river had turned it into a lush, verdant paradise, at least to travel-weary cowboys. That it also attracted the roughest elements of the frontier was to be expected. Vice of every kind was to be had in El Paso — the chief one being gambling.

The drovers made camp near the river about a mile from town. Once settled, Dud called a meeting — he and Ponder would go into Fort Bliss to try to sell what cattle they could. It was their hope the army would tell them where they could sell the rest.

"And hurry it up," Florine said. "I don't want to stay in this place any longer than I have to. There ain't no telling what kind of trouble Dud can stir up here."

"I resent that, Florine," Dud said.

But he let it drop. He was just as anxious to meet with the officers at Fort Bliss as Florine was to get out of town. To her tight-lipped fury, he told the men if he could sell some of the cattle, he would advance them part of their wages, and they could spend it on a few nights savoring what El Paso had to offer.

Toomey and Mutt exchanged glances. Dud didn't know if they were excited or terrified. He wasn't anxious to show off Jax or Ned to any would-be horse thieves in El Paso and saddled a dowdy brown instead. Ponder pulled himself up on the back of a similar nondescript mustang and waited for him.

"Don't forget," Dud said, putting his boot in the stirrup and swinging his leg over. "The Mescalero can still give trouble, even this close to a settlement. And keep your eyes on those kids."

They turned their horses and headed for Fort Bliss.

The streets of El Paso were wider and straighter than those of San Elizario. Flat roofed adobe houses dotted the landscape, and everywhere, there was color. Three-fourths of the city's inhabitants appeared to be of Mexican descent, and they showed their love of color in the striped serapes on their shoulders and in the bright blouses and brilliant patterns on the skirts the women wore. The mountains in the background made a majestic background for the green, irrigated crops that grew between dwellings. As Dud and Ponder rode through the streets, they heard a mixture of Spanish and English coming from all lips. The storekeeper at Birchville had said there was the inevitable class system — the white Anglos, the upper crust Hispanics, the lowly peons — but in the streets, there seemed to be no difference, and people talked and mingled without regard to color or caste.

El Pasoans were used to strangers traveling their pass. Nevertheless, Dud and Ponder earned a few curious stares, and as they rode by one group of men, Dud heard the whisper of, "El Escorpion." That they already knew of the incident at the river did not surprise him or Ponder.

The fort had been built north of town on the rented land of a local businessman. As they rode under the dappled shade of an occasional cottonwood, Dud and Ponder eyed the adobe huts spread out over the grounds. As they neared, two guards approached them.

"We're here to see about selling some cattle," Dud said.

One of the guards pointed toward the stables. "You can stable your horses over yonder." He moved his rifle and added, "There's the headquarters. They'll tell you who to talk to."

"Much obliged."

Unlike the deserted Fort Davis, the laid-back atmosphere of Fort Lancaster, or the minor activity surrounding Fort Clarke, Fort Bliss hummed with soldiers seemingly intent on a myriad of tasks. As they neared the stables, two soldiers immediately took possession of their horses and led them away. Dud and Ponder were so used to riding, walking the short distance to the building that housed the headquarters seemed like an imposition.

Their boots and clothes grew even dustier, but they weren't there to impress anybody with their looks. Opening the door of the headquarters, they could hear the sound of several men talking in another room. An agitated little second lieutenant at a desk rose to greet them and listen as they stated their business.

"Our contractor has been fired, but the quartermaster and an official from the government in Las Cruces are with the colonel now. I'll tell them you are here."

The lieutenant hurried down the hall to a door in the back. He opened the door and heated voices grew plainer. The door shut, and in a less than a minute, the door opened and the nervous lieutenant came back. He motioned them to follow him down a wide cool hall made of adobe. Dud was surprised they had heard anything through the thickness of the walls.

Their spurs clanged loudly on the wooden floor, announcing their arrival even before the lieutenant did.

Dud began to wonder if offices on every army post looked alike and how many prints of Abraham Lincoln had been distributed. Somebody was making good money selling flags. Surrounding the desk was a small man in a meticulous gray suit, a major who was evidently the quartermaster, and a seated colonel looking distracted and put out. On the other side, standing some steps away stood McHugh's right-hand man, Delgado. The only surprise he showed at seeing them was a slight widening and then narrowing of his eyelids.

Dud and Ponder nodded, neither denying their previous relationship with Delgado nor affirming it. The colonel spoke.

"What's this about cattle?"

"We've got a thousand head near the river to sell."

The colonel looked at Delgado.

"We've been doing business with Señor Delgado's boss, Charles McHugh. Delgado says he can have a thousand head to us in a few days."

Dud glanced at Delgado. The Birchville shopkeeper had warned them to stay out of the dirty politics that polluted El Paso. It would create a war that would solve nothing to announce that they had killed McHugh's other strongarm trying to steal their herd. Something Delgado was already guessing.

"We have the cattle here now, not in a few days," Dud said.

The colonel gave Delgado another look, one that said he did not care for him or his boss. He turned to the quartermaster.

"Go with them to look the cattle over and report back to me."

He turned to Dud and Ponder. "Come back at four. I'll have an answer for you then."

"But we need cattle in Las Cruces, too!" the small man in the suit said.

"Go with the quartermaster," the colonel ordered. "We can discuss it when you return."

The four men filed out of the office. Behind their backs, the colonel dismissed Delgado, telling him in curt tones he would see him the next day.

Once outside, Delgado overtook and passed them, giving Dud and Ponder nothing but a sharp glance on his way to the stables. By the time they reached their horses, Delgado was already mounted and leaving. Dud felt fairly certain he was heading back to the McHugh ranch, and the colonel would not be seeing him the next day.

The quartermaster, a beefy man with large forearms, a square jaw, and a sour face, said little as they rode out to look over the herd. The government man from Las Cruces was the opposite, with a smooth, oval face and a small dark mustache. He would have liked to engage them in conversation, but every time he started to speak, he took one look at the grim quartermaster and shut his mouth.

They had started out with twelve hundred head of cattle. A count that morning had confirmed they still possessed eleven hundred longhorns despite having sold some and losing others. Audie rode out to meet them.

"Everything all right?"

Audie nodded. Dud introduced him to the government man and quartermaster. Audie again nodded, and after giving the quartermaster a once-over glance, turned and left. Meanwhile, the quartermaster looked over the herd, his vinegary face showing disapproval with every sweeping glance.

"This is a sorry, lean looking bunch," he said.

Dud and Ponder made no comment. Dud was only glad Billy Sol and Shug weren't around to hear it, not the way they had struggled to keep the longhorns fed and watered in a land that had fought them almost every step of the way.

They waited on the quartermaster. After giving the cattle another inspection, he turned to Dud with a smirk tugging at his lips.

"How does it feel, Johnny Reb, to come crawling to the US Army to buy your pitiful cows?"

Dud stayed silent and still. As the silence deepened, the quartermaster glanced around — growing uneasy as he realized how conveniently he could be killed and his body gotten rid of with no one the wiser, except for the little government man from Las Cruces who would probably shut his eyes.

"How do you think it feels?" Dud said, staring in a quiet stillness that unnerved both visitors.

The quartermaster made up his mind. He whirled his horse northward.

"Be at the colonel's office at four sharp," he said, and rode away.

The little government man looked anxiously after him, unsure if he should try to catch up with him or stay with the lesser of two evils. Ponder solved his dilemma.

"Well, your honor, won't you join us in camp for a cup of coffee before you head back? We've got a cook that can burn a boiled egg, but maybe there will be a fruit cobbler we can swallow without choking too much."

The government man looked at the retreating back of the quartermaster. He turned to Dud and Ponder.

"Please, my name is Pedro Morales Hernandez Martin, but my friends call me Martin."

"Come on, Martin, let's see if we can rustle up some coffee."

Dud let Ponder take the lead, and before they reached camp, Martin had warmed up to the older man and was pouring out his woes. The government contractor had been a crook and believed to be on the take from

Charles McHugh, although the part about McHugh could not be proven. Martin disliked the quartermaster and considered him a brutal heathen, but not as corrupt as the contractor had been. The colonel, however, he found to be hard, but honest.

After they dismounted in camp, Henry and Darnell, curious about the visitor, offered to water the horses. Martin took one look at Florine and the two Hollister boys and crossed himself.

"You came across *el país del diablo* with a woman and children?"

"It was an accident and not planned." Ponder gave Florine a sour look of his own. "Do we have any cobbler left?"

"Get it yourself," she said and climbed into her wagon.

Ponder turned to Martin. "What can I say? She's kin."

Martin gave an understanding nod. *"Entiendo perfectamente."*

"I'll fetch the cobbler for you, Mr. Ponder," Jemmy said.

"Thank you, child."

Ponder found a stool for their guest and a small barrel of his own to sit on. Dud upturned an empty crate and sat while Will poured coffee for them. The two brothers, who had orders to stick to camp, retreated next to the wagon wheels to listen with grave eyes.

In almost no time, Ponder had the voluble government man telling them the circumstances of his visit.

"This part of the world, it is getting ready to explode now that the war is over," Martin explained. "The mail is going to start up again. They will have a wagon with eighteen guards, fifty mules and nearly that many horses. More will follow. The army is sending troops back to Fort Davis, and another unit of buffalo soldiers are coming to replace the 5th Infantry at Bliss."

It meant a massive number of mouths to feed, many of them coming through Las Cruces.

"And the Mescalero situation is terrible," he said with a moan. "What can we do? They are starved and treated miserably. But what can one do? Their warfare is so brutal, and their way of life so different, we cannot live together in peace. But to see their suffering is horrible."

Dud didn't know the answer and neither did Ponder. At the moment, just surviving filled all their thoughts.

"But you have risked life and limb bringing food to the Apache, and for that, *la Madre de Dios* will bless you."

Dud and Ponder looked at one another.

"I'm afraid we had a greedier motive," Dud said.

Martin dismissed this confession as unimportant. Dud and Ponder found themselves liking the little government man from Las Cruces, and as he continued to talk, every word gave them hope of selling their cattle at a good price.

Audie, Shug, and Billy Sol stayed with the cattle, but the others drifted into camp to listen, scrounging for whatever food they could find to gnaw on until Florine would emerge to cook supper. They listened to Ponder and the government man talking, and like Dud, did not interrupt the flow of conversation. Only once did Dud interject with a question.

"We had to kill a bandit and his men, El Escorpion. Is that going to mean trouble?"

Again, the government man waved this aside with a motion of his hand as of no importance. "The only thing that would make the people mad is if you preached to them that gambling is a sin. Me, I am a good Catholic. I tell them my beautiful wife does not want me to gamble, and they leave me alone. Otherwise, they would be angry."

He turned toward Mutt and Toomey. "You, you young men. They will win every cent you have. But do not get angry. Smile as if it was nothing, and you will be okay. You are better off to spend your money on the ladies of the evening first. But do not go to Rosa's house. They all have the bad disease. Go to Valentina's instead. They cost more, but they are cleaner."

Dud suppressed a grin at the looks on Mutt's and Toomey's faces.

Although not talked out by any means, Martin left an hour before Dud and Ponder were due back at the fort, saying he must work out the details of the cattle buy with the colonel.

"Things are looking mighty good, Boss," Mutt said.

"Don't get too excited. The deal's not done yet." It was only after the words left his mouth that Dud realized Mutt might not have been talking about cattle.

"Florine!" Ponder hollered. "Get on out here and start cooking. It looks like you are going to get your way. We may be taking some of these here cattle to New Mexico after all."

Delgado, dismissed and out of the picture, was not in the colonel's office when they returned. Now that they knew how badly the army needed their cattle, Dud and Ponder were prepared to dicker, and it took a better part of an hour. They did not allow any jubilation to bubble to the surface until they were riding away from the fort. And even then, they felt it bad luck to show they were happy about anything to the citizens of El Paso who would view them as prime rubes to be parted with their money as soon as possible.

"Ninety dollars a head," Ponder said in wonder when their backs were to El Paso.

"And ninety-three at Las Cruces," Dud added.

Florine had an early supper ready, and Dud asked Henry to gather everyone together. As they sat around the campfire, almost unable to eat because of the suspense and excitement, Dud and Ponder explained their deal.

"We'll cut six hundred head out for the army in the morning, taking them to Fort Bliss. Some of them will be going back to Fort Davis, others will stay at Bliss, still others will be butchered and distributed to Indian agents."

"And the other four hundred?" Barefoot asked.

"We're taking those to Las Cruces."

As soon as the words left his mouth, Dud saw the guarded looks Shug and Billy Sol exchanged. Florine didn't look at anybody, but her chest gave a great heave.

"You can take turns going into El Paso tonight if you want, but I won't have much money to advance you until tomorrow."

Dud paused. "I don't want to stop you from having a good time, but it would relieve my mind something powerful if everyone stayed with the herd tonight."

He thought the men would look at one another to make a decision, but instead, every man nodded his head. They had been through so much, the thought of losing everything so close to the finish line was something they could hardly bear either.

The next morning, however, there was no trouble, and they soon had the army's six hundred head separated, leaving the tougher specimens to make the trip to Las Cruces. It would be fifty more miles of open country, following the river. If bandits or Indians decided to swoop down on them, there would be no place to hide. It might mean a running fight.

Shug and Billy Sol cut the cattle without comment. Before heading to the fort, they approached Dud.

"You ain't planning on letting them have the General, are you, Dud?"

Dud shook his head. The General and Fitz's best horse, the one Ponder was using as his night horse, would be going back with them, and he told the brothers so.

The relief blooming over their faces was almost comical. Dud had never seen the brothers show so much feeling.

Despite their fears of a last-minute disaster, the drive to Fort Bliss in the morning happened without incident. The army took possession of the cattle, and the drovers went back to camp while Dud and Ponder waited to be paid. It took all Dud's willpower to keep his emotions from showing when the army put the bags of gold coins in his hand. There were no banks in El Paso, and they would have to carry the gold back across Texas. The gold, heavy in their saddlebags, weighed just as heavily on their minds, and they discussed different ways to hide it. They visited a tonsorial parlor, hefting their saddlebags on their shoulders, keeping them within a hand's reach at all times.

They returned to the camp only long enough to fetch a wagon. Once back in town, they loaded the wagon with boards and nails. Unsure of what Las Cruces had to offer and trying to make their purchase of lumber less conspicuous, they also bought a large number of supplies.

Once back at camp, Dud called another

meeting.

"I'm advancing part of your wages so you can spend it in El Paso. You've got one more night here. The government in Las Cruces wants those cattle as soon as possible, so we'll be heading out early tomorrow morning."

This time, the nodding faces were filled with excitement and relief.

"At Las Cruces, I'll give you the rest of your pay. We'll sell the mustangs we don't need and head home on the upper road, traveling by night. If you'd rather stay here in these parts, that's fine. But I would surely welcome your company on the way home. Those who return with us will get a bonus."

Dud didn't ask for an answer and didn't get one. Meanwhile, he set up a table with his ledger and a pencil. Audie wanted just enough money for a shave and haircut and a little to blow. The others followed his lead — fearful of losing everything in the wild and sinful El Paso. Shug and Billy Sol surprised Dud by deciding to go with Audie for a barbershop haircut instead of one of Florine's hack jobs.

Ponder said he would take the children into town early and return early, but only if they promised to stick to him. This they agreed to fast enough. The others had a mild and playful fight over who would get to go into town first. Dud and Barefoot volunteered to stay with the herd. Dud gave Darnell and Henry a hard look, and they agreed to let Toomey and Mutt go in first.

Dud was closing his ledger, about to put it away when Florine appeared before him.

"I want some of that there money that's mine."

Dud paused in surprise. "I thought you wanted us to keep your share until we sold the rest of the cattle in New Mexico?"

"I changed my mind. Now give me some money."

Dud agreed. "All right, Florine, how much do you want?"

The amount she requested would barely buy her a meal, so Dud had no idea what she was up to, but he gave it to her without further comment. She signed, making her mark for it with a set jaw, and he shut the book, looking after her as she walked away.

Chapter Twenty-Six

When Ponder returned to camp, they began working on the wagon. The boys helped remove the contents until everything was emptied. Dud and Ponder cut the boards to length, putting in a false bottom to hide the gold.

When they finished hammering, they rubbed the boards down with grease and dirt to disguise the newness. Satisfied they had done all they could, they put everything back in the wagon, and Dud told Ponder to return to town if he wanted to. After being warned over and over how difficult it would be to sell the cattle, to have the sale go through so smoothly seemed almost too good to be true.

"I'm so jumpy about something going wrong, I don't want to leave. I'll stay here on guard."

But Ponder didn't want to leave either. "In case you haven't noticed, Dud, me and

Florine are about wore out. Besides, I don't want to be in El Paso with that woman roaming around."

"What is she doing?"

"I don't know. Going here, going there on her old mule. It don't make no sense."

"Ponder, she needs new clothes."

Florine came back before dark wearing a mishmash of clothes that looked almost as old as the ones she went to town in. Dud could just imagine the scene she created in the store when they told her their prices. She said nothing, however, but went straight to her wagon. Ponder shrugged and left her alone.

Dud wondered if Mutt and Toomey would find the courage to visit Valentina's. What they drew in wages might not cover her services. Henry and Darnell presented a different set of problems. Paying for a night of love was abhorrent — a conquest to them had more meaning than a simple business transaction. It was the wooing and winning of the female sex they craved. It also meant complications with relatives and beaus.

"I may have to go in and fetch Toomey and Mutt so Darnell and Henry can take a turn."

But he didn't have to. Mutt and Toomey rode into camp in good spirits, but they came back early.

"We spent it all," Mutt told them. "Ain't got a cent left between us."

Barefoot left and returned early, as did the others, even Darnell and Henry — all of them clean shaven and smelling of soap. Unable to relax, they knew the last fifty miles might be the worst ones they would encounter. There were no secrets in El Paso, and every bandit there knew how much money they were carrying.

"Well, look at it this way, Dud," Audie said in the morning as Dud was about to give the signal to begin the drive. "Any smart bandit will wait until we get paid for these cattle in Las Cruces before trying to rob us."

"Yeah, but I've known some awful dumb outlaws," Dud said. He waved his hat to Shug and Billy Sol. "Head 'em out!"

They managed to keep the cattle from tearing up anyone's property on the way out of town. Once out of the pass, they found themselves on flat land that contained nothing but sand and poor grass. A hot wind picked up, and the baths they had were nothing but a distant memory as particles of dirt found their way into every hole and crevice. Bandannas went up, but the sand ripped at their eyes without mercy.

The cattle bawled and balked at moving forward. Dud rode ahead to Shug and Billy Sol, pulling down his bandanna so he could shout at them and getting a mouth full of grit before he could get the first word out.

"Let's stop here so they can put their backs to the wind. We'll start again at dusk and herd them by night. We ain't gonna get lost in the dark if we follow the river."

Shug and Billy Sol nodded and let the cattle slow to a halt. Dud rode down the line to tell the others.

Most nodded and began to nudge the cattle to move in closer, but Audie shouted something back. Dud rode closer, pulling down his bandanna.

"What did you say?"

"Ain't no outlaw with any sense gonna be out in this dust storm!"

Dud laughed and nodded, pulling up his bandanna to ride on to Barefoot and the boys. Audie was right. Their greatest danger would come in Las Cruces.

For two days and nights they pushed the cattle north, only stopping when the wind became unbearable for man and beast. There was always a need for guards, and rest was impossible anyway. Once the wind died down, they watered the longhorns and horses, trading mounts with more frequency than usual to keep from wearing them down. The cattle and horses were able to snatch at food, but not so the cowboys. The little jerky they had was soon gone, and it was impossible to even make coffee without having the pot become filled with sand.

At the end of the third day, the wind dwindled as the edge of darkness began to creep upon them. They were close enough to Las Cruces they no longer felt the need to push the herd so hard. Ponder and Florine got out the pots and pans, coffee was made, and the cowboys lolled and rested. Dud and Barefoot spelled Henry so he could eat and sleep for a while. The two men collapsed on the ground near the remuda, sitting with their own horses at hand. Dud touched his lips with his tongue, feeling nothing but caked grit.

"I've never been this filthy," Barefoot said. His hair was no longer black, but a sand covered mop like the rest.

Dud nodded in agreement. "Do you think you have earned your stripes? Do you think you can go back to San Antonio now, stand up to any man and win the heart of your little gal?"

"Yes. And what about you? Will you have made enough money to lure your wife back?"

To Dud's embarrassment, he felt tears of gratitude about to overtake him. He became so choked up; he was unable to speak for several moments. Barefoot did not press him for words, understanding the great emotion he was experiencing.

"Yes," Dud said after a long pause. "If we get the money in Las Cruces, too, I'll be able to build her the finest home in San Antonio."

They talked about the trip back in a desultory way — how hard it would be, the dangers that would await them. The only way they could make themselves stay awake was to let their lips move on occasion.

The long harsh scream of a barn owl sounding overhead caused them to jump. It circled, screeching several more times, and the horses began to make small movements of agitation. The owl flew away, and Dud expected the horses to settle, but instead they grew more disturbed, whinnying and pawing at the ground. He half rose, listening. Barefoot made to speak, but Dud shushed him with his hand.

A muffled cry came, and Dud knew in an instant it was Jemmy.

"Stay with the horses," Dud said, going for Ned, while Barefoot went for his rifle.

Once on Ned, Dud pulled his rifle from

his scabbard. He turned Ned in the direction of the wagons, but before they reached it, he could hear Will's screams.

"Stop! Stop! Leave her alone!"

Dud slid from Ned's back, still holding the rifle, intent on sneaking into camp. Will's cries grew muffled. Sensing someone was near, Dud started to whirl, but it was too late. A gun poked him in the back.

"Drop it and walk," a rough voice behind him said.

Dud put the rifle down, glancing over his shoulder long enough to get a look at a man whose age and stance screamed professional outlaw. The rifle poked him in the back again.

"Move."

Dud walked toward camp. It had grown dark, but the circle of fire illuminated his drovers, armed but paused. Shug and Billy Sol were with the cattle; Barefoot had stayed with the horses, but the rest of them were there, staring at a group of five outlaws, and the oldest one was a big man holding onto Jemmy.

He grinned at Dud. "Here's the boss man."

Jemmy struggled, but the old man kept a tight hold. The other hand held an ancient army pistol cocked at Jemmy's head. Ponder had Will by the arms. He leaned down and whispered in the boy's ear, and Will stopped struggling. Ponder let go, and Will stared at the man holding Jemmy with all the malevolent hatred a boy could muster.

"Good, good," the leader of the outlaws said in a jovial voice, his lips pulled back in a smile that showed a mouthful of blackened teeth. "Now hand over the gold and nothing will happen to this here little gal."

Dud blinked. Jemmy did look like a girl with his hair grown out over his ears. But Will had yelled let go of "her." He didn't have time to cipher it out.

"Come on, now, don't make us kill you all and have to search for that there gold," the leader said. "Just hand it over, and we'll leave pretty as you please."

Dud struggled to clear exhaustion and hunger from his brain. He looked at the men holding guns on them — the dirty older leader, a young Mexican, two sorry-looking young whites, and the last one, the one who had snuck up on him. He dressed as an Apache, but an uncommonly large physique and irregular features spoke of mixed blood. The whole bunch was a motley band of brutes he wouldn't be surprised to learn were McHugh's hired cutthroats.

Dud knew they weren't going to leave

quietly into the night. They were just lazy outlaws who demanded a shortcut to the gold rather than spend time searching. As soon as they had it, they would kill every last one of them. But the drovers still had their weapons in hand, waiting to see what he would decide.

"Boss man, make up your mind. What's it going to be? You play nice, or this here little gal gets it first."

Dud fought to wipe the cobwebs from his brain. In spite of the fog in his head and drained muscles, he knew lies told by El Paso ruffians when he heard them. What was it about outlaws in El Paso that he should be remembering? What did the men around El Paso live for? He took a gulp of air and spoke.

"This don't seem very sporting to me," Dud said, hoping to lure them into something that would lower their guard. "I tell you what, let's make a bet. I bet you I can whip this here Apache in a knife fight to the death. If he wins, I'm dead, and you take everything. If I win, you take half the gold and vamoose."

The Apache smirked. An avid look of interest crossed the leader's face. The eyes of the Mexican outlaw and one of the whites began to glow in vicious savagery. The other white objected.

"I don't know. Let's kill them, get the gold and get out of here."

"Shut up," the leader said. He looked at the Apache and gave a jerk of his head.

While one outlaw frowned, the other five began to quiver in bloodthirsty excitement. The cowboys stood like stone. Dud approached Henry.

"Give me your stiletto."

"Señor Dud, let me fight him," Henry said.

Dud gave a slight shake of his head. He gave a quick glance to make sure Henry was armed with a pistol in his belt. He spoke, saying the words so softly only Henry could hear them. "Be ready."

The Apache grinned, dropping his gun belt, and Dud did the same.

Henry handed him his knife, which Dud knew he kept razor sharp. Dud grasped the handle diagonally in the palm of his hand to better maneuver it in all directions. He crouched with his left hand outstretched, ready to guard against a blow, remembering the Cajuns he had fought in Louisiana. The Apache's actions mirrored his, except when he grinned again, Dud snatched a handful of sand and threw it in his face. The Cajuns had taught him a lot.

Dud charged, ready to send a thrust home, but the Apache recovered, blocking his blow and sending him backward. He barely had time to recover when the Apache rushed forward. Dud jumped back, but the blade of the knife grazed his abdomen. The blade-fighting Cajuns had also shown him never to let a landed blow stun him, and Dud responded with a slash to the Apache's wrist. But he was quick, and Dud's blow hadn't gone deep enough to cut the tendons.

It became a dance of meet and slash, blood flowing everywhere, but neither one was able to cut deeply enough to incapacitate the other nor maneuver closer to send in a deadly thrust. As Dud continued to crouch, waving the knife in his right hand and motioning with his left to distract his enemy, the overwhelming tiredness left him, and an unexpected rush of power coursed through his body. He had to get closer to Jemmy. Would Ponder and the others know what to do? Would they be ready?

Dud fought in a circle, moving ever closer to Jemmy. The Apache stared at him in hatred, his knife flashing so fast, it took everything Dud had left in him to parry his blows. But his were just as dangerous, and the Apache began to grimace in concentration, fighting with all his might to keep the deadly stiletto in Dud's hand from going in too deep.

The outlaws shouted with excitement — placing bets with one another. But their voices and shouts were like a faraway roar of a waterfall to Dud. Every particle of his being concentrated on one thing, killing the Apache.

Dud drew as close to Jemmy as he thought he could possibly get. And emulating an unknown assailant in New Orleans who had almost broken his leg, he shot out his left foot, landing his boot squarely on the Apache's knee. He crumbled, and Dud went in for the kill, thrusting his knife into the soft hollow of the Apache's throat.

In an instant, Dud snatched Jemmy, rolled away, and threw himself over the child, lying as flat on the ground as he could with Jemmy underneath.

The roar of gunfire over his head told him his drovers had known what to do. But this time, the unexpected commotion sent the cattle to their feet, and the rumbling of horns and hooves thundered past them.

Dud felt hands lifting him up, pushing him and Jemmy toward Ponder's wagon. He was shoved in the wagon, along the Jemmy and Will. The ground shook with the pounding of hooves, and the night roared with the sound of terrified longhorns racing ahead in one mass. Dud collapsed on a cot in the wagon, surrounded by a plethora of supplies shaking in the rumble and the nearby Hollister children staring at him in fright.

The sounds faded after a while, and Ponder looked into the back of the wagon.

"You kids move over and let me tend to Dud."

Ponder carried in a rag and a wash basin full of water. He handed the wash basin to Will to hold for him, while he removed Dud's shirt.

"Everybody?"

Ponder, concentrating on examining his wounds answered. "I don't know. We took them by surprise, so I'm hoping we got them before they could get any of us. You've lost a lot of blood."

Dud looked down at his bloody chest and arms. He had been cut more times than he realized. He could feel warm blood from his earlobe running down his neck. His eyes went to Jemmy and back to Ponder.

"Did you know?"

"I suspected, but I didn't know. Be quiet."

Dud felt like a dead man. Now that the fight was over, the jolt of energy had died, depleting him of all strength.

Ponder wrapped him in bandages. When he finished, he took the basin, giving orders to Will and Jemmy.

"Give him some water out of one of the canteens now and whenever he wants it. But don't let him try to get up."

Dud took a few sips of water, shut his eyes and drifted to sleep.

When he awakened, he knew the wagon had been moved, but he didn't know where or how long ago. He remained still, going over what had happened before he fell asleep. The tent flap opened, and Ponder peered in at him.

"You still living?" he asked, climbing into the wagon.

"How long have I been out?"

"Two days."

Dud tried to rise. "We've got to get those cattle to Las Cruces before something else happens."

Ponder put his hand on Dud's shoulder and gave him a firm downward push.

"They has already been delivered and paid for."

Dud leaned back and closed his eyes in relief. He opened them to watch Ponder, who was examining his dressings. After poking around, he leaned back, pleased and in good spirits.

Dud did not speak, but gave Ponder a questioning look.

"Everybody's okay. Barefoot and Henry kept the horses from running off, and Shug and Billy Sol had the herd circled and stopped before we could string together enough cuss words to make a sentence.

"Audie got a flesh wound in the leg, but it's more of a scratch than anything else."

Dud breathed another sigh of relief. They were all unharmed. But there was still the matter of the Hollister children.

"I want to talk to those kids."

Ponder nodded. He turned, poking his head out the wagon and hollering.

"Jemmy, Will, bring Mr. Dud some of that there broth out of the stew pot. He wants to talk to you."

In a few minutes, the two climbed into the wagon, Jemmy holding a cup with a dish rag around it. Ponder helped Dud sit. He took the cup from Jemmy and held it up to Dud's lips. Dud started to object, but his hand shook, and he thought he better accept Ponder's help. He drank it all, the Hollister children watching him with big eyes. When he finished, he reclined again, his head turned to them.

"What's this about you being a girl?"

Jemmy and Will started talking and blubbering, their voices mingling as Dud caught the words "Jemima" and "Mama told us to."

"One at a time. Will, you go first and start at the beginning."

Now that they no longer had to lie and hide, the truth tumbled out of the boy. Karling, the man who had come to the ranch, was an uncle — their mother's sister's husband. On visits, he had begun to fondle Jemmy, telling her he would kill Will if she told anybody. In a terrified turmoil, she eventually cried and confessed to Will, who insisted they tell their mother. The aunt was ill; the uncle was rich and powerful, and their mother knew she was dying. Hearing that Ponder and Dud planned on leaving on a cattle drive, she hit upon the only solution she could think of to get Jemmy away from a lecherous, evil man.

Jemmy looked from Ponder and Dud with tears in her eyes.

"Are you mad at us?"

Dud sighed and gave her a smile. "Now how can we be mad?"

Jemmy and Will began to cry, throwing themselves on Dud and hugging him. Ponder removed them with big, gentle hands.

"Now, now. Leave poor old Mr. Dud be for now. You can thank him later."

Ponder shooed them out of the wagon.

"Florine?"

Ponder turned back to Dud. "Never suspected a thing."

"Here, help me up. I'm starving."

Chapter Twenty-Seven

When Dud emerged from Ponder's wagon, he found they had made camp near the Rio Grande in a grove of cottonwoods. Ponder told him that Jemmy's story had moved the drovers almost to tears.

"Aw, they was a little embarrassed for pissing in front of her and everything else, but they got over it. They is so mad at that Karling feller, they is ready to whip his ass all over Texas."

Darnell and Henry had taken off as soon as possible to experience the delights of Las Cruces. They returned to camp late, in time for Mutt and Toomey to take a turn. While Henry and Darnell had roamed the cantinas and bars, Mutt and Toomey were determined to experience high-class living for at least one night.

"They say there is a big fine hotel smack in the middle of town," Mutt said. "And that is where we is headed. We's gonna get a room, go to a fancy restaurant and be high rollers for twenty-four hours."

"You'll have to buy some new clothes first, or they won't let you step foot in no fine hotel," Audie said with a laugh.

Dud watched the two younger men ride away in high spirits on two of the smaller mustangs. Toomey, still terrified something was going to happen to his uncle's horse, had made Henry promise to guard the gelding with his life. Dud looked around.

"Where's Florine?"

Ponder shrugged. "She went into town with Shug and Billy Sol."

"We've got to make plans. We can't stick around here long — it's too dangerous." Ponder, Will, and Jemmy started supper. Darkness fell, and the Higgins family still had not returned. Dud gave up waiting for them. With the campfire glowing, they sat eating and discussing what they should do next.

"Mutt and Toomey have already told me they are going back to Dewitt County."

"And I, San Antonio," Barefoot said.

"I ain't lost nothing in New Mexico," Audie said.

Dud looked at Darnell and Henry. "What about you two?"

Darnell grinned. "I's made a promise to

my sweethearts in San Antonio that I's would be back."

Dud laughed. "Henry?"

Henry shrugged and grinned. "Maybe by the time we get back, my sins will be forgotten."

Audie glanced at Jemmy and Will, who stood washing dishes near Ponder's wagon. "What about them?"

Dud shook his head. "I don't know. They know how dangerous it will be, but they don't want to be left behind."

"I can't see dragging a little girl through the territory we'll be going through," Audie said.

Ponder spit out his wad of tobacco. Dud and Audie both knew what that meant and braced themselves.

"We ain't got time to be interviewing no prospective parents, and I ain't leaving that child with just anybody."

No one wanted to argue with Ponder. Dud knew he was right — they couldn't throw Jemmy into another situation as bad as the one she left, but that in itself raised more questions.

"If we make it back in one piece, what are we going to do about this Karling fellow? He has enough say-so; he can throw us all in jail."

"You forget, you knucklehead, we'll have a first-class lawyer in Texas on our side."

All eyes turned to Barefoot, and in the flickering light of the campfire, they thought him blushing. His chest expanded a fraction of an inch.

"That is true," Dud conceded.

"Yeah, you would know," Audie said with a laugh. The others laughed with him, but left off hoorawing him to discuss the horses instead. They agreed to cull the mustangs the following morning. They all had favorites and each wanted to make sure his special pet wasn't sold.

"You better let me do the horse trading, Dud," Ponder said. "The way you're feeling, an eighty-year-old widow woman could take you."

Dud was about to retort when he heard the sound of horses. He had half risen when a familiar voice called out.

"Don't shoot, it's us."

Ponder shook his head. "Those two chuckleheads can't even spend one night in town without getting into trouble."

The two young drovers approached, garbed in new clothes. Toomey's neckerchief, blue shirt, vest, and leggings were more on the subdued side, but Mutt had gone all out on the brightest colors he could find along with leggings covered in fancy stitchwork and conchos.

"What happened this time?" Audie said, blinking at the display. "Did you get lost in a toggery and have to fight your way out?"

"Aw shucks," Mutt said. "We didn't know how much stuff would cost in this here place. We done spent everything we had on clothes before'n we could even get to the hotel."

"Mutt, yore hat's so big, I think you could take a bath in it," Ponder said.

The young men ducked their heads, looking sheepish.

"We sure are glad we left most of our wages with Mr. Dud, or we wouldn't have anything left to take home," Toomey said.

"Yeah, and then these here two fellers drug us in a saloon and kept trying to get us drunk and asking us a bunch of questions, so we decided we better get on back," Mutt added.

"What questions?" Dud asked, but before either of the cowboys answered, the sound of a horse and buggy approaching made Dud hold up his hand to stop them from speaking.

"That's not Florine," Audie said.

They reached for their guns and stood.

"Hello, the camp! It is I, Martin."

The shoulders of the drovers fell in relief.

"Come on in," Ponder called. "Light down and sit a spell."

The buggy drew closer. Martin was not alone. A dark shapeless mass sat next to him. Dud tensed, only partially relaxing when it became apparent the lump seemed to be a woman swathed in black clothes and wearing a heavy black veil.

Martin stepped down from the buggy and stopped to pat the person sitting on the seat before walking toward the campfire. His appearance with an unknown person made them all a little edgy. Martin sensed their tension. He removed his hat and gave a short bow of apology.

"Forgive me for coming to you in the darkness. But I heard a rumor in town today. My poor wife would not let me rest until I investigated it."

"What's that?" Ponder asked.

"That on the way here, you secured the release of a young Mexican woman from the Mescalero."

"That's right."

Ponder proceeded to give a brief description of how they came to help the señorita and her regrettable demise.

"I think she may have been the cousin of my wife."

Ponder gave a nod in Audie's direction. "Audie, here, nursed her. He can tell you more than anybody else."

Martin turned to Audie. "Would you mind, please, señor, talking to my wife about it?"

Audie nodded. He reached into his pocket, pulling out the Bull Durham tobacco bag where he kept the lock of hair and scrap of dress belonging to the girl he had tended with such care. He walked forward and spoke to Señora Martin. She pulled back the black veil, and in the dim light, the drovers took a deep breath at the sight of her beauty.

"My wife, she is an angel to me and to all our family. It cuts her so deep for something bad to happen to one of them."

"Have you been married long?" Ponder asked.

"*Si.* Many years. I don't know why she chose me, the poor runted son of a farmer. I did not believe I even had a chance with her. Through thick and thin, rich and poor, she has stood by me."

Unable to stop himself, Dud glanced at Barefoot. At the same time, Barefoot's eyes found his. They looked away, embarrassed to know each other's thoughts, and turned back to Señor Martin. He was speaking of something else.

"I also came to warn you. McHugh, his men, and no telling how many others will be waiting for you on the road to El Paso. You would be much better off leaving in the dead of night and going the long way."

"The long way?"

"*Si.* I brought you a map." He paused to remove a folded paper from his inside pocket. He opened it, smoothing it out before handing it to Dud. Ponder drew nearer and looked over Dud's shoulder as he examined it.

"There is a pass through the San Andres and Organ Mountains. On the other side is good water, the San Augustin Springs. There is an inn there also. Before the war, it was a terrible place of gambling, prostitution, and drunkenness. The roughest miners and worst outlaws gathered there. The war put a stop to it, and the soldiers are now forbidden to go there because of a regrettable incident during that time."

Dud knew of it – Confederates had captured a large number of Union soldiers in a humiliating defeat as they were dying of thirst trying to cross the dry Organ Mountains. The Confederates could not keep control of New Mexico, however, and soon, the Indians were rampaging against settlers with no troops to keep them at bay. But the surrender of so many Union soldiers had been an embarrassment to the army. He looked up from the map to watch Martin as he continued.

"With people pouring in, it will start up again and be worse than ever before. The owner is in Las Cruces now buying supplies. He will be here for many days. If you leave here soon, the only person you will find at the inn will be a drunken old desert rat who lives there for the whiskey and a place to stay."

"I'm surprised the Indians haven't killed him."

Martin shrugged. "Even drunk, he is a crack shot."

"And once we are through the pass?"

"Head south. See, here on the map," Martin said, pointing to a wye in the road. "When you get nearer El Paso, head east on the old stagecoach road."

He looked at them with keen, solemn eyes. "Take as many water barrels as you can haul and keep them as filled as you can. You will have need of all of them."

They gave him their thanks. Audie returned, and Martin bid them farewell. "Go with God, *mis amigos.*"

"And you and your wife also," Ponder said.

When the Martins had driven away, the horse's clopping fading into the darkness, Dud turned to Ponder.

"Do you think we can trust him?"

Ponder nodded. "Yes, I believe him. That's not to say we won't be followed or outwitted."

They stood silent for a moment, letting their predicament sink in. Mutt, however, thought he had waited long enough. He tugged at Audie's sleeve.

"Say, was that there woman as pretty up close as she looked from back here?"

Audie laughed. "She had thick coal black hair, with dark eyelashes longer than any heifer's you ever did see, and lips as red as rose petals and probably just as soft. Mutt, that was the most beautiful woman I have ever laid eyes on."

Mutt drooped in sorrow. "Dang, I wish I could have seen her up close."

The thick air dissipated into laughter. They were in danger, but Mutt's obsession with the female sex hadn't abated, much to their enjoyment. Mutt grew tired of them hoorawing him about women so he left to check on the horses. When he walked away, Dud turned to Audie.

"Was she really that beautiful up close?"

"She was until smallpox got a hold of her. She said she contracted it soon after she and Martin were married. He nursed her back to health and still treats her as if she was the same girl he married."

Ponder looked around. "Where's Henry and Darnell?"

Henry and Darnell moved closer. "We are right here, Señor Ponder."

"I want you to go back into town and find out who is the best whore at that there Valentina's in El Paso."

"Oh, we already know that, señor. All the men, they talk about Shady Sadie. She is supposed to be able to . . ."

"That's all I need to know."

"Why do you need to know that?" Dud demanded.

"Because tomorrow, I'm going into town to sell mustangs, buy water barrels, and spread the word that my good-for-nothing nephew wants to be debauched by Shady Sadie in El Paso as soon as possible."

Audie burst out laughing.

Dud, however, was not amused. "I would have liked to have had the pleasure if I'm going to bear the reputation.

"And bring me back some new clothes. Nothing as fancy as Mutt's. I don't want people to think I'm a millionaire or a refugee from a circus."

Florine, Shug, and Billy Sol came back to camp that night exhausted, their mouths turned down. They avoided looking and talking with the others, and Florine went straight into her wagon, staying there. Since they were about as socially backward as people could be, Dud at first wondered if they had lost their money to some shyster. But being socially backward didn't mean they were stupid, and Dud couldn't see any of the three losing hard-earned money to anybody.

"Maybe Florine's been out searching for wives for them and can't find any," Audie said.

"Oh, come on," Dud said. "She thinks they are still thirteen years old."

"Well, stranger things have happened."

Florine refused to come out of her wagon the next morning, leaving it to Jemmy to bake the biscuits and make gravy.

"Miss Jemmy, perhaps you'd better show me how to make biscuits and gravy," Barefoot said. "It's about time I learned."

Dud gave him a sharp look. "Does this mean you are forgetting about a certain little gal in San Antonio and embracing bachelorhood?"

"Maybe," Barefoot said, not looking at Dud. He took Jemmy by the hand and walked with her to Ponder's wagon.

The visit from the devoted Martins had rattled Barefoot, and Dud did not want to admit it had given him pause, too. But he put it from his mind, forcing himself to think about the map and the route they would be taking home.

Later, after breakfast, when Florine still didn't appear, Dud approached their wagon and asked the brothers if everything was all right.

"Ma's just feeling a little poorly."

"Should we send Ponder for a doctor?"

"No," Billy Sol said. "We done seen a bunch of doctors and whatnot yesterday."

"Shut up, Billy Sol," Shug said.

Dud paused, not sure how much to push it.

"Shug, is there something about your ma I need to know?"

"No, she's just wore out from the drive, that's all. Ain't it about time to split the mustangs?"

With the subject closed, Dud turned to the matter at hand. Every cowboy kept his favorite two horses. Henry and Darnell agreed to stay with the remaining remuda, while Barefoot and Toomey took the ones to be sold, riding alongside Ponder and his wagon. Audie, Mutt, and Barefoot would remain in the camp on guard. Before leaving, Ponder cautioned Dud about taking it easy.

"You need to get rested after that fight, because we're about to start another that's gonna make that one look like playing patty-cakes."

"How is it you get to go into town and have all the fun while I have to stay out here like an invalid?"

Ponder didn't bother to answer. He got in his wagon and turned to Audie.

"Don't let him overdo it."

Before they were out of sight, Dud hollered, "Bring us some decent food to eat for supper." Florine still had not gotten up.

Despite their precautions, or maybe because of them, they were not bothered in camp that afternoon. When Ponder returned minus the mustangs and carrying a wagonload of water barrels, they learned he had not only spread the word about Dud's supposed desire to go back to El Paso and partake of Shady Sadie's pleasures, he had explained away the water barrels.

"That was easy. We came up here in the spring when the creeks was running, but we'll be going back in the summer when the creeks is dried up."

"All too true," Audie said. "If we make it that far."

Ponder had traded for extra mules to add to Florine's wagon and gotten rid of the spare wagon he had coupled onto the back of his so that his oxen would only be pulling one.

"If I'd ah had two weeks, I could have got double the price, but an old man with a horny nephew has to take what he can get."

Dud frowned but said nothing. After all, he hoped the story would be swallowed by every bandit in Las Cruces, too.

Later, they built a large campfire, stuffing their faces with as much of the food Ponder had brought back as they could get in. Afterward, they loaded the campfire with more wood and retreated into the shadows to wait until the moon was high above them.

They left the campfire burning brightly for anyone watching to see. Without a word, Dud and Ned led the others east toward the mountains, General Sherman, minus his clapper, walking by his side. Ponder sat at the reins of his wagon, while Shug drove theirs with Florine still in the back. Somewhere closer to town, a pack of coyotes began to yipe, calling to smaller critters, "Come join us so we can eat you." The sound had always been both entrancing and repelling to Dud, but tonight, he felt only gratitude. It hid the sound of the horses' hoofbeats and the creaking of the wagon wheels along the barren soil.

They traveled the rest of the night, repeatedly sending someone to backtrack to see if they were being followed, but every time the rider returned, he affirmed they were alone. It was dawn when they reached the pass, and they had no trouble finding the springs. The water was unexpectedly clear and enticing, but the moccasin tracks around it took any joy away from it.

"They are not recent," Dud said. "Maybe two or three days old."

The water coming from the springs made a shallow stream that tumbled over rocks into a land where the tallest tree seemed to be only head high. The drovers began to fill their water barrels, each man silent, looking over his shoulder. Florine remained in her wagon, and Dud walked around the back where Shug stood. Billy Sol came out of the wagon.

"She's got fever."

"Do you want me to send Jemmy over to help?"

"No," Billy Sol said, reaching back into the wagon for a pail. "I'll tend to her. How far away are we from that there inn you were talking about?"

"Around the next bend across the creek according to the map."

Billy Sol nodded and headed for the springs. Shug swung his long legs over the back of the wagon and crawled in to check on his mother. Dud left to help the other men finish filling the barrels.

When they were done, Dud led the way to the inn, splashing across the shallow creek that would probably be the last good water they would see for a hundred miles.

When the inn came in view, every man's eyes blinked in surprise. A two-story rock and adobe structure surrounded by rock walls with tall wooden doors guarding its courtyard, it looked more like a fortress than a hotel. Dud rode in front and stopped before getting too close to the doors.

"Hello the house!" Dud said in a loud voice.

A bullet sang out and knocked his hat off. He got down from Jax, muttered a curse word, and fetched his hat.

"We ain't the enemy, old man!" he yelled. "We're cattle drovers from Texas heading home. Pedro Martin sent us this way."

"From Texas?" an old and rasping voice called.

"That's right."

"What's the name?"

Dud took a deep breath. How crazy drunk was the old man?

"Washburn!"

The old man repeated it, and Dud responded.

"That's right."

There was a brief silence before the voice hollered, "Fordie Washburn?"

Taken aback, Dud answered automatically. "No, his son, Dudford. His brother Ponder is with me."

"Ponder's with you?"

"Yes." Dud turned and looked back at Ponder, but Ponder's eyebrows were knitted together in puzzlement, and he wasn't noticing him. His eyes were on the doors.

They stayed closed, and Dud wondered if they should just ride on and forget about sleeping inside the fortress.

Just when he decided to give the word to head out, the doors moved and creaked, slowly opening. The old man pushing them came into view — a true desert rat with long dirty gray hair and covered in dust. He stepped aside.

"Come on in."

Dud stared down at him as he passed, but the lined face with its heavy brows and large watery eyes didn't ring any bells of recollection. He dismounted from Jax as Ponder and Shug brought the wagons into the courtyard. The old man shut the doors and bolted them after the last rider entered.

"We got a sick woman in the wagon," Dud said. "Do you have some kind of stretcher we can put her on to get her into a bed?"

"Yeah," the only man nodded. "Stay here. I'll rustle up something."

He disappeared into one of the rooms opening into the courtyard. Ponder watched with his mouth shut tight. Shug looked like he had seen a ghost. Audie's eyebrows creased in concern.

The old man reappeared dragging an old army cot that looked like it had been used in the War of 1812. Dud went to help him, and they maneuvered the cot to the back of Florine's wagon. Shug climbed into the back, and with Billy Sol's help, carried Florine out, placing her on the cot.

She lay with feverish eyes and beads of sweat covering her forehead. Her mouth sagged, saliva forming at the corners. She closed her lips, trying to focus on what was happening.

Shug and Billy Sol stood aside, backs stiff, and stared at the old man. He wasn't seeing them; however, he was looking down at their mother.

"Florine?"

Chapter Twenty-Eight

Florine looked up and recognition leaped into her eyes. She gasped.

"Zeb? Zeb, is that you? We've been looking all over for you."

Florine began to cry. The desert rat leaned down, searching her face. Florine grasped his hand, staring at him as if he was a vision that might fade away. His response was puzzlement.

"Florine, what are you doing way out here?"

"I had to come, Zeb. I had to find you. I had to see you one more time before I died, Zeb."

"Florine . . ."

"Zeb, I wanted to tell you. I wanted to tell how sorry I was for the way I treated you. I had to find you and tell you."

"Florine, you ought not feel that way. I was no account as a husband."

But Florine wept and shook her head. Zeb

continued to try to explain.

"I wanted to come home so many times, but I just didn't have the guts to face you after saying I was heading west for the cure and then being gone so long."

"You would have come home if I hadn't been so awful."

"That's not true, Florine. I'm just no good." He straightened and looked to Shug and Billy Sol. "Boys, carry your ma into that room yonder."

Shug stared at the old man, his face blank. Billy Sol scowled at him in resentment. But when Shug bent down without a word to lift up one end of the cot, Billy Sol did the same on the other end, carrying Florine without comment where they were instructed.

The drovers gathered around Ponder and watched the Higgins family disappear through one of the doors leading into the courtyard. Dud gave his head a shake, feeling as if he might have hallucinated the entire incident. Florine never apologized for anything.

The younger drovers stared with widened eyes, not bothering to hide their surprise and bewilderment. Dud exchanged glances with Audie before turning to Ponder.

"Was that Florine's husband? Is that why

she demanded to come out here? She was looking for him?"

"I reckon so. She must have heard he was in New Mexico. Come on, you knuckleheads, let's take care of these critters and get some rest. I'm bushed. Florine can handle her own dang problems."

The others nodded in dumb agreement. That Florine had feelings other than anger came as a shock to them, but their bodies and brains were too tired to dwell on it. Shug and Billy Sol joined them, refusing to look anyone in the eye, tending to the animals with the rest of them. Once the animals were put in the stables and fed, they found places underneath scrubby trees to sleep in the shade. Sleeping in a bed was for nighttime. Ponder climbed into the gold wagon, while Dud took the first watch, climbing a ladder onto a gallery that ran along a parapet encircling the fortress-like inn. He felt so tired he could hardly keep his eyes open as he stared at the monotonous landscape. He grunted in relief when Audie arrived to spell him. He climbed down and fell asleep in the shadow of Ponder's wagon.

When the drovers awakened, the heat was still so intense they moved around as little as possible, feeling almost unable to breathe and capable only of sweating. Ponder reluctantly built a fire in an outdoor beehive oven. Jemmy and Will helped while the others took turns standing guard. Shug and Billy Sol kept shooting looks at the door of the room they had left Florine in, but they refused to go in as long as their father remained with her.

Zeb came out when the fatback and cornpone were ready, sitting down with the others in the darkening courtyard. Shug and Billy Sol filled plates and took them in to their mother. Zeb paid them little attention, concentrating instead on his food.

When he finished, he announced that the men might as well sleep outside unless they wanted to tussle all night with the bedbugs.

"Hadn't had a chance to smoke them out yet. Put Florine in the onliest room that don't have them."

When Shug and Billy Sol came out of Florine's room and joined them, Dud sensed a diminished antagonism toward the old man. They weren't ready to throw their arms around his neck, but they had decided not to kill him.

Dud introduced the drovers to Zeb, being careful to leave off last names. Florine, Shug, and Billy Sol had come to an understanding with the Clampits, but it was almost a certainty that Zeb had not.

"How is Florine? We can't stay here long," Dud said.

Shug and Billy Sol opened their mouths to answer, but Zeb beat them to it.

"Plumb wore out. You boys had no business letting her come out here."

Since Dud seemed to be included in "the boys" reference, and it looked like Shug and Billy Sol may have forgotten whatever talking to Florine had given them about being nice to their pa, Dud answered.

"We tried to stop her, but can't nobody tell Florine what to do once she decides something, you know that."

In the shadows, Ponder snorted.

"This is true," Zeb said. "I'm going to get some shut-eye. This is too much for one old man to handle in one day anyhows."

He began to leave, but paused as he passed Ponder. "You got any whiskey with you?"

"No!"

Zeb gave Ponder a hurt look before withdrawing, mumbling to himself about Florine coming all the way to New Mexico to see him.

The next day, they discussed leaving. Dud and Ponder wanted to depart that evening.

"The horses have rested. We need to make

tracks before them danged bandits in Las Cruces figures out where we're at," Ponder said.

Dud put into words what everyone was wondering.

"Shug, are you and your ma and Billy Sol going to stay out here, or are you going back with us?"

Zeb interrupted.

"They's going." He looked at his sons. "Your lives ain't worth a plug nickel out here, now that every rotten, good-for-nothing bandito between here and El Paso knows you sold all them cattle."

Billy Sol began to shake with emotion. "You're just trying to get rid of us, Pa."

It shocked everyone, that Billy Sol had spoken without referring to Shug first.

"That ain't true. You got the ranch back home, family, friends. There ain't nothing out here for you."

"He's right, Billy Sol," Shug said. "We'uns belong back in Texas."

There was a long silence. Billy Sol broke it.

"Cousin Dud, Ma ain't doing too good."

The others waited for Dud to make the decision. It felt heavy on him — Florine's health or the safety of everyone?

"We'll stay one more day, then we're going."

No one objected, and the rest of the day was spent getting whatever preparations had to be made out of the way so they could spend the remainder of the time conserving their strength for what lie ahead.

Late in the afternoon, as they lounged in the courtyard under the shade of a clump of hackberry trees, Darnell began to talk about the girlfriends he had made in San Antonio. Not to be outdone, Henry went into detail about every cute little señorita he knew between Brownsville and San Antonio. Mutt and Toomey described for the umpteen time the women they had seen in the old town of Bexar and the stockinged ankle they caught a glimpse of. Audie began wondering out loud about the girl he had nursed, where she had come from, how she came to have relatives in Las Cruces. Ponder started in telling stories about his deceased wives.

"That black-haired woman from Louisiana almost did me in. I don't think I could have made it past sixty if she had lived."

Dud found himself getting angry at Barefoot for remaining silent about his plans. And then he was angry at himself for being angry with Barefoot.

"I'm going to take my money and build the biggest, finest house in San Antonio," Dud said, breaking into the conversation.

He continued on that theme, not understanding why he felt compelled to keep running off at the mouth about it. Shug, Billy Sol, and Zeb watched and listened in silence.

"Dud . . ." Ponder began, but Dud interrupted him.

"She'll have to be impressed. It will be the envy of all of her friends."

"Dudford," Ponder began again.

Dud ignored Ponder. "Even the mayor won't live in such a fine home. I'll let her decorate it with things straight from Paris."

The other drovers kept shooting looks at the two Washburns, trying not to stare at the fight brewing.

"Dudford! Leave it be. She's already remarried."

Ponder's words jolted Dud into silence. He had a hard time believing them. Ponder had to be lying, or he didn't hear right.

"What?"

"I said she's already married again. I did see her in San Antonio, I just didn't tell you the man she was with was her new husband."

"You are lying to me, Uncle Ponder! She

couldn't have gotten married again that quickly. We just got divorced!"

"Don't you be calling me a liar, boy. Somebody with influence talked a judge into letting them get married right away, that's what."

Dud had the wind knocked out of him. "But that would mean . . ."

It meant she had been seeing another man while still married to him. Getting his breath back, Dud exploded in anger.

"Why in thunderation didn't you tell me?!" Dud said, clinching his fist and moving closer to Ponder.

"Because you would have stopped the drive," Ponder yelled, standing up and not backing down.

"So what?" He and Ponder were now breathing fire almost in one another's face.

"Because. Because I needed it! Sitting in saloons playing one card game after another, about to go crazy. And poor Audie, what about him? And something was wrong with these here Hollister kids that their ma was desperate to get them out of the countryside. Callie and Fitz needed a new start and a good toehold. We all needed it!"

"So, you thought we'd all be better off being scalped by Indians?"

"Better than having you sitting around

and mooning over some snooty hussy."

Zeb stepped closer.

"Ponder, you lying old scuzz, you ought not to have lied to that boy."

Ponder whipped around. "Who are you calling a liar? You sorry worthless piece of trash, deserting your wife and children."

Shug jumped in with Billy Sol behind him. "Don't you be talking to our pa that way, Ponder."

"Put 'em up," Ponder said to Zeb, spitting out his chaw of tobacco and raising his fists.

Zeb raised his gnarled old hands in a fighting position, too, and he and Ponder began to circle, ready to start throwing punches.

Audie got up and sauntered away. From the corner of his eye, Dud saw him climb the ladder to the gallery. Dud ignored him, drawn back into the argument.

"Y'all ain't got no right to be butting into me and Uncle Ponder's business. If anybody is going to whip him, it's going to be me."

"Ain't nobody gonna talk trash about our pa," Shug said. "And that includes you and Ponder. Put 'em up, Dudford, because me and you is going to have it out."

Dud readied, but he was stopped by one quiet word.

"Apaches."

The would-be fighters paused. Every eye

turned upwards to Audie. Zeb went into a running hobble to the ladder and began climbing it. The others were fast behind him.

"Keep your heads down," Zeb hissed. "Spread out and don't fire unlessen I tell you to."

It took several minutes before Dud spotted a Mescalero hiding behind the low brush. Once his eyes grew accustomed to what they should be seeing, he found several more.

"They is spread out funny and acting peculiar," Zeb said. "Let me study on it."

They waited in silence, watching. At first, Dud couldn't see anything unusual except that the Apaches didn't seem tensed for an immediate charge. As he began to pick them out one by one, it struck him that they were leaving a wide gash on either side of the road leading up to the inn.

Keeping his eyes on the Mescalero, Zeb turned slightly toward Dud.

"They is waiting for a bigger payload than just the few little mustangs y'all is sporting. Shug said y'all is carrying gold."

"That's right."

"They wouldn't know nothing about the gold. But they is waiting for somebody with a lot more horses and supplies headed this way besides y'all's two wagons and a few measly mustangs."

"Somebody behind us?"

"That's right." He paused before continuing. "How come the army to buy from you and not Charles McHugh or one of them there other big ranchers around El Paso?"

"Because the thousand head McHugh promised the army happened to belong to us, and we didn't allow them to get stole."

Zeb shook his head and spat, never taking his eyes off the Apache in front of them.

"Charles McHugh and his bunch ain't gonna let y'all get off light, coming in here and taking over their business. He must have an army of men and horses behind him for the Apache to put off trying to get at you."

Dud thought for a minute, looking around him.

"Is there a back way out of this place?"

"Nope. Only one way in and one way out."

Dud looked down the parapet at the men with them, all of them tense and ready to fight. The Hollister children were below in the courtyard, looking up with anxious eyes.

"We could have it out with the Apache now."

"You is just seeing the tip. There might be hundreds of them out there."

Dud did not answer because there was nothing he could say. His mind became a whirl of ideas of escape that he rejected one by one. Zeb, in the meantime, seemed to be turning things over. He spat twice before making up his mind and speaking.

"McHugh generally likes his raiding at night." He looked around. "I got an idee. Keep four of your men up here to watch and bring the rest down. Including that big mouthed Ponder."

Dud crouched, running along the parapet, sending Ponder, Audie, and Barefoot down. Shug and Billy Sol followed their father. Dud, the last one down the ladder, joined them near the wagons.

Zeb was already explaining about the Mescalero waiting for a bigger catch.

"They is hoping to attack the men here because it offers good cover they can't get nowheres else. They figure they can overpower them, then turn on you all. There must be an unholy pack of them out there."

"Every second we stay here brings us that much closer to death," Ponder said.

"For once, Ponder, you're singing the right tune. We got to get you out of here."

"And how do you propose to do that?"

Zeb told them.

Shug and Billy Sol immediately set up

an uproar.

"No, Pa! You go on with Ma. I'll do it."

Billy Sol agreed. "That's right. That's right. And I'm sticking with Shug. You go on with Ma."

"I'm your pa, and you listen to me," Zeb called them down. "I ain't been much of a husband or a father, so you got to let me make up for it."

They wanted to argue more, but Zeb remained adamant. Giving in, they followed his instructions, bringing out an old wagon from a barn that looked about to fall to pieces. The horses they hitched to the wagon were just the opposite, slick, well-fed, and of surprisingly good blood. Ponder did his part by tossing every cast iron pan he owned out of the wagon. Will and Jemmy took old clothes and stuffed them with straw. Zeb found an old hat somebody had left at the inn and placed it on the dummy Will and Jemmy had made. He positioned the straw dummy in the driver's seat, winding rope around it so it would sit upright. He even went so far as to fashion a pair of mock reins to tie to the other ones.

Going inside the barn again, Zeb came out with two wooden silhouettes of gunmen.

"These here have come in mighty handy

fooling many a robber," he explained. "You'd be surprised how natural they look up yonder on the gallery. That and the straw dummy will give them three other things to aim at besides my old scaly hide."

He placed the silhouettes in the back of the wagon and turned to the drovers.

"I'll be in the first wagon. Shug, you, Billy Sol, and your ma be in the second, and let Ponder be in the third. They'll be looking at me busting out of the gate in my wagon. By the time they realized y'all have turned left and are heading the other way, Ponder will be behind you catching all the gunfire."

Ponder gave no objections to Zeb's lineup. Dud looked at his men.

"Do you all understand? We'll be fighting our way out, hoping the Apache stop McHugh's men from coming after us long enough for us to get away."

"I never thought I would be beholden to the Apache, but I reckon I am now," Audie said.

Zeb went with Shug and Billy Sol to fetch Florine and carry her outside to the wagon. They came out carrying her on the cot again, and to Dud's dismay, she looked worse, all drawn up and ghostly pale. At the wagon's bed, they paused so Zeb could talk to her.

"Florine, if I live, I promise this time, I'll come back home."

Florine could only shake her head. "Zeb, Zeb," she said, her voice weak and pleading.

"Don't you worry none, Florine. This old desert rat got a few tricks up his sleeve that don't nobody else know about."

He kissed her hand and told his sons to put her in the wagon. Once she was inside, he began tying the cast iron pans to his body. Shug climbed into the back of the wagon and came out with a small dutch oven.

"Here, Pa, this one might fit on your head."

"Much obliged, son," Zeb said, taking it and trying it on.

Dud walked to Ned, passing by Ponder.

"I still ought to whip your ass when this is over for not telling me."

"I'll be ready."

Dud reached Ned and stroked the mustang's neck. He leaned closer, thinking of all the things that might have been, but weren't. He reached inside his saddlebags, taking out Beatrice's letters. He stared at them, weighing them in his hand. Walking to the beehive oven, he threw the letters into the dying embers. He didn't wait to watch them catch and burn, but turned away to find Ponder observing him.

Dud gave him a nod, and Ponder nodded back.

Darkness came suddenly between the mountains. A half-moon was rising when Dud had his men get in line. He worried about Darnell, who had already suffered at the hands of the Comanche, but he dared not insult him in front of the other men to question if he was all right. Darnell knew though, and as Dud led Ned past him, he spoke.

"I be ready, Boss."

Dud nodded and walked on. The grim faces of the others told him they were prepared for what was to come. He hoped he did not let them down. He would climb to the parapet, watch for the McHugh riders from the gallery, and at the right time, run down, open the doors, and jump back on his horse to bring up the rear.

Once everyone was where they were supposed to be, Dud scrambled up the ladder to the parapet, rifle in hand, with Ned waiting for him below. The horse seemed to sense something important was about to happen, and there was a nobility about the mustang that brought up a lump in Dud's throat. He hadn't been any good at picking a wife, but he had picked two good horses.

Once on the gallery, he heard footsteps climbing up the ladder behind him. Barefoot paused at the top. "May I join you for a moment?"

Dud answered a quiet "yes," and Barefoot stepped upon the gallery, crouching down, joining him in staring into the inky darkness.

"I'm sorry about your ex-wife."

Dud didn't answer, and for a while, Barefoot watched the shadows with him before speaking again.

"I decided I wanted a Señora Martin instead of someone I was hoping would make me something I am not."

Dud wondered if that had been what he wanted, too. Somebody to turn him into something he wasn't and never would be.

"And if we manage to stay alive, what are your plans?"

"Go back to San Antonio and make Barefoot Sullivan the best lawyer he can be, and if he is lucky, find a woman who will love him just as he is.

"A good leader takes care of his men, but at the same time, always keeps the ultimate goal in mind. You are a good leader, Dudford Washburn."

Dud let out a long breath. "I have no goal left."

"Yes, you do. It is the same one you started with. To take longhorns to New Mexico, make money, and return home safely. The goal has not changed, only the motivation that you gave yourself to accomplish it."

Dud allowed himself the briefest of smiles before turning back to the waiting Mescalero.

"Thank you, my friend. But the time for reflection is over. We must be ready to act, so get down there, and when we bust out of here, ride and shoot like hell. If I make it back to San Antonio alive, I will need a good lawyer on my side."

"You will have one," Barefoot said, turning and going back to the ladder, climbing down and leaving Dud alone to once again make the final decision on when to act.

He heard the splashing of water as riders crossed the creek. He began to count the seconds that the spattering sounds of hooves made in water as they seemed to go on and on, realizing Zeb had been right about the number of men and horses McHugh had amassed in chasing them down.

The riders came into view, a dark mass of men and horses. Galvanized, Dud crouched and ran, reaching the ladder and racing down. He sped to the huge wooden double doors, throwing open the iron bars and grabbing the handles. He stood panting, one second, two seconds, three seconds. When they came, the screeching Apache yells on the other side rattled the metal on the doors. Dud flung them open as wide as he could and dashed to Ned while Zeb let out a war whoop of his own, cracking a bullwhip and hollering "Ha-ya!" to his horses at the top of his voice.

Zeb and his wagon raced down the road straight into the middle of the melee. Shug and Billy Sol did the same, but turned the wagon so sharply to the left, it almost toppled over. Ponder in his wagon was right behind them. General Sherman somehow managed to pass Ponder's wagon to catch up with Shug and Billy Sol.

Voices of Anglos could be heard above the yells of the Apache.

"There they are!"

Dud and his men made a run for it, shooting the Henrys as fast as they could, not bothering to aim, but firing wildly into the crowd and hoping they did not hit Old Man Higgins who seemed to have disappeared into the darkness.

But the Apaches were not letting the white

men follow, and the last Dud could see in the darkness behind him was a brutal battle between McHugh's men and the Mescalero.

The screams followed them for some time as the drovers raced on. Ned passed every horse with ease while Dud checked to see that all his men were with him. Jax was racing behind Ponder's wagon, nostrils flaring, appearing more alive than Dud had ever seen him. It occurred to him they all looked fuller of life than they had ever been before.

They were homeward bound.

ABOUT THE AUTHOR

Vicky J. Rose, who also writes under the pseudonyms of V. J. Rose and Easy Jackson, is the winner of two Will Rogers Medallion Awards, and runner up for the Western Writers of America Spur Awards, and the Western Fictioneer Peacemaker Awards. A former successful business owner, she graduated from a small West Texas university with a degree in journalism and a minor in history. She's also known locally for her dedicated volunteer work in preserving Texas history. Rose grew up in a small town with a wild past, full of stories about early outlaw gangs, lynchings, shootouts, and vigilantism that nurtured her love for the western genre. She strives to share that love of the Old West with her readers.

The employees of Thorndike Press hope you have enjoyed this Large Print book. All our Thorndike, Wheeler, and Kennebec Large Print titles are designed for easy reading, and all our books are made to last. Other Thorndike Press Large Print books are available at your library, through selected bookstores, or directly from us.

For information about titles, please call:
(800) 223-1244

or visit our website at:
gale.com/thorndike

To share your comments, please write:
Publisher
Thorndike Press
10 Water St., Suite 310
Waterville, ME 04901

CPSIA information can be obtained
at www.ICGtesting.com
Printed in the USA
BVHW042015170523
664396BV00001B/5